DECLARED A... ...us MUST
NOT ONLY F... ...ARVINNIUS'S RE-
LENTLESS EFF... ...TO FIND AND EXECUTE HIM,
BUT ALSO THE HOSTILITY AND DISTRUST OF THE
NATIVE TRIBES NORTH OF HADRIAN'S WALL.

General Arvinnius gave the tribune a hard look. *"Querinius, Arrius is to be taken alive no matter the cost. I want to be present when the treasonous bastard is crucified."*

Now an outcast and a fugitive of Rome, Arrius is not easily accepted by the Selgovi in spite of Ilya and his close friendship with her son, Joric, High Chieftain of the Selgovae Tribe. Arrius works hard to make the tribal clan chiefs understand the inevitable slaughter that is about to happen when the tribe confronts the legions about to march north. In time, he is able to convince the tribesmen to change their individual style of combat to a more unified approach and avoid pitch battles in favor of skirmish and ambush. When Joric is killed early in the conflict, Ilya becomes queen of the Selgovi. By now, Arrius has won the respect and confidence of the tribe. The subsequent invasion by the Roman legions is made more problematic by disaffection among the tribes. When Arrius is captured by Tribune Querinius, it becomes both a rallying cry for the Selgovae Tribe and a turning point in the war. Although the defeat of Querinius is significant, the tribe begins to accept the inevitable that Roman might is too great for the tribes to overcome; consequently, it falls to Arrius to play a key role in the Selgovi withdrawal north into Caledonia where the tribes already there intend to resist the southern migration.

i

"Historical fiction at its very best, Preston Holtry's *Enemy of Rome* provides a powerful and most satisfying conclusion to his *Arrius* trilogy. With effective dialogue, provocative male and female characters, and exhilarating sections of violence, this well researched book makes us feel as though we are on the inside looking around us rather than merely on the outside looking in. A must-read novel."—*John Vance, author of Echoes of November and Awake the Southern Wind*

"Preston Holtry has surpassed himself with Enemy of Rome, the final installment of the Arrius trilogy. Based on the first two novels, I expected a thrilling end and Preston did not disappoint! ... With realistic characters and unforgettable images of life in the Roman encampment and the tribal villages, Preston weaves a masterful tale, intertwining historical fact and riveting fiction. Be prepared to stay up late as you won't want to put it down. This is an exciting finale to the trilogy, right to the last page!"— *Randall Krzak, author of The Kurdish Connection and Dangerous Alliance*

"*Enemy of Rome* continues the story of the maverick Roman who is at odds with the men who command him... a most believable novel. He transports the reader to the northern frontier in the second century very well. The dramatic ending is satisfying and the writer teases the reader with literary pleasures to come. Preston Holtry has truly joined the ranks of those who write the better books about the Roman Empire."—*Griff Hosker, author of the Anarchy and Dragonheart book series.*

"A sprawling, multi-dimensional historical and epic novel in which Mr. Holtry exercises masterful control. He seamlessly weaves together history, adventure, passion, and family dynamics into a fascinating story that is always engaging, intriguing, and illuminating. It is also a helluva lot of fun."—*Hank Luce, author of A Darkness in the Pines, Secret of the Nightingale Madonna, Brainways, and Crown of Thorns*

ARRIUS
VOLUME III
ENEMY OF ROME

Preston Holtry

Moonshine Cove Publishing, LLC
Abbeville South Carolina, U.S.A.

FIRST MOONSHINE COVE EDITION JANUARY 2019

ISBN 978-1-945181-610
Library of Congress PCN 2018962665
Copyright 2019 by Preston Holtry

Map of Britannia 137-139 CE

For my wife, Judy, in deep appreciation for a lifetime of love
and friendship

Acknowledgement

Any writer of historical fiction depends on the professional historian to provide detail and context by which to craft a credible, entertaining tale of a bygone era. There are several authors who helped me draw inspiration and fact for a better understanding of the Romans and Brythonic Tribes. In particular, I want to acknowledge the scholarly works of two authors, whom I found to be especially helpful in understanding the Roman Army and the auxilia. Graham Webster's *Roman Imperial Army of the First and Second Centuries A.D.* offers detailed insights on every aspect of Roman military life including descriptions of armor, weapons, clothing, food, customs and religious beliefs. Edward N. Litvak and his book *The Grand Strategy of the Roman Empire from the First Century A.D. to the Third* provided a much-appreciated background regarding Roman organization, imperial strategy, tactics, mobility and so much more. Julius Caesars's *The Gallic War*, translated by H. J. Edwards, provided additional and near contemporary descriptions of the warfare, appearance and customs of the Britannia tribes that Arrius would have found quite similar. Other scholarly works I found helpful in capturing the second century of the Roman Empire are listed in the bibliography at the end of the novel along with a glossary of Roman terms and actual geographical locations where events in the novel take place.

I created the map for Britannia from a terrain map obtained off the internet from maps-for-free.com.

I appreciate the efforts of my wife, Judy, Bruce and Henri Filer and Don Ayers, D, Ed for the time they spent contributing ideas, needed criticism and trolling for the inevitable typos that often defy discovery before publication but are certain to be found by the reader.

Special thanks both to Florence Ah-Fa, Quebec, Canada for permission to use her image of the *Roman Helmet* for the jacket cover and Cynthia Guare for the front and back cover design. I'm grateful to Moonshine Cove for its support and willingness to complete the saga of Marcus Junius Arrius and especially Gene Robinson for making me a better writer.

Preston Holtry is the author of the Morgan Westphal period mystery series and the *ARRIUS* trilogy. He has a BA degree in English from the Virginia Military Institute and a graduate degree from Boston University. A career army officer, he served twice in Vietnam in addition to a variety of other infantry and intelligence-related assignments in Germany, England, and the United States. Retired from the army with the rank of colonel, he lives with his wife, Judith, in Oro Valley, Arizona. He now spends much of his time writing the next novel. Holtry is the author of four published mystery novels set in the Southwest during the period 1915-17 featuring the private detective Morgan Westphal.

Read more about his interests and writing approach at his website:

http://www.presholtry.webs.com.

Previous Works:

Historical Mysteries

Death in Emily 3
A Troublesome Affair
Seal of Confession
The Good Thief

Roman Historical Novels - The ARRIUS Trilogy:

Sacramentum (Oath) Volume One
Legacy Volume Two
Enemy of Rome Volume Three

Modern Thriller:

Looking for Steiner (under the name Wayne Preston)

Summaries of Volumes I and II

Volume I *Sacramentum*: The year is 135 C.E., and Marcus Junius Arrius, a 25-year veteran of the Roman Army, is the senior centurion of the XXII Legion, *Deiotariana* engaged in defeating the latest Jewish rebellion in Judaea. Without understanding why, Arrius is troubled by the carnage and brutality of the war. While the savagery on both sides is nothing new in his lifetime serving the legions, this conflict is somehow different. The fanaticism of the Jews in their efforts to win freedom from Rome puzzles him while the raw behavior of the legionaries he commands begins to disgust him as they disembowel Jewish dead looking for gems and gold coins. His precarious relationship with General Gallius, the legion commander, does not help. Gallius is insecure and resents Arrius's leadership abilities even while he feels dependent on the centurion. Tiberias Querinius, the legion's senior tribune tries to curry favor with Gallius by plotting to have Arrius killed; the plot fails. Arrius is convinced the tribune was behind the attempt.

The field commander of the Roman Army in Judaea develops a plan to lure the Jewish Army into consolidating its forces in a decisive battle to end the rebellion. The *Deiotariana* Legion is the unknowing bait to accomplish the latter objective. During the ensuing battle, Gallius is killed. When Arrius looks for Querinius to inform him he is now in command, he finds the tribune cowering in the medical tent. Following the battle and the defeat of the Jewish Army, Arrius is offered a position anywhere in the empire including command of the prestigious Praetorian Guard in Rome. Disillusioned, Arrius, instead, chooses an independent command in Britannia as far from Rome as he can go.

In Britannia, Arrius visits Eboracum where the VI Legion *Victrix,* responsible for command of Hadrian's Wall, is headquartered. He is shocked to find his command of Banna, one of fourteen wall forts, is subordinate to Tiberias Querinius. Upon his arrival at Banna, he sees two legionaries assaulting a woman and a young boy. He rescues Ilya and her son Joric, but his intervention is met with angry hostility rather than gratitude. His first impression of Banna and the centurions leading the Tungrian garrison is no more promising. Matius Betto, the centurion who has been interim commander, makes clear

Arrius has his work cut out for him to earn the loyalty of his centurions and to turn around a command suffering from low morale and prolonged neglect.

Realizing her initial reaction toward Arrius was unfair, Ilya goes to the fort to apologize; this meeting does nothing to abate their mutual antagonism. In time, Arrius has second thoughts about the beautiful native woman and spontaneously visits her. Their third meeting finds them both ready to seek common ground. For the first time since coming to Britannia, Arrius begins to look forward to a future rather than dwelling on a past he has yet to understand.

Volume II *Legacy*: As Arrius begins the slow process of turning around a dispirited and somewhat ineffective command, the hatred and jealousy of the centurion Matius Betto, the cohort's second in command, add to Arrius's problems. It does not take long for Betto and Querinius to enter into a conspiracy to ruin Arrius. In time, Arrius gains the respect and loyalty of the officers and legionaries at Banna with the exception of a few who remain committed to Betto. His success extends to Ilya who overcomes her strong hatred of Romans in general by falling in love with Arrius. Ilya eventually becomes pregnant and presents Arrius with a son. Unknown to both of them, Ilya unwittingly becomes the instrument of revenge for Querinius and Betto when her Selgovan heritage is revealed. The damage to Arrius is further increased when her close family relationship to Beldorach, the High Chieftain of the Selgovae Tribe is made known. Arrius returns to Banna from a campaign to find Betto holding Ilya brutally captive and Querinius accusing him of treason. An inquiry is held, and Querinius is both humiliated and enraged when Arrius is exonerated. In the aftermath, Ilya savagely attacks Betto, but it is Arrius's sword that kills him. Querinius is summarily relieved of his command, which contributes even more to the tribune's desire for revenge.

With the death of Beldorach, Joric is designated High Chieftain of the Selgovae Tribe. Ilya leaves Banna to go north with her son to assist him in assuming tribal leadership. She takes Arrius's infant son with her, creating a potentially irreversible breach between them. With her departure, Arrius realizes more clearly than ever he has become a prisoner behind a Wall that holds him captive to beliefs and symbols that no longer have any meaning for him. When Antoninus Pius, the Empire's new emperor, decides to abandon Hadrian's Wall and extend the frontier north, Arrius knows the Roman objective will provoke the Selgovi into a war they cannot win. If he remains in the Roman Army, he will be forced to be a part of a savage campaign that will threaten the lives of both Ilya and his son. He sees little choice except to leave the Roman Army, ostensibly to return to Rome. Instead, he secretly goes north to search for Ilya. Arrius is well aware he will be proscribed and declared an enemy of Rome when his destination is inevitably revealed.

Principal Characters

The Romans

Gaius Labinius Arvinnius, general and commander of Legion VI, *Victrix*, subsequently appointed field general commanding the II, VI, and XX Legions.

Marcus Junius Arrius, Former senior centurion (*primus pilus*) of Legion XXII, *Deiotariana* and commander (*Praefectus*) of an independent command at Banna

Marcellus Septimus, general and commander of Legion XX, *Valeria Victrix*

Rutilius Corbulo, general and commander of II Legion, *Augustus*

Plinius Flavius, centurion and commander, First Cohort of Tungrians

Rufus, *optio* (equivalent of a senior sergeant) First Cohort of Tungrians

Seugethis (Soo geth is), Praefectus and commander, I *Ala, Dacian* at Fanum Cocidii

Tiberius Querinius, Former commander of Uxellodonum and acting commander, Legion VI, *Victrix*

The Britannian Tribes immediately north of Hadrian's Wall

The *Selgovae*: The tribal lands are between the *Novanti* to the west and the *Votadini* to the east near the border between England and Scotland.

Athdara, principal wife of Beldorach

Beldorach, the deceased High Chieftain of the Selgovae and cousin of Ilya

Eugenius, son of Marcus Arrius and Ilya

Ilya, wife of Marcus Arrius and cousin of Beldorach,

Joric, Ilya's son and High Chieftain of the Selgovae Tribe

Tearlach (Chur lock), a close friend of Beldorach and later war chief of the Selgovi

Cuileán (Quil yon), clan chief of the Selgovi

The *Brigantes.* A large confederation of Britannian tribes occupying the territory south of Hadrian's Wall; the capitol was Isurium in the vicinity east of present day Leeds.

Decrius, a centurion in the Tungrian Auxilia
Iseult, wife of Decrius
Rialus, son of Decrius
Hudryn, senior tribal member

The *Novantae.* Occupied the territory immediately north of Hadrian's Wall and west of the Selgovi to the Irish Sea.

Bothan, High Chieftain of the Novanti
Neacal, clan Chief
Crixtacus, clan chief

The *Votadini.* Occupied the territory immediately northeast of Hadrian's Wall and east of the Selgovi

Darach, High Chieftain of the Votadini

The Far Northern Tribes

The *Venicones.* Occupied territory in the Scottish Lowlands, near Kirkcaldy. Indrecht, Tribal Leader

The *Epedi.* Occupied territory in the Scottish Lowlands, northwest of Glasgow.

The *Vocamagi.* Occupied territory in the Scottish Highlands, vicinity of Pitlochry, Vadrex, Tribal leader

The *Caledoni.* Occupied territory in the Scottish Highlands, vicinity of North Ballachulish.

ARRIUS VOL III

ENEMY OF ROME

Chapter 1

"Somehow I knew I would see you again, Marcus Arrius, but I never thought it would be here," Joric said. "But how can it be when you command the fort at Banna?"

"I am no longer a Roman officer in command of anything except Ferox here, and I wonder sometimes at that." When Arrius saw Joric was framing another question, he forestalled it by holding up a hand and adding, "There's time enough to say more of this later." He turned to Ilya and was suddenly tongue-tied. He searched for something to say and managed a banal "How are you?" before belatedly adding, "And Eugenius?"

"We are very well, Marcus, and even better now you've come."

He stood frozen, speechless, staring silently into her eyes, oblivious of the curious throng gathered around them. He wanted to reach out and take her in his arms but was unsure how she would react. A moment later, she decided the matter when she stepped forward and embraced him, clinging tightly to him. Arrius felt the swell of her breasts pressing against his chest.

"Marcus, it's been too long. Forgive me for what I've done," she said, voice husky with emotion.

"There's nothing to forgive, only a past to forget. What was done and said doesn't belong here. It's only the future that matters now," Arrius said in response, certain he never believed anything more strongly.

Their reunion was interrupted by Tearlach's surly voice, "Roman, your future here has yet to be decided. It remains for the High Chieftain and the clan chiefs to determine what will become of you."

"You forget, Tearlach, I'm now High Chieftain of the Selgovi, and the clan chiefs will provide advice and counsel only when I seek it."

Arrius was not the only one surprised by Joric's sharp comment. Far from showing any hostility at the rebuke, Tearlach looked more pleased than angered. After giving a brief nod in silent acknowledgement, the Selgovan abruptly turned his horse around and rode back toward the gate without so much as a backward glance.

Joric calmly watched Tearlach depart, his face expressionless. Arrius saw the resolute thrust of his jaw and realized there was nothing left of the youth he once knew. Joric had always seemed to him more mature and confident beyond his years, and it was even more evident now. He believed it was mainly circumstance that tested a man's mettle and contributed the most in developing character. Joric's assumption of tribal leadership surfaced inbred qualities that boded well for the Selgovi.

Arrius took a step back to look at Ilya. If anything, she was more beautiful than ever. Her green eyes were shining and told him more than words could she was happy to see him. She was dressed in a simple but elegant shift gathered at the waist that emphasized her lithe and becoming figure. It was apparent she had gained back the weight she lost as a result of Betto's cruel treatment followed by Eugenius's difficult birth that almost claimed her life. Except for a small braid on either side of her face, her honey-colored hair hung loosely down her back to her waist. The once livid welt across her cheek caused when Betto struck her with his *vitis* was now only a faint white line. He knew it was a mark she would bear the rest of her life.

Ilya thrust her arm through Arrius's and urged him through the inner gate leading to the upper level of the fort. As they walked along, Ilya spoke happily of the events that occurred since her and Joric's arrival in the village. Joric led Ferox and the pack horse, interjecting only brief comments while Ilya described the ceremonies elevating Joric to the tribal dais. It was evident from her uncharacteristic emotional description, she was both pleased to be back with her tribe and proud her son was its rightful leader.

Interested though he was, Arrius wanted to interrupt to ask of Eugenius but chose instead to let her chatter on until finally she stopped in mid-sentence and said in exclamation, "But I haven't said a word about Eugenius!"

From that point on, she spoke of nothing else. "Marcus, your son is perfect in every way. I'm certain he will have your size, and he will be handsome—that is if he can avoid scars to his face," referring to Arrius's prominent scar caused by a Parthian cavalry sword extending from the hairline on the right cheek down to the chin. He was used to people staring at the wide scar. However terrible the wound appeared, it was no more than most legionaries wore, seen or unseen, from having engaged in a lifetime of battles and campaigning. Even without the scar, his square-jawed face and the deep lines on either side of a prominent, hooked nose prompted some to say his face was more intimidating than handsome. In any event, he was satisfied that with his and Ilya's height Eugenius would be a large man when fully grown. Arrius also hoped for his sake he might bear the more regular and pleasing features of his Selgovan mother than his Roman father's heritage.

While Joric tied Ferox to a post outside, Arrius and Ilya entered the low doorway of the large, circular dwelling. Apart from the open door, the only natural light came from four narrow windows and the opening in the thatch roof allowing the smoke to escape from a raised and centrally-located hearth. After his eyes grew accustomed to the dark interior, he saw the room was rearranged somewhat since Ilya and Athdara brought him back from the brink of death. Cloth screens now separated the room into several compartments that now provided more privacy for the occupants.

When he began to distinguish form from shadow, he recognized Ulla sitting close to the doorway weaving. Ilya was forced to rely on the passive, heavy-set Brigantian woman as a wet nurse for Eugenius when she was unable to provide milk for the infant. Ulla paused in her task long enough to look up briefly with disinterest before continuing her work, her fingers a blur as she expertly wove the threads into an intricate design.

Athdara sat in profile on a stool near the fire holding an infant that he presumed was Eugenius. Older than Ilya, Athdara was still striking with aquiline features and high cheekbones not unlike Ilya and typical of Selgovan women in general. If her hair had not been streaked with gray, she would have looked much younger than her years. Her presence was somewhat surprising. Until now, he had given no thought to what would have become of her and Beldorach's other two wives following the tribal leader's death.

From the happy gurgles and toothless smile on Eugenius's face and Athdara's contented expression, it was clear to Arrius she was an accepted feature in the infant's life. Athadara looked in his direction. If she was pleased or displeased to see him, she gave no indication, nor did she make any comment. Silently she stood up and walked toward Arrius holding Eugenius in her outstretched arms. When he took the baby, he saw a look of regret in her eyes that made him realize the infant was a constant reminder of what Beldorach was unable to give her and why Joric had become the tribal leader of the Selgovi. He supposed she and Ilya reached some kind of accommodation. During his recuperation when Ilya came from Banna to nurse him, he recalled the relations between the two women had been strained.

Eugenius was everything Arrius hoped he would be. His eyes were neither blue nor gray but somewhere in between. Fixating on Arrius's nose, the infant's small fingers managed to find their target, and the prominent appendage received a vigorous squeeze that made his eyes water. Laughing at his distress, Ilya took the baby in her arms only to surrender him to Joric who entered the dwelling. While Ilya and Athdara watched calmly and Arrius with concern, Joric tossed the baby into the air several times in quick succession. From Eugenius's pleased reaction, it was evident he was accustomed to such treatment. It pleased Arrius to see the bond developing between the two of them, and he hoped it would continue during their lifetimes.

While Ilya poured cups of wine, Athdara served wooden platters heaped with generous portions of the stew from a pot hanging on an iron tripod over the fire. Arrius didn't realize how hungry he was until he tasted the delicious food. For the time being, conversation tapered off as they devoted their attention to the meal. Even Eugenius remained relatively quiet as he suckled greedily at one of Ulla's breasts. As appetites were satisfied, Ilya asked when he intended to return to Banna.

"I've left the Roman Army for good; I have no intention of returning to Banna. It's my hope you and Eugenius will come away with me when I leave Britannia."

He saw a cloud come over Ilya's face, and she glanced quickly at Joric. In an instant, he knew if he left Britannia, he would travel alone.

Joric quickly responded. "Marcus Arrius, while I lead the Selgovi, you will have a place with us for as long you wish. Let us have no more talk of departing when I have so much need of both of you here."

"Tell me, Marcus, was it my departure that caused you to decide to leave the army?" Ilya wore an anxious expression.

"I'll not deny it, but in truth, I think I would have left anyway."

Joric looked surprised. "But why?"

"I think it was Beldorach who finally caused me to think about what I had become although I realize now, Philos was the first to try when I think back to some of our past conversations." Arrius was still adjusting to the reality his former slave who eventually became his closest friend and died in this very settlement not long ago.

"Beldorach?" Ilya questioned.

"When I escorted him to Banna from Eboracum shortly after my arrival in Britannia, we argued about many things, usually over Roman intentions and tribal rights. He accused me of having nothing and said I defended what others own while he had fields and forests to claim. Ilya, I didn't understand him or how right he was until I met you. It's ironic that it was someone Rome considered an enemy who eventually made clear to me what Philos had been saying for years. After you left, I realized there was nothing left for me at Banna. I could no longer carry out orders in which I no longer believed much less execute as I once did without question."

"What orders?" Joric asked quickly, seeming to perceive there was more to Arrius's words than professing a desire for a new life and a place to live it.

"Several months ago, I attended a *consilium* convened by General Arvinnius, commander of the Sixth Legion. During the council, Arvinnius outlined Rome's plan to abandon the Wall and move north into Caledonia where a new wall will be constructed. The site for it is considerably farther north than where we are now. In the process, the tribes in the immediate proximity of the Wall are to be completely subjugated or driven farther north. Arvinnius doesn't care if the Selgovi and the other two tribes remain where they are or go north; however, if they remain where they are, they will be subject to the full measure of Roman authority."

"But why is such a thing being done now?" Joric asked without any sign of alarm. "It makes no sense to leave behind something that took so long to build."

"Arvinnius never explained why, and there was no reason to ask. It is not the province of Roman officers to question orders. But I suspect it has to do with ambition. General Arvinnius wants advancement, and the new emperor wants to establish his imperial reputation. Antoninus Pius has never served in the Roman Army. It's possible he seeks an easy military victory abroad to obtain it. And the northern tribes, including the Selgovi, continue to threaten *pax Romana.*"

"You said an easy military victory. Does the Roman emperor expect the tribes to simply accept Roman occupation without a fight?" Joric asked. "If so, he underestimates us. We will defend our lands."

"Then the Selgovi and the other tribes that resist will be annihilated. You will die fighting a war you can't possibly win. The alternative is to submit and avoid death or slavery."

"We have no choice but to fight! Do you think so little of our fighting abilities we will be defeated so easily?"

"You forget, Joric, I've fought for Rome for over thirty years in five different legions. I've fought both the Novanti and Selgovi. Believe what I say. You have no chance against the most disciplined army in the world. Even if the tribes were to join together and numbered many more times than I believe they do, you still can't win. In the end, you will be fortunate merely to survive."

Until then Ilya remained silent. Now she spoke dispassionately. "I've no doubt everything you say concerning the might of the legions is true; however, you misunderstand what Joric is saying. Our situation has little to do with pointless resolve and everything to do with practical necessity. The Selgovi simply have nowhere else to go. We either fight, or we make peace with Rome."

"Will the Selgovan clans consider an overture of peace? If so, I'll return to Banna and intercede on the tribe's behalf."

When Joric responded, his comments impressed Arrius by being devoid of the false bravado he might have expected from a young and inexperienced leader.

"There may be one or two clan chiefs who might consider a truce, but the rest will not. The clan chiefs think and act as warriors first, each concerned more with his clan than with the tribe in general. Talk of peace before fighting first would be interpreted as a sign of weakness."

"Why can't you go north?" Arrius asked logically.

"The northern tribes would prevent us from entering their territory," Ilya said. "The Epidii and Venicones have reason to hate us possibly more than the Romans. They stay in their hills, and we have always remained in the lowlands. It has always been so. There are many more tribes farther north than the Epidii and Venicones that we've never seen. The Caledonian Tribes can be depended on to resist any encroachment from the south, tribal or Roman."

Arrius was fast becoming exasperated at Joric and Ilya's fatalistic acceptance of what to him was an untenable position. "Seventy years ago, the tribes united against the Roman general, Agricola. Is it not possible to do so again?"

"I recall my father telling of this," Ilya commented. "Bathar was there and saw how badly the tribes were defeated even though they outnumbered the Romans by many times. The defeat had as much to do with tribal rivalry and failure to cooperate as it did with Roman fighting ability. The memory of that defeat surely still lives on as do the reasons for it."

"Then would it not be plain enough in the recollection of such a defeat to consider peace with Rome?"

"Marcus, you still have much to learn about us. We are a proud people and will not submit without attempting to defend what is our right to hold."

Arrius could think of nothing more to say, and a gloomy silence prevailed until Joric asked, "How much time do we have before the Romans begin their advance?"

"Preparations for the invasion began weeks ago. While no exact date has been set, I should think you have perhaps sixty days when the weather is better. The *auxilia* forces now positioned on the wall are ready now, but it will take time for the Sixth and Twentieth Legions to move forward from Eboracum and Deva. The legions will not be in the initial wave. The auxilia legionaries now stationed on the wall will be in the lead with the legions following close behind."

"Then it is likely your Tungrian and Dacian legionaries will be the first to fight us?" Ilya said, less a question than a statement of fact. "It's difficult to imagine Decrius and Rufus would fight us."

Arrius's expression was bleak, "Yes, it's true. They will do what they have to. Decrius must serve his twenty-five years to become a Roman citizen, and the only home and life Rufus knows is that of a Roman legionary."

"Were you involved in the planning?" Ilya asked. Arrius again nodded his head in grim silence. "And you were allowed to leave Banna to come here knowing you might likely reveal their plans?"

"I left at night in secret, and only a few I trusted knew where I was going. General Arvinnius will eventually learn of it."

"If he should learn of it sooner, will he advance the date of the attack?" Once again Arrius was impressed with Joric's logical question.

"It's possible; however, it will still require time for the legions to complete their preparations for the campaign. Arvinnius will not move until he's ready. Surprise is less important to the Roman Army than being prepared. He also knows as well as I do if the tribes had advance warning and another year to get ready, the outcome will still be the same. If the tribes resist, it will be like Judaea, and northern Britannia will be destroyed. Rome cannot afford to be defeated. Arvinnius plans for and expects only success. It will not end any other way."

"It seems you've made a poor bargain by coming here," Ilya said without any hint of bitterness.

"I had no choice. Whatever happens, the gods have decided for me, and for once, I do not question their wisdom as I once did."

"Well, whatever happens, I'm glad you're here," Ilya said."

"And I say the same, Marcus Arrius," Joric added. "Do not give up on us yet. We may yet find a way out of this dilemma, but I think the solution is not here with us tonight."

Arrius did not realize until Joric spoke how late the hour was. He also failed to notice that Athdara and Ulla left during the discussion taking Eugenius with them. Joric stood up and announced, "There is much to think about, and I've found I do my best thinking alone and on the back of a horse. I'll return when *Vindonnus* conquers the night sky," referring to the Selgovan sun god. His intent to leave them alone was transparent.

After Joric disappeared into the night, Arrius was grateful for his tactful declaration while filled with doubt concerning what to do now he was alone with Ilya. Their estrangement since Eugenius's birth made him feel awkward. He was afraid to say or do anything that would make things worse than they were already. Even dead, Betto remained a barrier between them. Ilya sat quietly staring into the fire, and Arrius knew her thoughts were similar to his. After a few moments passed, she looked at him and spoke.

"I know our separation has been as difficult for you as it has for me. I've tried to forget what happened to me, and I fear I never will. But I've also decided if I can remember something so horrible, I should be able to call to mind our time together with equal clarity. I think that will be much easier to do now that you've come here if you will only be patient with me."

"Ilya, I want you and Eugenius to leave here with me."

"Leave? But where would we go?"

"Anywhere you want as long as it's away from here. Perhaps to the far south where there is no threat of war."

"Marcus, I can't leave here. Joric needs me, and this is my home."

Her response was not unexpected. Arrius nodded his acceptance and saw the relief on her face as she stood up and came toward him. For a moment, they stood slightly apart gazing wordlessly at each other as if waiting for the other to say or do something to overcome their hesitation. With a sigh, she stepped into his arms and embraced him, holding him tightly. He breathed the scent of her hair and felt her warm breath on his neck, but the closeness of her did not arouse him as it once did. It was still too soon for her. He thought it was also true for him as well. They did not make love that night or many nights thereafter. For the time being, they were content simply to be together again.

Chapter 2

Dressed in a polished cuirass, his *sagum* flowing behind, General Gaius Labinius Arvinnius, commander of the Sixth Legion, *Victrix*, rode without helmet as was his custom. His composed features gave no hint of the rage boiling inside him as he rode swiftly toward the elaborate villa with his cavalry escort behind and hard-pressed to keep up. Arvinnius was far too disciplined to allow his emotions to give any hint of his inner thoughts; it was a trait he long cultivated knowing a neutral expression kept both subordinates and superiors alike slightly off balance and guessing what was on his mind.

The general's anger continued to fester until it now dominated nearly every waking moment. He felt betrayed. Since it was his plan to extend the northern boundary in Britannia, he deserved to be appointed governor of Britannia and given the responsibility for implementing the plan. He had worked out every detail down to the positioning of the last cohort. Success only required the emperor's approval. Hadrian's recent death was the opportunity to approach the new emperor. Hadrian made it clear after the recent and costly Judaean debacle there would be no further expansion of the empire under any circumstance. Consolidation and protection of the existing boundary was Hadrian's mandate as it was Trajan's before him. While Hadrian was alive, there would be no exception. And without an exception, there was no opportunity for glory and a chance of improving his own future and fortune.

Tall and lean with high cheekbones, Arvinnius cultivated a patrician look even though his lineal pedigree was not as distinguished as he would have wished. What remained of his prematurely white hair was combed forward over a wide brow. His nose was prominent and hooked giving him the appearance of a predatory raptor. He was not unaware that behind his back he was referred to as "the eagle," a reference he privately relished. If Arvinnius was not a brilliant general, he was considered capable enough and one of the few Roman generals who genuinely enjoyed command unlike many who served out of obligation and political expedience. He was also calculating and ruthless. Arvinnius thought destruction and a bloody *gladius* were more persuasive than peaceful words.

He thought Antoninus Pius was the answer to his prayer. The gods listened and placed a man on the throne with no previous military experience. The new emperor badly needed *dignitas*. A career politician, Pius would have to compensate for his own lack of military experience by achieving a victory over some enemy either real or perceived and regardless of how easily and cheaply it was achieved. After presenting the idea to the new emperor, Pius quickly approved it, realizing a victory in Britannia would justify adding the word *Imperator* after his name to the coinage that would soon bear his likeness. Before Arvinnius left Rome, he was virtually assured of becoming the new governor of Britannia. He arrived back in Britannia only to learn that while in transit, the perfidious piece of dung gave the governorship to Quintas Lollius Urbicus.

Arvinnius had never met Urbicus although he knew enough of him to resent his common birth. He found it difficult to believe the second or third son of a Berber would ever attain such rank and status. By comparison, his own lineage eclipsed that of Urbicus and should have counted for something, he thought sourly. It was clear Urbicus was favored by the gods and, even more unfortunately, by Antoninus Pius as well. He refused to admit he was jealous of him. Although Urbicus earned his reputation fairly while serving as both *legatus legionis* and provincial governor of lower *Germania*. Most recently, Urbicus had served in Judaea as a legion commander for which he was given high honors including a Gold Crown and Silver Spear. While Arvinnius was no longer enamored of such baubles after having been awarded similar battlefield recognition, he grudgingly acknowledged to have received both in one campaign was a significant accomplishment. There was no question Urbicus was highly deserving of being appointed governor, but it still irritated him that he had been.

He briefly considered resigning and returning to Rome. He'd begun to think he spent too much time in the legions, and until recently, he was content to do so. Then it occurred to him that while he was enduring the privations of frontier duty, lesser men were advancing faster than he was and achieving financial rewards that so far eluded him. Governor of Britannia would have changed that. He could leave

Britannia in three or four years with social status and more than enough to live well in one of the costliest villas in Rome.

When he arrived at the spacious governor's palace situated on a high knoll overlooking the *Tamesis River* and the sprawling settlement of *Londinium*, he was met with an unwelcome surprise. The escorts and personal standards of Marcellus Septimus, the legion commander of the XX Legion, *Valeria Victrix*, and Rutilius Corbulo, commander of the II Legion, *Augustus*, were arrayed outside the walls of the villa. He was under the impression the invitation was only for him, presumably to make overtures for the fact he had not been appointed governor. He viewed their presence with distaste, believing them both to be inferior to him in ability, intellect and most of all, family lineage. He had no doubt, and less concern, his dislike of them was fully reciprocated.

Arvinnius dismounted and handed the reins to his orderly. Ignoring the brisk salutes of the guards at the entrance, he followed a young *optio* into the courtyard, his white cape edged with a distinctive red stripe flowing behind him. His stride was brisk and his hobnailed boots echoed loudly on the flagstones. He paid no heed to the elaborate mosaics surrounding a large fountain in the center of the courtyard or the colorful murals painted on the walls. Nor did he take notice of the many statues of gods and goddesses placed in niches in the surrounding wall. His mind was on nothing except what he intended to say to Urbicus.

The presence of the other two legion commanders suggested his initial presumption of why he was there may have been wrong. Accordingly, he was already starting to adjust his thinking and expectations. He realized he must curb whatever personal feelings he might have concerning Urbicus. Prudence suggested biding his time when a more private occasion would give him the opportunity to vent in a less public forum. He was angry but not foolish.

Arvinnius was ushered through an inner doorway leading to a narrow, colonnaded courtyard with a long, shallow pool running nearly the length of the enclosure. A variety of plants grew in large pots positioned along both sides of the pool. Flanking the pool and centered on pedestals were marble busts of Hadrian and Antoninus Pius. Given the short time Pius was emperor, the bust was likely brought from Rome by Urbicus. From his previous visits, he knew the two doorways underneath the covered walkways bordering the pool led to the governor's private chambers, a latrine for guests, spacious dining and reception halls, and to the slave quarters that would be superior to what most ordinary Roman citizens could only dream of. The architecture and features were typical of an expensive Roman palace, elegant but not opulent and designed to impress the occupant and visitor alike with the image of an empire destined to last forever.

The optio led Arvinnius to one of the doors and announced loudly, "General Gaius Labinius Arvinnius, commander of the VI Legion *Victrix,*" then moved to one side to permit the legion commander to enter.

The chamber was illuminated by natural light from a large circular opening in the ceiling beneath which another small pool containing brightly colored fish reflected a blue sky dotted with white clouds. Arvinnius saw a group of men standing apart at the far side of the room garbed in a mixture of togas and ornate cuirasses. He recognized the familiar faces of the other two legion commanders in animated conversation with the new governor of Britannia dressed in a white toga sitting on an ivory stool placed in the center of a low dais. Behind Urbicus stood eight *lictors* each one holding the *fasces,* a bundle of birch rods tied around an axe symbolizing the governor's *imperium.* Standing nearby within earshot were other and more junior officers along with togated civilian administrators, undoubtedly part of the governor's personal staff.

As Arvinnius crossed the room, Urbicus stood up and came to meet him in a surprising show of unexpected cordiality. Urbicus was not a handsome man. Despite their similar age, the governor's hair was dark and thick and longer than was considered fashionable; the uniform color of his hair was clear indication it was dyed. His face was clean shaven. Close up, Arvinnius realized Urbicus was older by many years than he expected him to be. Of medium stature, he was physically undistinguished. If not for the fine cloth of his toga and the current setting, he might easily have been mistaken for a shopkeeper or tradesman in any market place. His ordinary appearance was compensated by an animated, charismatic presence. Despite his private feelings before he entered the room, Arvinnius felt himself caught off-guard when Urbicus reached out enthusiastically to seize the legion commander's forearm with a grip surprisingly hard and evidently intended to convey genuine welcome. Arvinnius noticed the apparent warmth of the governor's greeting did not reach his eyes.

"*Salve,* General Arvinnus, I bid you welcome," Urbicus said in a voice that was surprisingly deep for his relatively small stature. "I'm pleased you took the time to accept my invitation."

Arvinnius merely nodded coldly in acknowledgement, omitting the usual conventional response. Everyone in the room knew very well he had no choice but to accept the invitation. A provincial governor exercized absolute authority including imposing a death penalty at will without fear of censure from the emperor or the senate.

"Allow me to introduce you to my staff."

The governor took Arvinnius by the arm and steered him across the room. For the next few minutes, he exchanged brief, neutral comments with the governor's staff, carefully trying to discern which individuals might be worth getting to know, dismissing others as irrelevant to his future interests. He exchanged perfunctory nods with Corbulo and Septimus, both wearing sour expressions and then ignored them completely.

With the civilities observed, Urbicus resumed his seat and announced to the room in general. "Gentlemen, we are privileged today to have General Arvinnius in our presence. Many of you may not know, General Arvinnius is the architect of a bold plan to expand our northwest lines here in Britannia. And, I might add, it is a plan that when executed will extend the empire and add luster to the name of our emperor as well as our own reputations."

In spite of his earlier resolve to dislike Urbicus, Arvinnius was pleased to receive public praise, particularly when it seemed so genuinely given. Perhaps he had been too hasty in his earlier judgment. The next words uttered by Urbicus quickly erased the favorable impression for the new governor that was beginning to form.

"Although brilliant and well thought out, General Arvinnius's plan as presented to Caesar requires some modification." It took all of Arvinnius's inner discipline to keep silent as he stiffened in resentment at the implied criticism his plan was flawed.

"General Arvinnius envisioned a campaign consisting of two legions, the Sixth and Twentieth, reinforced by the auxiliary cavalry and infantry now positioned on the wall. The assault would move slowly forward destroying or pacifying once and for all the tribes encountered until reaching a point approximately 100 miles north of the current wall. There, I'm told, lies a narrow stretch between the two seas. If a wall is built at this location, it will reduce by half the length of the current frontier boundary in Britannia. What General Arvinnius presented has been approved by Caesar with the following changes. Where General Arvinnius proposed two legions, I will add a substantial part of the *II Augusta* to pacify and isolate pockets of resistance in the rear while the other two legions continue to press forward to establish the new border. The reason for adding the additional legion is to accelerate the progress of the campaign to achieve Caesar's objective faster than if a smaller force was used. Once the new frontier is secured, the attacking legions will commence construction of a turf and timber wall spanning the length of the border. The *Augusta* Legion will also assist in building the wall. I expect the new wall, along with necessary forts, to be completed within two years. I wish to make one final point. I'm assigning responsibility and giving full authority to General Arvinnius for command of the campaign." Arvinnius's earlier resentment was only marginally tempered by the governor's announcement he was appointed senior field commander for the campaign. No wonder Septimus and Corbulo looked as if they had been eating lemons.

"General Arvinnius will continue to refine the plan as necessary and present to me for final approval any major deviations from the concept I've outlined. I intend to be closely involved during the execution of the campaign as well," he added with a pointed look at Arvinnius. "I expect General Aravinnius will convene a *consilium* soon to present the details of his revised plan. I shall now ask you to enjoy yourselves for a few minutes while General Arvinnius and I adjourn for a private conversation. My steward will conduct you to the dining hall where wine and refreshments are available for your enjoyment. General Arvinnius and I will soon join you to celebrate the forthcoming venture." With that said, Urbicus stood up motioning for the lictors to remain where they were and made his way toward a side door nodding amiably to those he passed.

Tight-lipped, Arvinnius followed the governor down a short corridor leading to a small, windowless room conspicuously bare except for a small writing table, several stools and a larger table piled high with scrolls and wooden tablets. When the two men entered the room, a young man in a maroon-colored tunic stood up and bowed. "This is Ennius, my secretary," Urbicus announced. "He will record what is said here." Ennius nodded in acknowledgement of the introduction and resumed his seat without speaking.

The cryptic statement immediately placed Arvinnius on guard as he realized the meeting was not spontaneous.

Urbicus walked over to the large table and turned to face Arvinnius before taking a seat and motioning for him to be seated as well. Ignoring the governor's invitation, Arvinnius remained standing. Arvinnius saw a flash of annoyance appear on the smaller man's face.

"I thought it best if we met privately to ensure we understand each other."

"If this is a private meeting, what is he doing here?" Arvinnius replied bluntly, thumbing toward Ennius without looking at him.

"My secretary makes a record of all my proceedings, and this one is no exception."

"Then, governor, perhaps we should postpone our private meeting," emphasizing the word private, "until my *cornicularius* can be here to record the proceedings as well," Arvinnius responded in a grating voice.

An angry look crossed Urbicus's face, and for a moment, Urbicus said nothing, clearly weighing the situation. Finally, without taking his eyes off Arvinnius, Urbicus said, "That will be all, Ennius. I'll summon you when I need you." After the secretary left the room, he said, "Are you satisfied now, General Arvinnius?"

Arvinnius inclined his head in a curt nod. "For the time being, although I gather you did not invite me here to hear anything I might have to say; therefore, why don't you get on with whatever you intend to tell me?"

Urbicus's face assumed a hard expression as he replied coldly, "Your reputation precedes you, Arvinnius. I was told you were difficult to get along with, and now I see the truth of the accusation. Are you always so suspicious?"

"You gave me reason enough when you appointed me to command only to make it clear in front of my subordinate commanders you intend to look over my shoulder and keep me under your thumb."

The governor's face took on a calculating look and he hesitated before speaking as if considering how to respond. Then in a calm voice, he said, "I can see how you may have misinterpreted my comments as questioning your ability and judgment. It was not my purpose, I assure you. My intent was simply to emphasize my interest and support of the campaign and not to cast doubt on your capabilities."

Avinnius remained unconvinced. "Your words were ill-chosen if that is what you meant for that is not how they were understood by every man in that hall. I think you said exactly what you intended to say. And because of it, it would be best for both of us if you appointed someone else to lead the campaign. I prefer to be simply a legion commander than to have someone telling me what to do or questioning every order I give."

"General Arvinnius," Urbicus said forcefully, "you have no choice in the matter, and frankly, neither do I. That very point is why I wanted to talk to you in private. As far as refusing the command offered to you, I suggest you consider the consequences very carefully if you do. For the same reason, I hardly had a choice in coming here. You've been blunt with me, and I shall be equally so with you. It was the emperor's orders that sent me here; it is the emperor's orders that placed you in command of the campaign. Do you think you can say no to the emperor and survive? Even if you managed to keep from being publicly disgraced, you would be financially ruined and exiled to far worse places than this island."

It was Arvinnius's turn to look perplexed. "I don't understand," he responded, now unsure of himself.

"Then, General Arvinnius, I'll try to explain it in terms you can," Urbicus replied sharply, a note of sarcasm in his voice. "You were the architect of the plan to expand the border – an objective I might add that I personally believe is ill-conceived. Given the other and more pressing problems we continue to face in other border regions, expansion here is dangerous. Unfortunately, Antoninus Pius has visions of becoming another Hadrian without having to endure the discomfort, not to mention risk, of actually taking the field himself. Judaea was a disaster, but at least Hadrian had the balls to go there and straighten it out even if he was the major cause for the Jewish rebellion. Pius wants and needs a quick and easy victory. He thinks he can achieve *gravitas* by simply moving the border here farther north. He's convinced having an experienced field general and an equally experienced governor with proven military credentials virtually guarantees a fast and successful outcome. I knew enough of your reputation to predict you would protest at being placed in a position where you would be closely supervised. Unlike you, I've no experience with the native tribes here in Britannia, and that makes me uncomfortable. I also do not know of your capabilities first-hand, and that gives me reason for concern. In short, I am not in a position of my own choosing and neither are you. Were our positions reversed, I would probably voice the same complaint you've raised. General Arvinnius, both our careers are in jeopardy," emphasizing the point by jabbing his forefinger first toward Arvinnius then to his own chest. Urbicus then added with a sardonic smile, "Under the circumstances, we've little choice but to make the best of a poor bargain. General, do you think you understand the situation well enough now that we can get on with the practical matter of giving Pius what he wants?"

Arvinnius nodded slowly in assent, his lips pressed together in a thin line. "It seems I've misjudged the situation and accused you unjustly," he said stiffly, stopping short of an open apology.

Mollified, the expression on Urbicus's face softened slightly. "All right, then we can get down to the business at hand. First of all, I've no doubt you could have reached the new border location with the two legions you proposed. You realize now why I added most of the Second to expedite the campaign. The emperor is already considering the design of the new *sesterce* with his profile on it in anticipation of a victory in Britannia. We have little time to waste in planning the details. I invited Septimus and Corbulo here to provide you the opportunity to convene a consilium here. Now that you understand the circumstances, I urge you to do so. It would please me to announce that you will meet with Septimus and Corbulo to discuss the modifications to your original plan. I'm prepared to offer the accommodations of my palace in addition to the services of my own staff to assist you."

"When you put it like that, how can I possibly refuse?" Arvinnius replied dryly. "Would tomorrow be early enough to satisfy you, or did you expect to call in Septimus and Corbulo now?"

"Tomorrow will do," Urbicus replied, relief evident in the conciliatory tone of his voice. "We shall have to find a temporary replacement to command the Sixth as you assume field command. I have one or two tribunes for you to consider."

"Never mind, my second in command knows the legion, and he's already served nearly two years on the border."

"What's his name?"

"Tiberius Querinius. You may have heard of him. He was in Judaea, too," obliquely acknowledging the governor's service there as well.

"Yes, I recall the name. I believe he was one of the few survivors of the XXII Legion, *Deiotariana*. I understand he acquitted himself quite well. It was surprising anyone survived the way Vitellius Turbo sacrificed the legion to get the Jews to consolidate their army. Well, it worked and Hadrian got a quicker end to the war as a result even if the legionaries left alive in the *Deiotariana* might argue the point. Let Turbo be an example, General. I expect you to do whatever is necessary to get a quick and successful end to the campaign; however, I trust it will not be necessary to go to the extremes Turbo did."

General Arvinnius quickly scanned the faces of the group of men assembled in the palace dining hall consisting of senior members of the Second and Twentieth Legions along with principal members of the governor's staff. Septimus and Corbulo sat stone-faced, their rigid postures silently conveying displeasure at the prospect of serving under Arvinnius. Notably absent was the governor of Britannia. Arvinnius pointedly asked Urbicus not to attend on the concern the governor's presence would undermine his authority. The compromise was that Arvinnius had already outlined to Urbicus his concept for conducting the campaign, receiving immediate approval without suggesting the slightest change. Arvinnius's irritation over what he initially perceived as gratuitous meddling by the governor was replaced by a pragmatic acceptance of their common predicament. It was obvious to both of them their relationship would never be more than cordial at best. It was also clear it would be beneficial to them both to avoid taking positions where compromise was impossible.

"I will dispense with the details still to be worked out by our staffs and confine my remarks to the general concept of the campaign, missions for the major units involved and a projected time line for seizing and occupying the new border. The campaign will begin with the movement north by the auxilia units currently positioned on the Wall followed closely by the VI *Victrix* and *XX Valeria Victrix* Legions. The auxiliary forces west of *Aesica* including those legionaries positioned at Aesica will be under the command of the Sixth. Auxiliary forces east of Aesica will be under the control of the Twentieth. The Sixth will be closely followed by the II *Augusta* whose mission will be to guard the rear and engage any pockets of resistance. I anticipate it will be the Novantae Tribe in the west and the Selgovae Tribe east of the Novanti that will be the most troublesome. The Votadini along the eastern coastal region should prove to be the least problematic, and the Twentieth should have little difficulty subjugating the tribe quickly thereby creating an opportunity for the Twentieth to flank the Selgovi from the east. The cavalry wing at *Uxellodonum* will screen the left flank of the Sixth and protect the legion from any unexpected attack from the west. If the west flank of the Sixth becomes threatened, the Second Legion will move forward and engage, allowing the Sixth to continue north. Once the Sixth has reached the new border area, the Second will continue to engage any final pockets of resistence."

Arvinnius paused and looked around the hall to assess understanding of the concept. From their intent expressions, he was satisfied to see he held their interest.

"Once the border area has been secured, I'll give instructions how I want the new wall constructed, the precise location where it will be built and the number of forts required. At that time, I will also assign the section of the wall and the forts each legion will be responsible for building and defending. I expect construction to begin immediately. During construction, the entire auxilia will maintain security north of the construction site under command of the Sixth. Before, during and the post-campaign construction, each legion will be responsible for its own logistical support. The Sixth Legion will be responsible for supporting the auxilia."

"In preparation for the order to march, the Second Legion will move to the vicinity of *Voreda* twelve miles south of the Wall. The Twentieth Legion will proceed to *Vindomora* approximately ten miles south of the Wall. The Sixth will move to a position six miles south of

Banna. Once the legions are in place, I'll announce the date and time the movement north will begin." After a moment of silence, Arvinnius nodded and concluded the consilium by saying, "You have your orders; therefore, I suggest you return to your commands quickly to begin preparing for the campaign

Chapter 3

Arrius awakened just before dawn to find Ilya gone. Humming softly while she nursed Eugenius, Ulla looked up briefly in answer to his question and told him Ilya was with Athdara bathing in the nearby river.

Arrius always thought Romans were among the most insistent in the habit of frequent bathing. He since learned the native preoccupation with personal hygiene exceeded the Romans. Regardless of how foul the weather might be, the Selgovi were accustomed to frequent bathing. He learned it was not modesty that dictated separate bathing areas for men and women but rather to allow uninhibited conversation that mixed bathing would have discouraged. More than the village square would ever be, the bathing site for the Selgovi was the favored location for social interaction.

He heard a rustle at the doorway, and Joric stepped into the light of a flickering torch. By the shadows under his eyes and his furrowed brow, Arrius knew he hadn't slept well.

Without preamble, he said, "Marcus, we have no choice but to stand and fight."

Arrius nodded; it was a conclusion he expected to hear. "That's certainly one option, but it may not be the one that will serve the Selgovi the best."

"What do you suggest we do?" Joric asked with a perplexed expression. "The clan chiefs will not flee without first facing the Romans. I've been here only a short time but long enough to know their mind. If I propose any other alternative, I doubt I will be High Chieftain long after."

"The Selgovi will not survive much longer if they force you to make a fight of it."

"It seems I and the Selgovi are doomed with either choice," Joric replied bitterly. "If we stay and fight, the Romans will finish us. If we flee, the mountain tribes will do what the Romans did not."

"Not necessarily. I believe there's another alternative. Form an alliance with the other tribes and stand together. Even then the best you can hope for is to gain time until the Caledonian Tribes decide to join you in a larger confederation."

"What makes you think the Novanti and Votadini would agree to an alliance? In the best of circumstances, the tribes have never gotten along. And Beldorach's recent war against the Novanti gives them further reason to distrust the Selgovi."

"They'll understand the need soon enough if they try to fight the legions alone. You must also reach an agreement with the tribes farther north. The northern tribes will have reason enough to believe they will be next when they see what is happening in the south. Then they may be more willing to allow the Selgovi and the other southern tribes to come into their lands and become a barrier between them and the Romans."

"You still don't believe the Romans can be defeated no matter what we do?"

"No, but you can still keep from being slaughtered as you surely will if the Selgovi do not form an alliance with the other tribes."

"What if I'm not successful in forging an alliance?" Before Arrius could comment, he added, "I may not even be able to convince my own clans to do as you suggest."

"That may be, but you must try. If you fail, then it would be better for the Selgovi to make peace with Rome and live among them as the Briganti do now."

"The Romans may soon change their mind about how peaceful the Briganti have become," Joric said. "As you arrived, a Briganti delegation was just leaving. They came to seek our help. It seems they are planning to take up arms against the Romans and wish to enlist the help of the Selgovi and Novanti; they do not trust the Votadini Tribe, which they believe has become too used to Roman ways."

Arrius looked away and made no reply as he considered the possibilities the Brigantian initiative offered. After a few minutes, he said, "Did they say when they intend to do this?"

"This summer, but the precise date is dependent on enlisting the support of the Selgovi and Novanti. They want the northern tribes to attack the Wall when they make their move in the south. That way the legionaries stationed on the Wall will be tied down preventing them from reinforcing the legions."

"What was your answer?"

Joric shrugged, "I told them we would consider their proposal carefully, but we would not act until we were convinced their attempt was serious. Only then would we be inclined to join them."

"Were they traveling south, or were they on the way west to the Novanti?"

"They were on the way to see Bothan, the High Chieftain of the Novanti," Joric replied with a quizzical expression.

"Joric, I believe there may be an opportunity for both the Selgovi and the Briganti. The Briganti are unaware of Roman plans to extend the border. They should delay their uprising until the legions begin their move north. A Briganti attack will require the legions to look both north and south. Frankly, I do not believe it will accomplish anything but delay a final Roman victory. Yet, slowing the Roman advance can be used to your advantage by giving you more time to enlist the aid of the Caledonian Tribes, including moving as many families north that wish to go before the fighting begins."

It was apparent from Joric's relieved expression that he was pleased with the possibilities Arrius raised. "I will convene a tribal council and tell the clan chiefs what the Romans intend and what you have proposed."

Arrius looked doubtful. "How soon will that be?"

"It could be five or six days from now and perhaps longer. The clan chiefs are very independent. A few still resent that Beldorach named me High Chieftain. I think some might even have preferred my mother instead of me." Arrius noted the latter was said objectively without any trace of resentment.

"I think you do not have time to wait that long. I suggest you send someone you trust to go and meet with Bothan while the Briganti delegation is there. Your representative can reveal the Roman intention and give the Briganti a better opportunity to consider how and when to implement their plan."

"Marcus, will you go and see Bothan?"

The question took Arrius by surprise. "I don't think that's wise. First of all, I barely speak the Selgovan tongue, and I understand there are differences in the Novanti language. And why would they believe or trust anything a former Roman officer has to say, particularly one who fought them in a battle in which the Novanti suffered greatly?

More than likely, they would suspect my words were nothing but a Roman trick."

"I disagree, Marcus. I believe your presence here, your marriage to Ilya, and the fact you have a son by her will help to persuade them. You know and helped to develop the Roman plans. As far as the language is concerned you won't go alone. You will have an escort and interpreters to speak for you."

Arrius began to think Joric's idea had merit, and yet he remained unconvinced he would be an effective representative. "Who would you send with me?"

"Mother and I will go with you."

Arrius was persuaded. By the time Ilya and Athdara returned from the river, Joric had already alerted Tearlach to assemble a suitable escort for the journey west.

Tribune Tiberius Querinius hardly believed his good fortune at the prospect of taking command of the Sixth Legion. He tried to concentrate on what General Arvinnius was saying as he briefed the legion's senior staff concerning his recent meeting with Governor Urbicus. His mind began to wander. *General Tiberius Querinius.* The sound of it was grand. And to think he resented being sent to Britannia, an unwanted assignment that forced him to postpone taking his seat in the senate. To be sure, the senate no longer rated the status it once had under the republic, but it represented authority and the *dignitas* he coveted more than anything else. When first told he was to come to this rain-drenched island, he was convinced he was being punished. He even suspected Arrius was the cause of it and part of a plot to bring him down. Although Arrius denied it, he was convinced the centurion told General Vitellius Turbo of his less than admirable conduct in Judaea. Long since, he came to the belief that losing his nerve in Judaea was an isolated incident and an aberration that would never be repeated. Losing one's nerve could easily happen to anyone, he rationalized. He refused to accept the truth he was every bit the coward Arrius accused him of being.

In his mid-forties, the senior tribune of the Sixth Legion was not especially robust, but he carried himself well in either toga or armor. Clean-shaven and of medium stature, the tribune held his chin high. That and his thin lips gave him an outward demeanor of haughty disdain he carefully cultivated when talking to subordinates and anyone else deemed of inferior pedigree. He concealed a thinning hairline by combing his hair forward. Except for a slightly receding chin and eyes set too closely together, he might have been considered handsome. The product of privilege and wealth, he exploited rank and position as a right of his patrician birth.

General Arvinnius's next words abruptly took the joy away from the moment. "Tribune Querinius, since your position is a temporary one, you will not be accorded the rank of general. If you acquit yourself well, I'm certain even temporary command of a legion will be considered a sign you are favored by the gods. The emperor is sure to reward you well."

Querinius's face was a frozen mask in an effort to conceal his bitter disappointment. Completely ignoring the fact Urbicus and Arvinnius could have assigned someone else to the position, he focused only on his disappointment and the fact he was being denied what was rightfully his.

"I understand, General Arvinnius," he managed to say in reply, his throat constricted enough to make his voice sound strained. "You may depend on me to do my best."

Arvinnius looked at Querinius and replied sharply, "Make no mistake, Tribune, that's exactly what I expect." Arvinnius paused briefly as if assessing the other man's reaction before continuing briskly and directing his attention to Facilus Secundus, the legion's cornicularius.

"I intend to locate my headquarters with the *Victrix*. I'll make use of the legion's staff as necessary until I can assemble my own."

Querinius felt himself sinking even lower. He dared not look at the cornicularius for fear he would see the man smirking at his humiliation. Denied the rank, he was also going to be under Arvinnius's thumb and watchful eye. In the final analysis, he had just been relegated to a mere figurehead. It was always the same. *Fortuna* seemed to dangle high prospects in front of him only to snatch them away. A wave of self-pity engulfed him, plunging him into a fit of despair. He wished Arvinnius would finish so he could return to quarters and lie down to relieve the painful and blinding headache that suddenly come upon him. Mercifully with a curt nod of dismissal, the legion commander signaled the meeting was over. After saluting, which Arvinnius did not bother to return, Querinius walked stiff-legged from the room still not trusting himself to look at Secundus or any of the other officers.

Exiting the *principia* and making his way to his quarters, he fantasized about running his gladius through Arvinnius's belly in payment for humiliating him. The mental image of the general writhing on the end of his sword helped to lessen the anger and resentment that made his stomach churn. The only thing that would give him even greater satisfaction would be to have Arrius within his grasp. It seemed every misfortune that befell him since joining the *Deiotariana* Legion in Judaea was traceable directly or indirectly to the former centurion. He couldn't think of an act savage enough to inflict on Arrius to satisfy him. If the opportunity ever came, he would make certain Arrius would not have the luxury of a quick death. Unfortunately, he doubted he would have the chance anytime soon for by now he was probably in *Rutipiae* arranging passage back to the continent and Rome. It was rumored he was wealthy and intended returning to Italia, presumably to purchase a villa and live out the rest of his life in relative ease. He wondered what became of the attractive native woman Arrius was supposed to have married. The convenience of a local wife or concubine often became an unwelcome encumbrance when it was time for a legionary or officer to move on. No doubt she had been left behind in Banna. The thought filled his mind with possibilities. If he couldn't take revenge on Arrius directly, then the woman might be a pleasing alternative.

Noting the tribune's angry visage when he entered the colonnaded courtyard, the slaves tried to slip away to other parts of the spacious quarters knowing from experience it was best to keep out of sight when the master was upset. As steward, Varus had no such latitude and stood waiting silently to see what direction Querinius's obvious bad temper might take.

"Varus, tell Cyra to attend me in the bath," referring to the young woman he purchased in Deva during his recent and brief assignment with the XX Legion. "A massage may help to relieve the pain in my head."

The steward bowed in acknowledgement and gave a sigh of relief. Cyra was perhaps the only one in the household capable of calming the unpredictable nature of the high-strung, often bad-tempered tribune. Varus turned and beckoned to one of the other slaves lurking inconspicuously in the shadows of one of the porticos. Querinius strode past them and headed for the small bath at the far end of the villa where he stripped off his clothing. He stepped into the tepid water of the waist-deep heated pool and sat down on the lowest step submerging himself to the neck. He closed his eyes and did his best to forget what Arvinnius said and concentrate on the tactile pleasure of the warm water. He heard a slight rustling behind him, and without turning, he knew Cyra was removing her shift and waiting patiently for him. He enjoyed her fulsome charms and skills on frequent occasions, and there never was an occasion when she failed to please him.

Her hair was long and raven black. Full-breasted and shapely, her figure was nearly perfect. She would have been extraordinarily beautiful but for a disfiguring burn scar covering her left cheek which pulled down the corner of her mouth; it was a physical defect that considerably reduced the price he paid for her.

After a few minutes, Querinius stood up and without even so much as a glance at the naked woman, crossed the room to a narrow wooden table. He remained standing while Cyra dried him with a soft cloth. After lying down on the thin pallet covering the table, she began gently massaging his temple with soothing strokes. The throbbing pain in his head began to slowly recede, and the tension of a few minutes before was replaced by a pleasant languor. He sighed with pleasure as her expert fingers slowly worked their way down his chest and legs. Through half-opened eyes, he observed her impassive face completely devoid of any expression. Her apparent indifference began to counter the usual effect her swaying breasts and sensuous hands normally produed. He began to resent her impersonal attention even imagining she was taking secret delight in his failure to be stimulated. Resentment transitioned rapidly to unreasoning anger. Abruptly he sat up and struck her across the face.

Blaming his inability to become aroused on her, he shouted, "Clumsy bitch, get away from me!". She lurched backward into the tiled wall where she stood trembling, eyes wide with fright, hand pressed to the cheek already turning crimson from the sharp blow.

"Get out!"

Terrified, the slave ran to her shift and without taking time to put it on fled through the arched doorway. He was already beginning to regret allowing his rage to get the better of him although he felt no remorse for striking the slave. Slaves were no better than animals, essential but no longer tolerated when they offended. Another thought struck him. What if she told the rest of the household staff of his failure to become aroused? The way slaves gossiped, the story would be repeated again and likely exaggerated until it would be common knowledge and fuel speculation he was impotent. He would be ridiculed throughout Eboracum. His head pounded worse than before as his imagination took flight. He would not be made a laughingstock. He yelled for Varus.

Querinius heard a cough near the doorway and looked up to see Varus with a look of anxious concern on his face.

"Varus, bring me my sword and then send for Cyra. She no longer pleases me."

With a servile bow, Varus departed, careful not to give any sign of his revulsion for what was about to happen.

Querinius closed his eyes and leaned back on the pallet with a smile of anticipation. He realized a moment later his headache was gone.

Chapter 4

The four-day journey was largely uneventful. Ilya spurned any attention intended to make the effort less arduous and unpleasant for her. An accomplished rider, she easily kept pace with the others and did not complain when an occasional rain shower left them all shivering in the cold, damp air.

During the nightly camps, Ilya and Tearlach talked to Joric in a continuing effort to educate him in the customs and ways of the northern tribes. While Arrius's rudimentary knowledge of the Selgovan language did not allow him to follow the exchanges in detail, he was at least able to comprehend the general idea of what was being said. He found the more he listened and conversed in the native language the more comfortable and proficient he became in using it.

Surprisingly, it was Tearlach who was even more aggressive than Joric in questioning Arrius in detail concerning Roman tactics and fighting techniques. Arrius gradually overcame his initial unease in discussing such things by accepting the practical reality of his decision to join the Selgovi. He couldn't remain neutral during the impending conflict. As the days passed, his misgivings gradually disappeared, and he responded directly and without reservation to Tearlach's questions.

Arrius's previously-formed impression of Tearlach during his captivity the year before quickly began to change. Initially, he was convinced the Selgovan was nothing but a hot-headed warrior fixated on the next battle and intent on cutting off as many Roman heads as possible with Arrius as no exception. He was starting to believe his initial and unfavorable impression may not have been either fair or accurate. Tearlach's questions were shrewd, and he was impressed with his willingness to accept objective criticism of their fighting skills in comparison to Roman Army capabilities. He showed a willingness to step back and see the paramount weakness of tribal warfare that emphasized individual fighting skill in contrast to Roman practice where disciplined formations and organization were deeply ingrained. It did not escape Arrius's notice that from time to time Tearlach would glance in Joric's direction as if to assess whether the young tribal leader understood and was assimilating the information. Arrius soon realized many of the questions and ideas Tearlach posed were for Joric's benefit; the realization further elevated his opinion of the Selgovan.

For the most part, their progress was swift over the bare rolling hills and through the forests covering the lower elevations. Their pace was slow only in steep ravines where deep ponds or impassable bogs required them to take a slower and more circuitous route. One particular area seemed familiar. He saw a high escarpment in the distance and recognized it as the place Longinus intentionally pushed him over. Now looking at the almost sheer face, he marveled that he survived the fall. He supposed the centurion's bones still lay where Seugethis left him to die after the centurion tried to do the same to the Dacian commander. If not for the fortunate arrival of a Selgovan patrol that found him more dead than alive, his bones would be lying there as well. Thanks to Beldorach, he still lived to recall the incident, even though it was not motivated by mercy or compassion. Beldorach's reason for keeping him alive had everything to do with using him as an emissary to serve his own interests and that of the Selgovi. In spite of Beldorach's callous use of him, he believed under different circumstances, he and Beldorach could have been friends instead of cautious adversaries with conflicting objectives.

Arrius noticed by the end of the second day Tearlach preceded the main body by a short distance carrying a sheathed sword in his hand with the scabbard's point resting on his thigh. When he queried Ilya why he did so, she told him a sheathed sword carried in such manner was a universal symbol of peaceful intent among the tribes.

By nightfall of the third day, Arrius was certain their progress was being observed. When he drew Tearlach aside to inform him of his conviction, the warrior smiled and nodded approvingly. "For a Roman you're observant," he said. "Do you know how many there are and when they began following our trail?" Arrius shook his head. "There are five, and they began following us after we crossed the river at midday."

Arrius was somewhat taken aback at the precision of the Selgovan's response given without any hint of boastfulness. He was also impressed with the Novanti warriors, whom Tearlach confirmed them to be, and their ability to remain unseen, at least to him.

Late in the afternoon the next day, the loud, raucous noise of a *carnyx* announced the arrival of the Selgovan contingent as it approached the gates of Bothan's palisaded fortress. The sound of the trumpet-like instrument reminded him of those he heard on the occasions when he fought the Novanti. In battle and accompanied by drums, the noise they made started as a low-pitched rumble that rapidly escalated in scale to a near ear-shattering sustained blast. The sound was intended to unnerve and loosen the bowels of even the most steadfast enemy. His legionaries were no exception.

The Novanti capital was tucked away in a woodland area so dense that it contributed substantially to the security of the settlement. It was clear the narrow winding road through the forest was by design and not happenstance. Anyone approaching the settlement during the last several miles would have risked an ambush at every bend.

Apart from the fact the main Selgovan settlement was built on a dominant hill and the Novanti capital was located on flat terrain, the two villages were similar in the palisaded construction of the inner and outer walls and tall towers overlooking the gates. The trees and undergrowth had been cleared out to the distance of a bowshot from the log stockade enclosing the village.

Arrius was pleased at the good-natured reception they received. For traditional enemies, Selgovi and Novanti appeared to demonstrate less hostility and more curiosity at their arrival. To be sure, interspersed among the jocular and often ribald remarks called out as they passed through the outer palisade, there were occasional angry cries and dire imprecations for their bloody and painful deaths. Arrius was beginning to understand the nature of inter-tribal warfare and that it was not so much based on deeply rooted enmity or acquisition as it was on a traditional pattern of behavior that allowed clans and warriors to attain stature. The wholesale destruction of a tribe was not an objective nor was the acquisition of slaves since few Brythonic tribes supported or tolerated slavery. He later understood a peaceful visit by another tribal delegation was not an unwelcome event and hospitality was genuine enough even if did not imply lasting friendship.

Without pause, Tearlach continued on through the gate of the inner palisade. Inside there was a cleared area around which were clustered dwellings that differed little from those in the outer palisade except in their greater size suggesting they were domiciles of the more senior tribal members. Dominating these structures was a large, windowless and rectangular building made of stone with a thatch roof. It was toward this larger building they headed.

Before they were half way across the clearing, Arrius saw a large man emerge from the double-doorway centered on the long axis of the building. He had a mane of thick dark hair shot through with gray. The heavy gold torque around his neck was sufficient to tell Arrius the barrel-chested figure was Bothan. The tribal leader was imposing but not handsome. His nose was large and showed the red-veined effect of heavy drinking. His eyes were hooded and made small by heavy lids that drooped at the sides. Bothan's bare arms, nearly the size of a normal man's thighs, displayed numerous scars and tattoos. Although well-muscled, he was on the verge of being corpulent with a protruding belly that strained against a wide leather belt.

Arrius saw a man standing off to one side and immediately recognized the dark-faced Brigantian he saw leaving the Selgovan capital the day he arrived.

The Selgovan party had barely dismounted when Bothan's booming voice carried easily over the noise of the stamping and snorting horses. He regarded Ilya and said with a sneer, "Well, if isn't Bathar's whelp, and if I'm not mistaken, the young bastard puppy with her now calls himself High Chieftain of the Selgovi."

Arrius did not understand Bothan's words, but Ilya's taut face told him whatever Bothan said was not complimentary. He glanced at Joric and was pleased to see Joric was unruffled, carefully concealing his reaction with a neutral expression. Without the slightest hesitation, Joric approached Bothan and came to a stop within arm's reach of the muscular tribal chief. Looking Bothan in the eye, Joric said in a level voice, "I came here in peace to speak to the leader of the Novanti on a matter of great importance and not to be insulted. Your poor manners cause me to wonder if you are really Bothan or a loud-mouthed underling, and if I am bastard born, I'm relieved to see from the looks of you that you are clearly not the cause."

Because Joric spoke more slowly and distinctly, Arrius caught at least the gist of the sharp and disparaging retort. That it hit the mark was plain by Bothan's red face and his hand dropping to his sword hilt. Slowly, Arrius moved his hand toward his own sword.

The tense moment was diffused when Bothan threw back his head and laughed in genuine amusement. "Well, it seems the puppy has sharp teeth. Perhaps I should guard my tongue more carefully," Bothan added with a smile that did not reach his eyes before pointing his finger toward Arrius, his eyes narrowing in suspicion. "Who is this man whose short hair tells me he is no Selgovan. There's something about you that seems familiar, and I know that horse as well. Unless I'm mistaken, the last time I saw the beast Beldorach was riding it."

"I am Roman," Arrius replied before Joric spoke, "and for a time Beldorach did lay claim to the horse before he returned it to me. You saw me when I fought you not far from here."

"I remember you now," Bothan nodded slowly in recognition. "Your men fought well. I'll give you that," he added grudgingly.

"And your men fought poorly," Arrius replied bluntly.

Bothan's face flushed. "Do not provoke me, Roman. I gave you a compliment."

"I gave you the truth, not an insult."

"You had luck on your side that day, and I did not."

"A leader who depends on luck in battle is a fool."

"You may be the bigger fool by coming here believing you will be allowed to leave with your head on your shoulders," Bothan lashed out. "Now I advise you to hold that bold tongue of yours before I forget for the time being you are a guest." Bothan turned to Ilya and referring again to Beldorach said, "Your cousin was a noble adversary. It was too bad he was also ambitious. I've not entirely forgiven Crixtacus for failing to bring me Beldorach's head after his men killed him." Bothan gestured toward the smaller, even-featured man behind him.

"Then it is to Crixtacus the Solgovi owe their thanks for his generosity," Ilya said.

"Enough of this. It seems we are privileged to have so many visitors coming to see us. Pointing in the direction of the Brigantian, "I know what he wants from me, but I wonder what business the Selgovi have with the Novanti. Why a Roman is with you is most curious. I'm surprised a horse thief dares to come here," looking pointedly at Tearlach. Jerking his head toward the large doorway, Bothan said, "Come with me and you will tell me why you're here."

The Selgovan contingent followed Bothan into a cavernous hall illuminated only by torches. From the sound of the footsteps behind him, Arrius concluded the onlookers outside assumed the tribal chieftain's invitation included them as well.

Bothan strode purposefully toward a dais directly opposite the door and unceremoniously took a seat in the large, heavy throne-like chair positioned in the center. Seated, Bothan's bulk seemed to dwarf the high-backed wooden chair while giving him a more commanding presence in the flickering light of the torches than standing outside. Although there were several rows of wooden benches on either side of the dais, no one ventured to take advantage of them but remained standing in a semi-circle facing Bothan.

Without waiting for an invitation to speak, Joric announced in a clear voice that would have been easily heard in the farthest reaches of the hall. "I am Joric, son of Ilya, who was the daughter of Bathar," he said formally and Arrius thought unnecessarily. "I represent a long line of Selgovan leadership that extends back to when *Cernunnos* created the land we walk upon." In time, Arrius would understand the solemn formality and stilted oratory was a standard feature of tribal gatherings. Joric continued for sometime in like manner reciting what seemed an endless history of the Selgovae Tribe and its leaders. Finally, Joric signaled he was transitioning to the purpose of the visit when he said, "I've come to my cousins the Novanti to speak of urgent matters, matters that imperil both our tribes and make it necessary to suspend our hostilities and unite to a common purpose." Arrius saw Joric's words captured Bothan's interest. "We have been told the Romans plan to extend their claim north. If successful, they will occupy the tribal lands of the Selgovi, the Novanti and the Votadini."

"The Romans have tried before, and they will fail again," Bothan interjected with a sneer.

"Perhaps it is not the same as before, for the Romans plan to come in strength that will equal if not surpass in number that of all three tribes combined."

"This I find hard to believe. Why should they leave their great wall behind to attack us now? Who has told you of this thing? Is it the Roman who stands before me now?"

Joric nodded in assent. "It is, and he has great knowledge of these plans since he played a role in preparing for the Roman campaign."

"Why should I trust anything he says?" Bothan responded, tilting his chin in Arrius's direction. "I'll wager he's come here to satisfy Roman interests and not for the benefit of the Novanti or the Selgovi. Does this Roman have a name?" He ignored Arrius, directing the question to Joric.

"His name is Marcus Arrius. He was a Roman officer in command of the garrison at Banna and the fort the Romans call Fanum Cocidii."

"Is he then a traitor who expects to be somehow rewarded for his treachery," Bothan retorted sharply, "that is if what he says has any truth to it?"

Inwardly, Arrius bristled resenting being referred to as a traitor and suppressed an urge to draw his sword. Then objectively he realized that from Bothan's perspective, it was a fair assessment. He supposed he must get used to being so named.

Ilya spoke up assertively and with unmistakable pride. "Marcus Arrius is my husband and the father of my infant son who has come to live among us. He has turned his back on Rome, and when the Romans learn of what he's done, he will be their enemy for the remainder of his life."

For the first time, Bothan's face showed interest as he leaned forward and said, "Tell me then when and why the Romans intend to advance against us," looking directly at Arrius.

Arrius understood well enough to know he was expected to speak. "Noble Bothan," he began with what he hoped was an acceptable way to address the tribal leader, "I do not have enough of your language to speak in detail of how and when the Romans will begin their advance; therefore, I will tell you in the Roman tongue, and Ilya will translate my words to be certain that what I say is fully understood."

Pausing often enough to allow Ilya to keep pace, Arrius outlined General Antinnius's plans for invading the north. Apart from their two voices that more often than not were heard almost simultaneously, there was no other sound in the chamber. Occasionally, Ilya stopped to think of a word in the native tongue that closely approximated the

Latin meaning. Bothan listened closely, never taking his eyes off Arrius throughout the lengthy recitation. Arrius glanced over at Tearlach and saw the other man's brow wrinkled in concentration. Until now, he assumed Joric or even Ilya had told him the substance of what was now being related to Bothan.

When Arrius finished, he stood silently waiting for Bothan's reaction. For a few moments, complete silence reigned. Eventually, Bothan cleared his throat and said with an expression of genuine surprise, "But why would the Romans leave their great wall that we have never been able to overcome?"

"Rome has a new emperor who lacks battle honors. It may be that a successful campaign to enlarge the empire will give him dignitas." Arrius paused while Ilya looked at him quizzically. He substituted the word *stature*, and she finished the translation. "There is another and more practical reason for moving the border farther north. The new location will be less than half the length of the present wall and will require fewer legionaries to defend it."

"Will this new emperor lead the Romans in the march against us?"

Arrius shook his head and replied directly without the need for Ilya's translation. "The emperor is in Rome far away from this place. He will not come here for this."

"Then if he succeeds, how will he gain glory in a battle in which he does not fight?" Bothan asked.

Arrius shrugged and chose diplomatically not to say more for fear of intimating the campaign was too unimportant for the emperor to involve himself personally although he thought if Hadrian were still alive, it was conceivable he would come to Britannia.

Bothan shook his head in disgust. "This emperor is not much of a man if he does not fight beside his men." Again, Arrius did not respond, privately thinking Bothan had a point. "When will this Roman advance take place?"

"I believe it will begin soon when the weather improves and there is no longer a threat of snow."

Bothan grunted, nodding his head before commenting as much to himself as to the rest, "I think this emperor is not so wise as he believes himself to be. Even if he is successful, he risks having the Novanti, the Selgovi and the Briganti at his back while facing the tribes in the far north. I do not count the Votadini for they are already lapdogs of the Romans. This Roman emperor may find he has gained less than he expects in the unlikely event he does succeed in pushing us back. Already the Briganti are planning an uprising and want our help by attacking the Romans from the north."

Arrius's estimation of Bothan went up slightly. He privately harbored a similar concern when Arvinnius first broached the Roman plan. He wondered if Arvinnius and the others responsible for the campaign adequately considered the threat posed by the Briganti.

Bothan stood up and announced, "Until now, I've not been inclined to help the Briganti since they've never assisted the Novanti and Selgovi when we fought the Romans. It seems I may now have to reconsider my position." Arrius observed the relieved expression on the face of the Brigantian emissary. "We'll speak more of this tomorrow after I've consulted with my council and clan chiefs. Crixtacus will show you where you may stay the night. I'll have food sent to you." Bothan then glared at Tearlach. "I will keep a close eye on the horse thief while he is here." As Bothan stepped down from the dais and strode from the hall, Tearlach remained tactfully silent, a faint smile lifting the corners of his mouth.

"What if Bothan decides not to ally with us?" Joric absently poked the embers of the fire with a stick as Ilya sat nearby quietly observing the two men.

Arrius delayed his response while debating the best way to put into words what had been going through his mind since observing Bothan. He found himself in an awkward and unfamiliar position in taking on the role of advisor instead of commander. It was different now. The Selgovi were not under his command, and yet he felt keenly the responsibility that whatever he said or did not say might have a significant impact on the tribe's future.

"I believe Bothan will agree to an alliance with the Selgovi, but he will expect to lead it, which will present a problem for the Selgovi. In my opinion, Bothan is not skilled in warfare…"

"But then neither am I," Joric finished the statement. "However, I'll have your years of experience to help me."

Arrius inclined his head to acknowledge the obvious truth of Joric's inexperience. "True, although Bothan is hardly going to defer to a youthful tribal leader who depends on a Roman he has no particular reason to trust. The best way to resolve the matter may be to suggest Bothan assume the leadership role he expects to have anyway. If you were to propose it, he will be all the more receptive to receiving future counsel from the Selgovi, including the best way to aid the Briganti."

"I understand, although I do not see how the Selgovi and the Novanti combined could successfully attack the wall."

"They cannot, nor should it even be tried. It would be a futile effort and costly for the tribes."

"Then how can we aid the Briganti at all?"

"By waiting until the legions leave the wall and march north. That would be the best time for the Briganti to begin their uprising. Their attack would force the Romans to fight in the field in two directions without the benefit of the current wall defenses. The northern tribes would benefit as the Roman advance would be delayed. When Bothan convenes a council, you should propose the strategy for consideration."

"Marcus, you saw clearly what I did not. I'm fortunate to have you at my side. What if Bothan agrees to the Briganti plan?"

"Then I believe the Selgovi will be forced to deal with the Romans separately as best as possible. Under no circumstance should you agree to be part of such an attack."

"Marcus, if Bathar were here, he would approve of what you've said as do I," Ilya commented."

"You still do not believe the Roman advance can be stopped, do you?" Joric asked.

Arrius did not hesitate in shaking his head. "No, the most you can accomplish is to delay the Romans long enough to find sanctuary farther north. I still believe a treaty with Rome would serve the Selgovi best."

"I think a treaty cannot be considered until after we have fought them."

Reluctantly, Arrius agreed. "I fear you are right even as I believe many Selgovi will die as a result."

Several days later, the Selgovan delegation left a bellicose and over-confident Bothan acclaimed as the nominal war leader of the latest Novanti-Selgovan alliance. Arrius was pleased with Joric's success in maneuvering Bothan into accepting the strategy he and Joric agreed upon. Before the discussion was over, Bothan was convinced it was his idea all along. Arrius thought it unfortunate the tribal chief continued to be unshaken in his belief the Romans would ultimately be defeated. Bothan reluctantly agreed to send Novanti representatives to the Selgovan capital as part of a combined effort to go north and negotiate with the mountain tribes; he appointed Neacal and Crixtacus as his official representatives.

Two days from the Selgovan capital with Tearlach once again in his customary position a half mile in the lead, Arrius heard the distant drumming sound of hoofbeats becoming more distinct. Tearlach galloped into sight and brought his horse to a skidding stop. Tearlach's hurried warning of a Roman patrol was hardly necessary as by then Arrius saw a Dacian cavalry patrol emerging from the tree line ahead. He recognized the familiar figure of Seugethis thundering toward them wearing his gilded cuirass and white-plumed helmet.

Tearlach and the other Selgovan warriors had already drawn their swords and though badly outnumbered prepared to fight. Realizing flight was impractical at this point with the odds hopelessly one-sided, Arrius urged Ferox toward the oncoming horsemen with his hands raised in a desperate attempt to stop the charging Dacians.

For a brief moment, Arrius wasn't sure Seugethis was going to heed his silent plea to break off the attack. At the last minute, Seugethis held up a hand, and the troop came to a halt a short distance away. He noted the bewildered faces of the cavalrymen which matched the expression on the face of their commander now fully revealed when Seugethis reached up and removed his ornate helmet.

Arrius nudged Ferox forward until his mount was virtually nose to nose with the Dacian's horse. "Marcus Arrius! I imagined you were well on the way to Rome by now. What are you doing here, and who do you travel with?"

Up to a point, he thought truth would serve Selgovan interests better than a lie. By relying on the Dacian's past friendship, there was at least a chance Seugethis would not attempt to take them back as long as he remained unaware of Joric's identity.

"You're aware I married a native woman, and she bore my child?" Seugethis nodded. "You may also recall she is not Brigantian; she is by birth Selgovan. She left her native land to seek shelter with the

Brigantae Tribe many years ago. She now wishes to reestablish relations with her tribe, and I've pledged to assist her."

Seugethis stared at Arrius with an incredulous expression. "Who else knows of this?"

"A few, but it is better you do not know who. When I left Banna, I let it be understood I was leaving Britannia for Rome."

"Then Arvinnius does not know of this?"

"He does not although he will learn of it eventually."

"Arrius, I think you're a dead man. If the Selgovi don't end up taking your head, Arvinnius will stop at nothing to crucify you, and if he fails, Tribune Querinius will be right behind him to finish the job. You may not know Querinius is now commanding the Sixth Legion while Arvinnius takes overall command of the three legions once the northern invasion begins."

"Querinius is now a general?"

The Dacian shook his head. "Not exactly. He commands but still holds the rank of tribune."

"No matter, the fact he commands does not signify a pleasant time for the Sixth."

"Aye, he's a poor excuse for an officer as I've ever known. I don't care much for Arvinnius either, but I credited him with more sense than to put Querinius in charge of anything. You must know when they learn you're living with the Selgovi, they'll assume you are a traitor. Then I'll have little choice but to follow their orders to find you. If I were ambitious, I should probably take you back with me. On the other hand, I'm not ambitious, and I don't like Arvinnius or Querinius." Seugethis threw his head back and laughed. "I would give a year's pay to see his face when he eventually finds out you're in the north, but it won't be from my lips. That much I will do for you."

"Did you say three legions will march north?"

"I did. I'm told the II *Augusta* has been added by Governor Urbicus to accelerate the campaign to a successful conclusion."

"When will the invasion begin?"

Seugethis gave Arrius a shrewd look and ignored the question. "What will you do when the legions begin to march?"

"When that day comes, I'll do everything and anything to protect my wife and son."

"I see. Including fighting alongside the Selgovi?"

"If necessary I will, but I will avoid doing so."

Seugethis looked doubtful. "Arrius, I think it will be very difficult for you to live between two worlds – no longer a part of one and not entirely accepted in the other. Well, a man must do as the gods direct, and I wish you good fortune wherever you journey. If we meet again, I hope it will be in circumstances when our swords are sheathed. Now I shall pay my respects to the Lady Ilya. She will recall my handsome face in spite of the brief encounters we've had," he added immodestly and with complete sincerity.

"What will you tell your men?" Arrius asked as they walked their mounts toward the small Selgovan party that remained alert and mounted.

Seugethis dismissed the question with a peremptory wave of his hand. "They will not ask questions of their commander, nor will they say anything more than what I wish them to say. It will be said we encountered a small party of non-hostile villagers who were unable to say anything of importance concerning the Selgovi."

Seugethis reined in opposite Ilya and said with a dazzling smile, "No doubt you remember me. I am Seugethis, and after seeing you once again, I realize your beauty is reason enough for Arrius's refusal to return to Banna with me." Ilya graciously returned the smile, immediately captivated by the cavalryman's charming manner.

"I remember you quite well. Are all Dacians as handsome as you?" she asked, a glint of amusement in her eyes.

Seugethis beamed and replied immodestly, "I admit we are considered a handsome race, and some of us are even more favored than others." His gaze shifted to Joric. "And the young man here who bears such a striking resemblance to you? Who might you be, perhaps a cousin or nephew of the Lady Ilya?"

Arrius held his breath fearing what the young man would answer and was relieved to hear him say, "I am Joric, grandson of Bathar."

"It seems I've heard your name before, but I can't seem to recall it. It will probably come to me after we part." Arrius knew Seugethis recalled Joric's name well enough. Seugethis eyed Tearlach's surly face and remarked in an aside to Arrius, "I suspect not all in your party are non-hostile; this one looks as if he would smile while he cut my head off."

"You're probably right. It's possible the same could be said for me as well."

Seugethis turned and faced Arrius. "I'll leave you to your journey. I wish you well, Marcus Arrius," he said with sincerity. "My advice is to take your wife and young Joric and go far from here. Very soon these lands will no longer be safe for the casual traveler and most particularly for a former Roman officer." With a casual wave, the Dacian galloped back to his men and soon disappeared in the direction they had come.

Arrius continued to look after the Dacian troop long after they disappeared over a distant hill and the sound of their horses faded away. He felt a brief pang of regret for what the gods decreed for him. In a way, he envied the Dacian's freedom and his single-minded devotion to his beliefs vaguely realizing not long since he held a similar outlook. Shrugging off the momentary gloom, he turned and saw Ilya. Complicated it might be, but his fate was bound to this woman and the young man at her side. It was far too late to turn back now even if he wanted to.

The shadows were already lengthening when they made camp near a stream. Although the evening temperature was cool and the water was colder still from snow-melt, the stream offered a welcome respite following a long ride. After a quick meal of cold venison and hard bread, the men headed downstream and Ilya turned upstream in search of a convenient pool in which to bathe.

Arrius took only a few steps when he heard Ilya call his name. He turned and saw her motion for him to come with her. His blood quickened at the invitation, and he hastened to follow her as she threaded her way through the trees along the banks of the stream. Except for the first night when he arrived at the Selgovan capital, they had not been alone together. The communal living arrangements discouraged any intimacy or even the inclination for it.

The nearly full moon was just beginning to crest the treetops when he saw her disappear behind a stand of river willows. Catching up to her, he found her seated on a log in the process of pulling off her calf-length boots. Standing up, she loosened the belt that fastened the thigh-length kirtle around her waist and pulled the garment over her head. Underneath the kirtle, she wore a woven bodice tucked into

57

knee-long riding breeches made of animal skin and not unlike those worn by the Selgovi men. She started to undo the laces of the bodice until it gaped open revealing the shadowed cleavage and contours of her breasts. With mounting desire, Arrius watched her pull her breeches down over her hips. Unable to restrain himself any longer, he stepped toward her and gently slid the bodice from her shoulders until she stood fully revealed before him. For a moment longer, he stood without moving, content to take in the sight of her body glowing silver in the moonlight. He pulled her hard against him while their mouths met hungrily in unrestrained passion. It was so long since they were last together that it was as if their exploring hands were discovering each other for the first time. He felt her hard breasts tight against him as she pressed her hips urgently against his. They broke their embrace long enough for her to help him remove his heavy wool cloak and the rest of his clothing. After spreading the cloak on the leafy ground, they sank down upon it and were soon lost in a world where words were unnecessary.

They spoke little that night except to profess their love for each other. Both were only too willing to leave events they couldn't change shrouded in the past. They would never succeed in forgetting the horror of Betto's assault on her, but they would work together to overcome it.

Chapter 5

The two-day consilium was nearly over. General Arvinnius was pleased when the governor decided at the last minute not to attend citing the long distance he would have to travel from Londinium to the headquarters of the Sixth Legion at Eboracum. It was a decision Arvinnius counted on when he scheduled the meeting. The last thing he needed was Urbicus breathing down his neck and second-guessing his decisions. In addition to the tribunes and senior centurions from the three legions, the commanders of each of the sixteen garrisons located along the wall also attended. In a separate meeting following the council, General Arvinnius searched the faces of the three legion commanders and that of Gaius Cornelius, the tribune commanding the cavalry wing at *Uxellodonum* and quietly assessed their capability. His future and the success of the campaign rested on their shoulders.

Marcellus Septimus, the taciturn and overweight legion commander of the XX Legion, *Valeria Victrix,* was not particularly innovative, but he was competent enough. His fleshy, sagging jowls reminded Arvinnius of a hound. The fact the legion commander lacked imagination did not bother Arvinnius in the least; he preferred it when his subordinates followed his orders to the letter, confident he more than anyone else knew what should be done and when.

Rutilius Corbulo, commander of the II Legion, *Augustus,* was by far the more seasoned of the two legion generals. He was the very image of a Roman general. Resplendent in an elaborately engraved bronze cuirass, Corbulo was unabashedly vain in his appearance and the image he projected. Arvinnius guessed women found his dark features and square jaw irresistible, and he envied him in that respect. He thought Corbulo would never have dared to wear a cuirass such as that in the presence of Hadrian. The former emperor felt nothing but contempt for pretentious armor. As competent as Corbulo was, Arvinnius distrusted him. Corbulo was ambitious which ordinarily would have been a positive attribute. Arvinnius liked ambitious men and used their ambition to further his own. In his experience, such men would do whatever it took to succeed. Corbulo was an exception to this observation. He was convinced Corbulo shared the confidence of Urbicus to a degree he did not and never would. He suspected Corbulo would keep Urbicus fully informed of whatever was discussed during the consilium or occurred during the campaign.

Gaius Cornelius, commander of the thousand-man cavalry wing was a quiet but personable man with an impeccable birthright that extended far back in time and well before the first Caesar. Arvinnius felt an affinity to Cornelius based on his belief the tribune and others with similarly distinguished lineages were especially favored by Fortuna. That he himself was unable to trace his own lineage nearly as far only increased his admiration for the tribune's family bona fides. He was convinced a distinguished cognomen automatically conferred great *dignitas* to the individual who carried the name. Tall and spare, Cornelius had a broad forehead and prominent cheekbones. Physically the tribune might have resembled a younger version of himself. The tribune's beard was a notable difference in contrast to Arvinnius's clean-shaven face. It was not surprising to Arvinnius the tribune was a competent leader for that was to be expected of a man with such a noble heritage. Arvinnius would have been genuinely shocked to learn the Cornelian name resonated with him to an extent far greater than it ever had or would with Gaius Cornelius whose private beliefs were surprisingly and deeply rooted in more egalitarian views.

Strangely, Arvinnius's principal reservation concerning the four men before him focused principally on Tiberius Querinius. On impulse, he insisted Querinius assume command of the Sixth specifically to counter the governor's gratuitous offer to provide a replacement. The last thing he needed was a client of Urbicus serving as one of his senior officers. As the senior field commander, he believed his new position would provide ample opportunity to keep an eye on the relatively inexperienced tribune. Already he was beginning to have some private reservations and concerns he may have erred. There was something about the tribune that even naked ambition and an impressive family name couldn't entirely erase his growing doubts. Querinius was somewhat erratic in his behavior of late. He seemed distracted and did not appear to be focusing on his duties quite to the extent he should given the nature of his elevated responsibilities. There was also the incident of the slain slave girl. That in itself was not a particularly significant event. After all, the law gave slave owners the right to do anything they wanted to them. However, putting a slave to death was extreme and rarely done. He wondered what transgression the slave committed to merit such punishment. If he had made a mistake with Querinius, it was too late to do anything about it.

The thought he was consigned to an even closer supervision of the tribune was simply the latest irritant of a growing list of things bothering him, including the fact he would be getting fewer cohorts from the Second and Twentieth legions than he counted on. He suspected Septimus and Corbulo were responsible by going behind his back to Urbicus and persuading him local conditions in their sectors demanded a larger presence to remain behind. That he would have done the same if he commanded one of those legions was precisely why he was certain of it.

Arvinnius cleared his throat. "The reason we are meeting is for Tribune Gaius Cornelius to relay to you what he has already reported to me. The information has a direct and immediate bearing on the success of the campaign."

Even before Arvinnius nodded for the tribune to begin, Querinius felt the anger boiling inside. How dare his subordinate report directly to Arvinnius instead of him? It was simply another example that he was not being acknowledged as legion commander. It was unconscionable for Cornelius to bypass him, and he would neither forget nor forgive the slight. It took great self-control to conceal his feelings and pay attention to what the cavalry commander was saying.

The tribune began to speak with natural self-assurance. "Soon after I took command at Uxellodonum, I was approached by a native tribesman during one of my visits to *Blatobulgium*, twenty miles northwest of the Wall. As you may recall, Blatobulgium is our most distant fortress and well within Novanti tribal lands. This individual sought me out privately and offered to provide information about his tribe's activities in return for gold and an opportunity to relocate farther south of the Wall. Frankly, I mistrusted the man and doubted his credibility when he identified himself as a member of Bothan's war council. I agreed to pay him for any useful information, and he in turn consented to pass information on to the centurion in command of the fort. Since then the centurion has occasionally reported on matters that until now were of little consequence. Just before I left my post to come to Eboracum, I received the following report. I will read it and you may then judge its significance."

Salve Gaius Cornelius, Tribune and Commander of the Ala Petriana, I give you greetings.

I received information from our friend that a delegation of Briganti tribesmen recently visited the Selgovi and Novanti with an urgent plea to join them in a general uprising against the Romans. The Briganti are attempting to persuade the northern tribes to attack the Wall from the north while the Briganti mount a simultaneous attack in the south. I pressed him for the date when this would take place. He did not know, but he said it would be soon and before the Romans move north...

Arvinnius interrupted. "I can conclude only one thing from the last statement. Our plan for a campaign in the north is known. On a much more immediate note, we may also be facing a Briganti uprising at the very time we deplete our strength in the south. Continue, Gaius Cornelius."

The tribune began again where he left off.

What he said next may provide the explanation of why he had some knowledge of the plans for a campaign in the north. He claims three days ago a tall Roman with a prominent scar on his face visited the Novanti with representatives of the Selgovi tribe. From his physical description, and the fact he identified the Roman as a former commander on one of the wall forts suggests the individual may be the Praefectus Marcus Arrius, who was thought to have left Banna for Italia several weeks ago.

Cornelius put aside the wooden writing tablet and said, "The remainder of the report provides no additional information of any significance."

General Arvinnius spoke after a moment of stunned silence. "I sent a messenger to query Centurion Plinius Flavius, the present commander of Banna since the departure of the former Praefectus Marcus Arrius. Flavius professed to know nothing of his whereabouts indicating only that he believed him well on the way to the port of

Rutipiae if he has not already departed Britannia by now. I've dispatched couriers to the south who are ordered if necessary to go as far as Rutipiae to learn if anyone resembling Arrius passed by any of our depots or obtained passage to the mainland. In the meantime, I think it prudent to accept the strong possibility the report is accurate, including the speculation the Roman mentioned is none other than Arrius. Why a former Roman officer would leave the empire and treat with the enemy to the disadvantage of Rome is too heinous to contemplate and beyond comprehension. The one reason I can think of that makes it believable is that he was known to have married a Selgovan woman who apparently bore him a child. I also know from previous discussions with Arrius that he appeared overly sympathetic with the plight of the native people and once professed to me he was against unnecessary depredations against them — he failed to define what he meant by *unnecessary*. I recall thinking after the last time we talked of such matters, Arrius would bear watching. I was more than relieved when he decided to leave the army. It is inconceivable a highly decorated Roman officer would become a traitor to Rome. In any event, I offer a purse of 5000 *denarii* for any information leading to the capture of this Roman, whoever he may be. If by any chance this man turns out to be Arrius, I will double the amount. By the time I'm through with Arrius, he will curse his mother and the gods for giving him life."

Querinius was almost shaking from excitement at the possibility the unidentified man was Arrius. He fervently hoped it was. He would gladly give the same amount Arvinnius offered or even more for the privilege of watching Arrius suffer a painful and lingering death.

"I intend to proceed with the assumption the threat of a Briganti uprising is real. But if we have lost the element of surprise then so have the Briganti. We will continue with the redeployment of the Second and the Twentieth as now planned. Their presence closer to the Wall will simply aid the Sixth Legion in putting down any insurrection before it has a chance to mature. The advance of the auxiliary units on the Wall as presently scheduled will proceed within thirty days. In the event the Briganti unwisely decide to take up arms, I will order the Twentieth to halt its advance against the Votadini and deal with the insurrection as it occurs. In the meantime, while the Second and Twentieth legions are moving into their positions south of the wall in preparation for the move north, the Sixth will continue to patrol north of the wall. At the least indication of any hostile intent, I want action taken immediately with sufficient measures to insure these savages understand the consequences they face if they dare threaten Rome."

Following a brief discussion during which few questions were asked, General Arvinnius terminated the consilium. As the officers filed out of the principia, Querinius drew Gaius Cornelius aside under the colonnaded porch surrounding the courtyard and said stiffly, "I would speak with you in private, Tribune."

Cornelius stopped and regarded Querinius quizzically, responding politely, "Of course, Tiberius Querinius," and waited for the other to speak.

Controlling himself with effort, Querinius said, "I wonder why you did not see fit to report the information to your immediate commander.

Cornelius regarded Querinius with unfeigned surprise. "But, in fact, I did precisely that by telling General Arvinnius."

"What do you mean?"

"By order of General Arvinnius, I now report directly to him. He placed the *Ala Petriana* directly under his direct command days ago. It was not unexpected that he would do this although I did not think the command relationship would change until the invasion began. As you are aware, my task is to screen the west flank when the Sixth moves north. I thought of all people, you would have been the first to know of the order. I also assumed the general would share the information from Blatobulgium with you before presenting it to Septimus and Corbulo." Querinius was sure the last was said with a note of sympathy that made General Arvinnius's decision even more difficult to accept. When Querinius continued to say nothing in response, Cornelius said, "Is there anything else you wished to discuss?"

Querinius shook his head wordlessly and turned away in shock.

Chapter 6

Immediately after their return to the Selgovan capital, Joric sent messengers to the clan chiefs requesting their attendance at a tribal council. Several days later, the last of the eleven clan chiefs arrived and camped near the others in the fields outside the village gates.

If Arrius expected a solemn and subdued gathering, he was surprised at the festive air that prevailed in spite of the known purpose for the council. There were horse races, wrestling matches ending with the combatants bloody but laughing, and archery contests that left Arrius astonished at the deadly marksmanship of the participants. In the evenings, singing, dancing and drinking bouts continued and became noisier and more abandoned as the night wore on until the inebriated participants staggered off to whatever beds they had been invited to.

After observing the light-hearted behavior of the Selgovan clans over the last several days, Arrius was certain they held no real appreciation for what lay ahead. He said as much to Ilya the night before the council was to begin.

"You're wrong, Marcus. They understand very well what's in store for them. You think their behavior is child-like, but it would be a mistake to underestimate them. They celebrate because fighting is a part of our culture. Every young man when he comes of age expects to spend much of his life as a warrior first and farmer or herder second. Selgovan women understand the same and are reconciled to it. Now they expect to fight Romans and they prefer that to fighting the other tribes, or each other. If the Romans were not the immediate foe, they would be making plans to fight or steal livestock from the Novanti or Votadini. The other reason they celebrate is they know it may be a long time before they are able to do so again, if ever."

"Will they accept what Joric will say to them?"

Ilya shook her head and replied doubtfully, "Perhaps, although I don't think so. It may seem impractical and unwise to you to fight, but honor and tradition will prevent them from following a more realistic solution. Joric will have no choice but to give them what they wish while hoping they will agree to pursue efforts for enlisting the support of the mountain tribes."

"Is there any possibility the clan chiefs won't follow him?"

"It's possible. When his right to succeed Beldorach was confirmed, there was not the threat then that now exists. Joric is untried and undoubtedly, one or more clan chiefs will raise that point and demand he step down. If a majority of clans argue for that, Joric will have no choice but to either step aside or resolve the challenge to his leadership another way."

"What other way is there?"

"He may have to fight to remain High Chieftain."

Arrius knew and respected Joric's skill with gladius and dagger. Along with the help of Decrius and Rufus, he taught Joric over the past several years the use of sword, dagger and *pilum*, the heavy Roman spear that more than the short sword had become the signature weapon for establishing and maintaining the empire. He knew the young man was greatly skilled in the use of such weapons, but training was one thing and actual fighting was another. He tried to remember the first time he faced an opponent who was doing his best to kill him. It was in Germania, a skirmish during which he found himself face to face with a native tribesman as big as he was and by his lined face presumably more experienced. If not for the other man tripping over a wounded legionary from the first rank, he wouldn't be alive to recall the encounter. Fortunately, the automatic reflexes conditioned by hours of drill under the harsh and often brutal supervision of veteran optios came into play. Taking advantage of the opportunity provided, he ended the apparent one-sided contest with a quick, timely thrust of his gladius. He recalled at the time being amazed at how easily and quickly a man could die. He was sick after the battle was over. From that moment on, fighting and killing became as impersonal as it was routine. Arrius regarded Ilya's calm face and marveled at her quiet acceptance of her son's future, even possibly his life, might be in jeopardy before the Roman onslaught even began. He surmised her Selgovan heritage was responsible for the fatalistic outlook.

While Arrius was pondering Joric's dilemma, the young High Chieftain walked in accompanied by Tearlach. By now, Arrius was accustomed to seeing Tearlach close by Joric's side. He wondered if

Tearlach's close association with the young leader was a sign of loyalty or posed something entirely different. His own guarded relationship with Tearlach was reason enough to consider the possibility he was looking after his own interests. As long as Joric seemed unconcerned, he would remain a silent but cautious observer.

"Are you prepared for tomorrow, my son?" Ilya asked.

"Yes, I've talked separately with each of the clan chiefs, and I believe most will agree to what I will say. I've had to make concessions to win acceptance of my proposed strategy."

"What concessions?" Ilya and Arrius chorused almost in unison.

"I agreed that we will stand and fight." Joric held up a hand to forestall Arrius's quick response. "Let me finish. We will resist the Roman advance until Selgovan honor is satisfied. Then we will withdraw north."

"How and when will you know Selgovan honor has been achieved? After most of your warriors are dead and your women raped?" Arrius's voice carried equal measures of anger and exasperation.

Tearlach said, "What did you expect, Roman? That we would bow meekly to the invaders and flee like so many hares before the wolves?"

Ignoring Tearlach's outburst, Joric continued, "I admit the precise point cannot be clearly established, but I'm confident I'll know when the time comes. In return, I have agreement to approach the northern tribes to seek their support and a safe-haven if we are forced from our lands. There is one more thing. The clan chiefs have agreed to allow you and Mother to attend the council. Her presence will help to reinforce my own claim to the dais, and you will have the opportunity to tell the clan chiefs of your concerns and the Roman way of fighting."

Arrius was about to respond when Tearlach interjected sharply. "Roman, you would do well not to insult the clans by telling them how poorly they fight as you did with Bothan. We know of Roman success and have seen firsthand the cowardly manner in which they fight with no regard for individual honor and glory. You will be more successful if you first find things to praise them for before you tell them they must fight differently than they are used to. Perhaps then they will listen more carefully."

Arrius considered Tearlach's practical advice. He immediately understood the Selgovan was right but couldn't resist saying, "The Romans fight as one, and that is why they defeat their enemies who choose to fight individually. Romans want to win battles first instead of concentrating on personal glory."

Tearlach scowled and looked as if he was about to make a rebuttal. Evidently thinking better of it, he remained silent, and Arrius knew he made his point. For any chance at all to influence the Selgovi, he realized he must heed Tearlach's advice. He still wasn't convinced either Ilya or Joric fully understood just how desperate their situation was in facing Roman legions in battle.

Further reinforcing Tearlach's comment, Ilya said, "Marcus, Tearlach is right." She leaned toward him and placed a hand on his arm. "I'll translate for you and help to use our way of speaking to make them better understand you." He knew she was referring to the long-winded oratory favored by the native tribes in contrast to his tendency to speak directly to the point.

Arrius smiled. "Very well, I'll do my best to behave and curb any words of criticism and doom."

"Oh, there is one final thing," Joric interjected. "If you agree, I would like you to go north with Bothan's representatives to talk with the highland tribes."

"Am I then to be the Selgovi representative?"

Joric looked uncomfortable before replying, "No, Ilya will be my official representative."

Arrius was curious to see the inside of the great hall dominating the hill-fort that overlooked the palisaded village below. It differed little from Bothan's hall in size, but there the similarity ended. The door was on the end of the rectangular building, there were narrow windows spaced every few feet the length of the structure, and the roof was constructed of wooden shakes instead of thatch.

While he and Ilya stood outside waiting to be summoned, he speculated on the significance of the angry voices that occasionally drifted through the open doorway. Since Ilya seemed unconcerned, he concluded the heated exchanges going on inside were not out of the ordinary.

The clan chiefs and the warriors who accompanied them had already been inside for sometime before Tearlach emerged and curtly beckoned Ilya and Arrius to follow him. Arrius heard an undercurrent of restless noise as they entered the building.

The chamber was filled to capacity, and despite the cool temperature outside, the press of the standing crowd warmed the interior. The illumination provided by the narrow windows was supplemented by flickering torches that produced almost as much smoke as light.

They followed Tearlach down a center aisle defined by two parallel rows of huge logs supporting the high-pitched and smoke-blackened rafters above. At the far end of the hall, Joric sat on a worn, somewhat unimpressive wooden chair and modest in comparison to Bothan's throne. As he drew closer, Arrius observed the chair was centered on a low circular slab of polished stone carved with intricate designs. Earlier Ilya told him the carved stone even more than the chair represented the focal point of Selgovan authority and power. The stone slab was tall enough to place the chair's occupant slightly above any who stood before the circular platform. Joric projected an image of calm authority, and Arrius marveled again at his quick transition from youth to manhood.

As Arrius looked at the men standing closest to the dais, it was evident by their more elaborate attire and the heavy torques around their necks these were the clan leaders. Presumably, those standing just behind the clan leaders represented the more senior clan members. Some he vaguely recalled from the previous time he was here although he did not recall any names. With one exception, the expressions on their faces were uniformly grim; a few regarded him with suspicion and open hostility. The exception was a stocky man of medium height whose handsome features were marred by a scar almost as prominent as his own. The scar extended well into the hairline on the left side resulting in a white streak in his otherwise dark hair. Briefly their eyes met and Arrius saw only curious interest reflected in them.

There was a commotion at the far end of the hall, and for a moment, all attention was diverted to a confrontation between two men with drawn daggers angrily facing off in the center aisle. The disagreement was quickly fueled by the boisterous urging of the immediate bystanders while those farther back pressed in closer to observe the altercation. Two of the clan leaders strode toward the men, one of whom was already bleeding from a shallow gash on the arm. Occupied as they were, they did not see the approach of their clan chiefs until it was too late. One man was felled by a fist in a single blow to the side of the head while the other had his legs kicked out from under him followed by a second kick to the jaw. Without saying a word, the clan chiefs resumed their places while the two unconscious men were carried outside. Arrius determined from how quickly the noise subsided and the proceedings resumed, the outburst was a normal and frequent occurrence with the hot-tempered, combative tribesmen.

Joric began to speak, and the noisy din quickly died down to a muted hum as the men moved farther forward to hear what was being said. Joric's voice carried easily over the crowded hall aided by the height of the dais. The young tribal leader spoke too quickly for him to understand, and he assumed Joric was providing an introduction for him. His assumption proved correct, and after a few minutes, Joric looked at Arrius and said, "Arrius, I told them about you and why you came here. Except for the clan chiefs, the rest do not yet know the extent of the Roman emperor's plans. I left that for you to describe."

Arrius turned and faced the sea of faces. He suspected the sudden stillness that now prevailed was prompted more by curiosity and the novelty of having a Roman address them than any respect for him. He felt sure his presence and the opportunity for a Roman to speak was unprecedented.

He began first in the Selgovan language, greeting them formally by extolling their virtues as warriors of great renown. He had carefully rehearsed the beginning of what he wanted to say with Ilya. Even though he stumbled from time to time over the difficult, and compared to Latin, unmelodic language, he knew it was important that he make the attempt. He was rewarded by appreciative nods of encouragement from those who stood nearby. After switching to Latin, he paused frequently to allow Ilya to keep pace in her translation. He described the Roman plans to expand their frontier boundary and how it would be accomplished. Careful to avoid denigrating the fighting capabilities of the Selgovi, he concentrated on describing the battle tactics of the Roman legion in the field and hoped the description alone would be sufficient to emphasize the danger such an invasion presented. Occasionally, the hall would erupt in angry yells and fist shaking that obliged him to wait until the disruption subsided. He told them it would be futile to fight the Romans in open and close combat. The Roman Army wanted an enemy to fight in such manner for that was the way in which legionaries were trained to fight. Instead, he devised tactics designed to take advantage of Selgovan strengths and Roman weaknesses, tactics he successfully used against his own legionaries in Gaul, Parthia, Judaea and most recently in Britannia. He concluded by saying, "The Selgovi are fierce warriors and they fight bravely, but now they must learn to fight differently. You must restrain your desire to join Cernnunos for however noble it is to die in battle today, your tribe and your families depend on you to be there to fight again tomorrow and if necessary, the days after that."

For a brief moment, the chamber was comparatively still when Ilya finished translating his last words. He was completely unaware of what impression his words may have made. When he glanced at the faces of the clan chiefs, he saw neither approbation nor disapproval in their neutral expressions. Even Joric conveyed nothing of what he thought but merely acknowledged his thanks with a brief nod.

Told beforehand he and Ilya would be expected to leave after he spoke, they turned and proceeded back the way they came. It may have been his imagination, but the assemblage seemed more subdued than when they entered.

Once outside, Ilya complimented him. "Marcus, I think you made a very good impression."

"I'm not certain I did. Why should I expect them to believe a Roman? For all they know, I've been sent here to dupe them into doing things that will benefit the Romans."

"You misjudge them. If they believed that, you would have been dead by now regardless of my or Joric's influence."

"I'm surprised Tearlach hasn't already tried to."

"Tearlach? Why do you say that? Except for Joric and me, Tearlach is your greatest ally."

Arrius was skeptical. "He wanted to take my head the first time I met him, and nothing since has convinced me he's changed his mind."

"You're wrong. I've no doubt what you say may have been true enough before, but since your recent arrival here, he has seen how it is

71

with you and Joric and has changed his mind. Tearlach is pledged to support Joric because of Beldorach, and since you are here to help him, Tearlach regards you as an ally with the same purpose."

Arrius was dubious over Ilya's claim regarding Tearlach, but he chose to drop the matter of the Selgovan's questionable opinion of him and focus on more immediate concerns. "What will happen next, particularly if Joric is overruled?"

"It depends on what is decided. As High Chieftain he cannot be overruled except by a majority of clan chiefs. If one or more clan chiefs disagree and they feel strong enough about it, they have the right to leave and refuse to take part in any decision that is made. This does not happen often since all realize the strength of the tribe lies in unity. An individual clan is more vulnerable to the other tribes. Almost always, decisions are based and settled on compromise. As he should have, Joric has done much to minimize any public disagreement by negotiating ahead of time."

"Then all that went on in there," gesturing to the hall, "was all a show," he replied, more a statement than a question.

"Not entirely. If a clan chief senses his clan is not behind a decision, he may change his mind or risk the consequence he might be replaced."

"If he refuses to be replaced, what happens then?"

"A clan chief, including the High Chieftain, may have to fight any challenger to prove he's worthy. It seldom goes that far. Clan chiefs remain as head of their clan more by knowing when to negotiate than by relying solely on their fighting ability. Beldorach was challenged three times while High Chieftain."

"What was the outcome?"

"Two died, one changed his mind, and Beldorach remained as High Chieftain. I doubt Joric is in any danger of being challenged." When the men began to file out of the chamber hours later, Ilya learned just how wrong she was.

"It's my own fault. I should have suspected something like this," Joric said with furrowed brow as he regarded the sober faces staring at him.

Ilya's shock began to wear off, and her lips were compressed in cold anger. The expression on Arrius's face was thoughtfully sober as he listened to Joric tell what happened after he and Ilya left the council chamber. Sitting next to Joric, Tearlach was uncharacteristically subdued and said little, allowing Joric to relate the events leading up to Maredoc's challenge.

Joric continued, "Before the council, the clan chiefs seemed a little too quick to agree with what I proposed. Strangely, only Cuileán gave me the impression he was against what I intended to present, and yet he was the only clan chief who ended up siding with me. I now realize the others simply allowed me to believe I had their support to prevent me from canceling the council in order to avoid a public confrontation. Tearlach thinks Maredoc is behind it all. Evidently, he was the one who was most opposed to Beldorach naming me as tribal leader. If so, he may have seen the council as an opportunity to replace me. Perhaps he counted on me backing down and by doing so undermine my influence to the point it would force me to step aside. The clans would then choose another High Chieftain."

"When will this take place, and what are the conditions?" Arrius asked.

"Tomorrow at mid-day outside the village. The weapons will be sword and shield." Joric shrugged, "As far as conditions, I do not think Maredoc intends to kill me, rather only to defeat and exile me."

"Don't assume that! You must believe only that he intends to kill you, and you must do the same. You'll fight harder and smarter when you think your life will be forfeited if you lose."

Tearlach agreed. "The Roman is right. Even if Maredoc does not at first plan to kill you, he will if there is a chance he might not win. If you cannot afford to lose, neither can Maredoc."

'What kind of fighter is Maredoc?" Arrius probed, directing his question to Tearlach.

"He is not the best. It would be worse if Cuileán was the challenger. There is no better fighter among the Selgovi than Cuileán. Maredoc is not the most skilled swordsman, but he's more experienced than Joric," he added in obvious understatement.

Arrius rubbed the back of his neck and did his best to keep his face and voice from reflecting his concern. He knew the young tribal leader was proficient enough in sword and dagger from the long hours he and Decrius spent training both Joric and Decrius's son Rialus, Joric's closest friend. Of the two boys, Joric showed the greater talent indicating with more time and practice he would be among the best.

Unfortunately, many months had passed since he last saw Joric with a gladius in hand. He knew from experience without constant practice, sharp skills become dull, and Joric had never faced anyone who was bent on drawing his blood, least of all someone who might be intent on taking his life.

"Is there a way for someone else to fight for you – me, for instance?"

Joric squared his shoulders, and Tearlach grunted in disdain at the question. Arrius wasn't surprised at Joric's quick reply.

"Even if it were possible, I would not consider it. What kind of leader, or use for that matter, would I be to the Selgovi if I allowed someone else to fight for me? I know you mean well, but I have to be the one to face Maredoc."

Ilya gave Arrius an appreciative but regretful smile while Tearlach commented, "He's right, there is no other way. If Joric were to even propose such a thing, the clan chiefs would consider the fight to be over before it began and the position of tribal leader forfeit."

Arrius acknowledged the answer with a curt nod then said, "You may have at least one advantage. Maredoc doesn't know how well you fight. At first, make him believe your fighting skills are limited. Then he may become overconfident and careless."

Tearlach said, "What he says is true." He turned to Arrius and asked, "Roman, can he fight?"

"Joric was taught to use the sword we call the gladius. How well I taught him and how well he learned will be proven tomorrow. I'll wager Maredoc will find Joric a greater challenge than he thinks." Arrius hoped his words sounded more confident than he felt.

The sullen gray clouds hanging over the settlement the next day finally delivered their promise, and by late morning, a light rain began to fall with every indication it would continue throughout the day. The dark skies added to the somber mood of the throng gathered in a large circle around the soggy field outside the village gates. The stocky man with the scarred face whom Tearlach identified as Cuileán stood in the center of the circle ready to ensure the proper conduct of the combatants.

All those waiting for the two men to arrive on the field knew the seriousness of the occasion regardless of the outcome. In a short time, leadership of the tribe would be decided, and whether it was better if changed or remained the same, no one was prepared to say.

From his previous time with Beldorach, Arrius better understood the Selgovi. It was apparent to him there was always an undercurrent of conflict and bickering within and among the clans. Individual slights were quickly perceived and just as quickly action was taken to resolve them. On a number of occasions, he witnessed bloody fights only to see the participants talking amiably together a short time later. Their prickly nature, however, was balanced by an unqualified and fierce loyalty once it was given to another individual or cause.

Standing next to Tearlach, Arrius listened to the quiet conversations around him, and from what he was able to understand, he judged there was no appreciable support for one individual over the other. The restless villagers became silent as a barrel-chested, powerfully built man clad only in breeches and calf-length boots came into sight. The numerous scars on Maredoc's chest and arms provided mute evidence of his fighting experience. On his left forearm, he carried a round shield made of wood with elaborate designs painted on it. The shield was much smaller than the large rectangular Roman *scutum* or the more rounded shields carried by the auxilia. When he saw Arrius, Maredoc paused and began speaking at some length in a voice loud enough for all to hear. With a final glare, Maredoc continued on to the center of the circle where Cuileán waited. Although he didn't understand what Maredoc said, Arrius gathered from his belligerent manner it was not friendly. He turned to Tearlach. "What did he say?"

"He does not like you," Tearlach replied before adding, "He says you will be the next to die after he kills Joric."

Arrius made no response as the crowd's attention focused on Joric who walked alone through the village gate. He was relieved to see Ilya stayed behind as he advised. As did Maredoc, Joric carried a similar round shield that bore a simpler blue-green design consisting of three overlapping circles. In the center where all three circles joined, the intersection was solidly colored. The outer crescents of each circle were intertwined with vine-like curlicues. The design mirrored the nearly healed tattoo on Joric's bare chest and the smaller version above Ilya's right breast.

Although somewhat pale, Joric appeared calm with no outward sign of nervousness as he stopped a few paces away and faced Maredoc. Arrius heard Cuileán say a few words while glancing back and forth between the two men. That done, both acknowledged whatever was said with a slight nod and without any further preliminaries the three men drew their swords. Cuileán stepped back out of the way, bare sword at his side as the two men assumed a fighting crouch.

Maredoc made the first move by rushing toward Joric with upraised sword. The clan chief brought the blade down in a vicious arc which Joric barely managed to fend off as the attack left a deep gouge in the shield. Joric was hard pressed to deflect the rapid and continuous blows of Maredoc's aggressive attack that forced Joric backward across the field. So far, Joric had yet to strike an offensive blow. Arrius thought Joric might be overdoing the initial deception in concealing his sword-fighting capability until he realized the young man was simply outmatched. Belatedly, Arrius knew the shorter gladius Joric was using in comparison with his opponent's longer edged sword neutralized Joric's greater reach. Since the gladius was designed primarily for thrusting and not hacking, Maredoc's weapon was simply proving to be more effective in the apparent one-sided contest.

Arrius felt helpless as he observed the fight with a hollow feeling, believing now the outcome was only a matter of time before he finished the battle on his terms. He hoped the clan chief would be satisfied enough to win without taking Joric's life, but nothing so far gave him reason to expect a bloodless outcome, especially after Tearlach's translation of what Maredoc said to him before the fight. He was just as certain Joric would not concede the fight to spare his life.

By now, Joric was bleeding from several gashes on his sword arm. From his vantage point, Arrius was unable to assess how severe they might be. The scars on his own arm were reminders of how slippery a blood-soaked hilt became. Joric's face was taut with concentration with no sign of panic or resignation to an almost certain outcome. It was Maredoc who no longer appeared as confident and instead began to show signs of slowing his attack. The younger man's stamina was beginning to counter Maredoc's attempts to overpower him. Maredoc stepped back and said something to Joric. From Joric's brief head shake, Arrius suspected Maredoc invited him to yield. The refusal seemed to infuriate Maredoc who redoubled his efforts in a frenzied attempt to end the fight. Maredoc was starting to breathe hard and showed visible signs of tiring. Now it was Maredoc's turn to back away from Joric's relentless assault. Arrius started to relax when he perceived the increasing difficulty Maredoc was having. He saw Joric suddenly duck low as he stepped in close and deliver a bloody but not crippling blow to his opponent's left thigh. Caught off balance, Maredoc slipped on the sodden ground and fell heavily on his back. Joric took quick advantage of the mishap and stepped on Maredoc's sword just below the hilt while resting the point of his gladius on Maredoc's throat. The only sound to be heard was the heavy breathing of the two men as the onlookers watched silently waiting for Joric to end Maredoc's life as was his right. Arrius heard Joric speak clearly if somewhat hoarsely but did not understand what he said until Tearlach quietly translated, "Your life in return for loyalty and obedience. Which is it to be?"

Maredoc shook his head and said something in reply. Joric quickly thrust the blade into Maredoc's throat. Maredoc's body went rigid before falling back limply. In laconic understatement, Tearlach said, "Maredoc refused."

Silence prevailed as Joric slowly walked around the clearing eying the crowd, his sword at the ready as if in silent challenge to anyone who might further question his right to tribal leadership. Spontaneously, the crowd broke into a ragged cheer that swelled in volume. Arrius held his breath waiting to see if one of the other clan chiefs intended to take up the fight. To his dismay, two men stepped into the clearing followed by several more until all the remaining clan chiefs stood next to Cuileán. He tensed and reached for his sword only to have Tearlach restrain him. "No, Roman, there will be no more fighting. The clan chiefs accept Joric. Joric will remain High Chieftain."

Arrius breathed a sigh of relief as each clan chief stepped forward and touched Joric's sword which he gathered was as close to a formal acknowledgement of Joric's status as the proud and independent clan chiefs were likely to extend.

With Arrius on one side of Joric and Tearlach on the other, the three men walked soberly through the village and up the hill toward the council hall. They did not speak, each one lost in his own thoughts. Joric seemed oblivious of the blood still dripping from his arm despite the cloth Tearlach used to bind the deepest wound. Arrius had not really expected the fight would result in the death of one or the other. He assumed honor would be satisfied with an outcome considerably less final. It was apparent Joric believed otherwise. In any event, he thought, if there were any lingering vestiges of Joric's youth when he walked into the clearing, by the time the fight was ended, they were gone forever.

They were nearly to their destination when Arrius happened to look at Joric and saw how pale he was and how shallow and rapid his breathing was. He also noticed the young man was starting to shake. Recognizing that Joric was showing the initial signs of shock, Arrius grabbed him by the arm and steered him between two of the thatch-roofed dwellings bordering the central street. They walked but a few paces before Joric dropped his shield and vomited. Arrius waited a short distance away while Joric continued to retch until there was nothing left to bring up. Steadying himself against one of the houses, Joric finally turned and after retrieving his shield, looked sheepishly at Arrius. "Is it always like that after a battle?"

"Sometimes. I've seen it happen to the most seasoned veteran, particularly if he made a mistake in eating or drinking too much before the battle."

"Was it the same for you?"

Arrius laughed. "After my first kill, I heaved my guts so hard I thought my balls would follow." Then more soberly, he added, "But it is better when you are the one leading to refrain from doing so until the men do not see you." He gestured to the relative privacy of the narrow alley.

"I didn't know what it would be like to kill another man. It was easier than I thought, but now I regret I killed Maredoc. Did I do the right thing?"

"You did what you thought you had to do at the time. There's no profit in second-guessing the deed once it's done. Do you think Maredoc would have hesitated to do the same to you?"

"Perhaps not, but I've lost a clan chief whom I would have preferred at my side than at my feet."

"Possibly, but if you allowed Maredoc to live, he might easily have done more harm behind your back. Today, you won the respect of the other clan chiefs. They also know you will not hesitate to do what you think is right."

Joric didn't reply for a time, and Arrius was beginning to think there was nothing else to be said until the young man said thoughtfully, "Do you ever get used to killing?"

Caught off guard, Arrius hesitated before responding to the question. "I suppose. I've not thought about it, or at least not for a very long time. That may be the worst of it. Killing becomes easier and easier until you no longer think about such a question. But that isn't the same thing as enjoying the act. I've known some who did although most legionaries I've served with accepted death including the possibility of their own. In truth, the heat of battle does not encourage deep thinking on such things, and it does little good to dwell on them when the battle is over." Feeling somewhat uncomfortable with the introspective turn of the conversation, he said, "You did well out there. I thought at first you were over-matched."

"He was better than I, but I was luckier."

Arrius nodded approvingly at Joric's candid and realistic assessment. "Aye, you were at that, but then it is better to rely on skill than luck. The gods were kind to you, but next time they may not be. I think we should resume your sword-fighting lessons."

Joric smile was rueful, "I think Decrius and Rufus would agree."

A few days later, any chance for more lessons was lost when they learned the Roman Sixth Legion attacked the Briganti settlements. Hostilities began sooner than expected.

Chapter 7

Iseult watched Decrius and her son finish loading the cart. She was glad Rialus was coming along. She was dreading the long trip alone to the Brigantian capital the Romans called *Isurium*. It was almost three years since she last visited her parents while Decrius was serving in Judaea. She was feeling guilty she hadn't gone since. It was easy to find reasons for putting off the visits on one pretext or another. She had never gotten along well with her father from the time she was young as he focused on her brothers while seeming to barely tolerate her. She eventually admitted much of it was her fault. Her headstrong ways were a constant vexation to him. The final breach came after she met Decrius and moved to Eboracum to be near him while he was training to be a legionary in the auxilia. He bitterly resented her taking up with a Brigantian who decided to become Roman. Through the years, he was steadfast in refusing to allow Decrius into his home. For that reason, it was easier to come up with reasons not to go back for a visit simply to avoid the inevitable confrontations she would have with him.

Well, there would be no more confrontations. The news of his sudden death ten days before did not reach her until yesterday. She was determined to bring Nóinin back with her to live. Although her two brothers lived closer to Isurium than she did, she knew her mother would not be content to live with either one of her sons' wives. Fortunately, Decrius made no objection when she broached the idea to him.

When she suggested Rialus accompany her, she was not surprised her son quickly agreed. Ever since Joric left, she knew Rialus was restless. His eagerness to go with her was in part to escape the confines of the small settlement. She had a feeling Rialus would not come back with her when she returned to Banna. She suspected an added inducement for going was the proximity of the Sixth Legion at Eboracum and their destination only a few miles northwest of the Roman fort.

She always knew it was only a matter of time before Rialus would leave to pursue his dream of one day becoming a centurion like his father. She sensed the time had now come. The night before after feeding the livestock, she came back into the house and interrupted an earnest conversation between Decrius and Rialus. From their guilty looks and silence, the subject was obvious. She thought they were probably trying to spare her from any worries while her mind was occupied with other matters. It would have amazed them both to know if asked, she would have quickly agreed for Rialus's sake.

Out of the corner of her eye when they thought she wasn't looking, she saw Rialus and Decrius exchange broad smiles as her son buckled on the worn gladius Decrius gave him several years ago. Despite herself, she felt the sting of tears and surreptitiously wiped her eyes to keep Decrius and Rialus from noticing. Let the pretense continue for a while longer.

Their parting was not demonstrative in keeping with their mutual reluctance to show affection in front of anyone else. She turned to Decrius, and they briefly embraced before he helped her into the cart. She looked down at his broad face and lovingly traced the blue, spiral tattoo that covered his left cheek that wound downward around his neck until it disappeared underneath his neck scarf. She loved him now as passionately as when she was a young maiden. She knew without him saying the words it was the same for him.

"Iseult, it's possible when you return, I may not be here. Flavius has alerted the garrison we may go on campaign against the Selgovi. If we go, I'll hire Attorix to care for the animals."

"In that case, I may not hurry back. There are still those I would like to see before I return, and it may take time to convince Nóinin to come and stay with us. She's never lived anywhere else. It won't be easy for her to leave her home and friends behind."

"Rialus, take good care of your mother," Decrius called after them as Rialus urged the horse on with a slap of the reins.

As the cart wheels clattered and bumped over the cobbled road toward the bridge on the east side of the *vicus*, Iseult thought about what her husband said concerning the Selgovi. Decrius confided in her shortly after Ilya disappeared that she, Joric and the infant had gone north to rejoin the Selgovi. She believed Arrius left the island, but after swearing her to silence, Decrius told her where the former praefectus had gone. She realized Decrius and her son might one day face Joric and Arrius on a battlefield. The thought made her shudder at such an awful and cruel possibility.

Iseult wondered how Ilya was faring. She had been one of the few Brigantian women in the village who came to know the tall Selgovan woman and possibly the only one Ilya ever confided in. Their friendship deepened after she helped Ilya through the difficult birth of her son. She delivered many babies but never a birth as difficult as Ilya endured. That she and the infant survived signified the gods' intervention. Strangely, it was Joric who proposed the infant's name, Eusogenius, although she recalled Arrius later changed the name to Eugenius in the Roman manner. Ilya once confided to her she had been raped by Roman soldiers, and Joric was both the result and the cause for her exile from the Selgovae Tribe. Joric must have known he was bastard born for he was the one who proposed naming the infant Eusogenius meaning *well-born*. Clearly, the significance of the name to Joric had nothing to do with the difficult circumstances of the infant's birth.

As they crossed the bridge, Iseult looked back and saw Decrius walking toward the east gate of the fort. Even at this distance, his size made it easy for her to distinguish him from the others passing through the gate. She felt a sudden and terrible premonition she wouldn't see him again. Until today, the walls of the fort dominating the vicus were a familiar and accepted feature of their life at Banna; however, on this particular morning and in spite of a bright sun now rising over the hills, the fort looked sinister and foreboding. She felt a cold chill that caused her to shiver in spite of the comparatively mild temperature. Lost in thought, Rialus did not notice his mother's somber expression or see her lips moving in a silent plea to the gods to protect Decrius.

The four-day trip to the Briganti capital was slow and uneventful. Even the weather seemed to cooperate, and the days remained temperate with only a brief shower or two that did nothing to dampen their high spirits.

Iseult shook off her dire thoughts for Decrius's safety and concentrated on enjoying her son's company for the little time she was convinced they would have left together. The routine of every day living did not offer the opportunity to talk freely and comfortably as they did during the journey. It was Rialus who talked the most. She was entirely content to listen to him as he told her of his hopes and dreams.

Late on the fourth day, they arrived at their destination to find Nóinin stoic in her grief and obstinately stubborn in refusing to consider leaving. Iseult knew it would take even more time than she originally thought to persuade her to change her mind. For several days, she avoided the subject as she occupied her time looking after her mother and visiting with the few of her childhood friends who still lived in the settlement or close by.

Not unexpectedly, Rialus did not wait very long to tell her of his intent to leave for Eboracum and take the *sacramentum* in the auxilia. Even though she had braced herself, the reality he was leaving the next morning was still difficult for her to face. In spite of her resolve, she was unable to keep the tears back when he set off on foot in the direction of the huge stone fort, a day's journey to the east.

As Rialus walked, he occupied his mind with the anticipation of becoming a legionary. Barely a mile from the village, he was already regretting his decision to walk to Eboracum instead of waiting for a horse-drawn cart that might be going that way. But he was impatient for his adventure to begin, and the idea of waiting was intolerable.

He did not tell Iseult all of what he and Decrius talked about before leaving Banna, particularly his resolve not to return to Banna or to any other Wall fort. It was easier to allow her to continue believing he would remain in Britannia and possibly assigned to one of the forts along the wall. He looked forward to returning one day but not before he at least attained the rank of optio. He wanted more excitement than the prospect of dull, tiresome guard duty on the Wall. He planned to volunteer for any *vexillation* that would take him to some distant land far away from Britannia.

He imagined what it would be like to march in disciplined ranks and to carry a new gladius instead of the blade he now wore on his hip that showed the wear and tear of the training sessions with Joric and his father. He reached down and traced the scar on his thigh where an overeager Joric and his own inexperience had given him a permanent reminder of their time together. He saw himself one day riding in front of a column of legionaries wearing the transverse crest of a centurion, and his chest swelled at the thought.

It was the measured tread of marching feet he heard before he saw the long column of legionaries marching five abreast advancing down the road toward him. He knew the mounted man leading them must be an officer as his sweeping helmet crest looked like the one Arrius wore when he commanded the Banna garrison. Directly behind the mounted officer walked the *aquilfer* carrying the eagle standard and wearing the distinctive leopard skin headdress. Even at this distance, he recognized the standard of the Sixth Legion. The awesome grandeur of the formation made him even more eager to be marching with them. He watched the rhythmic swaying of their upright pila, the sharp points glinting in the sunlight. He admired the wall of red-painted scuta with the yellow eagle clutching jagged lightening bolts that each man carried on his left arm. He knew it would probably take years as a member of the auxilia before he would be permitted to join the ranks of a legion and be allowed to carry the eagle-lighting shield of a Roman legionary. Whatever it took, he was resolved to carry such a shield one day.

Most of the men looked to be much older than he was with some nearly as old as his father or Rufus, the optio that occasionally helped his father and Arrius train him and Joric. He heard the crunch of their hob-nailed boots, the creak of leather, the occasional hollow thump of a shield bumping a dagger hilt. One of the men in the outer rank turned to say something to the man behind him and seemingly from nowhere a centurion appeared and with his vitis delivered a stinging blow to the legionary's bare arm.

Rialus moved off the road to allow the column to march past. He saw the officer turn his head and fix him with a long steely look before yelling, "Centurion!"

The same centurion he saw before ran forward. "Yes, Tribune?"

Rialus saw the officer point in his direction. Thinking the officer noticed him at all was more than he expected. He wanted the opportunity to tell the mounted officer wearing the magnificent embossed cuirass to stop to be able to tell him where he was going and why. He was ready to follow this splendid looking man anywhere. He watched the centurion tap two of the legionaries on the shoulder but didn't hear what he told them. He was hopeful when the centurion with the two legionaries following close behind hurried toward him. He was completely unprepared for what happened next. One of the legionaries knocked him backward to the ground with enough force he felt momentarily dizzy. He looked up in mute shock as he saw them draw their swords and heard the centurion order, "Finish him!"

Rialus felt unbearable pain as the blades entered his body. Waves of blackness engulfed him before he could ask them why they did such a thing much less hear the centurion say to the mounted officer, "Tribune Querinius, that's one less to worry about."

Iseult looked up from the wool she was carding when she heard the muffled sound of trumpets and drums on the far side of the village and wondered what the fanfare was all about. No one mentioned a celebration, and it was still too early for the boisterous festival that traditionally banished the winter and welcomed the spring planting. She glanced quizzically at her mother but in return received only a silent shake of her head. Curiosity slowly grew to alarm as she heard terrified screams that were becoming progressively louder along with the rhythmic sound of beating drums.

She rushed outside and saw mainly women and children running past with older villagers hobbling along as fast as their aging limbs permitted. Iseult observed an old woman as she was bowled over by the throng and ran over to assist her. "What's the matter?" Iseult asked the woman, now thoroughly alarmed and infected by the panic surrounding her.

"The Romans, they are killing us!" the woman replied hysterically.

Iseult was stunned. It couldn't be she thought. Why would they do such a thing? The tribe had done nothing to provoke the Romans. The last Briganti rebellion was years ago. In fact, it was so long ago she was too young to remember much about it. Suddenly, it dawned on her why she had seen so few of the men since her arrival. The tribe must be planning another revolt, and somehow the Romans learned of it. When she asked where all the men were, her question was met with evasive answers. In retrospect, she realized her marriage to Decrius was the reason her own people didn't trust her. On the other hand, where did she belong? She wondered what Decrius would do? With some effort, she tried to clear her mind and think clearly. She could try to convince the Romans her husband was a centurion; however, she quickly discarded the idea as futile. How would she prove who she was? She curbed the waves of panic threatening to overwhelm her along with the urge to join the fleeing villagers. If she left, she'd have to abandon Nóinin for there was no way her mother would be able to keep up, nor did she have the strength to carry her. Oh, how she wished Decrius were here. The thought reminded her of Rialus, and icy fingers clutched her heart at the thought he may have encountered the Romans on his way to Eboracum. She envisioned him already dead. The image caused her to remain frozen with terror as the panic-stricken villagers streamed past her. It was the sound of her mother's voice that brought her back.

"Iseult, tell me what's happening," she asked in a plaintive voice.

Numbly, Iseult turned and entered the dwelling and replied in a voice that shook, "It seems the Romans are attacking the village."

Iseult was shocked to hear her mother cackle with glee thinking she was hysterical or confused. Nóinin quickly dispelled the thought by saying, "Now, we'll show them," vigorously clapping her hands together.

"What do you mean, Mother?"

"It means the revolt has started, and this time we'll throw the bastards out once and for all. No more will we feel the Roman boot on our necks!"

"Why wasn't I told about this?"

"You might have told Decrius."

Objectively, Iseult realized that is exactly what she would have done had she known about it. Her mother was right in not confiding in her. "I fear we're about to pay the price for your silence, and Rialus may have already done so."

A look of concern suddenly flashed across Nóinin's face. "Go, Iseult, before it's too late. Leave me, I beg you!"

Iseult hesitated, the anger at her mother beginning to dissipate replaced by a lingering sadness. By the time she turned to leave, she realized it was already too late when she saw a legionary standing in the doorway holding a bloody sword in one hand, his shield in the other. His eyes swept the room and came back to her, giving her a speculative look. He cast aside his shield and pulled off his helmet. Still holding the sword, he pulled aside the studded straps of his apron with his free hand and reached under his tunic. His intent was unmistakable. Desperately she looked about for something to use as a weapon as he moved slowly toward them. She started backing up to where Nóinin crouched against the far wall.

"Give me what I want without any trouble and no one will get hurt; resist and you die," he said in a lisp revealing several broken front teeth.

Iseult was repulsed at the sight of the soldier's nakedness, and she felt the bile rising in her throat. She was conscious of movement behind her just before Nóinin rushed past her toward the legionary screaming furiously and brandishing a kitchen knife.

Showing only momentary irritation, the legionary casually brought the tip of his gladius up in time for Nóinin to impale herself. Without taking his eyes off Iseult, he thrust her mother's lifeless body aside not bothering to withdraw the sword and continued his slow advance toward her.

Frozen with shock, she closed her eyes as if to make the horror go away. She opened them when she felt her shift being torn from her with enough force to send her sprawling to the floor next to her mother's body. A moment later, she felt the weight of his body and the sudden pain as he entered her. She tried to resist, but with her wrists pinned, she was unable to move. What seemed an eternity later, his harsh breathing and spasmodic movements indicated the ordeal was almost over. When he finally rolled off her and stood up with a grunt of satisfaction, Iseult was no longer able to control the nausea of her heaving stomach. She sat up and vomited.

The legionary jumped back in disgust, "Maybe you would have preferred the sword I gave the old woman than the one I shoved into you. It's fortunate for you, *cunnus*, I'm in a generous mood today, or you'd be as dead as her," gesturing toward Nóinin's body.

Struggling to stand up, Iseult's hand brushed the hilt of the knife her mother tried to use. In the pretext of picking up her shift to cover her nakedness, she grasped the knife and concealed it in the folds of the torn garment. The shock of Nóinin's brutal death and the shame of her rape were being replaced by an overpowering urge to strike back, but the segmented cuirass he wore presented little opportunity to deliver a mortal wound. Her chance came when he reached down to pick up his helmet. She had killed many hogs by slitting their throat, and she quickly found sweeping the edge of the blade under the legionary's neck was no different including the rush of blood that splashed on the floor at her feet. Without a sound, the legionary collapsed lifeless at her mother's feet.

For a moment longer, Iseult stood motionless still gripping the bloody knife. Then she began to shake uncontrollably when the full realization of what happened sunk in. She looked at her mother's body, and her eyes filled with tears. She heard screams and yelling outside the dwelling, and the sounds jarred her back to reality. It would not do to be found naked and bloody with a dead legionary. Her thoughts quickly turned to Rialus; and it was enough to prompt her to action. There was nothing she could do for Nóinin, but Rialus was another matter. He couldn't have gotten far. She refused to consider the possibility he might already be dead. She lifted Nóinin's featherweight body and laid it lovingly on one of the beds. She dragged the dead legionary behind one of the other beds and covered him with a blanket. She hid his sword and helmet in a large basket.

After wiping the legionary's blood off her feet and legs, she rummaged among her things and found another shift to replace the one the legionary ripped off her. These tasks completed, her thoughts turned once again to her son. There was little choice except to wait until the Romans left before she could look for him.

For what seemed an eternity, she heard the screams and sounds of the town being ransacked. Alternating between anger and despair over the fate of her mother and Rialus, she stifled her sobs afraid other legionaries would hear her. She huddled in a corner as the morning wore on until finally the village began to grow quiet indicating the Romans were gone.

Unable to wait any longer, she ran out the door and around to the rear of the house to get her horse only to find the animal lying dead, the surrounding ground dark with blood. There was no point served in shedding more tears at the wanton slaughter. She set out on foot in the direction of Eboracum ignoring the dead bodies lying about and the pitifully few pleas for help from those she passed. She thought of only one purpose now, and that was to find her son.

Iseult found Rialus where the Romans left him. His motionless body and deathly pale face confirmed her worst fears.

She fell to her knees beside him and covered her face. She felt the tears she no longer held back stinging her eyes. Suddenly, she heard Rialus moan and through her tears saw one of his fingers twitching. She bent down to examine him more closely. His forehead was abraded and swollen. She found a wound high on his right chest and a second one lower down on the left side. Upon closer examination, she decided the wound in his side was less severe than first thought. It was the other wound that was the more serious. That he had not yet bled to death and the wounds were only seeping she thought were good signs. He might yet have a chance providing she got him back to the village and tended him properly.

She carefully lifted him to a sitting position to better examine whether the sword wounds, for that was what she assumed they were, penetrated all the way through his body. To her relief, she found they had not. Rialus groaned and opened his eyes. As she gently laid him back down, she saw a flicker of recognition in his eyes. He managed a wan smile.

"I don't believe I will go to Eboracum unless it's to fight Romans," he said in a voice barely above a whisper. "Did they attack the village?"

Iseult nodded. Her voice shook as she said, "Don't move. I've got to get you back to the village, but I need to find a cart to take you. You'll have to stay here until I can get help."

Rialus acknowledged by saying faintly with a flash of humor, "I think I've walked enough for today. Unless the Romans come back, I'll still be here when you return."

Rejuvenated at finding Rialus alive, she ran back toward the village in search of a horse and cart. To her dismay, she passed the carcasses of both oxen and horses that she failed to notice before. As she reentered the village, Iseult was horrified at the wholesale destruction the Romans inflicted on the Brigantian capital. Homes were burning and human bodies of all ages and sex were strewn about lying in the streets or spilling out of doorways. Not content to simply slay the inhabitants, many of the bodies were hacked to pieces. It was evident the Romans came to destroy the village and equally clear they achieved their objective.

Nearing despair at the dimming prospect of finding a horse left alive, she was close to her mother's house when she heard a horse whinny. She darted toward the sound. In a clump of trees, she saw a small corral and a horse regarding her calmly, its ears fanned forward as if waiting for her to arrive. Relief flooded over her as she ran toward the animal mouthing a silent prayer of thanks to *Epona*, profoundly grateful the horse goddess was looking after her. Close up, she realized the horse was old and long past its prime. She thought it was still sound enough for her purpose. She found a rope hanging on one of the rails and looped one end around the animal's neck before opening the gate.

Iseult led the horse to the back of her mother's house where to her relief the cart she had brought from Banna remained intact. Quickly harnessing the animal, she ran inside to find blankets to place in the cart. She finished making up a pallet on the cart bed then paused in her efforts as a thought occurred to her. There was no point in returning to the village in case the Romans decided to return. She would be better off taking Rialus back to Banna or at least away from here. Her decision made, she began to consider the necessity of taking food and water. It required only a brief delay to load enough water and provisions for the two of them and to prepare a pallet for Rialus. The horse would have to do with what it could find along the way. She was about to leave when she glanced at Nóinin's body lying on the bed. Iseult felt her eyes sting with tears. She hesitated, reluctant to leave her behind. Unable to bear the thought she might be mutilated and deprived of proper burial rites, she returned to where her mother lay. After wrapping the body in a blanket, Iseult carried it outside and gently placed it in the cart.

Iseult was relieved to find Rialus still conscious and somewhat more alert. With her assistance he was able to climb into the cart where he collapsed, drained of his last reservoir of strength.

It was late in the day, and the evening shadows were just beginning to lengthen when she felt they were far enough away from the village to risk stopping for the night. She would have preferred continuing on to get that much closer to Banna, but she also knew the aging horse needed to rest, or the chance of them reaching Banna at all would be further reduced. It was also obvious Rialus was in no condition to walk.

She tethered the horse in a grassy clearing then left it to graze contentedly while she followed a faint trail downhill carrying the empty water jar in hopes it would lead to a stream. To her relief she didn't have to go far before she found a natural spring bubbling into a small pool from a rocky outcropping above. After filling the jar, she looked about the glade and decided this was a suitable location to bury Nóinin. The essential presence of trees and water was reassuring. Here *Brigantia* would watch over her in the next world. Although there was no possibility of encasing her mother's body in a hollow oak log according to custom, the presence of oak trees would at least allow her to wrap Nóinin in peeled branches in token observance of the proper burial rites.

When she returned to the cart she was alarmed to find Rialus awake but burning up with fever. She gave him as much water as he would take and cleaned the wounds as best she could, knowing there was little else she could do for him. The gods alone would decide his fate now.

As soon as she saw Rialus drift off in a restless sleep, she carried her mother's body down to the glade and found a spot above the spring where the ground was moist and soft enough to dig. Using Rialus's worn gladius, she dug as deep as her rapidly declining strength would allow. She cut enough oak branches to line the grave. Iseult then laid the blanket-wrapped body in the shallow depression and tried to remember all the prayers tradition demanded. After pushing the dirt back into the hole, she placed rocks as large as she was able to carry on top of the mound to keep the wolves and wild pigs from getting to the body. When she finished, she went to the stream and washed off the worst of the grime from the trip and her recent labors. She was too tired and emotionally drained to cry any more tears. She took one last look at the rocky mound before retracing her steps up the hill to the cart.

Throughout the night, she woke frequently every time she heard Rialus cry out. Each time he roused, she made him drink more water. She was gratified to find in the morning the fever had subsided, and his regular breathing indicated he was sleeping more peacefully.

Between mouthfuls of bread, Iseult finished harnessing the horse and climbed up on the seat. Without looking back, she slapped the reins and guided the horse back onto the narrow road in the direction of Banna.

Decrius went numb when Flavius informed him of the imminent assault on the Brigantian capital. The acting praefectus of the Banna fort observed Decrius's reaction with a mixture of sympathy and wary speculation. Mindful of his Brigantian heritage, Flavius was privately concerned over what the huge centurion might do when he learned of Querinius's plan for a preemptive strike.

"When will it happen?"

"I'm not sure, but I think it's imminent."

"Praefectus, I must take a leave of absence to attend to a personal matter."

"What personal matter?"

"My wife and son left two days ago for Isurium."

"Well, I should think they will be all right because of your position here," Flavius responded with false assurance.

"On the contrary, it is because of me they risk not only the Romans but any tribal retaliation as well. I'm not exactly looked upon with great admiration or fondness for taking the Roman sacramentum."

"Very well, since you put it that way, I can hardly refuse your request. I expect you back here just as soon as you've seen to their safety."

Without further comment, Decrius acknowledged his agreement with a nod, saluted and headed for the stable for his horse.

Flavius watched him go. If their situations were reversed, he had no idea what he might do faced with similar conflicting loyalties. He hoped Decrius would come back, but something told him he would not.

Within the hour, still wearing his armor and leading a spare horse, Decrius was in full gallop heading south on the road to Isurium. It would take him almost two days of hard riding to reach the tribe's capital city. If he pushed hard enough and changed horses frequently, he thought there might still be a good chance to get there before the attack took place.

He rode all night and stopped only long enough to change mounts or to allow the horses a brief rest. As dawn approached, he was starting to become more confident with each mile he would reach his destination in time. Unfortunately, a long night and fatigue made him less vigilant. A pothole he should have avoided proved deeper than he believed. The next thing he knew he was catapulted out of the saddle as the horse stumbled and fell beneath him. He got up slowly and was relieved to find beyond a few abrasions and a sore knee nothing seemed to be broken. This was not the case with the horse that was lying on its side and whinnying piteously as it struggled to stand. Decrius limped over to the horse with a sinking feeling. It required only a cursory examination to confirm the right foreleg was broken just above the fetlock. He drew his pugio and after a brief prayer and apology to Epona, mercifully cut the pulsing vein on the horse's neck.

He looked about and was relieved to see the other horse cropping grass a short distance away. The horse looked up curiously at his approach but remained where it was allowing Decrius to grab the reins before the animal bolted. After recovering the saddle from the dead horse, he was soon galloping south again and taking more notice of any potential hazards.

His optimism of a short time ago was now replaced with the growing doubt he would reach Isurium in time. The few settlements he knew to be located along the route were unlikely to have a horse available let alone one large enough to accommodate his bulk. He dared not risk the remaining horse by overtaxing it; consequently, the rest stops became longer and longer throughout the day. Late in the day, both horse and rider were beginning to show the rigors of the long, grueling ride. Grimly he pressed on and did his best to quell thoughts of what he might find when he reached Isurium.

Iseult didn't see the legionary until he stepped out from behind a large bush to block her way. Before she knew it, more soldiers closed in from the sides until she counted six ringing the cart. She recognized from the knobbed staff one of the legionaries carried he held optio rank and was probably in charge of the patrol. With little else she could do, she tried to put a bold face on her predicament by saying as calmly as she could, "Please allow me to pass. I still have a long journey ahead to join my husband, Centurion Decrius, at Banna."

The optio guffawed loudly, eliciting smiles from the other legionaries. "You'll pass when I say you can and not before. That is if

I allow you to go. As for *Centurion Decrius*, whoever the hell he might be, he has little taste in wives. I've bought better looking wenches than you for two *asses*," referring to the lowest denomination of Roman coinage, "or even a cup of wine." Considering how she undoubtedly looked, Iseult thought it was probably true.

"I think you're a Brigantian bitch out looking for some Roman cock. Well, this is your lucky day. You just found six of the best and most willing the Sixth Legion has to offer."

Iseult resisted the fear welling up inside and tried not to show it. So far, their attention was focused on her and not on Rialus. She had to keep it that way. "Very well, but it will cost you each a sesterce. I don't give my favors for free or a few asses."

"A sesterce each!" the optio exclaimed in feigned outrage then with a humorless laugh, "I think if there is any payment, it will be you paying us for the privilege. Now, climb down off that cart and be quick about it! You there," he ordered, pointing to one of the legionaries, "see what's in the cart. If there's any wine, I'll have it first along with the woman."

Iseult's heart sank as she quickly said, "Be careful, my son is hurt and cannot be moved."

The optio shot her a suspicious look and walked over to the cart to look inside. After peering over the side and prodding Rialus none too gently, he looked up at Iseult and said brusquely, "Woman, you don't need to worry about him anymore – he's crow meat now."

Their helmets, shields and pila stacked to one side, the other legionaries watched and called out ribald encouragement to the legionary last to take his turn satisfying himself with the dead woman. They were oblivious of the sound of the galloping horse until it was nearly upon them. Belatedly, the optio called out a warning when he recognized the rider's transverse crest. He quickly ordered the men to form a rank on the side of the road. With no time to retrieve their equipment, they left it where it was and hurried to comply with the order. The one legionary was still hastily pulling up his linen drawers when Decrius rode up.

Decrius took in the cart and the old horse, its head drooping tiredly, and wondered where the owner was. Something was terribly wrong. His eyes hard as flint, he looked down at the legionaries noting their spears and shields stacked a short distance away. Slowly he dismounted and walked toward the optio who saluted by bringing his staff horizontally across his body. Ignoring the salute, Decrius stopped a pace in front of the optio, his hand resting on the hilt of his sword. The optio's eyes widened slightly at the size of the tall officer, regarding him with growing unease. When Decrius did not return the salute, he nervously brought his staff back to his side

"What is your unit, and what are you men doing here?" Decrius asked, his voice sounding somewhat hoarse from the long ride.

"We're on patrol with the second century, fourth cohort, Sixth Legion now on campaign to put down a Briganti revolt. We were returning from patrol when we came across a Briganti woman driving that cart over there," he said nodding his head in the direction of the cart.

Decrius suddenly felt cold. "Go on," he urged dreading to probe further.

"Well, we stopped the woman to learn where she was going. I was talking to her, but she got upset when one of the men discovered the body of a man in the cart. She claimed the man was her son. We had nothing to do with that – he was already dead when we stopped her. All of a sudden, she screams and pulls out a knife and stuck it right in her throat, just like that," the optio added, pantomiming the act.

Decrius's hand gripped his sword hilt until his knuckles were white. For a moment, he couldn't speak and stood rooted, staring at the optio.

"Where's the woman?"

"Over there in the trees," the optio replied gesturing toward a small grove of trees a short distance away then said with a suggestive leer, "Centurion, you can have all you want of her. We're finished with her. You'll find her well used and uncomplaining," he added eliciting chuckles from the other legionaries.

"Shut your mouth, swine. Don't speak to me like that again."

The optio flushed a deep crimson and compressed his lips in sullen anger while taking in details of the centurion's appearance. He glimpsed part of Decrius's facial tattoo not entirely covered by the helmet cheek-guard and the long hair gathered at the neck. A shadow of suspicion flashed across his face.

"You're an officer in the auxilia," he said more of an accusation than a question. With the revelation, the optio immediately relaxed his posture while a condescending smirk pulled his mouth to one side. "Then I hold you're not really a proper officer at all so, *Centurion*," emphasizing the rank in a sarcastic tone of voice, "it might be best if you let real legionaries go about their business while you tend to your own." Emboldened by the optio's disrespectful remarks, the other legionaries laughed and turned their heads to see what would happen next.

The optio opened his mouth to say something more when Decrius's fist caught him full in the face. Knocked senseless, his nose and mouth bleeding, the optio dropped without making a sound. One look at their optio lying on the ground and Decrius's stony face was enough. The legionaries stared straight ahead while remaining at rigid attention.

Decrius walked toward the trees silently beseeching the gods not to confirm what he already knew he would find.

Iseult's lifeless and naked body, legs splayed grotesquely, was partly hidden in the tall grass at the edge of the trees. The hilt of the small dagger he gave her years ago protruded from her throat. In marked contrast to her violated body, the expression on her face was serene, almost as if she was asleep. His eyes blurred as he unfastened his sagum and covered her with it. He then turned and walked stiffly over to the cart and looked down at the face of his son. He pulled the blanket down covering Rialus's chest and noted the wounds. He had seen enough dead men to know the optio told the truth. Iseult had been unaware Rialus was dead of the wounds before she encountered the legionaries. The nature of the wounds made clear Rialus had become another casualty of the Roman assault on Isurium. Somehow, Iseult managed to get him away and this far before being stopped by the legionaries. He had been too late. Even if the other horse held up, he would not have reached Isurium in time, and he suspected Flavius already knew he would be.

Woodenly, he stalked back to where the legionaries remained at attention. Although these men had not killed his wife and son, the distinction was not enough to still a cold rage. The violation of Iseult's body alone was sufficient to demand a price be paid. Decrius approached the nearest legionary standing closest to the unconscious optio.

"Did you take her?" he asked the legionary.

The legionary shrugged, regarding Decrius with a wary look. "We all did. What does it matter anyway? She was…"

Whatever the legionary intended to say further was cut short when Decrius's fingers gripped the legionary's throat with one hand and enough force to crush it. The remaining four legionaries, their eyes still fixed straight ahead were not immediately aware of what happened until they heard their comrade's body fall to the ground and the sound of the legionary struggling to breathe. They turned and were momentarily bewildered to see the centurion, gladius in hand, regarding them with a fixed expression.

"Here now, Centurion, what're you doing?" one of the men said in alarm.

Ignoring the question, Decrius asked, "Did the woman say who she was?"

The legionaries looked at each other puzzled by the question. "She may have, but I don't remember," one of the men blurted out.

"I remember," said another stepping back and drawing his gladius. "She said her husband was a centurion, and we didn't believe her..." The legionary paused as he regarded Decrius closely and then added in a softer voice, "I think now she was telling the truth."

Another legionary asked in alarm, "What're you going to do with us? We didn't kill your son or your wife."

Decrius gave a slight nod and replied quietly, "I know, but you did enough."

Decrius tenderly wrapped Iseult's body in one of the blankets and placed her on the cart next to Rialus. Tired and bleeding from several gashes on both arms and his shoulder, he leaned against the side of the cart and watched the optio slowly regaining his senses.

The optio struggled to his feet holding his throbbing head. The first thing he saw was the tall centurion staring at him. When his vision began to clear, he looked about in confusion for the other men. He was shocked to see their headless bodies lying in a row by the side of the road. The heads of the legionaries were impaled on their spears thrust in the ground beside their bodies. It was clear from the optio's face he understood who the centurion was.

"By all the gods, I didn't believe she was telling the truth." Then once again looking about him, he added, "If you were able to do this," indicating the bodies, "then I'm a dead man," he said in a low voice, apparently resigned to his fate.

"I'll not kill you, at least not today," Decrius replied, his voice flat. "Go back to your legion and tell them a Brigantian by the name of Decrius did this. Tell them he was once a centurion and loyal to Rome. After today, he is neither and will spend the rest of his life killing Romans. Now, go before I change my mind and kill you instead."

Decrius watched without moving until the optio disappeared down the road in the direction of Eboracum. He felt numb and recalled almost nothing of the fight with the legionaries. He almost wished the legionaries had succeeded in killing him. The only feeling left was a cold hatred for those he served for so many years. Strangely, he recalled once when there was a perceived threat of a Briganti revolt two years before, Arrius had asked him what he would do if the Briganti did rebel. It was a fair question, and at the time, he said he didn't know. Today, the answer was no longer in doubt.

He tied his horse to the back of the cart and climbed slowly up on the seat. First, he would find a suitable place to bury his wife and son. After that, he would find who was leading the Briganti revolt.

Chapter 8

Since Cuileán's clan occupied the extreme northern boundary of the Selgovan tribal lands, it was only natural for Arrius and Ilya to accompany him when he returned to his village. Arrius knew Ilya's purpose in going north was to attempt to fulfill Joric's objective in achieving an alliance with the northern tribes; Arrius's was a different purpose –ensure no harm came to Ilya.

During the two days required to reach Cuileán's village, Arrius found the clan chief to be an invaluable source of information about the tribes occupying the northern regions the Romans called Caledonia. Since Ilya never had occasion to venture there, she also listened closely to what the clan chief said. Both Arrius and Cuileán depended on her to interpret for both of them, although each day Arrius required her to do so less and less; therefore, he was dismayed to learn the language of the Caledonian Tribes was different from that of the Selgovi. He and Ilya would have to depend on Cuileán who spoke the northern dialects to be their voice.

"They paint their bodies with animal designs, and for that reason we call them the painted people," Cuileán said as they made their way through a deep and rocky ravine. "They trust no one, especially the tribes south of them. Neither do they trust the tribes dwelling in the far north where I've never been."

Arrius maintained a tactful silence at this revelation since he thought Cuileán could easily have been describing the Selgovi and the other southern tribes.

"Many of their clan chiefs are women, and lineage is traced more often through the female side. They depend principally on sheep, goats and oxen for their food. The land is too rocky to grow many crops. They have few horses so they travel mainly by foot. You will find the north is not as thickly forested as it is here; consequently, their houses are built of stone."

"How well do they fight?" Arrius asked and waited for the answer while Ilya translated.

Cuileán shrugged. "They are physically big like you and are fierce in battle. The Caledonians seldom launch an attack unless their numbers are sufficient to guarantee they will prevail. They prefer the sword and spear where we rely on bow and arrow to kill as many as we can before they can throw their spears or use their long swords. If they get close enough for swords, it is difficult to defeat them. Wounds that would fell other men are nothing to them." Arrius listened attentively asking frequent questions in an effort to learn as much as he could about these primitive-sounding and apparently intractable northern tribes. The more he heard about the Caledonian tribesmen, his skepticism only increased that an alliance was possible.

Rather than spend another night in camp, Cuileán indicated his intention of pressing on to his village. It was well into the night when they reached their destination. Earlier, Cuileán had dispatched one of the warriors to alert the village of their impending late arrival allowing the inhabitants to slumber on undisturbed by the unexpected arrival of their clan chief.

Cuileán led Ilya and Arrius to the largest dwelling where the clan chief was greeted enthusiastically by a bare-breasted, dark-haired woman nursing a swaddled infant. The clan chief identified her as Moriath, his senior wife. In the torchlight, Arrius saw the small forms of two more children who remained fast asleep in spite of the noisy reception. From the shadows, another attractive woman, taller, younger and completely naked greeted Cuileán affectionately. Both women acknowledged Cuileán's introduction to Ilya and Arrius with slight nods without making any effort to cover their bodies. Arrius gave Ilya a side glance and saw her lips pressed firmly together in disapproval at the ample display of female flesh.

The tall woman whose name was Igerna walked toward the shadows on the far side of the dwelling motioning for them to follow. Arrius struggled unsuccessfully to keep his eyes off her breasts and hips swaying far too provocatively as they followed her. He was still not used to the Selgovan custom of multiple wives much less their general lack of modesty. It was even more difficult to become accustomed to the tolerance for sexual liaisons as long as it was done openly and with the consent of all those affected. Adultery committed in secret was a different matter, and if discovered, the punishment would be severe for both man and woman. According to Ilya, it was common practice for the injured parties to dictate the punishment which included banishment or, in more extreme cases, even death.

Igerna indicated an open space to unfold their pallets on the stone floor. In no time, Ilya's steady breathing signified she drifted off while Arrius remained awake and doing his best to ignore the sounds of lovemaking on the other side of the room. When sleep eventually came, it was fitful and accompanied by erotic dreams. By morning, Arrius wished they had simply camped one more night before continuing on to the village.

Since Bothan's indispensable guide was yet to make an appearance, there was nothing to do but wait. Sensing his impatience, Ilya suggested they saddle the horses and explore the countryside leaving Cuileán to see to the details of preparing for their journey north. Arrius was surly and not at all interested in the idea, and he agreed only after Ilya insisted she would go alone if he remained behind.

When he went to get the horses, he found a throng silently watching Ferox energetically mounting one of the local mares. He cursed in irritation, reminded of his sleepless night. His mood became even more truculent when he considered the stallion was faring better than he was. He soon realized the fascination was caused not by the common sight of two horses copulating but rather by the size of the stallion that in comparison dwarfed the considerably smaller ones native to Britannia. Arrius thought Ferox was only too eager to do his part to increase the size of the local stock. The one consolation of waiting for Ferox to consummate his latest conquest was the expectation the horse would be more docile than usual. He credited Beldorach after the horse's capture by the Selgovi for having done much to curb the animal's former ill-tempered and unpredictable behavior. He had known no one before or since who handled horses the way Beldorach could. He smiled when he recalled how the animal's spirited behavior several years ago nearly destroyed the boat carrying them across the wide channel from Gaul to Rutipiae.

As they rode away from the village with Arrius in the lead, they headed in a westerly direction, heeding Cuileán's warning not to venture north. Arrius thought Ilya was especially radiant and good natured in contrast to his dark mood. She was clearly refreshed from an uninterrupted night's sleep. He remained silent and morose as she chattered on, responding cryptically to her occasional questions. Gradually the crisp brightness of the day began to have an effect, and he started enjoying Ferox's even gait while taking note of his surroundings. With a practiced eye, he unconsciously and by force of habit surveyed the passing terrain looking for potential ambush sites or likely places suitable for a hasty defense.

Preoccupied as he was, Arrius at first was unaware Ilya was no longer behind him. In sudden panic and none too gently, he turned Ferox around and galloped back while frantically searching both sides of the trail for any sign of her. He was beginning to imagine the worst when he topped a tree-lined creek bank and found Ilya's mount grazing placidly in a small clearing. When he saw no evident sign of her he called her name, the concern evident in his voice.

"I'm over here," came her reply in a husky voice with a hint of amusement.

He turned in the direction of her voice and saw Ilya appear into the dappled sunlight from behind a massive oak tree. The sharp rebuke he intended for alarming him died on his lips. She stood waiting for him wearing only a broad smile.

"I was beginning to think you didn't care enough to come looking for me."

At first, Arrius only stared mutely at her alabaster figure. Until now, he had never seen her fully naked except in the moonlight or the flickering light of an oil lamp. She was breathtakingly beautiful. Her hair was unbraided and cascaded over her shoulders. Arrius slid off Ferox and unbuckled his sword belt. A mischievous smile curved her lips as she watched him come toward her.

"I sensed you were restless last night, and I thought perhaps Igerna may have had something to do with it."

"I didn't think you noticed since you fell asleep so quickly," he replied accusingly, his voice thick with mounting desire as he took her into his arms.

"The way you were thrashing about I feared you were going to wake the entire village," she murmured in response, pressing her body urgently into him.

"It would seem you had more than seeing the countryside on your mind," he said appreciatively.

"I think you talk too much," she replied while helping to remove his tunic.

The morning shadows were long disappeared when Arrius was roused by a loud thunk as something struck the tree just above him. Instantly awake, he opened his eyes and saw a feathered shaft still quivering only a few inches above his face. Naked, he rolled over and reached for his sword while at the same time calling out to Ilya. As Ilya ducked behind the oak tree, Arrius stood up in a crouch, sword at the ready and looked across the clearing where he saw several men on horseback each leading a packhorse and silently watching him. He immediately recognized the grinning man holding the bow as Neacal, the heavy-browed clan chief Bothan said would accompany them north. He thought the solemn-looking man slightly apart from the other two might be Crixtacus but wasn't sure.

Neacal said something in an undertone causing the man nearest him to lean back and roar with laughter. Unamused, Crixtacus merely shot Neacal a disgusted look and remained silent. Arrius thought he must indeed present a ludicrous sight. He dropped the gladius and reached down to retrieve his tunic. While he pulled the tunic over his head, the three men walked their horses slowly across the clearing toward him. Arrius was aware Ilya silently joined him. He glanced at her and saw she had not taken the time to put on her riding breeches. Barefoot and clad only in her woolen shift that reached just above mid-thigh, she presented an alluring if somewhat disheveled appearance. Arrius bristled at Neacal's appreciative leer.

Neacal spoke first. "It's a good thing we come in peace. It was not long ago when my arrow would have found another target than a tree. You are careless, Roman, or has your attention been on other matters?"

Ignoring the remark, Arrius said, "Your destination is not far away," pointing in the general direction of Cuileán's village.

"I thought you might wish for some company. That is why we were waiting patiently for you to wake up, but it did not seem as if either one of you was in any hurry to leave."

"We aren't; therefore, you should be on your way."

Crixtacus turned his horse around and started back toward the trail only to have Neacal call sharply after him, "Hold, Crixtacus! We go when I'm ready."

Crixtacus looked over his shoulder and shot Neacal a contemptuous look without pausing. "I think you should do as the Roman says and leave while you're still able to. I've seen this man fight. You would do well not to provoke him."

"I think the Roman does not look too dangerous to me, and the woman might be willing to spread her legs as a welcome gesture—"

Whatever else Neacal intended to say, he never got the chance. In two steps, Arrius reached Neacal's horse and grabbed a handful of the Novantean's woolen vest. Arrius threw rather than pulled Neacal from the saddle. With a thud, Neacal landed on his back with enough force to knock the wind out of him. In a cold fury, Arrius placed one bare foot on Neacal's throat and pressed down hard. Red-faced, eyes bulging, Neacal tried unsuccessfully to dislodge the foot. In a matter of moments, Neacal's efforts were reduced to ineffective scrabbling until finally his entire body went limp. Only then did Arrius remove his foot, eyeing the two other Novanti to gauge their intentions.

"Was it necessary to kill him?" Ilya said, an edge to her voice.

"He'll live, but he won't feel much like talking for a few days."

"It wasn't necessary to treat him that way. He intended no harm," Ilya added, lips turned down in disapproval.

"It was necessary to teach him to be more careful what he says in the future."

Crixtacus walked his horse over to Neacal who by now was groaning audibly. The smaller man looked down at Neacal unsympathetically and offered no assistance when the injured man tried to stand. Neacal regained his feet and stumbled unsteadily toward his horse and with difficulty climbed into the saddle. Massaging his throat with one hand and guiding the horse with the other, he faced Arrius and in a voice no louder than a whisper said, "I'll not forget this, Roman. One day you'll regret you didn't kill me when you had the chance."

"Leave now while you can and hope you never give me a reason to regret my good nature."

Ilya and Arrius watched the three men disappear into the forest. He glanced at Ilya and noted her worried frown.

"I fear you've made an enemy."

"I have many, and one more is no great concern."

"All the same, I think it better if you did not go north. Neacal must go as he is Bothan's ambassador. If you're with me, there will only be more trouble."

"If I don't go, then you will not," he retorted with an edge to his voice.

"You don't understand Marcus, I'm Joric's representative, and I've no choice in the matter."

"You aren't listening to me. You are my wife, and I have no intention of allowing you to go without me. You saw the way Neacal looked at you. If nothing else, he'll use you to get back at me. No, I'll not permit it!"

"You would jeopardize Joric's chance for an alliance because of some misguided idea I need protection?" she replied, eyes flashing.

"Have you thought the alliance could be jeopardized even more if Neacal decides somewhere along the way a Selgovan ambassador is no longer necessary?"

"You're making more of this than is merited. I appreciate your concern, but I can take care of myself," Ilya said in a more moderate tone in an attempt to placate him.

Arrius tried to curb his rising anger, replying in what he thought was a reasonable tone. "We'll speak no more about it. When you've calmed down, you'll realize I'm right."

Her reaction was enough to convince him he had probably said the wrong thing. Ilya stood glaring at him, hands on her hips in resolute defiance. Twice she attempted to respond but was too angry to get the words out. In silent frustration, she began pulling on her breeches and boots. He was still fastening the lacing on his boots when she vaulted onto her horse and galloped back the way they came.

He buckled on his sword belt and walked slowly to where Ferox was tethered. Rubbing the animal's nose, he muttered as he looked back at the oak tree, "Ferox, I think it was a fine morning, my friend, but now I think the rest of the day will not go as well as I hoped."

He took his time riding back to the village, arriving in time to find his things were in the process of being moved to another dwelling. Under the present circumstances, Arrius thought it was probably just as well.

Chapter 9

Three days into the journey and the pall enveloping the group since leaving Cuileán's village was yet to dissipate.

Arrius and Ilya had exchanged barely a word since their altercation four days before, the one just as stubborn as the other in refusing to make any overtures. During the day, Ilya rode well back in the column while Arrius remained close to the front behind Neacal and Cuileán. At night, they maintained their distance with each choosing opposite sides of the camp to spread their blankets.

By tacit agreement, Arrius and Neacal avoided each other to the extent the confines of the small camp allowed and essential coordination of routine tasks dictated. During the day, it was Cuileán and occasionally Crixtacus who acted as intermediaries between the two men. Neacal spoke little, and on the few occasions he did, his hoarse voice was an audible reminder of what Arrius had done to him. Privately, Arrius was beginning to think Ilya may have been right about her insistence he remain behind; however, he wasn't ready to voice his misgivings and least of all to Ilya.

The terrain was becoming more open the farther north they traveled. Gradually, the steep hills and dense forests were left behind as the party descended into a low, relatively open and rolling countryside. Where the streams and small rivers flowed swift and clear in the upper regions, by comparison the streams in the lower elevation seemed turgid and muddy as they emptied into stagnant bogs. The swampy ground often proved even too treacherous for the horses, forcing them to take circuitous routes. The forests were noticeably thinning as the landscape transitioned to grassland interspersed with isolated and sparse stands of trees found along the banks of the numerous streams they crossed. What other vegetation there was consisted mainly of fern-like bracken and gorse bushes just beginning to show the buds that would soon burst into yellow flowers.

Occasionally, they passed isolated settlements consisting of a few crude hovels inhabited by no more than three or four families struggling to maintain a marginal existence. Arrius asked Cuileán why there were no visible signs of the occupants. Cuileán told him the people who lived between the Selgovi and the Venicones distrusted both tribes with ample justification. They were loyal to either the Selgovi or Venicones depending on which tribal representatives they might encounter. If possible, they considered it best for their continued welfare to avoid interaction with either tribe. Arrius thought about the coming invasion and pitied the unfortunate natives who were about to be caught between the clash of two cultures.

That evening while the sun was still low over the hills, Cuileán drew Arrius aside and motioned for him to follow as he ascended a low hill a short distance away from the camp. Reaching the summit, Arrius saw a wide river ahead flowing into an estuary that progressively widened until it spilled into the sea beyond. Farther north, he saw mountains and the glint of snow on the crests of the tallest peaks.

Pointing first to the east and then due west, the Selgovan said, "It is here or close by, I believe, where the Romans intend to come and build their wall. It is the narrowest stretch between the two seas that lie on either side." Cuileán pointed to the snowcapped mountains ahead. We will not go that far. The tribes we will visit are located not far from here, and it will be better for them to contact the tribes farther north on our behalf. The high mountain tribes are fierce and primitive, and they do not like strangers, particularly Romans. My grandfather along with the other Caledonian Tribes fought the Romans in those mountains almost seventy years ago."

Arrius knew Cuileán was referring to the spectacular success Agricola achieved for a brief time which marked the extent of the Roman advance before or since.

"Even though the Romans were badly outnumbered, they were still victorious." Cuileán added further, "It was a humiliation that has not yet been forgotten by the mountain people. For that reason, it would not be counted against you if you were to turn back. From here on, it will not be safe," he added neutrally.

"Does that mean me, or does it include the others as well?"

Cuileán shrugged. "Possibly if the upland tribes kill you, they will be satisfied to let the rest of us live."

Amused, Arrius smiled. "That may be reason enough for me to continue. I thank you for your counsel, but I will take the risk one Roman does not look like an invasion."

Cuileán accepted the answer without showing either disappointment or satisfaction. "Tomorrow we'll be deep in the lands of the Venicones. It is they and the Epedi in the west who will be the first of the northern tribes to face the Romans when they come. If the Venicones do not kill us, we will go to the Epedi. The Caledoni claim the lands north of the Epedi, and the Vacomagi occupy the land immediately north of the Venicones. I hope these four tribes will listen carefully to what we have to say then help persuade the remaining tribes to assist in defeating the Roman occupation."

"You don't sound very confident of our success."

"We will say what we have come to say, but in the end, it will be others," gesturing north, "who will decide if they choose to believe they are in jeopardy and allow us to return unharmed to our own lands."

On that solemn note, the two men silently watched the sun slowly dipping below the far hills while each pondered what the gods might be arranging for them in the days to come.

There was no indication anything was amiss as the party followed Cuileán single file along a narrow path bisecting a long stretch of chest-high marsh grass. Suddenly from both sides of the path, near-naked warriors seemed to spring forth from nowhere in numbers that made resistence futile.

No less surprised than the others, Arrius was impressed with how effectively the ambush had been prepared and executed. Most of the warriors were armed only with a light spear while some brandished a variety of swords. He noticed a few carried badly-worn Roman swords undoubtedly acquired during the Agricola campaign. He saw why they were called the "painted people." Visible on all parts of their bodies were various designs painted on with different colored pigment. The crudely drawn designs predominantly depicted the profile of various animals while some appeared to be only geometrical shapes. The men were rough-looking and hirsute, sporting bristling beards some of which were long enough to be braided. A majority of the warriors had sandy-colored hair while a few had bright red hair, which he thought at first was dyed but learned later it was natural. What was most remarkable was their size. Most of the warriors were easily as tall if not taller than he was.

Arrius was pulled roughly from the saddle, and his hands bound behind him. He heard Neacal and Cuileán speaking earnestly in a tongue that bore little resemblance to the Selgovan language. Whatever they were saying seemed to have no effect as they were also bound and led away. He jerked away from the two men flanking him long enough to turn and see if Ilya was all right. He was relieved to see she was still astride her horse although the reins were held by one of the warriors. If she was frightened, she concealed it well with a haughty, disdainful expression.

He was sent sprawling and received several painful blows from a spear shaft for his efforts. He was pulled to his feet accompanied by angry shouts requiring no translation to understand the intent. Arrius heard a shrill whinny and scream behind him. He turned and saw a man with a bloody shoulder from a bite Ferox gave him. The man was taking out his anger on the horse by beating it across the flank with his spear shaft. Another man held the reins of the plunging horse. Enraged, the stallion managed to lift both back legs and caught the warrior with the spear in a vicious kick that sent him sprawling with nothing left of his face but bloody pulp. The stillness of the body and the unnatural position of the head made it clear the man's neck was broken. Arrius was horrified to see another warrior, bare sword in hand, advance toward the maddened horse.

Distracted by the unfolding spectacle, the two men on either side of him relaxed their grip allowing Arrius to twist free and run awkwardly toward the young man holding the sword. Ignoring Ilya's scream and Cuileán's shout of alarm, he shouldered an older man with a gray beard roughly aside who attempted to stop him and sent him tumbling into the tall grass. The man with the sword turned too late to prevent being bowled over by the momentum of his attack. The first to regain his feet, Arrius delivered a well-aimed kick that caught the warrior full on the chin hard enough to knock him senseless to the ground. He turned quickly around and saw tribesmen cautiously coming toward him from all directions but careful to remain out of range of the bucking horse. Frantically, Arrius worked to loosen the bonds around his wrists and was relieved to feel them beginning to loosen.

Arrius broke free in time to sidestep the first of three men closing in on him from all sides. A moment later, he was on the ground with all three men on top of him doing their best to pin his arms and legs while the other warriors shouted encouragement. Oblivious to the blows he received, he stood up leaving one man writhing on the ground from a painful kick to the groin, another was unconscious and the third man was limping away cradling a broken arm. Arrius quickly knelt down and retrieved the sword of the first warrior he kicked and pointed the blade meaningfully at the unconscious man's throat. Other men running toward him immediately came to a halt, uncertain what to do next. One of the men carrying a spear slowly hefted the weapon only to be waived back by the gray-bearded man he had sent tumbling into the marsh grass. The older man wore a heavy torque around his neck. Arrius focused on him assuming the neck ornament marked him as the leader.

Arrius heard Cuileán's voice shouting urgently in the strange, incomprehensible language. Whatever the Selgovan was saying appeared to have some effect. All but the gray-bearded man began to relax as they moved back a pace before stopping to regard him with silent speculation. The gray-bearded warrior spoke tersely without once taking his eyes off Arrius. When he finished speaking, Cuileán said, "Arrius, drop the sword. Indrecht is the tribal chief of the Venicones. He says no one will harm you or the horse if you spare his son's life. If you kill him, we will all die."

"Then tell them I will spare his son only if we are treated not as captives but as guests who come in peace to talk to the Venicones. Cuileán, make him understand we have important matters to discuss."

Cuileán spoke at some length while the men around him listened attentively. Finally, Arrius saw Indrecht nod reluctantly. Visibly irritated at the turn of events, Indrecht said something that immediately caused the other warriors to relax. Arrius hesitated then tossed the sword aside hoping the Venicones, although savage in appearance, were trustworthy. Turning his back on Indrecht, Arrius stepped toward Ferox and examined the nervous stallion for any apparent wounds. He was relieved to find nothing but a few superficial lacerations. He resumed calming the animal with soothing words and gentle strokes, and gradually, the stallion ceased its nervous prancing.

His attention focused on the horse, Arrius wasn't at first aware of becoming an object of intense interest until he turned around and saw Indrecht and many of the other Venicones tribesmen quietly staring at him. Indrecht spoke a few words while Cuileán translated. "Indrecht wants to know if the horse is all right."

"Arrius nodded and said, "Tell him and his warriors not to come near him, or they may die like him," gesturing in the direction of the man Ferox killed.

After Cuileán finished translating his response, Indrecht spoke again, a curious expression on his face.

"Indrecht asks if you would have killed his son."

Arrius nodded. "Now ask him if he treats all visitors to his land so ill."

"Strangers are not welcome here, particularly if they are Roman," Cuileán said after waiting until Indrecht finished speaking. "They have no reason to like or trust Romans."

"I am only one Roman. Am I then such a threat to the Venicones?"

Arrius was not expecting to see a brief smile soften Indrecht's stern face before he replied. When he finished speaking, Cuileán said, "After what you and the horse did to his men, he thinks perhaps you are. He is willing to treat you as a guest and listen to what you have to say. He is also curious to know why you risked your life for a horse when the odds were so against you."

Arrius smiled. "Tell him I thought the odds were in my favor."

After Cuileán translated, Indrecht threw back his head and laughed before saying something else. He was still chuckling as he walked away.

"What did he say?"

"He said the Venicones may have to treat you as a friend because they cannot risk having you as an enemy."

"Marcus, you could have been killed!" Ilya said in low tones as they walked side by side. They were her first words spoken directly to him since their departure, and they seemed to him more rebuke than an expression of concern for his safety.

"What would you have me do? Stand by meekly and watch my horse killed?"

"If necessary, yes. Besides he wasn't going to kill the horse. He merely held the sword in his hand."

"How was it you knew that, and I did not?" He was thoroughly angered at her unreasonable argument.

"Because the Venicones do not believe in the needless death of animals, and unlike the Romans, they do not kill them in arenas for sport as I am told they do in Rome."

"It might have been useful if someone bothered to tell me," he said sounding defensive. "It would appear I risked my life for no reason at all."

"I know the horse means much to you, but our purpose here is more important. Your actions may have jeopardized everything."

"Apparently, your concern has little to do with the possibility I might have been been killed." He was irritated at her unfair criticism. "I believe had I not acted as I did, we would still be captives and in far worse position to achieve an alliance with the Venicones."

Ilya attempted a more accommodating approach, realizing belatedly her words sounded far too critical. She knew the reason for lashing out at him was the aftermath of her paralyzing fear when it looked as if he was about to be killed.

"I cannot deny what you say is true," she replied in a softer tone of voice. "I simply meant I don't want you taking any unnecessary risks. I couldn't bear it if anything should happen to you."

Somewhat mollified at her overture and hopeful it signaled a thaw in their relations, he decided to respond in kind. "For me the *unnecessary* risk would have been to do nothing. I admit it seemed to have turned out better than I expected, and perhaps if I thought more about it, I might not have acted as I did," privately thinking just the opposite.

Ilya tactfully shifted the conversation to less controversial subjects.

That night, Neacal and Cuileán talked at length with Indrecht while Cuileán or Neacal provided cryptic translations for Arrius and Ilya. If Indrecht harbored any animosity concerning the Venicones warrior Ferox killed, he did not show it indicating what Cuileán said to him earlier in the day was true. Since the Venicones revered animals, their gods simply punished the tribesman for having mistreated the horse. After hearing the explanation, he resolved his gods would have to wait until he went farther south before he performed any animal sacrifices.

Arrius tried to determine whether the tribal leader was supportive or against what Ilya was telling him, but Indrecht's face was inscrutable. He asked few questions and gave no indication of what he might be thinking. Once Indrecht looked in Arrius's direction and said something which Neacal with a contemptuous sneer was quick to translate.

"Indrecht wants to know why he should trust a man who turned on his own people."

Arrius thought the question was fair and not unexpected. "Tell him Rome's interests and mine were no longer the same, and that I was no longer fighting for the things I once thought important."

Indrecht listened to Neacal translate, his face showing impatience. Ilya and Cuileán shifted uneasily, and it was apparent they were just as uncomfortable with the ambiguity of his response.

Indrecht spoke again, and Neacal turned to Arrius with a gloating expression. "He said the answer is not clear. He thinks you are being evasive and wants to know what you believe in now."

Arrius looked directly at Indrecht and replied pointing at Ilya, "I believe in this woman and our son. Her other son Joric is now High Chieftain of the Selgovi. When the Romans invade, the Selgovi and Novanti will be defeated without the help of the northern tribes and possibly my help as well. It is my destiny to prevent the slaughter that will surely come if the tribes do not unite."

After Cuileán finished translating, Indrecht's eyes narrowed thoughtfully. A few moments later, he spoke cryptically, and Arrius, anticipating what he would be asked, did not wait for either Neacal or Cuileán to translate.

"He asked how I can help. Tell him I can teach the tribes how best to fight the Romans. The Romans cannot be stopped, but they can be prevented from destroying the tribes one by one including the Venicones when the southern tribes have been defeated."

Indrecht's next question with doubt plainly reflected in his expression was immediate. Cuileán translated. "He wants to know if you intend to teach us to fight like Romans?"

"No! There is no quicker way for the Romans to defeat the tribes than to try to fight as the Romans do. First, the Romans cannot be stopped in one battle or many battles, but they can be delayed. If the tribes strike suddenly and often, it will slow the Roman advance. The way you attacked today was successful; that is one of the ways to fight the Romans. It is better to strike when they least expect it."

The discussion went long into the night with Indrecht showing no sign of fatigue as he continued to probe with incisive questions indicative of a keen intellect. It was not until much later when the tribal chief stood up and turned as if to leave only to pause and look thoughtfully at Arrius. When Indrecht finally spoke, he pointed to his cheek.

Cuileán translated. "He wants to know how you got the great scar on your face."

"Tell him I was once careless in battle."

When Cuileán finished the cryptic answer, Indrecht spoke and pointed down to the puckered scar on his right side. Cuileán said, "He says he, too, was careless once, but the other man was more careless."

Indrecht had disappeared into the darkness by the time Cuileán finished the translation.

After a brief silence, Arrius looked at Neacal and Cuileán. "What will he do?"

Yawning, Neacal replied, "I do not know, but I think he will not say until he has the advice of his council and possibly not before he talks to the Epedi."

Cuileán was more optimistic. "I believe he will agree to help us, but I also think Neacal is right about talking to the Epedi. They do not get along; however, they trust them more than they do us. It's possible the tribes here will do nothing until the Romans begin to move north. Then they will decide. I fear if they delay, it will be too late to help us." The faces of Ilya and the three men reflected their gloom over the tenuous outcome of the discussion.

Ilya eventually left to settle in for the night followed quickly thereafter by Cuileán and Neacal. Arrius remained for a time staring morosely into the embers of the dying fire. Soon he began to feel the effects of the chilly night air and realized it was past time he, too, got some rest. With some effort, he stood up and experienced twinges throughout his tired body he managed successfully to ignore until then. Some of the aches and pains resulted from the ambush earlier in the day, but the cold night air was beginning to aggravate wounds received from past campaigns and battles. He limped through the sleeping camp massaging his left thigh as he walked. The leg was still a painful reminder of the Jewish arrow that struck him during the *Deiotariana* legion's last battle in Judaea. When he reached his blanket, the sliver of a moon cast enough light to see Ilya fast asleep under it. Her presence seemed to signal a truce between them.

She didn't wake up when he stretched out beside her.

According to Cuileán, the principal settlement of the Venicones was situated near a lake directly north and not far from where they were presently located. Unfortunately, because of the deep river ahead, it would require nearly a day traveling northwest to reach a safe place to cross. The crossing site was then almost another full day's march west of the village.

When they camped that night as well as the next night, Indrecht asked even more questions. Some were the same as if he was testing to see if the answers would be consistent. Arrius's respect for the canny tribal chief continued to increase with each discussion. He was impressed with Indrecht's calm, pragmatic views. In many ways, Indrecht reminded him of Beldorach. Indrecht was also charismatic and possessed similar leadership qualities in sharp contrast to Bothan, the bellicose leader of the Novanti.

The first indication they were nearing their destination was the presence of large fields defined by low stone fences containing primarily sheep except for occasional small herds of shaggy cattle with long, widely-spaced horns. The herds were being looked after by older men or young boys who watched curiously as the column passed by. Not a single horse was in sight.

Surrounded by a chest-high stone wall, the village sprawled haphazardly across several small, nearly treeless hills on the shore of a lake glistening like wet slate under the gray hues of a cloudy, overcast day. A hill-fort was centrally located not unlike those common throughout Britannia. Compared to the Selgovan and Novantean dwellings, the much lower walls of the round, thatch-roofed houses were made entirely of rocks instead of the mud and wattle construction more typical of villages in the south. A small corral abutting each house contained rooting hogs and chickens living in symbiotic harmony. Radiating out from the village were more fields in which more livestock grazed placidly. Since he saw no crops being grown and there were no significant forests for game to live in, Arrius concluded the Venicones depended mainly on the animals for their livelihood. He discounted the presence of the lake and the fish it contained as a food source. He learned soon after his arrival in Britannia the northern islanders seemed to have a strange and near universal aversion to consuming anything with scales.

Arrius's first impression confirmed Cuileán's description of a culture considerably more primitive than the tribes dwelling in the southern regions. The clan chief said the tribes living farther north were even less advanced and more intractable than the Venicones.

In spite of the comparatively cool temperature, the men he observed were lightly clad in breeches made from animal skins and simple sleeveless vests of sheep's wool. Although some of the men wore calf-length boots, there were nearly as many who were barefoot. The women were uniformly garbed in shapeless wool shifts reaching to just below the knee. Most women were barefoot, but here and there were exceptions with a few wearing sandals or leather wraps gathered and secured at the ankle. Similar to other native people inhabiting the island, both men and women wore their hair long and loose although he noticed some of the women braided their hair in one long, thick braid that hung down their back. From the grime on the villager's faces and arms and the proximity of the lake, it did not look as if the Venicones regarded personal cleanliness as reverently as did the Selgovi.

Chattering excitedly and completely ignoring the misty rain beginning to fall, the villagers drifted toward the procession as it headed in the direction of the hill-fort. The excitement was tempered when the corpse of the man Ferox killed was noticed draped across one of the pack horses. The discovery was the occasion for one of the women, whom Arrius assumed to be the dead man's wife, to begin a keening wail. After the distraught woman was led away, the silence that quickly descended on the festive throng lifted, and once again the mood became festive over the unexpected but welcome diversion.

Indrecht stopped the procession in a level area below the hill-fort and motioned for Ilya and the others to stand off to one side. The presence of flat rocks arranged in a semi-circle, and the beaten earth suggested this was where the villagers gathered for meetings and ceremonial occasions. As the horses were taken away, the men took up seats on the rocks while the women stood well back. All directed their attention to Indrecht when he began to speak at length. While he spoke, Indrecht frequently gestured toward Ilya. It wasn't necessary

116

for Cuileán to translate to understand the tribal leader was explaining the purpose of the delegation from the southern tribes.

At one point, Indrecht pointed to Arrius and said something that drew angry scowls and jeers which Neacal took great satisfaction in translating.

"He said you're a Roman. They do not like Romans. I have more in common with the Venicones than I thought," he added with a humorless smile.

Indrecht continued to speak, smiling as he did. It was obvious he was still referring to Arrius, and whatever he said produced a spontaneous and enthusiastic response from the men with some jumping to their feet in excitement.

Neacal started laughing as Cuileán turned to Arrius, regarding him with a sober look and said, "Indrecht complimented your fighting abilities. He has challenged his men to test their skills against you in various contests. This is not a good thing for you, Arrius. One of their favorite contests is wrestling, and there are none better than the Venicones."

Chapter 10

"Tiberius Querinius, I congratulate you on your success!" Arvinnius said approvingly after having surveyed the bodies and destruction of the latest Briganti village virtually razed that morning. The two officers drew their horses to a stop beneath one of the more than fifty wooden crucifixes lining the road upon which only a few of the men and women continued to writhe in agony. Farther down the line of crosses, several legionaries under the supervision of an optio were nailing another captive to a cross. The victim's screams were punctuated by the metallic sound of the hammer driving in the large nails made exclusively for the purpose.

Praise from Arvinnius was seldom given. His approval was signified more often by the absence of pointed criticism than complimentary words. Querinius had difficulty concealing both his surprise and his pleasure at the unexpected praise.

"I trust this will be an object lesson for any further thoughts of rebellion," Arvinnius commented in satisfaction as he idly watched the dying man above them twitching spasmodically. "Querinius, do you not find it curious the so-called Christians have come to revere an object we have been using for executions since the early days of Rome?" Then evidently not really interested in the tribune's opinion on the matter, Arvinnius turned in the saddle and signaled to the centurion in charge of his escort it was time to return to Eboracum. Querinius was pleased when Arvinnius, clearly in an expansive mood, invited him to return to the fort with him.

Feeling the need to break an awkward silence as they rode, Querinius commented, "I think your information the Briganti were on the verge of revolt was accurate as there were few young men in the village, mainly old men, women, and children."

"What information?" Arvinnius asked with a puzzled look.

"Why the information you evidently had when you ordered me to attack Isurium," Querinius replied, clearly puzzled at the question.

"I was given no such information, Querinius. For all I know, the Briganti men may have been off somewhere performing one of their outlandish rituals as they seem prone to do. I've heard it said they even practice human sacrifice," Arvinnius added in profound disgust.

"But I thought the report Tribune Gaius Cornelius presented at the consilium warned of an imminent Briganti attack!"

"Oh, that," Arvinnius replied, waving his hand if brushing off a fly. "I really didn't give the report much thought."

"Then why did we attack?" Querinius asked, completely perplexed.

Irritated by the question, Arvinnius retorted, "Why, it should be obvious enough to you, Querinius. The Sixth hasn't seen a fight in some time, and I'm certain some of our newer replacements have yet to be blooded. Before the real battles come, I want the legion to remember what it's like to smell and see blood dripping from a gladius. It tones the men up, and it's good for morale. Besides, you provided an object lesson in Roman efficiency if the bastards ever dare to challenge us."

"What if the Briganti are provoked into fighting?"

"Then we shall deal with it, of course. To be honest, I hope they do as the Sixth could use some practical training, and I imagine the Second and Twentieth would profit as well. Neutralizing the Briganti now only ensures the south is more secure when we move north."

"When do you intend to order the advance?"

"We march as soon as the Second Legion is within a day's march of Eboracum. Corbulo has been delayed and will not be in place for at least another week," the last said in disgust. "When Corbulo's in position, that will be the time to order the auxiliaries on the wall to begin their advance. In the meantime, I've ordered Marcellus Septimus to begin moving the Twentieth Legion to its forward position in the vicinity of Vindomora. I suggest you send Secundus Avitus," citing the legion's *praefectus castrorum*, "on to Voreda with a quartering party in the next day or so to prepare for the legion's arrival. In the meantime, I want you to keep patrols moving about the area just in case the Briganti decide to do anything unwise."

Anticipating nearly everything Arvinnius said, Querinius smugly replied, "General, I've already ordered Avitus and the second cohort to leave for Voreda tomorrow. Four cohorts will remain in the field for the next three days until they're replaced by the cohorts remaining in Eboracum."

Arvinnius glanced at the tribune. "The plan is sound enough, although I believe it would be better to leave only two cohorts behind in the garrison. The Eboracum fort would be the last place the Briganti would consider attacking, and even if they did, eight hundred legionaries would be more than enough to defend it. I suggest it would be better to place extra legionaries out in the field and ensure the security of the signal towers. The towers are vulnerable and are likely to become easy targets in retaliation for your success today."

Querinius winced at the implied criticism for neglecting the signal towers. Arvinnius's comment was particularly painful since he had dismissed the same suggestion made by the grizzled praefectus castrorum. When Avitus recommended something similar the day before, he dismissed it arbitrarily only because he had not thought of it. Now he would have to endure the knowing look of the old prick when he amended his orders.

"Very well, I'll make the adjustments." Then in an attempt to divert the general's attention to other and more neutral matters, he asked, "What news is there from Rutipiae concerning Arrius?" He referred to the general's recent efforts to verify if Arrius had left Britannia.

"As I suspected, there is no indication the bastard ever left the island which is enough to confirm the individual who visited the Novanti was undoubtedly Arrius. I received a reply from Lollius Urbicus agreeing with my recommendation that Arrius be proclaimed an enemy of Rome." Arvinnius then regarded Querinius with narrowed eyes. "You didn't get along with Arrius as I recall. It was plain enough the first time I saw the two of you together at Banna. Why?"

Caught off guard, Querinius struggled to think of a reply that would satisfy the general's question without having to go into details — details that if known would not serve his interests at all. On the other hand, he didn't know how much Arvinnius knew of the events in Judaea that eventually turned them into bitter enemies. The last thing he needed was Arvinnius probing into what happened in Judaea in the final hour of the *Deiotariana* Legion. Even now, Arrius's scathing condemnation when the centurion found him skulking in the medical tent continued to haunt him.

Trying to sound off-hand, Querinius replied, "I found Arrius to be opinionated, insubordinate and self-serving."

Arvinnius chuckled, "By Jupiter's balls, you just described half the men in the army above the rank of optio and every general including me! Come, Tribune, there's more to it than that. I warrant he saw occasion to pin your ears a time or two. Every primus pilus I ever knew was a sore on the ass of every tribune in every legion I served. And if he wasn't, he probably wasn't doing his job."

Presented with a face-saving opening, Querinius seized the opportunity with relief.

"Aye, you have the essence of it. He was as you say an insufferable bastard, made worse because he was undeserving of the honor of being *Primus Pilus*. I blame Arrius for what happened to the *Deiotariana*. It was his recommendation to locate the camp where we did and too far forward to be reinforced. The location placed us in an untenable position when the Jews attacked in force and overran us."

Arvinnius glanced sharply at Querinius in open disbelief. "I find it strange to hear it was the primus pilus who located the camp position. It's the responsibility of the *praefectus castrorum* or the legion commander to select the location for the night camp, and if for any reason either man is not able, it is the legion's senior tribune who does so. If I recall correctly, you were the senior tribune," Arvinnius added pointedly.

To Querinius's profound relief, a mounted legionary pulled up on a lathered horse beside him, saluted and reported the first cohort had contacted a sizable Briganti force. Silently giving thanks to every god he could think of, he quickly took leave of Arvinnius and followed the courier in the opposite direction of Eboracum.

It was late in the day, and the afternoon shadows were beginning to lengthen when Decrius finished the last of the prayers over the rock-covered grave of his wife and son. His attention was suddenly drawn to the faint but unmistakable clamor of battle. Without a backward look at the graves, he mounted and guided the horse in the direction from where the sounds were coming from. He hoped when he found the Briganti, they would recognize his Brigantian facial tattoo and long hair before noticing the distinctive sword belt and red tunic.

He was in no hurry and did not urge the horse to go any faster than a walk. There was no need to join a battle already in progress when he might be mistaken for an enemy by either side. In fact, there was every reason to expect a less than warm reception by his own tribe. He was not unaware of the tribal attitude toward him for having served Rome by choice. If Iseult's father would have nothing to do with him, there was no reason to expect any warmer reception from anyone else in the tribal federation.

Decrius had gone less than a mile when he saw a flash of movement in the trees ahead. The battle sounds stopped, clear indication one side or the other prevailed. The comparative brief conflict seemed to indicate a one-sided advantage. He thought the odds did not favor the Briganti. As if to confirm his prediction, he saw a group of men, their torsos and faces daubed liberally with blue paint, silently threading their way through the trees toward him. Wounded men hobbled along as best they could with other more seriously injured being supported or carried on makeshift litters. Their drawn faces and anxious glances behind them were enough to confirm the outcome of the battle.

He reined in the horse and after dismounting silently, waited for them to draw closer. The first man to see him stopped in his tracks, an expression of alarm on his face. Undoubtedly thinking the Romans had outflanked them, the warrior gave a warning cry alerting those close to him that prompted several men to run toward him with swords at the ready.

Decrius raised both hands and called out in the Briganti tongue, "I'm not a Roman. I'm one of you." The men slowed their run to a walk but still approached cautiously until they completely surrounded him. Without lowering his sword, a lean-built warrior with wide, deep-set eyes and bleeding from a gash on the shoulder asked in a harsh, grating voice, "Who are you?"

"I am Decrius, a Brigantian by birth."

"You look more Roman than Briganti, and that looks like a Roman horse and saddle."

"It was a Roman horse. Now it belongs to me."

Another man standing behind Decrius spoke up excitedly. "Wait, I know this man. He's a member of the Roman auxilia."

"Is this true, and if so, can you think of any reason why we shouldn't kill you now?"

"It was true, but since the death of my wife and son today, I no longer serve Rome. It is my intention now to kill as many Romans as I can. I've already started," he added.

"Are you the one who killed the legionaries we found by the road?"

"I killed some legionaries this morning." He didn't elaborate further.

"How many were there, and how did you leave them?" the other man asked with a suspicious expression.

"Five with their heads on their spears," Decrius replied.

The answer seemed to reassure the man as he asked in a less belligerent manner, "Was the centurion's helmet yours as well?"

"It was."

"Well, there's no time now to talk of this. There are too many Romans behind us to delay any longer. I'm certain you won't mind if the wounded use your horse," the man said and without waiting for agreement, he helped the nearest wounded man to get on the horse. Moments later with Decrius leading the horse and two more wounded men holding on to the saddle blanket on either side, the march resumed toward the setting sun.

"Why should I trust you?" Hudryn asked bluntly. As the senior council member of the northern Briganti, Hudryn now claimed the position of tribal leader since the death of Tadg that afternoon. Since the Brigantes Tribe was in reality a federation of separate tribes, the identification and ratification of Tadg's replacement was a weighty matter that would not be settled easily, and until it was, the Romans enjoyed more of an advantage than they possibly knew.

Decrius regarded the man on the opposite side of the fire with the deep-set eyes and responded logically, "If I wasn't telling the truth, why would I have waited for you to come to me when I could have easily ridden away?"

"Yesterday a Roman centurion and today a loyal Briganti tribesman? It's difficult to believe."

"What would I gain by lying?"

"Our confidence while you spy for the Romans," Hudryn countered.

"I suppose what you say is true," Decrius conceded. "Unfortunately, I do not know of a way to convince you I am not a spy."

Hudryn made no immediate response as he silently considered the response. Taking a new tact, he said, "How do you account for the Romans' sudden attack unless they knew we were on the verge of rebellion?"

Decrius shrugged. "Until now, I didn't know the tribe was planning to revolt. It's possible the Romans learned of it and attacked first. Yesterday, I was at Banna when I learned of the planned attack on Isurium. I left there soon after to find my wife and son who had recently gone there. I was too late," he said, face bleak.

"What do you intend to do?" Hudryn asked in a more conciliatory tone.

"I intend to spend the rest of my life killing as many Romans as I can."

Hudryn gave Decrius an appraising look and did not immediately reply. When he did speak again, he said, "If what you told me is true, then we have need of you and your skills. We did not fare well today. We were not ready, and the Romans killed many more of us than we did of them. I also fear the settlement is destroyed. With the loss of Tadg, we are not well positioned to fight the Romans."

Decrius did not know Tadg well enough to disagree with Hudryn. Privately, he thought if Tadg was more of a warrior, he would not have allowed the Romans to catch them so unprepared.

"It may be much worse than you think," Decrius said quietly. "The Romans are planning to abandon the wall and build another farther north. The legion in the far south and the one in the west will soon join the Sixth Legion at Eboracum."

Hudryn kneaded his forehead, a look of discouragement replacing his previous resolute expression.

"If we have so little success against one legion, we will surely have no chance against three."

Silently agreeing with the assessment, Decrius did not respond, reluctant to say anything in the belief he had neither the right to criticize nor to offer advice. Evidently, Hudryn felt no such reservation and asked, "What would you do if you were in my position?"

After a few minutes, Decrius said, "I think the Briganti would be better off if they were to make overtures of peace to the Romans then wait until the tribe is better prepared for war."

"And what will you do if we make peace with the Romans?"

Decrius did not hesitate. "I will never make peace with the Romans."

"Well, I think it's too late or too soon to deal with the Romans except with sword and arrow," Hudryn added objectively.

Decrius did not reply thinking Hudryn was probably right.

Hudryn gave Decrius a searching look then said, "You are experienced in the Roman way of fighting, and I think that knowledge would benefit the tribe. Will you stay and help us?"

"Yes," Decrius answered simply without emotion or further comment.

Before the night was over, Decrius was the nominal leader of the Briganti revolt.

Chapter 11

Arrius drew the arrow back to his ear and briefly sighted down the shaft before releasing the bowstring. He had the satisfaction of seeing the arrow run true and strike three fingers from the center of the target. It was a credible shot although it was not as good as either of the arrows Neacal and Crixtacus launched both of which struck the center. The archery contest quickly came down to him, Neacal and Crixtacus representing the southern tribes facing three Venicones tribesmen. He had never excelled in archery and considered himself no better than average in the use of the weapon. He was therefore pleased at how well he did. The close match ended several arrows later with Crixtacus declared the overall winner to Neacal's obvious disgust.

In the mock swordfights, Arrius was the clear and undisputed winner. He realized early on even the better swordsmen were less proficient than the typical legionary after completing his initial training. Had wounds been the sole criteria for determining a winner, the soggy ground would have been redder still with Venicones blood. Fortunately, the outcome of the sword fights did not require the shedding of blood to determine the winner, which was settled by three men watching every movement carefully. At some point, the judges declared a winner when they believed one of the contestants clearly prevailed over the other. It was evident from the enthusiasm shone by the Venicones, they enjoyed contests of any kind even those where they were clearly outmatched. There was never the slightest hint of bias shown by the judges for the local competitors as he first assumed would be the case.

Arrius thought between the spear-throwing and wrestling contests yet to come, he would have the easiest time with the spear. He surmised he would have difficulty holding his own in a physical contest with opponents who were at least as big as he was and with most of them looking considerably younger. A few contestants were taller than he was.

Hefting the spear confidently, he took note of its balance and shifted his hand accordingly. Longer and lighter than the Roman pilum, he was confident he would do well. After all, the pilum, more so than the gladius, was the premier offensive weapon of the Roman Army and decided more battles in favor of Rome than either sword or arrow combined. The distance to the target, an animal hide stuffed with straw the size of a man's torso, was farther than it would have been for a Roman training field, but the pilum was a much heavier weapon to throw.

In recognition of his performance so far, Arrius was given the honor of the first throw. He backed up several paces from the line scratched in the dirt and assumed a slight crouch leaning back as he did with his left foot forward in preparation for a conventional two-step launch. After compensating for not having the weight of a shield on his left arm, he cocked his arm, tightened his stomach muscles, and launched the spear. He watched the spear brush the left side of the target and come down solidly to earth a spear-length behind the target. He was well satisfied with the throw. When he turned around to allow the first Venicones contestant to take his turn, he noted the crowd of spectators was strangely subdued. Until now, there had been no discrimination or hesitation in expressing praise over a contestant's performance.

Arrius watched the young tribesman glance briefly at the target and without any preliminaries almost casually throw the spear. He then turned and walked confidently away while it was still in the air. To his amazement, Arrius saw the spear pierce the target. Out of the next five competitors, only one individual failed to make a direct hit when he had only pierced the right edge of the target. Soon the target was moved farther back, and Cuileán remained the only competitor representing the southern tribes until he too was eliminated after the target was moved still farther. Only one contestant managed to strike the target at that range although all the other spears fell closer than his at the outset of the competition. Arrius was positive he had seen nothing to compare with the accuracy and the distance the Venicones were able to hurl the spears. He knew now the silence that greeted his attempt reflected a stunned response to his unimpressive performance.

By the time the contestants stripped down to leather breeches and paired off for the initial wrestling bout, Arrius was having second thoughts about participating; unfortunately, he saw no graceful way to avoid the contest without inviting ridicule. The rules did not take long to explain as there were essentially none unless the enjoinment against severe injury or death counted. Arrius surmised it was no accident he was paired with Indrecht's son whom he kicked unconscious the day before; his jaw was still swollen and bruised. The grim, determined face of his opponent was indication enough this was not going to be just another match, and the way in which the onlookers closed in on them confirmed it. Their size was nearly equal but he had the advantage of weight while the other man was younger and in his prime.

In his young legionary days as a ranker, he had achieved a modest reputation for his skill in the Greek-style form of wrestling, but subsequent years and age gave him little reason to be confident. Slowly circling his opponent, Arrius was still trying to recall some of his previous and more successful holds and maneuvers when the younger man made the first move with lighting speed. He found himself hard pressed to remain upright after being grappled around the waist in a bone-crushing grip that also pinned one of his arms just above the elbow. Unless he broke the hold, he would be forced to bend backward until he fell. With his one free hand, he grabbed the other man's throat and began pushing until it was his opponent who now risked losing his balance. The hold broken, both men stepped back breathing hard, regarding each other warily. Several more times they locked together with neither man gaining an advantage. Finally, the younger man made the mistake of launching himself in a running attack designed to knock him off balance. Arrius quickly sidestepped and caught the man in the throat with his forearm as he went by. The tribesman's momentum and the force of the blow was enough to knock him to the ground where he remained and desperately trying to breathe.

Declared the winner, Arrius looked around and found there were three other competitors declared winners of their bouts. He became concerned when all three began walking toward him. To his relief, Indrecht stepped forward and motioned for only one of the three to pair off with him. Invigorated and confident his skills were returning, he was no longer aware of sore muscles as he crouched and faced his next opponent. A few minutes later, the last thing he remembered was watching the gray sky above rapidly fading to black.

Arrius opened his eyes and saw the silhouette of someone kneeling over him. As his vision began to clear, he realized it was Ilya peering down at him, the concern plain to see on her face.

"Marcus, are you all right?"

His mouth felt dry and his head throbbed painfully. He managed a feeble "Yes" that sounded more like a croak. The truth was he was certain he had not felt so bad since Longinus pushed him off the escarpment.

Ilya's voice changed quickly from concern to angry exasperation as he heard her say next, "What were you thinking? You're far too old to be doing such foolish things and trying to prove you're as strong as you used to be."

He closed his eyes and made no response. Even if he had the strength to do so, which he did not, it was unlikely he could think of anything to say that would convince Ilya, or himself for that matter. While she daubed a cool cloth on his head, she continued to berate him, and he had no choice but to endure it vaguely thinking he might even deserve it. He was grateful when she finally stopped lecturing him, apparently satisfied her point was well and truly made.

He then made the mistake of saying, "Since I don't remember the end of the match, I gather I did not win."

"You didn't," was the sharp response.

"I won the first one – I think."

"You were lucky," Ilya retorted, an edge to her voice.

"I can tell you're not happy with me."

"I didn't realize it showed."

Becoming more irritated with her cryptic, unsympathetic responses, he closed his eyes in defense, taking refuge in silence and hoped when he opened them again, she would be gone. He finally heard her leave and cautiously opened his eyes to verify she was gone. He saw Cuileán's face peering down at him.

"I think all wives sound much alike. It is even worse when you have more than one."

"Perhaps that was the reason I delayed taking one."

"The truth is when you were unconscious, she cried. She thought you were going to die."

"I think she had reason enough to believe it," Arrius responded with a wry smile. "What happened?"

"You fought Gaithan. I'm told he is their best wrestler and has never been defeated. You were praised for having lasted as long as you did."

"Did we manage to impress the Venicones with our efforts?"

"I think we held our own, thanks to you."

"What about Indrecht? Will he agree to join the alliance?"

Cuileán frowned. "Indrecht says the Venicones will not fight the Romans until they come north. He does not believe the Romans will come here. If they do, he will fight them with us."

Arrius was disappointed for Ilya and Joric. Indrecht's position virtually assured there would be no significant military alliance in place to resist the Roman advance. He realized now he had been extremely naive in thinking the prospect of a Roman invasion would be incentive enough to set aside tribal differences in favor of the larger effort to survive the legions.

A few days later, their visit with the Epedi Tribe located west of the Venicones proved no more successful. Although both tribes did not want the Romans on their doorstep, it was also clear they were not eager to share their lands on a permanent basis with anyone. The two tribal leaders reluctantly granted permission for a temporary migration of the southern tribes into their land but left unanswered the question of what would happen should the southern tribes have to take up permanent residence. Arrius would have liked to have gone farther north to meet with the Caledoni and Vacomagi in hopes they would be more accommodating, but Indrecht advised against it, citing the hostile welcome they were certain to receive.

Despite the overall disappointment of a lukewarm reception in the north, there was still enough progress achieved by the visits to maintain a degree of optimism that at least a tentative understanding with the northern tribes had been accomplished. Ilya put things in perspective by commenting they could now focus attention on a Roman attack without fearing one from the north as well. The ten days spent in the north also provided him with an excellent opportunity to become familiar with the region. The contrast between the lowland region and the more mountainous terrain in the north was dramatic. Some of the lakes he saw were larger than any he had seen so far in Britannia. The mountain sides were rocky and steep and blankets of snow remained where the early spring sun failed to reach the shadowed canyons. Vegetation on the upper rocky slopes consisted mainly of bracken and waist-high bushes that in some areas were so thick it made traveling on foot almost impossible. The dense forests in the valleys and ravines made passage by foot or horse difficult, and Arrius led Ferox more often than he rode. It was apparent the highland country was more suitable for infantry, offering as it did few places where cavalry would be capable of maneuvering effectively.

During the return trip south, Neacal apparently decided not to antagonize Arrius. By tacit agreement, the two men avoided each other except when it was impossible to do so. He didn't trust Neacal and did not doubt the Novantean was merely biding his time waiting for the day and opportunity to settle matters between them.

The closer they got to the Selgovan capital, the more eager Ilya was to see Eugenius. It was she who now urged a faster pace, chafing at each delay. The pace quickened after they reached Cuileán's village and learned the Roman advance had begun, and Joric had been badly wounded.

Chapter 12

Arrius and Ilya remained at Cuileán's village only long enough to rest the horses before pressing on to the Selgovan capital. Accompanied by Cuileán, they rode all night and reached the gates of the settlement at sunrise. Ilya was beside herself with worry over Joric's condition. Arrius kept his own concerns to himself for the extent the invasion may have already progressed. It was possible the Selgovan capital, or what was left of it, was now a Roman settlement. He had participated in enough such campaigns to know there would be no mercy shown for infants such as Eugenius; older children would be spared for they were marketable as slaves.

While there were no smoking ruins, there was also none of the usual noisy clamor of villagers passing back and forth as they went about their usual daily routine. Instead, the settlement was ominously quiet except for low chanting coming from the council hall at the top of the hill. The few villagers to be seen consisted of women and a few old men standing in small knots talking quietly. As soon as they saw Ilya pass by, they fell silent and stared solemnly as the small band of horsemen ascended the hill toward the council hall. Arrius glanced at Ilya and saw her mouth compressed in a thin line from apprehension and the fatigue of the long ride. His initial relief the settlement was not ravaged was replaced by the feeling they had arrived too late.

The chanting abruptly stopped as they entered the upper enclosure. By the time Ilya and Arrius dismounted, the door of the council hall opened, and a grim-faced Tearlach emerged followed by the senior council members and clan leaders. Their bleak faces confirmed the worst before Tearlach said to Ilya, "Your son now rides with Cernnunos."

"When?" Ilya asked quietly, her face composed.

"As the sun left the sky yesterday."

"How did it happen?"

"It was a Roman spear. He was struck in the chest while leading an attack on the Romans two days ago. There was nothing we could do to save him; the wound was too severe. He named you to succeed him."

"Where is he?"

"Inside," Tearlach replied and stepped aside as Ilya walked silently past him.

Arrius started to follow but was restrained by Cuileán. "Later you will be permitted to enter when the doors of the hall are opened to the villagers." Reluctantly, he remained where he was and watched Ilya disappear inside the cavernous hall.

Arrius approached Tearlach and asked, "How close are the Romans?"

"They remain where they are, two days ride from here."

"What are the Novanti and the Votadini doing?"

"They like us are watching to see what the Romans will do. I believe the Votadini will make overtures of peace. They do not believe the Romans will do them harm because of their peaceful relations with Rome."

"It might save them, but if I were them, I would prepare for the worst."

"Why do you think the Romans are moving so slow?" Tearlach asked with a puzzled expression.

"I don't know. The original plan called for a fast march by the auxilia with the legions coming behind to eliminate any resistance the auxilia was unable to overcome. It's possible the legions were delayed after the initial assault, and it may be the Briganti are responsible for it. In any event, I would not count on the delay lasting for long. What has been done to ready the villages and those who wish to evacuate north?"

Tearlach shifted uncomfortably. "The clans are reluctant to go. I think many do not believe the Romans intend to come any farther, and the fact their advance has not progressed much beyond Fanum Cocidii has merely contributed to their unwillingness to abandon their homes. Others believe it may be time to do as the Votadini have done and seek an understanding with Rome in hopes they will be left alone."

"To assume that would be a mistake along with any idea of Roman forgiveness for past Selgovan behavior. The invasion provides an opportunity to reinforce the might of Rome. Rome never completely trusts a local population. It cannot afford to. The empire is vast and the legions by comparison are small in number. A doubtful allegiance, which Rome would consider applies to the Selgovi, is considered a

133

rebellion waiting to start; consequently, it is in Rome's interest to make certain there is no capability to rebel. The lucky survivors will be conscripted for duty as legionaries in Gaul, Dacia, or some other distant place and far enough away they will not be able to cause trouble. The not-so-fortunate will be sold as slaves. Those remaining in Britannia will be too few to do anything but submit."

Tearlach did not reply. Arrius changed the subject believing he had said enough on the matter.

"How many others were killed with Joric?"

Tearlach did not reply immediately. Finally, he looked away and replied, "Joric was the only one."

"How can that be?"

"We engaged the Roman advance two days ago. Joric refused to remain behind some of the more experienced warriors and stayed several paces in front of the rest. He became the main target for most of the spears the Romans threw."

"Why didn't you stop him? He was inexperienced, and you should have kept him from—"

Face flushed, Tearlach bristled. "His place was where he thought it should be. A leader who is unwilling to fight shoulder to shoulder with his men is no leader at all but a coward who depends on others to take the risks."

Arrius knew Tearlach was right. He realized he was simply railing against an outcome the gods had determined more than either the legionary who had thrown the spear or Tearlach's failure to restrain the young leader. He relented and softened his criticism.

"There's much right in what you say. At times there is naught else to be done but wade into the fight. The trick is in knowing when, and Joric did not have time to learn it. You must know Joric was like a son to me. I wanted to adopt him as such; Ilya would not allow it."

Tearlach relaxed, and the anger disappeared from his face. Neither man spoke for a time allowing the heat of the moment to pass. Tearlach was the first to break the silence.

"What success did you and Ilya have with the northern tribes?"

Arrius summarized the outcome of their visits north and ended by saying, "In time, and if it comes to it, they will join the Selgovi. Regrettably, it will not be soon and not before the Selgovi and Novanti have either been subjugated or pushed from their lands."

"I hoped for more."

"Hope is like a prayer to the gods. Sometimes the gods listen, sometimes they do not. It would be best to depend more on what the Selgovi can do than what the gods might grant." Then changing the subject, he asked, "What of Bothan? Is he remaining steadfast, or will he try to make peace with the Romans?"

"Bothan will fight. So far, he has done much as we have, waiting to see what the Romans will do next. He hates the Romans and will never forgive them for killing most of his family including two of his sons."

"Can the Votadini be persuaded to join the Selgovi and Novanti?"

"Darach insists his tribe is in no danger and has refused to entertain an alliance. He believes he has nothing to fear from the Romans unless he joins us in resisting them, and he may be right."

Arrius shook his head. "Perhaps, but if Darach allows the Romans to progress unimpeded, or if he resists and is quickly defeated, the Selgovi and eventually the Novanti will be further threatened. The Romans will then be in position to flank the Selgovi from the east while at the same time pressing from the south. The Selgovi and then the Novanti will have no chance and no other choice but to withdraw north."

"You make it sound hopeless, Roman. Your words are words of defeat. What would you have us do, surrender or withdraw before the fight has even begun?"

"I speak of what I know will happen if the Votadini do nothing or prove to be no obstacle at all. I do not believe in fighting useless battles where there is no chance of winning."

"I can see you have little regard for our ability to fight."

Arrius suppressed his anger and tried to sound reasonable. "If the Votadini will not fight, you must withdraw before you are cut off from the north. How you withdraw is the question not if, for eventually you must."

"The Selgovi will not meekly step aside and invite the Romans to occupy us."

Further discussion ended when Ilya, dry-eyed, emerged from the council hall. Arrius was struck by her calm, almost serene expression. If the senior tribesmen expected a tearful, emotional collapse, her composure dispelled the notion. When she spoke, her voice was strong and steady.

"We will take time to bury my son in a manner befitting a High Chieftain of the Selgovi. Then we must prepare for the difficult days ahead. The Romans are marching, and the northern tribes have made no promises to help us. We will resist the Roman invasion as best we can even as our women and children must make ready to move farther north to safer lands. The clans must either confirm my leadership or select another among you to ascend the dais. Either way we cannot afford to delay or to leave the tribe without a leader in this dangerous time. If the clan chiefs support me becoming queen, then know I will do all I can to justify their confidence in the spirit and tradition of my son, Beldorach, and Bathar whose daughter I am. I ask the clan chiefs to decide now inside the council hall and according to tradition and in the presence of Joric to decide who will be seated in the sacred chair." Ilya stepped away from the doorway as the clan chiefs and tribal elders filed back inside the hall. A moment later, the door banged shut leaving Ilya and Arrius alone outside.

"I am sorry, Ilya. Joric was a fine and brave young man. It is possible if I had been here at his side, this would not have happened."

"Perhaps, but I see no point in dwelling on things the gods decide."

He acknowledged the truth of what she said with a silent nod. "Tearlach indicated you were the successor. Do you expect they will choose you?"

"I think it's possible. It's a logical choice for I have a strong lineal claim. Occasionally, and particularly now when there is the prospect of war, that is not enough. The wise choice might be to select one of the clan chiefs who can better lead the warriors in battle. If I were a clan chief, I would place much importance on such a thing."

He was impressed with her objective insight. "Will you accept if leadership is offered?"

"Yes," she replied without hesitation.

"What if you're not chosen?"

"I must leave here since my presence would be considered a threat to whoever is chosen. You and I will take Eugenius and go wherever you wish."

"Then I hope they choose another, for I believe there are terrible times ahead for the Selgovi, and I would wish you and the infant in a safer place. What happens next?"

"If I am invited back inside, it will be as queen of the Selgovi; if I am not asked, we must leave."

Arrius was again impressed with her poise. Except for Tearlach and Cuileán, he did not know the other clan chiefs well enough to judge their abilities. In spite of his own desire that she not be chosen, he was convinced the Selgovi would be making a mistake if they did not recognize her claim.

The matter was resolved when the door opened, and Tearlach beckoned her to enter. Ilya paused and looked at Arrius as if waiting for him to tell her not to go. He nodded silently in encouragement and watched as she entered the hall.

He looked at the closed door for several minutes, thinking what it meant, processing the effect on his life he never anticipated not so long ago. Thoughts, memories of expectations, aspirations from the time he first took the sacramentum as a legionary to the Empire of Rome. All the campaigns, the hardships in the belief there was somehow a nobility that justified sacrificing private thought and personal gain to a larger purpose. Not for the first time in recent months he had cause to recall what the previous primus pilus of the Sixth Legion so many years ago told him when he was about to be promoted to centurion. He didn't recall the exact words, but it was about rejecting symbols, implying there were more important things to believe in than the Roman eagle atop a legionary standard he once carried proudly and without question.

He walked to the stone wall dominating the village below and noted the stark contrast to the grandeur of the Roman Empire he was familiar with and the comparative primitive conditions of the Selgovan settlement. He heard a plaintive cry in the direction of Beldorach's former dwelling and knew Ulla was being attentive to his son. Ilya's decision in assuming responsibility of the Selgovae Tribe was both understandable and unpredictable, but then the gods always were and always would be capricious, leaving mere mortals to wonder why.

During the rest of the day, Ilya was busy presiding over the ceremonies of Joric's funeral and participating in the formalities required in assuming tribal leadership. Tearlach told Arrius the ceremonies for Joric's funeral rites and Ilya's investiture were considerably reduced as she stipulated. He was permitted to witness only the rites and ceremonies held outside the council hall. Throughout the day, he glimpsed Ilya only from a distance. It wasn't until late that night when they found themselves alone that she allowed herself to surrender briefly to the loss of her son. Arrius said nothing and continued to hold her until no more tears were left.

Finally, after she calmed, she said, "Marcus, it might be best if you took our son away."

"The time for leaving is past. I chose to come here to be with you, and today your choice has given me even more reason to remain. Besides, what do you think your people would say and do if I were to take Eugenius away when today he became the future leader of the Selgovi?"

Her silence signified practical acceptance of his argument.

"Marcus, I need your help."

"You will have it in any way you ask."

"It would have been better for all had Joric lived. I cannot lead the warriors in battle."

"It is better you cannot. Joric did, and he died for it. The Selgovi is best served now by a leader who thinks and acts beyond the battlefield. Unfortunately, the gods did not give Joric enough years to understand that."

"Will you be my war chief, Marcus?"

"No, and if you think on it, you will know the answer why I cannot."

"You think the clan leaders would resent the choice?"

"Yes. This is the time when more than ever you need the loyalty of the clans. Do not risk undermining that loyalty by appointing a Roman to lead them. One day when I have earned their trust and they no longer see me as I once was, it may be different."

"That day may come sooner than you think."

"The gods will decide that."

"No, Marcus, I will decide," she replied quietly but firmly.

Arrius observed the Roman campfires lazily rising through the trees across a wide front. He shook his head in wonder. It was a sight that made no sense at all. He estimated the wall was no more than fifteen miles farther to the south, and if the visibility were better, he was certain he would be able to see a portion of it from their concealed position on a tree-covered hill.

"They have remained like this for three days?" He asked Tearlach, the new war chief of the Selgovi.

"Yes. I thought they would have come farther."

"It can only be because the legions have yet to come forward. What you see in front of you represents only the auxilia."

"How many men are in the auxilia?"

Arrius thought for a moment and replied, "Assuming some have been left behind at each of the forts to protect the gates, I estimate a force of eight to nine thousand men. The legions are not at full strength; therefore, I believe they collectively represent another twelve thousand legionaries. What is the combined strength of the Novanti and Selgovi?"

"Less than half that number," Tearlach said with a resigned expression.

"Well, numbers don't always tell the end of the tale," rationalizing that at least in his experience it had occasionally been true.

"We know the hills and forests, and a few men can stop many," Tearlach replied with hopeful bravado.

"Aye, it is an important advantage." He paused before continuing, choosing his words carefully. "How have you and Bothan deployed your warriors, and how do you intend to fight when they," indicating the Roman encampment ahead, "begin to march?"

"They are in groups of one hundred warriors spaced a mile apart with smaller units in between. If a group is attacked, then runners will be sent to adjacent groups to alert the others. In that way, we can reinforce wherever the Romans are concentrating their attack."

Arrius acknowledged Tearlach's explanation with a lifted eyebrow as he silently considered what to say without sounding harshly critical. Rather than tell Tearlach the strategy was doomed to failure, he decided a more indirect approach might be more effective.

Almost as if thinking aloud, Arrius began to speak. "When the attack begins, we can expect the auxilia to march forward in a series of columns, probably three cohorts abreast, with each cohort consisting of about four to five hundred men. The cohorts will be preceded by cavalry. The cohorts on the outside will be screened by additional cavalry as they advance in sight of the center cohort. Distances will be adjusted as the terrain allows. The main column will follow behind the lead cohorts, which in turn will be followed by the units whose responsibility it is to provide provisions and fodder. The legions will follow the auxilia in similar formations up to two miles behind but centered in order to deploy forward or laterally anywhere across the front when the auxilia has been decisively engaged. In this way, the Romans can advance across a wide front without the necessity of having to position legionaries along the entire line of advance."

"I think you may be suggesting there is a better way to meet the Roman invasion than the way I described."

"Possibly not better, but different. Consider what you said earlier. The Novanti and Selgovi know the terrain better than the Romans. Since we are outnumbered, we cannot fight them on their terms and in the way that will mean certain defeat for the tribes."

"Then what do you propose?"

Arrius replied slowly and deliberately, occasionally hesitating and sketching in the dirt to better describe what he meant when his proficiency in the language failed him.

"Rather than allow the Romans to attack you while trying to defend that which you cannot, attack them and attack them often. If you attack them with one hundred warriors, the Romans will counterattack with five hundred. By the time they deploy in attack formation, it is time to disengage and disappear in the forest or ride over the next hill. You cannot stop them, but you can wear them down, for each time they maneuver into an assault formation, it requires time and effort to do so. Time is what you need, and the effort to constantly maneuver will tire and discourage them. You must attack them in the rear and force the legions to deploy unnecessarily in the belief they face greater numbers than they do. Destroy their supply wagons and provisions for no army can fight for long on empty stomachs. At no time must you join in a close-in, prolonged battle where the Romans have the greatest advantage. When the Romans attempt to use spear and gladius, you must use stealth, surprise and the arrow. When the

Romans want to fight in an open field, use the forest, the swamps and the ambush to force them to fight and go where they are at a disadvantage."

After he finished speaking, Tearlach remained silent in reflection. When he finally spoke, he regarded Arrius with renewed respect.

"I think you have described a better way to fight. We will do as you advise, and I will try to convince Bothan to do the same."

Chapter 13

"I'll piss on your graves if you fail me again!" Tiberius Querinius screamed at the legion's assembled centurions who stood grim-faced below the tribunal on which the livid tribune stood. The three tribunes remaining in the legion following Arvinnius's conscription of the other two stood off to one side and tried to remain inconspicuous. This was the second tongue-lashing they had been subjected to, the first having been delivered to them in private.

"I do not have to remind you it has been two weeks since we destroyed the Briganti capital, and we have yet to find, much less kill, a significant number of their warriors. So far, they've managed to kill almost a hundred legionaries, legionaries that will not be replaced before we march north. Needless to say, General Arvinnius is not pleased over the poor results, and if he is not pleased then I surely am not. I fail to see why barbaric tribesmen have so far managed to out-maneuver, out-fight and escape the talons of the Sixth Legion. Can it be the *Victrix* eagle is nothing more than a sparrow hawk?" he said scathingly. Querinius ignored the many scowls on the faces of the centurions at the disparaging reference to the legion's symbol which came dangerously close to sacrilege.

"Have a care, Tribune," the voice of Quintas Livius boomed in the colonnaded inner hall of the legion's basilica. "It is ill-advised to taunt Jupiter by insulting the eagle of Rome."

There was shocked silence at the audacity of the legion's primus pilus to speak in such manner even though there was not a man there who had not thought the same.

"Ah, Centurion Quintas Livius," Querinius responded in a deceptively mild voice, regarding the legion's senior centurion with cold eyes. "I think it likely Jupiter is more concerned with how poorly the legion has performed than over any words I've spoken. But since you've seen fit to interrupt, perhaps you would like to explain to me why you think the legion has been so spectacularly unsuccessful." As soon as he made the statement, Querinius regretted it. Too late, he realized he had tacitly invited public criticism of his own orders and tactical dispositions to date. The centurion's response confirmed his worst fear. Even more objectionable was the centurion's typical outspoken manner and refusal to be intimidated that reminded him too much of Marcus Arrius.

"Tribune Querinius, we tire ourselves with constant marching to places where the Briganti are not. They are shadows in the trees, and their arrows pick off our legionaries one by one. They know our strengths and avoid fighting battles they know they cannot win. It would be better to locate their camps and strongholds with smaller and mounted patrols and then march to destroy them from several dispersed and fortified positions away from Eboracum."

Querinius heard a murmur of agreement among the other centurions and was chagrinned he had allowed himself to be upstaged. He called the officers together to challenge them into trying harder to improve the legion's success which had steadily declined since the initial attack on the Briganti capitol. He misjudged the mood of the officers and now placed himself in an awkward predicament. He couldn't ignore the merit of Livius's concept without risking the possibility of looking even more a fool. Perhaps the centurion's plan or some variation thereof might prove exactly what was needed to break the tactical stalemate, and if it failed, he would place the blame on having relied too much on the recommendations of his more battle-experienced centurions. Querinius placed his hand on his hips in what he hoped was a convincing posture of martial confidence and forced an encouraging smile.

"Salve, Centurion Quintas Livius! Now that's the kind of thinking I want to encourage in the *Victrix*. The idea has merit, and we will see how best to implement it." Querinius was too pleased with the smoothness of his recovery to note the disgusted expression on the face of Livius and the other centurions.

From the concealment of a small hill nearby, Decrius watched the small stockaded fort nearing completion and noted the similarity to the two other cohort-sized forts under construction farther to the west. He estimated when finished it would be large enough for five hundred legionaries. The purpose of the forts was obvious, and he wondered why the legion commander took so long before ordering them built.

So far, the Briganti's luck was holding following the destruction of the capitol. Ironically, the disorganization of the tribe and subsequent leadership void following the initial Roman attack worked to the tribe's advantage. By avoiding large pitched battles and relying instead on ambush and small engagements, Briganti casualties were light in comparison to the Romans. He curbed his own urge to fight the Romans more aggressively in practical recognition the tribesmen were not yet organized and trained enough to take on the enemy in open battle. He was tireless in his efforts over the past weeks to better prepare the tribesmen to engage the Romans more effectively. He did not make the mistake of trying to instill Roman tactics and practices which time would not allow them to master since with each passing day, the legion from Deva drew closer.

Silently, Decrius motioned for the others to follow as he backed down the reverse slope of the hill and headed for the horses concealed in a stand of trees. The genesis of an idea was starting to form in his head, and he ignored the comments and questions of the four other men as they headed back to the main Briganti camp located a few miles north of Isurium. By the time they reached the camp an hour later, Decrius was ready to convene a war council. It was time to raise the stakes and increase the tempo of the war.

"Will we be successful?" Hudryn asked as he gave Decrius a worried look across the small campfire. The Council had been over for hours during which Decrius outlined his plan for a simultaneous attack on each of the three Roman forts under construction. The attack was scheduled to take place in three days.

It was the second time Hudryn asked the question since the clan leaders had gone back to their own camps to prepare their warriors. Decrius resisted the urge for a caustic reply, irritated at Hudryn's constant need for reassurance. Decrius was reluctant to give voice to some deep reservations of his own. He did what he could to prepare the Briganti in the time he had. Was it enough? Well, they would find out soon enough. For now, let Hudryn and the others keep thinking the Briganti would do well enough. There was no point in going into battle thinking otherwise even if the odds did not favor them. He silently enjoined the gods to intervene on their behalf.

"Yes, I believe we have a chance to take the forts, and even if we fail, it will tell the Romans we intend to fight."

For a moment, Hudryn appeared ready to accept the answer as Decrius hoped, if only so that he would go away and leave him alone.

"You do not sound overly optimistic."

Decrius shrugged and considered how best to respond. "Only the gods can say."

"Perhaps we are not yet ready for a major attack. It might be better to keep on the way we have."

Decrius regarded Hudryn with contempt. "Then the Briganti might as well crawl on their bellies to the Romans and seek terms."

"You misunderstand me, Decrius. While you've been living the life of a Roman all these years, we've bided our time for this day. I simply want to ensure we have a reasonable chance to succeed. I confess I have doubts, not of our resolve, but our capability. We've been thrust into a war sooner than we expected to be, and I am not yet convinced we are ready."

Decrius looked at Hudryn and relented knowing Hudryn spoke the truth and was merely echoing his own inner thoughts. When he answered, his voice was more moderate.

"It's true our chances would be far better if we had the luxury of time to better prepare. Unfortunately, in my opinion, that is not the case. In a matter of days, or at best a few weeks, the Romans will be here in far greater strength. Then we will have little choice in the matter of when and where to fight – the Romans will be the ones to decide. The tribe wants revenge for what happened to Isurium. Our young warriors grow impatient and expect to take their revenge."

"I think you do not believe the Briganti can prevail against the Romans," Hudryn said, more a statement than a question.

Decrius recalled what happened several years before in Judaea when the relentless Roman war machine made Judaea into a virtual wasteland. He couldn't escape the feeling the same thing was going to happen here.

"No, I do not think the Briganti will prevail even if we take the forts or win many battles after that. In time, the Briganti will be obliged to seek peace with Rome and that is why when we first met, I suggested seeking terms with them."

"Possibly that is what we should do so now?"

"The opportunity for that has come and gone. Since then we've killed a lot of Romans. They will not be ready to listen until they believe they have truly defeated us."

"If you do not think we can defeat the Romans, why attack the forts at all if it will change nothing?" Hudryn asked, genuinely perplexed.

Decrius shrugged. "The warriors want to fight and kill Romans, and because I want the same thing."

Fortunately, Arvinnius had given nominal approval for the construction of the forts and thought the concept of positioning the cohorts forward was worth the attempt to force the elusive Briganti to battle. Otherwise, when the survivors of the three cohorts returned to Eboracum greatly reduced in number, Querinius wouldn't have given a sesterce for his chance of remaining in command of the Sixth. Had the Briganti attack been more coordinated and aggressive, the outposts would have been annihilated. Instead, the centurions managed to hold the forts but only at considerable cost. Roman casualties were sufficient that it was necessary to abandon the forts once the Briganti withdrew. Although Briganti casualties greatly exceeded Roman losses, it did not soften Arvinnius's icy stare.

"In spite of your stirring speech to the returning cohorts, Querinius, the Sixth has suffered grievously. It is providential the Twentieth Legion arrives in a few days to continue the efforts against the Briganti. I cannot delay the advance north any longer; therefore, you will begin moving the Sixth north in two days time while readying Eboracum for occupation by the *Valeria Victrix*."

The general's order was a positive indication he was still in command of the legion. He intended to offer additional sacrifices to the gods for having avoided being at one of the forts when they were attacked. When the reports came in of how close the Briganti came to taking them, he had nervous flashbacks of what happened to the *Deiotariana* in the Sorek Valley. He had not slept well the last two nights. He couldn't banish the horrible images of the wholesale carnage the Jews inflicted. Even more, he couldn't suppress the memory of Arrius confronting him after the battle was joined and accusing him of cowardice for remaining with the wounded. No matter how hard he tried to forget or to justify his behavior, he knew

Arrius had been right. He was afraid. His introspection was interrupted when Arvinnius continued sharply.

"It's unfortunate the Sixth must march with only dubious success in the campaign against the Briganti. I expect you to ensure legion morale recovers on the way north. When the Sixth marches, it must be seen by the Briganti and the northern tribes it is worthy of the name *Victrix*. Do not disappoint me, Querinius, and do not make me regret I refused the governor's offer to find a replacement for me as legion commander. I would hate to think Urbicus would be given reason to doubt my judgment," he added meaningfully.

"General Arvinnius, you will have no cause to regret my appointment."

"See that I don't," was the stern reply.

Querinius swallowed audibly and attempted to make his exit before the general said anything else to undermine his confidence. "If you will excuse me, general, I have much to do to ready the legion."

"You'll leave when I say you can go. Now, attend me closely. I have confirmation one of the Briganti leaders was a former centurion at Banna under Marcus Arrius. A large brute with tattoos on his face by the name of Decrius – I seem to recall him when I visited Banna. Speaking of Arrius, there is no longer any doubt he's assisting the northern tribes in some capacity." General Arvinnius gave the tribune a hard look, "Querinius, Arrius is to be taken alive no matter the cost. I want to be present when the treasonous bastard is crucified. I hold you personally responsible that I have the pleasure to see his execution. Now you may go."

Querinius saluted and thought if General Arvinnius wanted to watch Arrius nailed to a cross, he more than anything intended to wield the hammer. Just as quickly he considered a quick death after capture would be in his best interests rather than risk the possibility Arrius would speak of events in Judaea.

Without expression, Decrius listened to the grim reports of the attacks on the other two Roman forts. The results were even worse than what happened during the attack he led on the third fort. Hudryn and the rest of the council who survived the bloody battles were downcast and avoided looking in his direction. No one laid blame for the failure on him, but he knew it was his fault, and worse, he had privately expected the attacks might not succeed but clearly not to the extent they failed. Perhaps if they confined the attack to one fort, it might have been different. Objectively, he realized he used the tribe more for exacting his own personal revenge than any real regard for the final outcome. He suspected they were waiting for him to speak, something to stir their flagging morale. He didn't have the words or the inclination to do so. At this point, the Briganti would probably be better off without him and to follow someone who believed more that the Briganti could eventually defeat the Romans.

"Decrius, what should we do?"

Decrius looked up and saw Hudryn standing a few feet away. Lost in his own thoughts, Decrius had not heard the other man approach. He saw the confusion and doubt on Hudryn's face, and the same reflected on the other council members. He knew they were waiting for him to give them direction. He almost felt resentment building within himself for their dependency on him. Ignoring the throbbing sword cut on his right arm and the aching muscles, he stood up and considered what he should tell them.

"Today the Briganti fought well and bravely, but the Romans fought better. We should learn from our failure in order not to repeat it. I am to blame for ordering an attack too ambitious to be successfully carried out. There is much to do to prepare for the next battle." His short speech sounded hollow and unconvincing to him, and he knew by the disappointed expressions it did not inspire them.

"The next battle!" Elatha exclaimed. "Another battle such as the one today, and there will be nothing left of the Briganti except old men, women and children. We proved we cannot fight the Romans on their terms and expect to defeat them. We should have kept on fighting them as we have been doing."

"I agree with Elatha," added another council member whose name Decrius didn't remember. "We must choose more carefully the manner and the location for battle and look for circumstances that minimize their capabilities and our weaknesses. For the time being, the Briganti must survive and allow our wounded to recover. The clans should disperse into the hills and forests and avoid any contact with the Romans. Let them think we're afraid. When our warriors are ready and the Romans believe the rebellion has been abandoned, that's when we will strike again. But instead of large battles, we will destroy their signal towers, raid supply depots and ambush their patrols."

Decrius heard the words and couldn't disagree with the logic. Under the present circumstances, the summary was not only a prudent course of action, it was the only practical thing to do. Before the death of his wife and son, he might have counseled the same. He realized since their deaths his focus was mainly on killing Romans without taking a longer view of the tribe's future. He saw Hudryn watching him silently, his expression guarded.

Behellagh was the next to register his disapproval. "If we were victorious today, I do not think we can afford any more victories. I also agree with Elatha."

Decrius decided it was time for him to speak. "What you suggest makes sense for now," he conceded, "but it will not overcome the Romans. It is a strategy of defeat not victory." There were mutters of agreement. "You say we must survive, and I say you must achieve more than that for it is all you have been doing since the Romans came here."

"Perhaps what you say is true," Hudryn said thoughtfully, "but to continue as we did today will doom the Briganti to extinction. Elatha and Behellagh have spoken for me as well. We respect what you have done for us, but we must proceed more slowly than you would have us go."

The short speech was met with widespread agreement. Decrius thought under different circumstances, he would have said much the same. Instead of resentment, he felt only relief. He was too overwhelmed with the loss of Iseult and Rialus to lead them properly.

"I cannot argue against what any of you have said, for I think much of what has been spoken is true. I am not yet one of you, but nor am I Roman. I have spoken to you truthfully as someone who has fought alongside the Romans and who knows firsthand what they are capable of. For me to have merely told you what you wanted to hear would have been foolish and dishonest. I think it would be better to select a new war leader, one who is more willing to follow a strategy such as Elatha has proposed."

The silence that followed was sufficient for Decrius to know the council members were in uniform agreement. There was nothing left to say and no reason to remain any longer. He turned and walked to the picket line where his saddled horse was tethered. He heard footsteps behind him and then Hudryn's voice, "Decrius, where are you going?"

"North to the Selgovi and fight Romans."

"But why? We need you here."

"We both know it's better for all if I leave now. My presence here may bring more harm to the tribe than my departure. You and the others must do what you think is right, and so must I."

"Then may the gods be with you, Decrius."

"And with the Briganti as well," he replied and vaulted into the saddle. He did not believe once he was able to transit the wall it would be difficult to find Arrius.

Chapter 14

Standing on the village rampart near the east gate, Arrius squinted in the bright morning sun as he watched the returning patrol and thought even at this distance there was something familiar about the large man riding with it. No man in the Selgovae Tribe was that large. If it was Decrius, he wondered why he was coming here instead of remaining in the south with his tribe now in revolt or with the Tungrian Cohort at Banna. Long before the patrol reached the gates, there was no longer any doubt it was Decrius.

Arrius descended the rampart steps and was waiting by the gate when the patrol entered the settlement. A smile wreathing his face, Arrius called out a greeting.

"Salve, Decrius, it's good to see you again. I bid you welcome even as I wonder why you've come."

It was a stone-faced Decrius who regarded Arrius silently, acknowledging the warm greeting with the barest hint of a nod and without any change in expression.

The smile dying on his face, eyes narrowed in speculation, Arrius waited while the Brigantian dismounted. Already it was apparent from his cold and silent demeanor this was not the Decrius he had known before.

Arrius extended his arm in welcome and saw Decrius hesitate briefly before responding in kind. In awkward silence, they gripped each other's arm.

"I did not expect to see you here."

After a moment of silence, Decrius spoke. "A few weeks ago, the Sixth legion made the choice to come here an easy one. For a time, I helped the Briganti fight the Romans until it became clear they did not wish to pursue the rebellion as much as I did. I had no place to go but here. If the Selgovi allow, I will help them fight the Romans."

"I'm certain they will welcome your offer for they will need all the help they can get in the days that lie ahead." Arrius hesitated before asking, "What of Iseult and Rialus?" already dreading the answer.

"Because of the Sixth Legion, they are with the gods. Ask me no more."

Arrius reached out impulsively and grasped Decrius' shoulder in wordless sympathy. "Come with me. Ilya will be happy to see you even though her joy will be lessened when she hears of Iseult and Rialus.

"Is Joric now High Chieftain?" Decrius asked.

"Joric was killed in battle a short time ago. Ilya now leads the Selgovi." Briefly, Arrius described what happened. In a deliberate effort to change the subject to less painful matters, he said, "I'm anxious to learn what the legions are doing and when we can expect the assault to begin."

As they walked uphill toward the inner fort, Decrius described the progress of the Briganti rebellion.

"Apparently, Arvinnius must have known something about the Briganti plans to rebel and ordered an attack on Isurium led by none other than Tiberius Querinius." Decrius paused briefly before continuing. "You should know Arvinnius and Querinius are aware you didn't go to Rutipiae. Arvinnius has personally offered a price of 10,000 denari for your capture. He wants to make an example of you by having you crucified; he intends to be present when they nail you to a cross."

"I'm flattered to know I am worth so much. Does Arvinnius know or suspect Flavius knew where I went?"

"Querinius came to Banna and talked to the officers and optios. No one admitted to knowing anything except of your intention to go to Rome."

"Good, I don't want Flavius or any of the others to suffer for what I've done. Now tell me about Isurium."

"I'm told Isurium was completely destroyed, and the road to Eboracum was lined with crucified Briganti. The Romans showed no mercy. The tribal chief was killed, and the Briganti will to resist was severely weakened. For a time, the Briganti fought well enough, and the Sixth suffered for it. Unfortunately, the Briganti sustained many casualties as well. In my opinion, I think the rebellion is all but over."

"In that case, Arvinnius will begin the advance."

"Will the Selgovi fight?"

"The Selgovi and Novanti have formed an alliance, but even together there is no chance of winning. I've counseled the tribes to withdraw north to Caledonia if they are to survive. The alternative is to seek peace with Arvinnius as the Votadini intend to do." Arrius quickly summarized the dilemma facing the Selgovi and the reluctance of the Caledonian Tribes to allow migration of the southern tribes.

When he finished, Decrius said with a sour expression, "You talk as if you've been defeated before the Romans begin their invasion."

Annoyed by the implied criticism of his strategy, Arrius curbed his irritation. "Ilya must be more concerned with the survival of the tribe than merely killing Romans." Noting the look on Decrius's face, he said, "Decrius, you've suffered a great loss with the deaths of your wife and son, and you want to avenge their deaths. I realize that; however, if you are to be of value to the Selgovi, you must temper your hatred with reality. There will be many battles in the days to come and ample opportunity for you to shed Roman blood, but I would charge you to look beyond the fighting to what is best for the tribes."

"I understand what you're saying, and it's similar to what the leaders of the Briganti said. Perhaps in time I'll be able to see things your way, but for now I want to fight, and I want to be where that is most likely to happen."

Arrius concluded this was not the time to convince Decrius to embrace a more pragmatic approach to the impending Roman onslaught. The challenge was to find a way to use Decrius that would both satisfy the former centurion and the need of the Selgovi. Already an idea was beginning to take shape to achieve both ends.

Arrius watched the forward skirmishers crest the hill more than a mile away. Soon after, the cohorts came into view accompanied by the faint but ominous sound of drums. He noted objectively in spite of the uneven terrain, the legionaries marching in columns five abreast maintained a precision that added further intimidation to the awe - inspiring display of Roman power. Cavalry *turmae* screened the flanks of the five advancing columns stretching across a wide front. Until recently, he never imagined the day when he would view such a sight as an adversary. The rounded shields visible in the forward columns indicated Arvinnius was following the usual Roman practice of placing non-Roman cohorts in front with the legions following behind. To his relief, he did not see the Tungrian standard.

In the far distance, he identified the eagle standard of the Sixth Legion slowly rising above the crest of the hill as if it was moving upward toward the sky. He saw the aquilfer wearing the traditional headdress come into view. For a brief moment, the standard bearer's body was fully silhouetted against the azure blue of the afternoon sky. He recalled the last time he carried that same standard nearly twenty years ago. It had been underneath the eagle and below the escarpment where the fort at Banna now stood when Hadrian presented him with a *vitis*, the twisted vine stick signifying the rank of centurion.

A small group of horsemen followed behind the standard bearer, and Arrius was certain he recognized the ornate curaiss Querinius favored. He observed a lone rider just ahead of Querinius. The fact he wore no helmet indicated it was General Arvinnius. He hoped Decrius would one day have the chance to open Querinius's belly – he deserved it for what was done to Iseult and Rialus. Strangely, he felt detached with no personal animus for either Querinius or Arvinnius.

He looked at the other Selgovi within his range of vision and noticed they were taking in the spectacle of the advancing infantry with restrained silence. Heretofore, they would have been running toward the legionaries with no other thought than to engage in individual combat. He credited Tearlach far more than he did his own efforts for their current patience. Athough resistant at first, the Selgovan warriors eventually accepted the need to modify their style of fighting to the extent of better coordinating their efforts and attack according to a prearranged plan. It remained to be seen when the battle was joined if they reverted to their more traditional and individual style of fighting rather than attacking in a coordinated effort.

"Is it time, Arrius?" Tearlach asked without taking his eyes off the formations that were slowly closing the gap to where the Selgovan warriors lay hidden. The initial battle line consisted of shallow trenches dug on the reverse slope of the hill to their front and below the tree line in which they were now concealed. From the Roman camp the night before, he predicted the route the Roman advance would take, consisting as it usually did along a straight line, deviating only when the terrain mandated a more circuitous route.

"Not yet. Wait until the skirmishers are virtually on top of the trenches. The main body will then be in arrow range. The Romans will not expect to be attacked in the open; they'll believe the attack won't come until they enter the trees."

The strategy he outlined to the war council weeks ago was simple and designed to keep the Romans off-balance. The hit and run tactics he convinced the council to adopt were designed to tire the legionaries by forcing them to constantly deploy in battle formation. Such tactics would not defeat the legions, but they would slow the Roman advance and provide more opportunity for the Selgovi to use their superior mobility and knowledge of the terrain. The ultimate objective, he emphasized, was to conduct a war of attrition. Key to this was launching attacks behind the Roman advance and directed primarily at the rear camps where supplies and stores would be maintained. He suggested to Tearlach that Decrius should be given overall responsibility for the latter raids. He intuitively recognized such a task would be viewed as insufficiently important and too inglorious to satisfy Selgovan ideas of personal glory; consequently, the senior Selgovan war leaders were only too willing to support his recommendation. Equally important was that Decrius was pleased with the task and leadership of the one hundred mounted warriors assigned to him to accomplish it.

In the time Decrius spent with the Selgovi in preparation for the conflict, the tall Brigantian pushed himself and his horsemen tirelessly. Until now, Arrius had not realized how proficient Decrius was on the back of a horse, furthering his growing impression the Britannians seemed to have a natural affinity for horses foreign to Romans in general, which explained why the Roman Empire always depended on non-Roman cavalry. Decrius was quick to perceive and take advantage of the riding ability of the Selgovi along with the strong bond that existed between the tribesmen and their highly trained and disciplined horses. He thought they were easily a match for the Parthian and Dacian cavalry.

Decrius took pains in describing the manner in which Roman supply camps were organized, how the supply convoys were deployed and guarded and in identifying the priority items such as grain and oil that should be destroyed first in the event there was no time for a more thorough effort. Arrius was relying on the disruption in the legion rear areas to cause a significant delay in the Roman advance.

Tearlach rose up in the stirrups and leaned forward in the saddle, eyes focused on the rapidly closing line of skirmishers. Without turning his head, he motioned for the carnyx player to come forward.

"Gráda, let the signal be heard all the way to Rome," Tearlach commanded.

The young warrior lifted the mouthpiece of the trumpet to his lips and blew a long, sustained blast that swelled in intensity from a low moaning sound to a cacophonous shriek reverberating throughout the surrounding hills. Even though Arrius was prepared for the ethereal sound, he still felt a cold chill down his spine. By the gods, he thought, the noise was enough to summon the dead.

As the last notes of the carnyx faded away, the Roman skirmishers were either lying dead on the grassy slopes or running back toward the marching columns with a wavy line of Selgovan warriors in hot pursuit. A hundred yards from the Roman columns, Arrius watched as the Selgovan warriors stopped and nocked arrows in preparation for the next volley. The second volley caught the legionaries in the process of forming a battleline with machine-like precision and before the rear ranks could raise their shields above their heads in defense against the descending arrows. He saw a number of legionaries felled by the missiles. Gaps in the lines were quickly filled by legionaries moving forward from the rear ranks. The Selgovan and Roman lines continued to close in toward each other until they were less than a hundred feet apart. Tearlach signaled to the carnyx player to sound the recall. He held his breath to see if the next phase of the plan would be executed or if the Selgovan warriors would fall victim to their own bloodlust. He was dismayed to see not all the warriors heeded the signal to fall back and instead continued to run toward the line of auxiliary shields; most of them never got much closer when the first rank of legionaries hurled their pila with deadly results. The second rank of legionaries moved forward through the spaces between the legionaries in the front rank and loosed a second volley of spears. A few Selgovan warriors reached the Roman lines but were swiftly cut down with virtually no effect to the advancing legionaries.

Arrius shook his head in disappointment. "I hope those who would consider such folly in the next engagement are watching carefully."

"Most obeyed the signal."

"Too many did not, and they will fight no more. Such results if they continue to be repeated will doom the Selgovi. They must learn they cannot fight on Roman terms. The next phase must be more successful," he added grimly. He hoped the Novanti in the west were faring better but had no confidence they would. He feared the lessons so clear to him were going to be costly until the tribesmen finally took them to heart.

They watched the Roman lines reform into marching columns when there was no sign the Selgovan attack would continue. The Romans got barely a quarter-mile further when they were attacked again and forced to deploy into battlelines. While there were few significant casualties on either side, Arrius was pleased to see the Selgovi were beginning to follow the order not to engage the Roman formations in close combat.

Following the initial attack, he suggested to Tearlach that by reducing the assault force by half and alternating each half, the Selgovi warriors would have a chance to rest between assaults, an advantage the Romans did not have. He thought by the time the legionaries prepared their marching camp that night, the sentinels would have a difficult time staying awake. Tiberius Querinius would not be happy with the day's progress, and if all went as planned for the Selgovi tomorrow and the days after that, he would be even less satisfied.

That night Arrius drew Tearlach aside and said, "We must have news of what is happening with the Novanti and the Votadini. No matter how successful we are here, if our flanks are not secure, we will be in great jeopardy. Send runners to Bothan and Darach and find out how they fare." Tearlach agreed, and riders were quickly dispatched.

Tearlach looked at Arrius. "How do you think it went today?"

"As well as can be expected. I'll wager the legion covered only half the distance the commander intended, and his legionaries will be just as tired."

"But we cannot defeat them by fighting in such manner. We've accomplished little today except to show the Romans how well we can run from their spears and arrows. There were muted comments in agreement among the men sitting or standing nearby.

Concealing his irritation, Arrius said, "You've done more than you realize. The Selgovi have reduced the pace of a Roman legion to that of a snail, and that is no small achievement."

"But in time even the snail can travel a great distance," Tearlach said.

"Take each day as it comes. The Selgovi have done well today, and because of it, you will be able to fight again tomorrow."

By late in the third day, the Selgovan strategy had begun to fray the nerves of the most resolute centurion in the Sixth Legion and none more so than those of Tiberius Querinius. The lack of sleep, the chronic headaches he suffered from and the continued presence of General Arvinnius was taking its toll. What he needed was more cavalry to break up the constant attacks the Selgovi were launching thus reducing forward progress to a crawl. To make matters worse, he had been forced to send half the cavalry back to deal with the Selgovan raids on his supply caravans. But so far, General Arvinnius persisted in refusing his repeated recommendations to give him three or four turmae to augment his depleted cavalry force. What was truly surprising was that Arvinnius had not taken him to task for the legion's slow advance. Curiously, he seemed content to say little and not at all provoked by the frustrating Selgovan tactics. Had their roles been reversed, he would have been looking for a new commander of the Sixth Legion.

Querinius heard rapid hoofbeats behind him and looked over as a courier rode up to General Arvinnius and saluted.

"Salve, General Arvinnius. General Marcellus Septimus sends you greetings from the Twentieth Legion and good news on the progress against the Votadini," the courier announced before handing Arvinnius a wooden tablet.

A smile briefly relieved Arvinnius typical expressionless features after reading the message.

"General Septimus has routed the Votadini and in less time than I anticipated." Then turning to the courier, he said, "I'll send my congratulations and new orders to the *Valeria Victrix*." Arvinnius called for his cornucularius riding just behind him to send up one of the clerks. The clerk barely arrived with tablet and stylus in hand when Arviniius began dictating a brief reply.

Salve, Marcellus Septimus,

The news of your success is welcome. I congratulate you and the legion for achieving a quick and decisive victory. I expect you will impress upon the Votadini that any continuation of hostilities by them will be dealt with harshly. I leave it to your discretion the degree to which you will convince them of the futility of resisting Rome now and in the future.

With your victory, there is now the opportunity to combine the efforts of the Twentieth and Sixth Legions against the Selgovi who continue to slow the advance of the Sixth Legion. As planned, you will now proceed in a northwest direction with the major part of the legion and attack the Selgovan eastern flank.

General Gaius Labinius Arvinnius

When the scribe finished, he handed the tablet to Arvinnius who pressed his seal into the wax without bothering to read the short message.

Following the courier's departure, Arvinnius, in obvious good humor, turned to Querinius and announced, "With the Sixth to their front and the Twentieth flanking them, we will soon route the bastards. Now they will have little choice but to submit or be destroyed. I will sacrifice to Fortuna for their continued resistence. Crush them now, and there will be no chance of an uprising later."

As Querinius listened to Arvinnius, he understood the general's tolerance of their slow progress. He had been waiting for the message from Septimus, anticipating the Votadini would not put up much if any resistance thus making the Selgovan position completely untenable. He considered making a sacrifice to Fortuna as well except his would be a request for a quick but painful death for Arrius.

Chapter 15

Arrius listened without expression as the Votadini messenger, lines of exhaustion creasing his face, described to the Selgovan war council what had happened to the tribe during the last five days.

"Darach sought to continue the peace the Votadini long enjoyed with the Romans. He sent emissaries to the legion to assure them of his continued loyalty. The Romans beheaded all but one and sent the remaining emissary back with the heads of the others. It was clear they did not want peace, only the destruction of the Votadini. Although it was hopeless from the start, we did what we could to defend ourselves. Darach believed the Romans would be content to pass peacefully through his lands, and because of that, we had not prepared ourselves to fight them as we should have. Nearly every village has been destroyed. Those who survived the fighting and executions were either taken away as slaves or they hide in the forest, afraid to show themselves for fear they will suffer the same fate."

"And what of Darach, does he live?" Ilya asked.

"He was among the first to fall in battle and was captured by the Romans. It was unfortunate he lived – he was executed in the Roman way. They nailed him by his feet and hands to cross-timbers where he remains now."

Shocked silence prevailed for several moments broken finally by Ilya as she turned to Arrius and said, "Unfortunately, Marcus, what you have been saying has been proven correct. Why didn't the Romans simply accept the offer of peace made by the Votadini?"

"To make an example of the Votadini and remind the tribes of what is in store for them. Rome worries less about hostility beyond the frontier than rebellion within its borders."

Ilya directed her attention to the clan chiefs. "Tell your clans those who thought to remain behind should reconsider their decision. Tearlach, send a messenger to Bothan and tell them what happened. If he decides to remain where he is, the Novanti will suffer for it."

While Ilya spoke, Arrius was thinking quickly about what the Votadini defeat implied. For him, the most disturbing news the messenger gave was the Votadini had been defeated so quickly. Tearlach warned him the Votadini could not be relied upon, but he had counted on a few weeks before the predictable result would occur.

"Marcus, what will the Romans do now?" Ilya asked.

"The Twentieth Legion will begin to move against our flank. We must break off contact with the Sixth Legion and withdraw quickly north until our flank is once again secure."

"Then Bothan will have little choice but to fall back as well," Tearlach commented thoughtfully.

"That is so," Arrius agreed. "This was the original strategy General Arvinnius planned."

"Then what we've accomplished against the Sixth Legion so far has been wasted," Tearlach said.

"Not at all," Arrius replied sharply. "Your warriors have gained experience in the way the legions fight and deploy. The knowledge and experience will prove useful in the days ahead. It's true the legions will be able to move farther north and faster than before, but the farther they move north, the greater the distance between their forward position and their rear supply depots. We will intensify the attacks behind their advance concentrating on the forward supply stations. If we're successful, Arvinnius will have no choice but to divert more legionaries and cavalry from the advance to protect his rear area."

Arrius noted the skeptical looks on the faces of many of the clan chiefs and heard a number of disgruntled comments break out among them. He remained patiently silent. He was becoming used to the capacity of the Selgovi clan chiefs for lengthy debate no matter the subject in contrast to the typical legion consilium in which the senior centurions' participation was comparatively straight forward and mercifully brief. When there was dissension, it was quickly resolved by the legion commander's decision unlike Ilya's authority as queen that was far from being as absolute.

After a seemingly endless discussion, the clan chiefs gradually lapsed into silence. Since none of the clansmen proposed an alternate plan than the one broached by Arrius, Ilya stood up and said, "We'll go north tomorrow for whatever distance it requires until we're no longer threatened by an attack from the east. Tearlach, I'll leave it to you how best to manage our withdrawal. Those who decided to stay behind must be persuaded to leave with us."

It was an uncharacteristically somber group of clansmen that stood up to leave. For a brief while after Tearlach and the others left, Ilya stared morosely into the fire. It was apparent the burden of tribal leadership was weighing heavily on her shoulders. Arrius sought to reassure her.

"There is little else you can do, Ilya. For now, the Romans have the upper hand. It's unfortunate the Votadini were defeated so quickly, but it does not really change anything except to accelerate the move north."

"You knew this was going to happen, didn't you, Marcus?"

"Yes. The only hope for the Selgovi and the other tribes was to enlist the help of the tribes in the north. Only that would have presented a real problem to Rome. Arvinnius counted on the history of tribal warfare here in Britannia to prevent the tribes from coming together in organized resistance. Unless the tribes can overcome their distrust of each other and hate Rome more, Rome will prevail."

"Then I fear Rome will be here for a long time."

"That may well be, but Beldorach believed otherwise. He knew it would take a strong leader to unite the tribes. His ambition was to be that leader. His death was a blessing to Rome even though he was attempting to forge a peace and use me to bring it about."

"What do you mean?"

"He saved my life by not allowing Tearlach to take my head. He allowed me to leave so that I would go back and tell of his desire for peace. I knew his real intention was to gain time to convince the tribes to join together to defeat the Romans."

"Could Beldorach have succeeded?"

"Perhaps, but I think not. The culture of the tribes cannot be changed quickly. Even as resourceful and visionary as Beldorach was, it would have been difficult for him to change things."

Ilya made no response and continued to stare introspectively into the fire. Arrius knew she was weighing the implication of his words. After a moment of silence, Ilya said with a thoughtful expression, "If I am not the one to achieve what you say then perhaps Eugenius will be."

Deciding this was not the time to indulge in a subject better left for future discussion, he stood up and announced, "It's time for me to take a more active role."

Startled, Ilya said, "What do you mean?"

"I will not be going north with you. Instead, I will join Decrius with additional men. More than ever, we must slow down the Romans with more aggressive attacks behind them. I must find Decrius and tell him what happened to the Votadini. The Twentieth Legion is virtually unopposed, and we must do what we can to slow it down.

"But, Marcus, I need you with me," Ilya said with a hint of uncertainty.

"You have Tearlach and the other clan chiefs to advise you. Listen to their counsel but don't hesitate to make your own decisions. Remember what I've said to you and the council several times before. The Selgovi cannot win this fight, you can only survive it. For that reason, you must urge the clans to keep moving north.

Arrius left to find Tearlach to enlist his help in selecting the men who would go with him. He was delighted when Cuileán was the first to volunteer.

Arrius found Decrius late in the day after he had led his two hundred warriors around the Sixth Legion's west flank the previous night. The Brigantian was presiding over the complete destruction of a small supply camp. It was also apparent he was fulfilling his desire to kill Romans for none of the two dozen or more legionaries survived the assault. Their decapitated bodies lay where they were struck down. A score of oxen lay motionless on the ground in a small corral where they had been slaughtered. The Selgovan warriors were still in the process of smashing wine amphorae, strewing the contents of grain sacks over the ground and stuffing their leather satchels with as much food as they could carry. The remaining supplies the warriors couldn't carry were being burned using the wagons and carts to fuel the pyre.

If Decrius was shocked to see Arrius and the two hundred horsemen behind him, he didn't show it; rather, out of habit, he saluted then waited silently for him to speak.

"I see you're causing the legion some inconvenience," Arrius said. "You've done well for on the way here I found two other camps in similar condition."

"There was a third camp."

Arrius acknowledged the comment with a nod. "What casualties have you suffered?"

"A few but not as many as the Romans. Have you come here because you've run out of Romans in the north?" eyeing the horsemen arrayed behind Arrius.

"No, in fact, there will soon be even more than when you left." Quickly, he summarized what happened to the Votadini and ended by saying, "The real threat to the Selgovi is now the Twentieth Legion. We must combine our forces and do what we can to slow the legion down by attacking it from the rear."

"Then the gods better be with us for the odds are not," Decrius responded with a sardonic smile, encompassing the three hundred tribesmen with a sweep of his hand.

"True, but I couldn't risk bringing more. Ilya and Tearlach will need every warrior in the days ahead." Then eying the column of dense black smoke spiraling skyward, Arrius said, "It's time we were on our way," and without further comment urged Ferox in a northeasterly direction.

After several days of hard riding, Arrius knew it was time to rest the horses. Even Ferox was showing the effects of the hard ride. The evening shadows were lengthening when he signaled a halt in a valley with a small stream and sufficient grass to graze the horses.

The route the Twentieth Legion took north was easy to find. The abandoned rectangular-shaped night marching camps were readily recognizable by the low earthern walls and shallow trenches left behind. In addition, there were the blackened remains of villages and bloated bodies, human and animal, giving evidence of the legion's passage. The tribesmen destroyed several more supply camps as they made their way, but instead of destroying all of the food, some was saved to distribute to small groups of Votodini who somehow managed to escape the Roman depredations. Generally, the survivors consisted mainly of women and children looking gaunt and dazed from their ordeal.

The Votadini capital they passed by that morning had been systematically destroyed with nothing remaining except knee-high rubble. On either side of the main road leading into the settlement was the gruesome spectacle of crucified bodies arrayed in lines with military precision. Arrius heard the angry muttering behind him and assumed it was the wanton destruction the Romans caused that angered them. Later, he was confronted by Cuileán who wanted to know why the Romans employed such a cruel way to execute prisoners.

"Because it is cruel and provides a clear message what happens to Rome's enemies."

"But the Vatadini were friends of the Romans. They would have been more likely to seek an alliance with Rome than with the Selgovi."

"The Votadini made the mistake of trying to stay in the middle and have suffered for it. Is crucifixtion any worse than what the tribes have done to the Romans they've captured?" recalling past incidents in which some of his men had been unfortunate enough to be taken alive before being brutally tortured and killed. To his relief, his answer apparently was enough to silence the Selgovan who turned away without further response. He was too tired to debate much less defend the diverse ways various cultures used to strike fear in the hearts of their enemies. He had seen it all, and the worst of it was that he no longer thought about it. The only curious thing about Cuileán's question was in the asking.

Arrius circled the encampment to check the positioning of the sentinels. He hadn't gone far when he encountered Decrius doing the same. Decrius, uncharacteristically taciturn since the death of his wife and son, seemed inclined to talk.

"Arrius, what will we do when we catch up to the legion? Three hundred horsemen can do little against more than ten times that number. I think when we're done, there will be few of us left alive to tell of it."

"What you say is true; therefore, I don't plan on attacking them in a conventional way. Our horsemen would have little effect against trained legionaries."

"I don't understand."

"Once we catch up to the legion, we'll attack their flanks and rear and sting them with arrows. We'll form the tribesmen into thirty-man teams; ten men will be assigned to hold the horses while twenty warriors will advance on foot to take up concealed positions. After each member of the attack team launches a volley of arrows, they will quickly move back to the horses and make their escape. By employing a small number of teams at any given time, the tribesmen will be able to rest themselves and the horses more frequently than the Roman forces can. Perhaps then we can slow the legion down long enough to prevent attack on Ilya's flank. If we are able to accomplish that, we will have served our purpose."

General Marcellus Septimus's fleshy jowls were flushed with anger. He hurled the latest message tablet from Arvinnius to the ground and crushed it with his boot heel. The courier who brought the offending missive shifted uneasily wishing he could slip outside the tent before he became the focus of the legion commander's wrath. Since the general was not known for temper displays, the tribunes and senior centurions standing nearby exchanged significant looks. Without reading the cryptic message, they knew full well what it said. The legion's advance had slowed to a crawl caused by the incessant attacks during the past several days, and not unexpectedly, General Arvinnius was out of patience.

At first, the attacks were perceived as a nuisance, but when casualties began to steadily increase, the attacks were soon taken seriously and nerves became frayed. The silence of the Selgovan attacks was unnerving and punctuated only by the near silent hiss of well-aimed arrows shot from unseen positions. All too often, the arrows found their mark. Occasionally, only a few arrows were launched, and yet the small volley was enough to prompt the cohorts into forming the *testudo.* The tortoise formation required the legionaries marching in the center files to raise their scuta above their heads while the outside ranks faced their shields outward. Although protective, the formation required time to assume, and the tightness of the formation slowed the forward pace of the columns. In time, the centurions began to ignore the isolated volleys and accepted the risk of an occasional casualty simply to keep up the momentum of the march. At other times without warning, a sudden and dense volley of arrows descended on the marching columns. While many of the missiles thudded harmlessly into the shields, there were still enough that struck an unprotected neck, face or leg. Even more unsettling were the night sentries found with their throats cut.

"General Arvinnius is of the opinion we move too slowly," General Septimus announced with supreme disgust to no one in particular. "By Neptune's scaly balls, I'm forced to agree." Then turning to the legion's primus pilus with a glowering look, he said, "Well, Quintas Calidius, what have you to say? More to the point, what do you advise we do to speed up the march?"

The grizzled senior centurion showing numerous battle scars on face and arms was unperturbed. Calidius already anticipated the question and was prepared.

"I suggest we reposition the auxilia cohorts from the vanguard to the flanks and rear and at a greater distance farther out than our flank guards have been so far. Leave a single cavalry turmae to screen the forward cohorts. Since the attacks seldom come from the forward line, there is little need for the auxilia or most of the cavalry to lead the advance. The auxilia are also better equipped to deal with the attacks because of their lighter equipment and greater proficiency with bow and arrow. Instead of stopping or slowing down when we're attacked, leave the auxilia and cavalry to deal with it. Finally, keep the main body moving at an increased pace regardless of what happens on the flanks. It's clear the enemy numbers are small, or by now, they would have attacked in force." He did not need to point out the obvious that repositioning the foreign auxilia would shift the brunt of the casualties to them. It was understood the auxilia legionaries and the cavalry were more expendable than the Roman legionaries.

Metellus Septimus stared at the centurion for a full minute before replying, a thoughtful look gradually replacing the angry expression of a moment ago.

"Sensible counsel, primus pilus. Give the necessary orders, but I wonder you waited so long to offer it."

Even as the recommendations made to General Metellus by Centurion Quintas Calidius were about to be executed, it was obvious to Arrius that with each passing day the men were becoming more fatigued, and he was concerned the toll on men and horses was starting to contribute to their mounting casualties. The terrain was also becoming more open making it difficult to get within arrow range of the Roman columns without detection. It was also apparent the coastline they were occasionally glimpsing was becoming closer each day as it curved northwest. Cuileán warned if they continued as they were, they would be squeezed by the legion's advance and the sea as the land in front of them began narrowing appreciably.

Arrius assembled the senior warriors that night and announced his decision to disengage and make their way north to the lands of the Venicones where he hoped Ilya and the rest of the Selgovae Tribe were now located. That no ensuing discussion or disagreement followed was enough to indicate tacit approval. Even Decrius, for the time being, seemed to have had his fill of fighting.

With Cuileán in the lead, they left a few hours before dawn and made their way toward the coast. Except for brief stops to rest and feed the horses, Arrius urged a fast pace intended to avoid any chance encounter with Roman cavalry. By the next day, Arrius recognized landmarks from his previous trip with Ilya and the Novanti delegation. The following night, they camped near the spot where the Venicones ambushed them. With no sign of the Roman advance, Arrius was reassured they were sufficiently far enough to allow campfires and a more leisurely start the next morning. Extra sleep, the first hot food in more than two weeks, and the close proximity to their destination did much to lift flagging morale. He looked forward to being reunited with Ilya but worried the reception the northern tribes would extend to the migrating lowland tribes might pose as big a risk as the pursuing Romans. He recalled the less than enthusiastic pledge Indrecht gave to permit occupation of Venicones land and the more guarded acquiesence by the Epedi to do the same. Now that the Roman advance had commenced, would the pledges be honored or cast aside? Rejection would be disastrous for both the Selgovi and Novanti if caught between the Romans and hostile northern tribes. His concerns increased even more when they crossed the river and found the Selgovan encampment; it was located where the new wall was likely to be constructed.

Chapter 16

The grim expressions and subdued manner of the encampment confirmed Marcus's worst fears something was terribly wrong. He was somewhat reassured to see Ilya emerge from a rude shelter constructed of hides stretched over a pole frame. Her solemn face was further indication all was not well.

Arrius dismounted and briefly embraced Ilya before asking, "Why are you camped here and not farther north?"

"This is the land Indrecht assigned to the Selgovi; Bothan's camp is an hour's ride to the west of us."

"We cannot stay here. This place is too close to where the new wall will be built."

"Our options are limited, Marcus. We'll either fight the Romans in a few days, or we'll fight the local tribes if we continue north to a safer location."

"What have you decided to do?"

"I've only been waiting for your arrival before going farther. We'll need every man to push on."

"So, your decision is to continue on and face whatever the northern tribes are prepared to do," he responded neutrally, avoiding any influence in her decision.

"Yes," Ilya replied without hesitation. Then indicating the generally flat and open countryside surrounding the camp, she added, "Even as inexperienced as I am, I can see this is no place to make a stand against the Romans. I believe our odds are better there," gesturing north toward the snow-capped mountains.

"Then I think we should not delay. There is still much of the day left. What will Bothan do?"

"He also intends to press on and only waits for us to begin moving. Tearlach is with him now to coordinate our progress and arrange for mutual support in the event either tribe is attacked."

"It seems you've planned well. What can I do to help?"

"I would have you and Cuileán take a force of your choosing to go on ahead and find a suitable location to build a settlement. Decrius can remain here and assist in our defense in case the Roman approach is faster than expected or in the event Indrecht objects to our moving farther north."

Arrius turned to Cuileán and said, "Pick twenty men and be ready to leave as soon as they can be ready. Each man will take a second mount and enough provisions to last for a week."

Ilya and Cuileán exchanged looks of concern. Cuileán spoke first. "Twenty men will have no chance if we're attacked."

"I doubt a hundred more will make a difference if we are. A small party will not be perceived the threat a larger force would and may encourage talking instead of fighting."

"What if you're wrong, and you're attacked anyway?" Ilya asked.

"Then I would wish I had taken more men, or that I had not offended the gods. Now I want to spend a few minutes with Eugenius before I leave."

Ulla, placid as ever, was holding the infant when Arrius entered the shelter while Athdara, who evidently heard the conversation outside, was busy filling a leather bag with provisions in preparation for his departure. Arrius reached for Eugenius and cradled the sleeping baby briefly before reluctantly giving the infant back to the wet nurse. He already regretted the need to leave his son and Ilya so quickly.

Her packing completed, Athdara took Ulla by the arm and led her outside leaving Arrius alone with Ilya.

"Be careful, my love," she said softly, embracing him.

"I will, and soon we'll have time to spend together in a beautiful and peaceful valley with nothing to do but watch the clouds passing above us."

She sighed and leaned back with a wistful expression. "You make it sound too wonderful to be true. Do you think there is such a place where we can live without the threat of war?"

'I fear there will always be a threat of war. If the tribes are not busy fighting Romans, they seem all too willing to fight each other. Perhaps one day you and Eugenius can make a difference, but I don't think I'll live long enough to see that day." He intended to sound reassuring, yet even to his ears his words sounded gloomy. He thought it best not to say anything more lest he make the future appear bleaker than it did already.

"I should go or everyone will think we're doing more than saying goodbye."

The lighthearted comment drew a responding smile and softened the planes of her face. "Perhaps the next time we see each other, we need not waste time talking at all although I will insist you first take time to bathe," wrinkling her nose in mock disgust.

"Already you place conditions on our next meeting. I warrant you'll be happy enough to see me even if I've just climbed out of a bog."

Playfully, she slapped him on the chest. "You may be right at that."

A few miles from camp, Arrius rounded a small hill and found Cuileán and the other two outriders dismounted and talking heatedly with several bare-chested men, one of whom was Indrecht. He expected an early encounter with the tribal leader of the Venicones and only hoped there would be an opportunity to talk first before spears were cast and blades were crossed.

The men on foot watched silently as Arrius and the others rode toward them. As he came closer, Arrius recognized one of the three men was Indrecht's son. The faces of the Venicones tribesmen were uniformly grim if not overtly threatening.

Cuileán did not wait for Arrius to ask what the Venicones wanted. "Indrecht says we must remain where we are. He will not allow us to go farther."

"Tell him we cannot remain here since it is near here where the Romans plan to build their wall. Does he then intend that we make peace with the Romans and thereby become the enemy of the Venicones? If so, then the Venicones will have more to be concerned about than the Selgovi."

Arrius waited for Cuileán to translate. It was apparent from Indrecht's obdurate expression, the argument was not persuasive. Following a rapid exchange between the Selgovan clansman and the tribal leader, Cuileán turned and said, "He says the Venicones do not wish war with either the Selgovi or the Romans, but it will be war if the Selgovi try to take what belongs to the Venicones."

"Indrecht must understand we have no choice but to go on or risk death or slavery from the Romans. Already many Selgovan and Novanti warriors have died, and the Votadini have been destroyed.

What will it matter if the Selgovi die at the hands of the Venicones or the Romans? The result will be the same. The difference will be there will be fewer Venicones to stand against the Romans. Tell him it is the Venicones who will bear the brunt of the Roman presence; therefore, they would do well to have the Selgovi and the Novanti as allies to help stop them. If the tribes fight each other, only the Romans will win. The better bargain is to allow us to go on and find a more defensible place to live than here."

This time after Cuileán finished translating, Arrius detected a subtle change in the tribal chief's manner, a slight relaxing that suggested his argument was at least being considered. Indrecht's next words confirmed as much.

Cuileán said, "Indrecht thinks you talk as well as you fight."

"Does that mean he intends to let us go on?"

After Cuileán finished translating, Indrecht hawked and spat and briefly looked away before replying at length.

"Indrecht says for now there will be peace between the Selgovi and the Venicones until he sees what the Romans will do. If the Romans come here then he will help us fight them. If the Romans do not come, then there will be war between our tribes. Indrecht warns it may be more difficult to persuade Vadrex, Chief of the Vacomagi, and Bericus, King of the Caledoni. He warns the Vacomagi are hostile to the Venicones and says it is a mistake to enter their lands."

"Tell Indrecht we must go and talk with Vadrex. It may well be his mistake if he chooses to fight the Selgovi rather than allow us to live in peace."

Indrecht made no response except to shake his head doubtfully after Cuileán finished translating. The tribal leader watched silently as the Selgovan horsemen rode north.

The rest of the day and well into the next as they drew closer to the mountainous region ahead, Arrius saw no sign of the Vacomagi. Despite the lack of human presence beyond isolated homesteads long abandoned and covered with undergrowth, he couldn't shake the feeling watchful eyes were observing their every movement. As a precaution and to indicate peaceful intention, he or Cuileán occasionally raised a sheathed sword in hopes it would forestall a hostile reception they would have little chance of surviving. If it were not for the familiar prickly sensation at the back of his neck, he would have believed they were traveling through a deserted landscape. Their previous trip north with Ilya had not extended this far; consequently, they had no idea where Vadrex's settlement might be and counted on the Vacomagi finding them.

The comparatively flat terrain where Ilya remained with the tribe transitioned from gentle rolling hills to steeper, densely forested hillsides with swift flowing streams frigid from snowmelt flowing down from the higher, snowcapped mountains ahead. More often than not, they were obliged to dismount and proceed on foot to spare the horses when crossing rocky streams or negotiating the more precipitous slopes. Eventually, they entered a wide valley through which a large river flowed southward. Arrius decided to remain near the river in hopes of making easier and faster progress than trying to negotiate the mountains through which the river twisted and turned. By late afternoon of the third day, the main river channel swung abruptly west at the confluence of another and smaller river flowing from the northeast. It was where the two rivers joined that Indrecht had said they must turn and follow the smaller river northeast where it began a series of serpentine loops marking the western boundary of the Vacomagi. Late in the afternoon the next day, the sudden curving of the smaller river indicated they had reached their destination. From the bluffs overlooking the river, the land stretching to the east transitioned to a coastal plain.

Arrius thought it would be better to wait until the next morning to attempt a crossing. He was standing silently regarding the opposite bank as the shadows lengthened when Cuileán joined him.

"Arrius, how much farther do you think we will have to go to find the Vacomagi?"

"I believe we will find them tomorrow."

"What do you mean?"

"A short time ago, I saw movement in the trees across the river. I believe the Vacomagi are waiting for us over there."

Cuileán looked speculatively at the far bank. "If they're hostile, we'll have no chance once we enter the river."

"I agree, and that is why only you and I will cross tomorrow. I would go alone, but I need you to speak for me. If it does not go well, the men should return and warn the clans to come north but to expect to fight when they do."

"Arrius, I don't know if you're bold or simply foolish. I think it is not much of a plan. We may never get to the other side before they decide we've gone far enough."

"We'll be permitted to cross because by now Vadrex is curious. It is also possible we won't be allowed to return once his curiosity is satisfied."

In a misting rain early the next morning, Arrius and Cuileán guided their skittish mounts into the river that fortunately proved not as deep as they originally thought. Once the horses also realized it, they quickly settled down allowing both men to focus their attention on the bank ahead. Halfway across, Arrius saw a dozen rough-looking and bearded men emerge from the trees and stand silently watching as they drew near the bank. The men were garbed only in breeches and calf-length boots similar to the Venicones. Some wore painted symbols on their chests and arms. With the exception of a large man armed with what appeared to be a Roman-style gladius standing slightly in front of the rest, each man was armed with a spear or an axe; all carried a small, round-shaped shield. Their forbidding expressions offered no encouragement.

Ferox surged out of the water and up the shallow bank with ease at the same time the rain began falling in greater intensity. Arrius reined in and held up his sheathed gladius hoping the gesture would be recognized as peaceful and forestall a volley of spears. Without waiting for Cuileán, whose smaller horse was having more difficulty negotiating the steep bank, he dismounted and walked toward the tall, heavyset man with the sword. As he drew closer, Arrius realized the man was older than he first appeared. Despite his age, his powerful build and large size presented an intimidating presence. His face, upper chest and arms were badly scarred, and his left eye was nothing more than a puckered scar. Curiously, Arrius saw the hilt and scabbard of the gladius the huge man carried at his side were ornate enough to have been worn by a Roman general. He stopped a few feet away, and for a moment, the two men silently regarded each other. Arrius spoke first asking in Selgovan, "Are you Vadrex, Chief of the Vacomagi?"

Arrius was taken aback when the man responded in a deep voice in heavily accented but easily understood Latin. "Roman, to your misfortune, I am Vadrex. You are either very brave or very foolish to come here. It is widely known I would almost rather kill a Roman than take a woman. Why have you come?"

"I've come as an ambassador bearing greetings from the Queen of the Selgovi."

"Beldorach was leader of the Selgovi. What has become of him?"

"He was killed, and his cousin, Ilya, now rules the Selgovi."

"Bathar had a daughter by that name. Is she Bathar's daughter?"

"She is and my wife as well."

"The Selgovi now have a queen whose ambassador and husband is Roman? This is strange news and curious enough to spare your life long enough to hear what you have to say. Then I will kill you."

"You may find it will not be as easy as you think."

Vadrex's lip curled in a contemptuous sneer. "I only need to lift a finger, and my warriors would send you to your gods."

"True enough, but you would go to your gods before I reach mine."

"You see these scars, Roman? Do you think one Roman can kill me when so many others have tried and failed? You have the balls of an ox to challenge me." Vadrex's voice became dangerously mild. "Why have you come here?"

"I came to speak on behalf of the Selgovi, not to challenge you or to listen to your idle boasts." Arrius didn't attempt to conceal his irritation.

"Do not try my patience, Roman."

Arrius thought it was time to call Vadrex's bluff. "Then do not try mine. I was told Vadrex was a formidable man and a great leader of the Vacomagi. So far I see only an old man who brays like an ass and brags of what he probably never was."

"I think now we'll fight instead of talking, and it will be my pleasure to kill you myself."

Already beginning to regret his impulsive words, Arrius realized he had pushed the Vacomagi tribal leader farther than he intended. He was risking the success of the Selgovan embassy by either killing the man he came to ask for assistance or humiliating him in front of his men. There was no benefit to the Selgovi for either outcome. He cursed himself for allowing the situation to get out of hand.

"Very well, but what of them if I should kill you?" he asked, gesturing to the other Vacomagi warriors.

Vadrex smiled. "Do not worry, Roman, you will not kill me, but in the unlikely chance you do, they will let you and your men leave unharmed." Without taking his eyes off Arrius, Vadrex said something to his men that drew howls of laughter.

Unable to follow the exchange between Arrius and Vadrex, Cuileán asked in a tense voice, "What is happening?"

"It seems Vadrex would rather fight than talk. I'm afraid any chance for a peaceful alliance between the Selgovi and Vacomagi is finished."

Vadrex interrupted. "Why does the Selgovi wish an alliance with the Vacomagi?"

"I have come a long way to tell you why; however, you seem more willing to fight than to listen. Perhaps it would benefit both the Vacomagi and the Selgovi if we talk first and then fight." When he saw the huge tribal leader hesitate, Arrius dared to hope reason and curiosity might yet prevail.

"I'll listen to what you have to say only out of respect for Bathar who was much admired even by the Vacomagi."

Arrius breathed a sigh of relief.

Under a large tree whose broad canopy provided some shelter from the rain, Arrius told of the Roman plans that necessitated the northern migration of the Selgovi, Novanti and what was left of the Votadini, pausing occasionally when Vadrex translated what he said for the benefit of the Vacomagi warriors. When he finished speaking, Vadrex stared thoughtfully into space without speaking.

"How does it come to pass a Roman speaks for the Selgovi?"

It was an obvious question so Arrius briefly described the circumstances and his reason for leaving the Roman Army.

"You left your people for a woman?" Vadrex asked in amazement.

"And for the son she bore me."

"I have many sons I know and many more I do not. Most of the sons I do recognize would see me dead if they had the courage to try. Instead, they wait for me to grow old and weak before one attempts to take my place as leader of the Vacomagi." The dispassionate comment gave Arrius some insight into the tribe's culture, which apparently regarded fighting ability as the essential qualification for tribal leadership.

Believing the interchange was drifting, he attempted to refocus the discussion. "Will you allow the Selgovi to live here in peace?"

"No." The answer was brief and uttered in a way that left no room for doubt it was final. "I'll help the Selgovi fight the Romans, but I will not give them any of my lands unless they are willing to acknowledge me as their leader."

"Ilya is the leader of the Selgovi."

"Then have her come here, and I will take her to wife if she is comely enough then she will be queen of both the Selgovi and Vacomagi. Perhaps she will give me better sons than I now have, sons who do not wish me dead."

Feeling the anger building inside, Arrius said, "I fight for Bathar's daughter, and as long as I live, she will remain my wife."

Vadrex's one eye narrowed. "Careful what you say, Roman, or you may not see your queen again. You continue to live now only because I permit it."

Arrius concluded there was no longer anything left to lose. "Then it's settled. I will send Cuileán back to inform Ilya of your decision. If the Selgovi and Vacomagi are destined to fight, let it begin now with the two of us. If I lose, the Vacomagi will have one less warrior to fight. If I kill you, then there will be peace between the tribes."

Vadrex smiled and instead of speaking directly to Arrius, he addressed his own men. Whatever he said evoked smiles and mocking laughter. No translation was required to understand his challenge was not being taken as a serious threat to Vacomagi leadership. Cuileán who understood the gist of Arrius's proposal from Vadrex's comment said in a soft undertone, "Arrius, you've gone too far. Even if you should defeat him, there are too many for us to fight."

"Leave now and wait for me on the other side of the river. If I do not return, go back and tell Ilya what happened. She and the clans must be warned and prepared to fight the Vacomagi."

"I can't leave you here to fight them alone."

"You will do it because there is no other alternative." Then in an attempt to soften the harsh reply, he said, "Do you then think so little of my fighting skills that you consign me to the gods before my blade is even drawn?"

"I think you face long odds, Arrius. Even if you kill Vadrex, I think they will not let you live long enough to celebrate the victory."

"Perhaps, but I think it's too late to argue the point. If I win, it may save both the Selgovi and Vacomagi from a tribal war neither tribe can afford," He hoped to sound more optimistic than he felt.

"You will not win, Roman. Your companion should not bother to wait for you. He should go back to your queen and tell her she is now a widow." Vadrex then addressed Cuileán. "Tell Ilya I am willing to take her as my queen as a condition for the Selgovi to live here in peace."

Cuileán glanced at Arrius and shrugged in resignation. "Shall I take your horse with me?"

Nettled at the Selgovan's pointed inference, he said, "I'll need Ferox when I finish here."

"Leave the horse," Vadrex interjected. "After I take your head, I'll take your horse and in time possibly your wife as well — if she comes here."

"We'll soon see if your sword is as sharp as your tongue."

Vadrex responded with a mocking smile. "You will know sooner than you would wish, Roman. You should have asked why I speak your tongue and how I got these scars before being foolish enough to challenge me. When I was young, I was captured by the Romans and made a slave. Because I was bigger than most, I was eventually sold to a gladiator school. In time, I was taken to Rome where I fought in the arena for ten years. I killed many men, and although wounded many times, I was never defeated. Because of my success, your emperor gave me freedom and this sword. Now make peace with your gods for you are about to see them."

Chapter 17

With a small escort, Tiberias Querinius rode slowly along the road paralleling the stone foundation upon which the new wall would be built. Already in a few places the stone foundation was nearly complete and teams of legionaries were cutting large rectangular turves from the grassy soil with which to construct the earthen wall. Where the soil was too thin or too porous for cutting, loose earth was being placed between revetted clay cheeks. Other *dolabrae*-wielding legionaries were busy excavating a deep slope-sided ditch twenty paces forward of the stone foundation. The spoil was being placed on top of the outer edge to add further difficulty in overcoming the obstacle. Forward of the ditch, the *lilia* had already been dug; the deep, round pits with sharpened wood stakes placed in the bottom would present an additional obstacle for the overall defense of the wall. Concurrently at various points along the wall, the foundations of forts were also being constructed. Similar to the purpose of the larger and more impressive stone wall farther south, the turf wall when completed would serve principally as a means to define the frontier and to control the local population rather than serving as a defensive barrier.

Progress was ahead of schedule thanks to a spate of uncharacteristic and welcome clement weather. When General Arvinnius returned from Londinium, Querinius was certain he would be pleased at the results, particularly for the section the Victrix Legion was responsible for in comparison to those being built by the Second and Twentieth Legions. It was widely rumored Governor Urbicus might accompany the general to formally designate the new boundary as The Antonine Wall in honor of the emperor and the military victory credited to Antoninus Pius. All considered, Querinius reflected, the emperor's new designation, "*Imperator*," had been cheaply won. Apart from a relatively slow start in the campaign, once the Twentieth Legion successfully destroyed the Votadini and flanked the Selgovi, resistance virtually melted away. The rest of the advance had been made with relative ease. The cavalry patrolling north of the wall continued to report little or no significant contact with the fleeing tribes.

He heard the drum of hoofbeats and looked back to see a turma of cavalry rapidly overtaking his small band. He turned and noted with distaste the troop was being led by Seugethis, the flamboyant commander of the Dacian cohort formerly stationed at Fanum Cocidii a few miles north of Banna. He disliked the cavalryman's overbearing nature, but even more, he resented that Seugethis witnessed his humiliation at Banna when he failed in his attempt to have Arrius convicted and executed as a traitor. Thinking the cavalry officer had just returned from patrol, he signaled for his escort to halt and waited for the troop to come to a halt.

"Salve, Tribune." Seugethis omitted the customary salute.

With effort, Querinius controlled his irritation and ignored the casual manner of the greeting. "What have you to report?"

"Unfortunately, very little. It seems the Selgovi and Novanti do not wish to fight. My patrols have made only isolated sightings and no significant contact."

Querinius was torn between relief and disappointment. If the tribes decided not to attack again while he remained in Britannia, he would be more than satisfied. Unlike the Dacian, he would not feel deprived if he was spared the risks of further hostilities even though the opportunity to see Arrius dead might well be slipping away.

"Have your men heard or seen anything of the traitor Marcus Arrius?"

"Not a trace, Tribune. Why do you ask?"

"Because General Arvinnius has offered a reward of 10,000 denari for Arrius's death or capture, and I would prefer the reward go to the Victrix Legion. I will also pay a similar amount to anyone who shows me his head."

"That's a handsome offer, Tribune," Seugethis commented thoughtfully. "Do you have a personal score to settle with Arrius that you offer such a fortune?"

As soon as the question was asked, Querinius realized his mistake. He had opened the door to suspicion his motive was more than a desire for justice. "Not at all, I merely want to ensure he pays for his treasonous conduct and for bringing dishonor to the legion."

"To place such a large sum on Arrius's head from your own purse is curious. What lies between you and Arrius that you dislike him so much?" Seugethis leaned forward in the saddle and regarded Querinius with a penetrating look.

Querinius's face flushed as he replied, "I do not hate Arrius at all. He's nothing to me, but by his actions he brought disgrace to every Roman officer. For that alone, he must be held accountable."

"Tribune, somehow I think there is much more to it than that; however, I'll keep in mind what you said. If my Dacians capture Arrius alive, it may be interesting to hear what Arrius has to say." Without waiting for a response from Querinius, the cavalry officer galloped off with the troop thundering after him.

A chill swept over Querinius. He had inadvertently aroused the Dacian's curiosity, thereby increasing the danger his cowardice in Judaea would be exposed. A savage headache started throbbing in his head. The splendid weather and progress of the wall construction was forgotten. Even with Arrius proscribed, he continued to risk the threat of exposure and the public humiliation it would bring. He became aware the centurion commanding the escort was staring at him. With effort, he shrugged off the disquieting effects of the conversation and without comment urged his horse on down the road.

Vadrex's revelation was sobering. As he drew his sword, Arrius thought his chances for surviving a fight with the tribal leader were not very good. Vadrex drew his sword and lifted his shield in readiness while his men moved to encircle the two combatants. Without taking his one eye off Arrius, Vadrex said something to one of the warriors closest to him. The man quickly tossed his shield toward Arrius. The shield landed between the two men although closer to Vadrex than to Arrius. Vadrex gestured with his sword toward the shield saying, "Take it, Roman" he said with a humorless laugh, "I don't want to take advantage of you."

Arrius thought under the circumstances it would be prudent to accept the invitation even though the shield was suspiciously closer to Vadrex than to him. Without taking his eyes off Vadrex's face, he moved cautiously toward the shield. As he bent down to pick it up, he saw Vadrex tense just before he rushed forward with his sword stretched out. Reacting instinctively, Marcus grasped the shield and hurled it toward Vadrex. The shield struck the Vacomagi leader a painful blow just below the left knee that slowed his charge long enough for Marcus to leap safely to one side.

Showing no concern for the bloody gash on his shin, Vadrex said, "You are quick, Roman, but no matter, you only prolong the end a little longer."

Vadrex allowed Arrius to move to the far side of the circle then in a deliberate act of contempt, Vadrex dropped his sword and shield and pulled down his breeches. Encouraged by the raucous laughter of his men, Vadrex took his time emptying his bladder.

Arrius took advantage of the delay to size up his opponent. In spite of Vadrex's larger size and claimed experience in the arena, he thought his adversary's greatest weakness was in being overly confident in an outcome Vadrex believed was entirely in his favor. To bolster his own confidence, he recalled his fight with Aculineus four years ago in Judaea. Despite the younger man's agility and experience fighting in non-lethal legionary contests, he killed the centurion. Unfortunately, Vadrex's experience was in the public arena where death for one of the combatants was routine, expected and gave added incentive to fight hard.

Out of the corner of his eye, Arrius saw he was close to one of the Vacomagi warriors standing in a relaxed position next to his spear, thrust butt-first in the muddy ground. Shifting his sword to his left hand, he moved closer to the man while pretending to be unaware of how near he was. A moment later, he heard the warrior exclaim and felt his hand on his back pushing him toward Vadrex. Arrius reached out and quickly pulled the spear shaft free before moving out of reach of the warrior. Warning shouts alerted Vadrex who managed to retrieve his shield in time to ward off the thrown spear. The spear struck the shield just above the boss. He heard Vadrex grunt with pain and saw him drop the now unbalanced shield. He was gratified to see the spear point had penetrated the shield far enough to draw blood from Vadrex's left forearm. Although a minor wound, he thought perhaps it was a psychological advantage to draw first blood.

Vadrex rushed toward Arrius with an angry bellow. During the next few minutes, it was all he could do to defend himself against the tribal chief's aggressive and persistent attacks. It wasn't long before both men were bleeding from various wounds to the arms and shoulders. Arrius's sword arm was numb from parrying Vadrex's brutal slashes, and occasionally, he was obliged to use both hands to ward off the hacking blows. However, as skillful a fighter as Vadrex claimed to be, Arrius thought his opponent was not as proficient with a gladius as Vadrex thought he was. Designed as a thrusting weapon for close-in fighting, the short sword was less effective as a slashing weapon as Vadrex tended to employ it. The technique left his upper body dangerously exposed each time he lifted the sword to deliver a blow and particularly so without a shield. Arrius guessed Vadrex used many different weapons in the arena, but the gladius evidently was not the one he used often or possibly even at all. Perhaps the sword had been given to him as a traditional symbol for prowess in the arena. Vadrex's failure to replace the shield was either because he was too confident of the outcome, or the wound to his forearm precluded holding it. In either case, it was a mistake that made him vulnerable. Arrius believed his chances might not be as hopeless as he first assumed.

By now, the circle of warriors was silent with the ring of metal blades and the labored breathing of the combatants the only sounds heard above the soft patter of the rain. Arrius thought it strange Vadrex's warriors were unusually reticent. He would have expected shouts of encouragement in support of their leader, but instead, they remained silent observers and seemingly indifferent to the outcome of the fight.

Arrius kept waiting for signs of fatigue in his opponent, but between the two of them, he was the one beginning to feel and show the effects of the fight. Vadrex was built like a bull and seemed to have the strength of one. Even as his own strength and confidence began to wane, Vadrex's seemed to be increasing. It was obvious his stamina contributed to his survival in the arena. Vadrex stepped back and smiled confidently at Arrius.

"You fight well, Roman. You might have survived one or two contests in the arena. But I can tell you're finished, and I grow tired of the sport. Because you fought well enough, I'll give you a clean kill and let you keep your head so your gods will know you."

Arrius did not respond, concluding it was better to conserve what little strength he had remaining rather than make boastful threats that would sound empty even to his own ears. Instead, he took advantage of the brief respite to force several deep breaths into his heaving lungs. If he didn't do something soon, there was little doubt the contest would end on Vadrex's terms. He wondered if he could somehow maneuver Vadrex close enough to Ferox to mount and make his way back across the river. The thought was an idle one. Even if he was able to get close to the horse, he doubted he had the strength to climb on the horse fast enough to make his escape.

"What's the matter, Roman," Vadrex taunted, "are you so ready to die you have nothing to say?"

When there was still no reply, Vadrex started walking slowly toward Arrius. Still holding the gladius in both hands as if prepared to stop another one of Vadrex's powerful chopping blows, Arrius backed away stalling as long as possible in an effort to draw a few more breaths in his heaving lungs. The tribal leader frowned in annoyance and quickened his pace. Arrius knew time and his strength was fast running out to withstand his opponent's arm-numbing attacks. From the confident expression on Vadrex's face, it was apparent he thought the same as he raised his gladius high above his head in preparation for a killing stroke. Knowing this was his last and only chance to survive the one-sided fight, Arrius drew his dagger and stepped in close to Vadrex lifting the gladius only with his left hand to meet the descending blade. Even as he plunged the dagger into Vadrex's belly, Arrius was unable to completely deflect Vadrex's descending blade from slicing deeply into his left shoulder.

With a look of complete shock, Vadrex dropped his sword and fell to his knees, both hands clutching the hilt of the dagger. Arrius walked slowly toward Vadrex to finish him. He barely took a step when he was pushed roughly aside by one of the Vacomagi warriors carrying an axe. Thinking he was about to be killed where he stood, Arrius was caught by surprise when the warrior ignored him and instead moved swiftly toward Vadrex. The warrior shouted something incomprehensible before burying the heavy blade in Vadrex's head with enough force to nearly split it in half. Even though the stomach wound was mortal, Vadrex might have lived for days. That the Vocamagi warrior finished Vadrex instead of preventing him from doing so was strange enough, but even more mystifying were the actions of the other warriors. One by one, each man struck the corpse with spear and axe repeatedly until there was nothing left but a mound of bloody flesh.

His lungs still heaving, Arrius lifted his sword and waited as the man who finished Vadrex came toward him still carrying the bloody axe.

"Put down your sword, Roman," the man said in stilted Selgovan. "There will be no more fighting today. You've won the right to live – at least for now. I am Gelchar. I am Vadrex's oldest son. I have claimed leadership of the Vocamagi." Arrius wondered if Gelchar had killed his father out of mercy or simply to accelerate his claim to tribal leadership. "Tell your queen the Vacomagi will fight the Romans only if they come this far. I will let the Selgovi live in peace as long as they remain west of the river that flows behind you. Do you understand me, Roman?"

"I do."

"Good, then go now before I change my mind and decide to finish what Vadrex could not."

Arrius walked over to Vadrex's body and retrieved his pugio now covered in gore. After climbing into the saddle, he looked down at Gelchar and asked, "Where will I find the Caledoni if I decide to look for them?"

"Across the river and more than two days away in that direction," pointing west. "The river separates the Caledoni lands from the Vocamagi. You have been traveling in their land for the past day."

"You are generous in allowing the Selgovi to live in land you do not claim."

With a sardonic smile, Gelchar said, "You must make your own peace with the Caledoni."

"Will they be willing to talk instead of fight?"

"I do not know, Roman. The Vocamagi and Caledoni seldom talk — we prefer to fight instead."

Realizing there was no more to be said, Arrius headed for the river. He saw Cuileán and the others silently observing him as he made his way across the river to the opposite bank. When the horse reached the shore, he thought Cuileán's look of surprise he was still alive was fully justified.

"It's deep, but it will heal," Cuileán said after examining the gash on Arrius's left shoulder. "I thought you were a dead man when I left you."

"But you remained here instead of going back to Ilya?"

"The reason was to recover your body to take back to her."

Arrius was irritated by the Selgovan's matter of fact assumption he had no chance against Vadrex. He was about to make a caustic remark when he thought better of it. After all, before the fight was over, he also had concluded the same. "I suppose there was reason to believe Vadrex would win," suppressing his injured pride at the intimation his fighting abilities had been underestimated. He then related what happened to the Vacomagi leader and the conditions by which the Selgovi would be left alone.

"At great personal risk, you've done well, Arrius," Cuileán said. "The Selgovi owe you much for what you've done. Songs telling of your courage will be sung for many years." The comment did much to reduce the resentment he felt for the Selgovan's lack of faith in his fighting ability. All considered, he was lucky to have Fortuna watching over him. Arrius looked at the open wound that was still bleeding profusely and realized how deep the wound was. "I believe it may be difficult to hold a shield for a few days."

Cuileán looked at Arrius. "It will be a long time before you will be able to use it." The clan chief turned to one of the men. "Serghine, build a fire. We need to cauterize the wound to stop the bleeding."

With a small fire kindled, Cuileán held his dagger blade in the flames until it glowed a dull red. The clan chief looked at Arrius and after seeing him nod silently, stood up and swiftly pressed the heated blade to the wound. Arrius involuntarily clenched his fists in reaction to the searing pain. After what seemed an interminable amount of time, Cuileán grunted in satisfaction and removed the smoking blade.

Trying to ignore his throbbing shoulder and the nauseating smell of burnt flesh, Arrius said, "There's still much of the day remaining. We'll leave now. We'll travel west before heading south to find Ilya and the others."

"Why not go back the way we came?" Cuileán asked. "It will take less time, and we know the way."

"True, but then we won't have the opportunity to see more of the northern country. And while we've made peace of sorts with the Venicones and the Vocamagi, we haven't contacted the Caledoni."

"If we find the Caledoni, I hope they prove friendlier than the Vocamagi," Cuileán said over his shoulder as he walked toward his horse. "You aren't fit to accept another challenge," he added objectively.

"True, and for that reason I believe I'll let you have that honor."

Chapter 18

It was after sunset when Querinius dismounted inside the main gate of the fort that when completed would be the main supply depot for the northern region. The fort was centrally located several miles south of the earthen wall that daily rose higher and continued to advance impressively across the countryside. The wall was being constructed quickly and ahead of schedule as the legions rushed to finish their assigned sections. The speed of the construction had less to do with legionary zeal and competition among the legions as it was attributed to the relentless and harsh supervison of General Arvinnius. In recognition of the campaign's overall success, Governor Urbicus invited all the legionary officers to an official banquet in honor of General Arvinnius.

A legionary led Querinius's horse away while an optio holding a torch escorted him to one of several large and hastily constructed buildings ablaze with flickering torches. In front of the main entrance, an honor guard stood in stiff ranks under the supervision of a centurion. Preoccupied as he was with his own thoughts, Querinius was unaware of the centurion's salute as he walked past him to the door. Full of nervous expectation, he was focused only on the possibilities the evening might provide. Surely before the banquet was over, the legion commanders would also be recognized for their part in the successful outcome of the emperor's first military venture. But it was more than recognition he wanted this night. He intended to take advantage of the occasion to approach Arvinnius when he would be in a predictably expansive, and more importantly, a receptive mood. He intended to solicit Arvinnius's support in obtaining the governor's approval to leave Britannia for Rome. The sooner he left this miserable island the better. His private opinion was he had acquitted himself well enough, and there was no reason to prolong what could only be termed a tedious and exceedingly unpleasant assignment. The only regret in leaving would be in forgoing the pleasure of seeing Arrius executed; it was a sacrifice he was willing to make in return for a quick departure. Perhaps the governor would even send him back as his personal emissary to report the progress of the wall to the emperor.

Although the exterior of the storage building was plain, the interior had been transformed to a passable facsimile of a banquet hall reminiscent of a villa in Rome. It was apparent the governor spared no expense in the cloth furnishings that covered the walls in soft folds including the tables ranged on either side of the room. In place of the usual earthen plates and vessels common to the legions, porcelain and silver graced the tables. Instead of the usual clay drinking cups, there were metal goblets of burnished bronze. It was evident Urbicus intended the guest of honor would be suitably recognized.

The hall was already filled with senior commanders and staff officers from the legions. The officers assigned to the governor's personal staff were readily distinguishable from the others by the spotless condition of their linen tunics in contrast to the worn and stained tunics of the legionary officers. With the exception of the commanders and tribunes assigned to the Sixth, he had only a passing acquaintance with most of those present. He saw Tribune Gaius Cornelius speaking to Praefectus Plinius Flavius, the newly appointed commander of Banna following the departure of Arrius. He observed Marcellus Septimus, the legion commander of the Twentieth Legion, and Rutilius Corbulo, commander of the Second Legion, were keeping their distance from each other. The rumor was the only common ground between the two men was an implacable dislike of General Arvinnius. It was also rumored there was little mutual regard between Urbicus and Arvinnius. Protocol dictated he should greet the two legion commanders, yet he was reluctant to subject himself to the possibility of being publicly rebuffed. The cold manner in which he was treated during past encounters with the two legion commanders gave sufficient reason for his hesitation. He quickly became aware during the first consilium he attended with Septimus and Corbulo they did not consider him as anything more than the titular and very temporary commander of the Sixth Legion.

He wondered if the legion commanders would be seated near Arvinnius and the governor. After all, he reasoned, Arvinnius owed his success to the legions and to the three men who commanded them. The thought suddenly occurred to him that tonight might well be the occasion when his promotion to general would be announced, the rank he coveted so badly and which Arvinnius thus far denied him. Just as quickly, a sudden chill swept over him. With promotion would be the expectation he would continue to serve as commander of the Sixth Legion. Gone would be any chance of leaving Britannia, possibly for years. The specter of remaining here on the island was simply too awful to contemplate, and he began to make silent promises of lavish sacrifices to every god he could think of if only he would be allowed to leave for Rome.

Since neither the guest of honor or Governor Urbicus was present, he joined a group of officers listening attentively to a tribune newly arrived from Rome and describing Antoninus Pius. If the verbal portrait of the emperor was accurate, he was a paragon of virtue with no use for sycophants. His only problem so far had been his unpopular but eventually successful effort to persuade the senate to proclaim Hadrian a god. According to the narrator, Hadrian's ascendancy to the pantheon of gods was achieved solely on the basis of the emperor's personal popularity which finally overcame Hadrian's many detractors. Querinius wondered how well he would fare in an environment of such virtue.

A sudden trumpet blast announced the arrival of Governor Urbicus accompanied by General Arvinnius whose grim expression was in sharp contrast to that of the serene-faced governor. A third man followed behind Arvinnius. Younger, and with an autocratic bearing, the individual regarded the crowded hall with a calm, self-satisfied expression. The whispered conversations around Querinius indicated no one knew who the third man was. The last note of the trumpet faded, and Urbicus began to speak.

"I give you greetings and extend my welcome on this most auspicious occasion to honor one who has earned my gratitude and the appreciation of our emperor. General Labinius Sulla Arvinnius has led three legions in a masterful and ultimately successful campaign to expand the empire in Britannia. The emperor praises General Arvinnius for his careful planning and bold execution of the advance and consolidation of the new frontier. General Arvinnius, you have earned the admiration of Rome, and they clamor for your presence so that they, too, may honor you as well. For that reason, I am pleased to announce Emperor Antoninus Pius has recalled you to Rome where he will personally reward you for the victory you have given him and the empire."

The cheers were loud and boisterous. Querinius thought the purpose of the noisy reaction to the announcement was more to do with the thought of Arvinnius's departure than praise and admiration for the emperor's recognition. The reason for the contrasting expressions on the faces of Urbicus and Arvinnius was now apparent. Urbicus was probably just as happy Arvinnius was leaving Britannia as Arvinnius was displeased at the prospect. Why Arvinnius would react unfavorably to a triumphant return to Rome and an opportunity to bask in the favor of the emperor was curious. He did not pay attention to the governor's last comments as he considered whether the news of the general's return to Rome was beneficial or prejudicial to his own chances of leaving.

"And now it is my great pleasure to introduce General Titus Marius Felix who by personal direction of the emperor will assume command of the Sixth Legion, *Victrix*."

The announcement was met with approving cheers slightly more muted than those accompanying the news concerning Arvinnius; however, the reaction was sufficiently loud to convey respectful approval. Querinius went numb from shock. The public announcement he was about to be replaced without the benefit of any advance knowledge was humiliating. He struggled to keep his face expressionless and restrained the impulse to leave the hall as quickly as possible to escape the smug looks that he imagined he would be subjected to. Had Querinius bothered to look around, he might have been even more disappointed to find he was not attracting any attention at all. The rest of the governor's comments lauding the credentials of General Felix were lost on Querinius as his mind began to re-examine the possibilities before him. Apart from the embarrassment of having no idea he was to be replaced as commander of the Sixth, he began to rationalize there was no longer any reason for him to remain in Britannia. In fact, the arrival of General Felix now made it more likely his request would meet with approval. He grew impatient waiting for the governor to finish speaking. He did not want to wait a moment longer to broach the idea of his own departure under the pretext of congratulating both generals on their good fortune.

It was much later before the circle of officers surrounding the three men began to thin and Querinius was able make his way to General Arvinnius.

"General Arvinnius, my congratulations to you for your good fortune," Querinius said when he finally caught the attention of the hawk-faced general standing apart from Felix and Urbicus.

"Ah, Querinius, there you are. It seems we've both been taken unaware. Until General Felix arrived this morning, I had no idea I was leaving or that you were to be replaced."

"Still, for you to be honored by the emperor is high praise," Querinius replied with an ingratiating smile.

"The emperor's praise is no more than a fart in the wind. To be sure, he will present me with some bauble and a minor estate somewhere in an obscure province where I will never go. I'll be publically and briefly acknowledged at the games after which I will be dismissed and soon forgotten. In the end, that will be the extent of my reward for the Britannian victory. I'm told I will be denied the triumph I deserve while Urbicus sitting on his ass in Londinium gets the credit for what we did here."

The bitterness in Arvinnius's voice was evident and should have been a warning for Querinius to postpone his request. But intent as he was on his own purpose, he failed to appreciate fully the general's dour mood.

"General Arvinnius, since I am to turn command of the Sixth over to General Felix, perhaps it's time I, too, returned to Rome. If you would intercede with Governor Urbicus on my behalf for permission to leave Britannia, I can claim my seat in the senate."

Arvinnius gave Querinius a sharp look, and when he responded, his irritation was obvious. "So, Querinius, it's as I always suspected. You have a taste for the idleness of Rome over the rigors of field duty. I find it strange you wish to go to Rome while I prefer remaining here." Arvinnius paused and a calculating look glittered in his deep-set eyes. "I may be in a position to help you, but there is some unfinished business you must attend to before I advance your petition. I'll see you are permitted to return to Rome as soon as I'm told the traitor Marcus Arrius has been executed."

"But, General Arvinnius, as I will no longer have command of the Sixth, I have no authority and no legionaries with which to pursue

Arrius." It was the only thing he could think of to say for an excuse short of refusing the offer. He dreaded the idea of a prolonged campaign possibly deep in the mountains where the tribes would have an advantage.

"Tribune, you almost persuade me you're not eager to undertake the task. Were I to ask any of the senior officers, they would consider finding and killing the traitor a great honor."

Arvinnius's tone of voice and words were sufficient to end any further attempt to refuse the mission unless he was willing to accept the consequences of a failed career. "Of course, I look forward to the task. I was merely pointing out the practical matter of no longer having any legionaries to command."

Waiving his hand impatiently, Arvinnius dismissed the concern. "Nonsense, I still command here in Britannia, and I intend to take my time in leaving. You will have the legionaries you need. I think a cohort should do. I'm certain they will be eager enough to go and find the bastard if only to be spared the toil of working on the emperor's worthless wall."

Querinius was almost as appalled at the General's disparaging comment concerning the wall as he was at the prospect of being given such a small contingent. He quickly responded. "I think three possibly four cohorts will be necessary to accomplish what you ask. I've no doubt it will take time and great effort to locate and capture him in the mountainous region where he is presumably hiding. General, I must insist on a larger force."

Arvinnius considered the request thoughtfully before responding. "Perhaps you're right. I'll see to it that you also have cavalry as well. A force any larger will merely slow your movements and reduce the opportunity of finding Arrius. I think you should concentrate on how to encourage the tribes to aid you rather than using hostile means. Now then, Tribune, I see no reason to delay. The sooner you depart and find Arrius, the closer you get to Rome. I'll have your orders prepared and ready for you in the morning."

Arvinnius ended further discussion by abruptly turning away to join General Felix talking to a cluster of officers eager to make themselves known to the new commander. He reflected on the assignment he had given Querinius and speculated on the chances of the tribune's success. He thought it unlikely Arrius would be captured or that Querinius would survive the attempt, and yet the matter of Arrius represented unfinished business. He hated the idea of leaving Britannia without the matter of Arrius being resolved. Even if Querinius managed to come back with the former praefectus, he wouldn't be here to receive him. He had already decided under the circumstances there was no reason to delay his departure as he so intimated to Querinius. The island now seemed far too small to accommodate both him and Urbicus. It was better to leave now when it would appear to be his decision rather than suffer the humiliation of waiting until Urbicus told him to go. There was another reason to get back to Rome. The thought suddenly occurred to him, he might be in a better position to influence his future by being in Rome close to the emperor than remaining in the far reaches of the empire. After all, perhaps the gods were smiling and about to give him possibilities he would otherwise not have if he remained in Britannia.

Chapter 19

After leaving the Vocamagi lands and traveling west, Arrius was dismayed to find the terrain was quickly becoming increasingly more difficult to negotiate than any so far encountered. During the first day and into the next, they crossed a series of mountain ridges separated by narrow valleys with some no wider than a ravine and defined by treeless slopes far too steep for mounted passage. It was no wonder the northern tribes had so few horses. In the rugged mountains they crossed, horses were more an impediment than an asset. Frequently, there was no alternative but to accept the reality of long, time-consuming detours to avoid places where even foot travel would have been daunting. To the north and now quite close were the tall peaks he saw at a distance from the isthmus where the new wall was being constructed. Now there were only traces of snow left on the highest rocky crags.

There was little sign of habitation apart from isolated family homesteads consisting of one or two round dwellings constructed of stone and roofed with straw thatch. The inhabitants had fled in haste leaving behind hearths still warm and sheep browsing on the grassy hillsides. Finding the Caledoni was proving to be more difficult than expected. At the end of the third day, Arrius concluded it was time to abandon the effort and begin heading south the next morning.

Just as darkness began to envelop them, Arrius heard a soft thud and saw the quivering shaft of a spear appear without warning a few feet from the small fire flickering in the center of the campsite. He stood up with his sword half drawn before Cuileán restrained him.

"No, Arrius, I think the Caledoni only want to talk. If they wanted to kill us, we would already be dead."

"What if you're wrong?"

"Then you won't have long to worry about it," the Selgovan replied calmly as he tossed several pieces of wood on the fire to build the flames higher.

Reluctantly, Arrius thrust the sword back into the scabbard and waited to see what would happen next, expecting at any moment a volley of spears and arrows would come hurtling at them from the surrounding blackness. With the fire once again burning brightly, the campsite was fully illuminated. The men showed no sign of alarm although he noted each man was alert with his weapons close at hand. Apart from the muted crackling of the fire and the occasional clomp of hooves from the direction of the tethered horses, there were no sounds until a voice from somewhere beyond the edge of the firelight broke the silence. Whatever the invisible speaker said was unintelligible to Arrius, but evidently not to Cuileán who replied tersely in the same guttural language. A moment later, a tall bearded man dressed in leather breeches and knee-length woolen tunic emerged from the shadows and walked calmly into the light of the campfire and retrieved the spear. He carried a small shield of animal hide; a sword on his back easily twice the length of a Roman gladius was secured under the hilt by a wide leather baldric belted diagonally across his bare chest. A narrow leather headband restrained the shock of unruly black hair hanging past his shoulders.

In an undertone to Cuileán, Arrius said, "He's either foolish or brave to come here alone."

Cuileán apparently translated some version of the remark for the man's mouth curved in a humorless smile. The visitor turned to Cuileán and spoke, but before the clan chief finished translating, the man struck his spear shaft several times on the side of his shield. From all around the camp, there was a similar response that increased in tempo until it rolled like thunder through the surrounding mountains.

While still looking at Arrius, he spoke briefly to Cuileán.

"His name is Urthaile, and he is a clan chief of the Caledoni. He's been sent by Bericus, King of the Caledoni, to learn who we are and why we are here. He also thinks you are more foolish than he is for coming here with so few warriors while he has many."

Cuileán and Urthaile then engaged in a lengthy exchange during which Urthaile occasionally glanced at Arrius with interest. Eventually, Cuileán turned to Arrius and summarized the conversation.

"I told him about the Roman invasion and explained why we came. Urthaile is pleased to hear of Vadrex's death and praises you for causing it although he does not believe Gelchar will do anything to improve relations between the two tribes. He does not fear the

196

Romans and says he does not think they will come here. If they do, they will not defeat the Caledoni. He says they know the mountains, and the Romans do not."

"Ask him if the Caledoni will let the Selgovi live here in peace."

Once again Cuileán addressed the Caledonian. During the course of the conversation, Arrius was dismayed to see Urthaile frown and shake his head.

"Urthaile says the Selgovi will have difficulty living here, not so much because of the Caledoni, but rather he thinks we will not find the high country an easy place to live. He advises south of here is a more suitable place where the Romans used to have a large fort. He thinks it is far enough away to keep a safe distance between the Caledoni and the Selgovi. Urthaile says if we remain there and do not come into the mountains except to trade, he thinks Bericus will leave us alone as long as the Selgovi do not make trouble."

"Ask him if we settle near the Roman fort, will there be peace between the two tribes?"

Urthaile directed his attention to Arrius as Cuileán spoke. When the Caledonian slowly shook his head and smiled sardonically, he knew he wasn't going to get the answer he wanted.

"He says he does not have the authority to make peace; however, if the Selgovi are willing to join him in attacking the Vocamagi then Bericus may be more inclined to have a favorable opinion of the Selgovi and be willing to talk of peace."

Arrius frowned. "He must tell Bericus the Selgovi will not fight either the Vocamagi or the Caledoni unless they are hostile to us. We are at war with the Romans and for now, that is enough."

After acknowledging the reply with a curt nod, Urthaile turned and without a backward glance strode away into the darkness. The next morning, there was no trace of the Caledonians.

A few tortuous days later, on a bluff overlooking a wide river below, Arrius scanned the familiar outline of the low rectangular-shaped berms and partially filled-in ditches and knew he was looking at the remains of the Roman fort Urthaile had mentioned. From its large size, he realized this was no small outpost and surmised he was looking at what once was large enough to accommodate a legion.

There was an unnerving stillness and desolation about the ruins that seemed to have an unsettling effect on both the Selgovi and the horses which snorted and stamped nervously. He thought from its size and location this far north, it must be *Pinnata Castra* built by the Twentieth Legion following Agricola's defeat of the mountain tribes. That the fort had been razed and abandoned soon after it was completed was silent evidence of Rome's inability to maintain a tenuous foothold in the highland mountains in spite of Agricola's overwhelming victory at *Mons Graupius* presumably not far from where the fort once stood. Arrius thought Urthaile's reason to believe the Caledoni had little to fear from a Roman invasion was justifiable. Nothing had really changed in the more than seven decades since the Roman invasion of Caledonia. The native tribes were still unable to defeat the Roman Army in battle, but it was also true Rome would never truly pacify the Britannian tribes unless Rome decided to double or triple the number of legions now occupying the island. He hoped for the future of the Selgovi and his son that day would never come. He took a last look around and was struck by the stillness of the place. Where once a beehive of activity existed, there was only the sound of the wind rustling the tall grass covering the ruins. By the time they made their way down the bluff and across the river, he had already dismissed using the site for the Selgovan capital; it was too much a part of the past, and a future was what the Selgovi needed to secure.

A day later after breaking camp, Arrius agreed with Cuileán's proposal to press on the rest of the day and that night in expectation of reaching the main Selgovan camp the next day. Except for brief stops to rest the horses, their progress was fast except where the steep terrain obliged them to dismount and lead the horses. He marveled at the cat-like ability of the Selgovi to travel confidently and silently at night. The only sounds of their movement were those made by the horses or an occasional dislodged stone rattling down a rocky hillside. By contrast, the Roman Army preferred day patrols and generally avoided moving at night except where extreme necessity dictated. Then such travel depended on open terrain or a well-constructed road.

It was with a collective sigh of relief they finally crested a hill shortly after daybreak and came upon a Selgovan patrol that informed them the main encampment was but a few hills farther on.

When they reached the camp in a narrow, tree-studded valley, Arrius was surprised to find that it was much smaller than the last time he saw it. He noted with approval horse patrols were maintaining a watchful presence on the surrounding hillsides. He saw Ilya's large tent and made directly for it. She was talking to Athdara and Decrius with her back to him. It was Athdara who said something to Ilya; she quickly turned around and began running toward him. He was barely dismounted before Ilya reached him. Entirely oblivious of the amused laughter and ribald comments from those observing nearby, she threw her arms around his neck and kissed him passionately. He ignored the pain as her arm pressed down on his shoulder, not wishing to interrupt the pleasure of her tight embrace.

Inside the tent a short time later with Ilya listening attentively, he recounted all that occurred during his journey. He omitted his role in Vadrex's death saying only that he was slain by his own men apparently as a result of a power struggle. She gave him a suspicious look over the cryptic explanation of the Vocamagi leaders's demise then eyed the stain on the left shoulder of his tunic. When he finished, Ilya's relief was clearly evident as she commented thoughtfully, "If we have peace with the Vacomagi and the Caledoni then we have reduced the number of tribes we may yet have to fight."

"Only if we do not attempt to locate within their lands three or four days march from here."

"Then it seems we've come far enough. I'll inform the clan chiefs who are here to begin claiming their holdings. It's late in the planting season, and already there is concern we will have a difficult winter ahead if the crops are small or worse if there are no crops at all. For that reason, some of the clans decided to remain in the lower valleys and begin building their villages where the horse herds have ample forage. Tearlach who has been to see Bothan said—," Ilya stopped in mid-sentence when she realized Arrius was asleep.

Arrius awakened some time later to find his left shoulder throbbing painfully. He probed it gingerly and decided it was time Athdara took a look at the wound. He heard Ilya and Decrius talking quietly outside the tent. "Marcus needs to know what the Romans are doing," he heard Decrius insist.

"True, but he's exhausted and needs sleep. There's time enough to tell him what's happened."

He sat up and called out, "What is it I should know?"

The conversation outside abruptly stopped, and a moment later, Ilya and Decrius entered the tent. "Marcus, it's nothing that can't wait until you've rested."

"I've slept enough. Tell me what the Romans are doing now."

After a brief hesitation, she said, "So far there's been little change since we last saw you. Their patrols have not ventured very far from where the new wall is being built. For now, the Romans seem to be concentrating their efforts on building the wall and forts."

Arrius waited for Ilya to continue, but she apparently had said all she was going to say. "I think there is more to what Decrius said," he said with an edge to his voice. "It would be best to hear it now as later."

With a resigned look, Ilya turned to Decrius. "All right, you may as well tell him."

"What Ilya told you about the patrols is true, and the fighting, what there has been so far, has been occasional and isolated with no great effort on the part of the Romans to mount any strong attacks on the Selgovi or the Novanti. There is a report from Bothan and confirmed by Tearlach that a Roman column is moving slowly through the valleys. At first, the column was thought to be a trick to lure us into attacking so the legions could destroy both tribes in one final battle. However, there has been no change in the activities of the legions which as Ilya has said continue to be occupied mainly in wall and fort construction. It is also strange that so far the column has avoided battle and instead remains in camp for several days at a time while delegations visit the settlements under a flag of truce before moving on to another camp."

"The Romans want to make peace with the tribes?" Arrius asked.

"Not exactly," Decrius replied and hesitated before adding, "They want you. Tribune Querinius is leading the column and is offering 20,000 denari for you alive and half that amount for you dead. The column consists of the First Cohort of Tungrians under the command of Plinius Flavius, and the Cavalry with him is the Dacian Ala led by Seugethis."

He was stunned. He knew his presence in the north would eventually be known to Arvinnius, but he never imagined the Roman general would go to such extraordinary lengths to capture him much less offer a reward in such a staggering amount. He doubted the money would be a persuasive factor as Roman coinage held no great value with the northern tribesmen except to be melted down to make jewelry or decorate the hilts of their daggers and swords.

"So, Arvinnius thinks to use my former legionaries to capture me, and to think I'm worth so much - why it's a small fortune. Arvinnius must think it's clever to use the Tungrians and Dacians for the purpose. I wager he believes they have more incentive to see my head on a pole. Perhaps he's right at that although I would hope that is not the case for most of them. Still, there are bound to be some in both cohorts who probably do not recall me in the most favorable terms and would throw dice for a chance to settle past scores."

"I don't believe Flavius or Seugethis are pleased with their orders, nor do the centurions who served under you," Decrius said.

"What do the Selgovi think?" Arrius asked, looking pointedly first at Ilya then Decrius.

"The people are puzzled by the offer and do not understand why it has been made," Ilya said.

"The Novanti, what do they say?" addressing the question to Decrius.

"It's difficult to say. Bothan thinks it's a trick and doesn't trust the Romans. I've heard there are some among the Novanti who are interested if by giving you up, it will persuade the Romans to leave them alone until they've had a chance to rebuild their villages and plant their crops."

"Will Bothan keep on fighting?"

Decrius shook his head. "He's having enough trouble keeping his distance from the Epedi who are less hospitable to the Novanti than the Venicones have so far been to the Selgovi. Bothan claims one day he will resume his fight with the Romans, but it will not be soon."

"For the time being, Bothan and I are of similar mind," Ilya said.

"Do not hold Tearlach back because of me and for the reason I once commanded the Tungrians and Dacians."

Ilya shook her head emphatically, "It's already late in the year, and for the time being the tribe must concentrate on preparing for the winter."

"That is a valid reason. I don't want you to decide what is best for the Selgovi based on me."

Ilya's reply was ambiguous, "It depends on the circumstances." He thought it might be best not to pursue what circumstances she might have in mind.

Decrius turned to leave the tent but paused at the entrance and asked, "How is the wound?"

Arrius shot Decrius a meaningful look and hoped Ilya did not notice. He tried to brush the question off with a casual remark. "It's nothing but a scratch."

"What wound?" Ilya asked sharply.

Decrius failed to comprehend Arrius's response. "The one Vadrex gave him. Cuileán says he fought well."

Ilya gave Arrius an accusing look. "I thought you said Vadrex was killed by his men."

Suddenly aware he had broached a sensitive subject, Decrius made a hasty departure.

"It's true, but only after I put my dagger blade in his belly," he replied, sounding defensive.

"Marcus, what am I going to do with you?" she asked rhetorically with a mix of exasperation and concern.

"First, you can come over here and remove your dress, and then much later you may send for Athdara to tend my shoulder."

A slow smile erased Ilya's disapproving expression, and she delayed only long enough to secure the tent flap before slipping off her shift.

Chapter 20

The first night watch had been posted when Flavius approached Tribune Querinius's tent. He was hesitant to tell Querinius what was on his mind expecting it would be a vain attempt to reason with the tribune and another opportunity for the him to make some disparaging comment about the cohort. It was obvious from the time they left the Antonine Wall the tribune held a low opinion of the Tungrians and made little effort to conceal it. He thought it would be a waste of time to speak of his concerns, but his position as commander of the cohort obliged him to try.

The orderly on duty announced him, and Flavius entered the tent. He stood quietly waiting for Querinius to acknowledge his presence. The tribune predictably kept him standing while he took his time reading the tablet he was holding. The petty exercise of rank and position was irritating, but he had come to expect such behavior and endured it with stoic self-control. Eventually, Querinius put the tablet down and acknowledged the centurión's presence with a look of annoyance bordering on resentment at the intrusion.

"Tribune, it's difficult to find any of the tribesmen, and when we do, they run away. Those we've talked with either say they do not know Arrius, or they aren't interested in helping. I believe we're wasting our time."

"Centurion Flavius, I can assure you Emperor Antoninus and General Arvinnius do not care what you think, and if they do not, why by Minerva's nether parts, would you believe I do?"

The stinging retort caused the centurion's face to flush in anger, the knuckles of his hand turned white as he grasped the hilt of his gladius, resisting the impulse to draw it. Nothing would give him greater satisfaction than thrusting it into the tribune's throat.

"But you may have a point at that. If good will and peaceful offers do not influence the barbarians to cooperate then we may have to try something else. Perhaps taking some hostages might be the answer. Yes, I do believe it's worth trying," he said with growing enthusiasm. "Bring me some hostages — 20 or 30 should do. Then spread the word they will be released when Arrius is brought to me either dead or alive but preferably alive. We'll give them a few days then begin executing one hostage each day until Arrius either comes here voluntarily, or he's brought to me."

"I'm not sure that's wise, Tribune. Our numbers are not great, and we would be hard pressed to withstand a major attack if the natives decide to retaliate."

"Nonsense, the scum have been thoroughly subdued. If the barbarians intend further hostilities, we would have been attacked by now. Be careful, Flavius, lest you persuade me you have little stomach for the task. I suggest you begin to look like you're more eager to get the job done than you've shown me so far. Now go and inform Suegethis what I want done."

Flavius clamped his mouth tight to keep from saying anything that might be interpreted as disrespect. He saluted and left without speaking. He had a sinking feeling as he left the tent the cohort was now living on borrowed time. Suegethis would be no more pleased than he was over the new orders. He envied the cavalryman who was fortunate to spend most of the time on patrol and far away from the tribune. In just a few hours after the tribune's arrival at the Tungrian camp, Flavius's poor impression of Querinius formed two years ago was confirmed. Then Querinius had been the senior commander of a campaign that included the Tungrians. The campaign against the Novanti had been singularly unsuccessful, principally because of the inept leadership of the tribune. The Tungrian Cohort suffered heavy casualties because of the tribune's failure to provide timely support when the Novanti attacked. Flavius was badly wounded, and Decrius, his opto at the time, was forced to take over the century. His initial opinion of Querinius had not only been confirmed but continued to sink to new depths. In the seventeen years since taking the sacramentum, Flavius had seen superiors who inspired either profound contempt or hatred, but none managed to achieve both to the extent reached by Tiberias Querinius. The mission alone was distasteful enough without the constant verbal and physical abuse Querinius imposed on the men. He found fault with everything. His requirements for uniform and equipment appearance, normally relaxed in the field for practical considerations, were expected to be maintained as if they were in garrison. After the marching camp was prepared, the legionaries were forced to spend additional time cleaning their equipment for inspection the next morning. The centurions were expected to punish the slightest infraction. On one occasion, Querinius demanded a centurion's twisted vine stick in order to personally administer the *castigato* to a legionary for an infraction slight enough that usually would have merited only a verbal rebuke.

Flavius was more worried over the cohort's plummeting morale than the threat of a native attack. For the first time in over a year, a legionary had deserted early that morning. That the desertion occurred so far from the wall merely emphasized the depth of the problem. The legionary was quickly apprehended by a cavalry section detailed to find him. The tribune did not waste any time in making the deserter an object lesson to discourage any further attempts. The cohort did not resent the *fustuarium* the legionary was to be subjected to. In fact, the century to which the legionary was assigned had expected it and had brought cudgels to the formation to administer the gauntlet. It was the fifty lashes with the *flagula* preceding the cudgeling that was unexpected and drew an undercurrent of protest within the ranks. The flogging virtually guaranteed the legionary would not survive the punishment as occasionally some who suffered the fustuarium managed to do. His back a bloody mess, the legionary managed to stagger only a few steps before he fell and started to crawl the length of the fort to the south gate which if he could reach it alive, he would be allowed to live. It was obvious from the light cudgel blows being given the legionaries were doing their best to see their comrade made it to the gate. Querinius quickly became enraged, interpreting the actions of the legionaries tantamount to mutiny, a conclusion Flavius privately thought was valid. The tribune ordered the legionary's centurion to take matters in hand. Cotta ended the charade with one blow to the legionary's head.

As he walked back to his tent, Flavius was positive there would be additional attempts to desert regardless of what happened that morning. The hostility of the legionaries to the purpose of the patrol was only partly overcome by the promise of a generous *donativum*. Arrius had been widely admired, and they did not relish the task of being responsible for his demise. For that matter, neither did he. Arrius had been instrumental in having Arvinnius appoint him to command the Tungrian Cohort before he left Banna. He thought the chances of success for the current mission from the outset were not good, and he was beginning to think they were becoming even less so each day. Before they started the march, the tribune's promise of a generous reward if the campaign was successful was greeted without any noticeable enthusiasm. Some went so far as to express near mutinous opposition to the task. The most outspoken was Rufus whose rank as optio made him both influential within the cohort and doubly vulnerable should Querinius become aware of some of the things the stocky legionary had been saying.

Flavius should have anticipated Rufus's open opposition. In hindsight, it was a mistake not ordering him to remain behind. The problem was Rufus was one of the best optios in the cohort and due in no small part to Arrius and his capability to turn even the most incorrigible legionary into an asset. Not that Rufus was exactly a model legionary or that he would ever rise to the rank of centurion. His fondness for gambling with the rankers and love of a wine flask provided frequent occasions requiring his centurion to look the other way simply because in the field there was none better. Decrius was the one who told him how Rufus had been responsible for saving Arrius's life in Judaea which explained the tight bond between the two men. He decided it was time to have a private word with Rufus, less out of personal concern for the man's welfare than concern Rufus might further aggravate an already tense situation.

Flavius found a grim-faced Rufus supervising his century as they prepared for inspection the next morning. The silence of the legionaries was ominous enough. This was usually the time after the first night watch was posted when the legionaries were allowed to relax, play dice or talk quietly among themselves.

"Rufus, come with me," Flavius summoned the optio to walk with him out of earshot of the men.

Rufus regarded the centurion's serious face in the light of a flickering torch and decided he was not going to like what the centurion was going to tell him. He wondered if Flavius was going to order him to surrender his knobbed optio staff. As far as centurions went, Flavius was not a bad sort. He knew Flavius could have done more than restrict him or dock his pay for infractions that would have meant demotion or much worse. In fact, he was grateful he hadn't been pulled aside before now. His outspoken reaction to what happened to the deserter caused his own centurion to warn him to be more careful. If the deserter was in his century, he would have refused to have the men carry it out. By and large, he thought he had behaved himself well enough until then. He knew his basic problem was he was still a ranker at heart and tended to view everything from that perspective. He thought he was a good enough optio, but he resented having to order the men to do things he didn't like or that had no purpose. He was beginning to miss the anonymity and comparative freedom of the ranks and thought maybe it would be just as well if he was sent back to them.

Flavius stopped in the shadows and faced Rufus. "I've been hearing too much of what you've been telling the men. I don't suppose it will do any good to tell you to keep your opinions to yourself and your mouth shut except to carry out orders. It was your voice I recognized this afternoon. It was fortunate Tribune Querinius did not, or you would have been in front of the formation, and the flagula would have skinned your back. You're a good optio, but you try my patience." Flavius's irritation was clear from the tone of his voice.

Unable to restrain himself, Rufus blurted out, "What the tribune did was wrong. The man deserved to be punished, but to lash him first wasn't right. He had no chance of making it to the gate."

"Rufus, you've been a legionary longer than I have. What a commander will order has little to do with what's right or wrong. He holds our lives in the palm of his hand and has the authority to do just about anything he wishes. All Querinius has to do is think there is mutinous behavior and those he believes are guilty will be lucky if the lash and cudgel are enough to satisfy him. More likely he will crucify the offenders. It's one thing for you to risk your own position and life, but keep in mind you risk others by encouraging the men to do the same. Even if they don't believe as you do, they will blindly follow your lead and at their peril."

Rufus reluctantly conceded the centurion's point and that he didn't consider the consequences of his actions. He resolved to be more careful in the future.

"Now what have you to say for yourself?"

"Centurion, it isn't just me talking or that resents why we're out here. We know what the tribune intends to do to Arrius if we should find him, and they don't like it. It's one thing to kill Arrius in battle; the gods will have their say there, but I'll have no part in anything Querinius will order us to do to him, and I'm not alone in saying so. If by chance we do find Arrius, we won't bring him back."

"Rufus, you're not listening to me," Flavius said in exasperation. "You and the rest of the cohort, including me, have no choice. Personally, it's my hope we never find Arrius. If we do, then it will be his misfortune. I strongly advise you to reconsider what you've told me and never say anything like that again. The next time I cannot and will not overlook it. I regret what I've said seems not to have any effect in your attitude. I only hope for your sake as well as for those who might be foolish enough to follow you that you'll consider carefully what I've said. I'll not warn you again."

Rufus watched the centurion as he stalked off in the direction of the cavalry camp. He didn't resent what Flavius said and accepted the centurion's comments were true and well-intentioned. Grudgingly, he realized few other officers he'd known would have taken the time to make such a gesture. However, it changed nothing concerning his hatred of Tribune Querinius and widely shared by most other legionaries in the cohort. By the time he finished his recruit training, he had developed and since maintained a universal dislike of all officers. Over the years, there were some exceptions with Arrius among the very few officers who had earned both his loyalty and respect. By contrast, Querinius embodied everything he despised in most officers. His dislike was further compounded by the tribune's single-minded purpose of finding and executing Arrius. He vowed if Querinius succeeded in getting his hands on Arrius, he would see the former praefectus got a clean death with a gladius or a pugio before he would see him subjected to a painful and humiliating execution. What Flavius did not know and would not be told is the patrols that went out looking for Arrius were making no real effort to find him. With a little help from the Tungrian legionaries and the gods, Arrius would remain safe where he was, wherever he might be.

Seugethis slowly combed his fingers through his short but luxuriant beard as he listened impassively while Flavius relayed Querinius's orders. Flavius was unable to tell whether the cavalryman approved or disapproved of the new direction. After a moment of reflective silence, Seugethis commented objectively, "Aye, it makes sense. I never believed the tribes would give up Arrius for Roman coin. Querinius is right. We must give them a better reason, or we'll continue to waste our time as we already have. Sooner or later the tribes will decide we've been here long enough, and one infantry cohort and one cavalry wing will be hard-pressed to resist a major attack. We must have hurt them more than we thought else we would have been attacked by now. I suppose Arvinnius has little care what happens to two auxilia units and thinks if he loses them, it's a small risk to achieve his purpose." Seugethis made the comment without rancor in acceptance of the prevailing Roman perception the auxilia was inferior to regular legionary units.

"Your cavalry will have a better opportunity of rounding up some prisoners than my Tungrians."

"True, although so far I've seen few natives during the last several days, and those we've encountered are too old or too lame to be of much value. The healthy ones are like goats that can quickly climb a steep, rocky slope or disappear into dense forests where my horses cannot follow. We need to increase the number of patrols and go farther north. We're hardly more than a hard day's ride from the wall, and the way we keep traveling east and west, it doesn't appear Querinius intends going any farther," he said with obvious disgust.

Flavius nodded. "I think as concerned as Querinius is with his own personal safety, he'll not venture farther, nor will he allow more than one infantry century at a time to leave the camp as he requires now. Any chance of taking hostages will be mainly up to your cavalry."

"You're probably right even though I believe there is still little or no chance in capturing Arrius. I wager if he's alive, he's far enough away Querinius will never find him, and I'll sacrifice to Zalmoxis the tribune never does."

"That's my hope as well," Flavius said, causing Suegethis to look sharply at the centurion.

"What do you mean?"

"Frankly, I care not if we ever find Arrius. I've no stomach for this campaign and neither do the men. I believe my Tungrians are on the verge of mutiny, and it wouldn't take much to push them over the edge. They resent Querinius as much as they still admire Arrius, and the tribune continues to make it worse each day." After making the comment, Flavius thought he sounded much like Rufus.

"Have a care Querinius doesn't learn of your sentiments," Suegethis cautioned. "You have the worst of it, Flavius, and I do not envy you for it. At least I am able to mount my horse each day and ride away while you're always within his reach."

"Don't you have reservations for why we are here?"

The cavalryman replied neutrally, "It's not for me to judge. I have my orders and will obey them, and whether I like them is not something I intend to dwell upon. I, too, have respect for Arrius and don't believe he has done wrong by choosing to live with the Selgovi. But if I see him with a sword in his hand leading tribesmen against my cavalrymen, I'll cut him down as fast as I would swat a fly and with no more concern. Now, if the gods were to ask me, I would tell them to keep Arrius far away from my sword. In the meantime, I'll do what I can to locate and capture him." The forceful way he spoke and the hard glint in his eye left little doubt in Flavius's mind Suegethis meant what he said.

Arrius was encouraged by how quickly the swelling in his shoulder went down. The angry-looking flesh around the wound noticeably improved each day thanks to Athdara's careful attention.

Feeling useless while the Selgovi were busy constructing dwellings and clearing fields in preparation for planting, he resolved to do something about it. Ignoring Ilya's protest that it was too soon to ride, he left with Decrius ostensibly to visit the settlements of those clans that remained farther south of the main settlement. He assured her they would be gone only a few days.

After several hours, they paused briefly to give the horses a rest. The two men exchanged only a few words. Since Decrius was naturally reticent, he didn't attach any significance to the man's silence. He was about to ask Decrius what was bothering him when the Brigantian spoke first. "Arrius, if we are looking for the other clan villages, we won't find them in this direction."

"True if that's what I intend, but it isn't. I'm looking for Tearlach to see for myself if Flavius and Suegethis give any indication of coming farther north. There is still the possibility Bothan is right that the real purpose of such a small force is to lure the tribes south to attack it, much like what happened to the *Deiotariana* in the Sorek Valley. We were the bait, and if the legion was sacrificed, I suppose it was a small price for Hadrian to win the Judaean war. Arvinnius has successfully pushed the tribes north, but he's hardly achieved a lasting peace. Until he thinks he has, I believe he will continue to look for a way to achieve a decisive victory. Tearlach is impulsive, and I'm concerned he won't resist the temptation to attack."

"There have been no reports the legions are preparing to take to the field."

"It doesn't require much time for a legion to march, and if the information we have is accurate, Flavius and Suegethis may be remaining close to the wall for a reason. There is also the thousand-man cavalry ala commanded by Gaius Cornelius. In all probability, it remains positioned on the left flank so it can move quickly to join the battle and protect their western flank."

Decrius reached up and massaged his neck before saying, "I hope you're wrong."

Arrius turned to Decrius, his surprise evident. "What do you mean? I imagined you would be pleased at the prospect of a battle."

Decrius frowned. "I've other things to occupy my mind, and I think I have seen enough fighting for now."

Completely mystified at the sudden change in the former centurion, he asked, "Is it because we may have to face the Tungrians and Dacian cavalry?"

"That is certainly part of it. I've no wish to fight men who are not Roman and particularly those I once served with. That alone, however, is not the main reason. There's a woman back at the camp that I will take to wife. Her husband was killed, and she has small children. It will not be the same as it was with Iseult, but we get along well enough, and the children have taken to me. Perhaps it isn't too late to make a new life instead of finding more Romans to kill because of what they did to Rialus and Iseult."

Arrius responded sympathetically. "Perhaps you understood better than the others why I left Banna and came to Caledonia."

Decrius inclined his head in acknowledgement. "It's true. I had Iseult and Rialus then, and that made it clear enough to me why you left and would not be coming back. You would have surprised me only if you had not."

After a moment of thoughtful silence, Arrius stopped and faced Decrius. "My friend, I think it would be better for you to go back to your woman. I can get along well enough until I find Tearlach."

"If you run into one of Querinius's patrols, you'll have no chance."

"Will it make such a difference if you're with me? I don't believe the Tungrian or Dacian patrols are likely to come farther than they have, and I'll have Tearlach and his men to see I come to no harm. I'll probably find Tearlach tomorrow or the next day." Decrius's hesitation was enough to convince him of the Brigantian's true preference. He added the final inducement. "By returning, you can tell Ilya where I'll be in case she wonders why I haven't shown up at any of the villages."

Decrius smiled uncertainly and said, "I think Ilya will not be overly pleased I left you."

Arrius laughed. "No doubt she'll be even more displeased with me. Now go and think no more of it."

With a grateful look, Decrius mounted his horse and headed back in the direction of the main Selgovan settlement.

Still mounted, Seugethis watched impassively as the cavalrymen finished herding the villagers together. Until now, his patrols had managed to capture only a few men fit enough to survive what was in store for them. Most of the natives they found so far were too old, too infirm, or too young. They needed healthy men whose loss to their villages would provide more incentive to give up Arrius. After many days of sweeping the countryside, the early morning raid had caught the sleeping village completely unprepared. Resistance was brief and ineffectual, and the final tally was enough captives to serve the tribune's purpose.

Only the young children showed distress, wailing hysterically as they huddled together and clutched their mothers pathetically. Carefully observing the reactions of the men, Seugethis had already decided which captives he intended to take. He would select the men with hatred in their eyes and who held their heads high in defiance. Such men were the ones most likely to hold out the longest. Since it would require time for word of what was being done to circulate, he wanted hostages with the will to resist and possibly survive although he suspected Querinius had no intention of allowing any of the captives to go free even if Arrius was handed over.

Seugethis urged his horse forward toward the circle of captives and pointed to the ones he intended to take. When fifteen men of various ages had been segregated from the rest, Seugethis called out to one of the cavalrymen using the point of his sword to quicken the pace of a tall, lean tribesman with a bloody head wound.

"Comigius, ask that man what tribe they belong to."

The cavalryman nodded and spoke rapidly and incomprehensibly in one of the native tongues to the man he had just pushed into the growing circle of captives. Ignoring Comigius, the man responded directly to Suegethis.

"We are Novanti," the man replied calmly in Latin. Suegethis was impressed with the man's quiet but commanding presence and wondered if by any chance he was one of the Novanti leaders.

"What's your name, and are you the leader of these people?"

"My name is Crixtacus, and I am their clan chief."

"Good, then translate what I say. Tell your people they will not be harmed. I regret those who were killed and do not wish to see anymore needless deaths."

"Why, because there are now fewer of us to sell on the slave market? My people would prefer death to becoming a Roman slave."

"We are not looking for slaves. We will take you and these men as hostages. They will be released unharmed in exchange for the Roman Marcus Arrius who has been proclaimed an enemy of Rome. Do you know of this man?"

"I know him. You will not find him here with the Novanti. If that is the man you seek then it is among the Selgovi you should look. The Selgovi will not give up Arrius for Novanti warriors, nor would we do the same if Arrius were living with the Novanti and you took Selgovan hostages."

Seugethis silently wondered if Querinius had considered the point Crixtacus just made or merely assumed the tribes would be willing to turn over a Roman to save any tribesmen regardless of tribal membership. Well, it was a point past considering now, he reflected. He thought from the beginning the entire effort had little chance of success, and by the time Querinius realized it, these men would all be dead with Arrius far away somewhere in the mountains – that is if Arrius was still alive.

"Those I leave behind must tell the rest of the Novanti and Selgovi what we want. We will wait long enough to ensure the tribes have heard our request then each day Arrius has not been turned over will see the death of one hostage. I can assure you their deaths will not be quick or painless. Now, tell your people what I've said."

"Roman, you may as well kill us now and be done with it. You'll not get Arrius this way."

"I'm no Roman. I'm a Dacian not a Roman. Now tell your people what I said."

"You're nothing more than a Roman lapdog," Crixtacus said contemptuously, "and fit only to kneel at the feet of the Romans."

"Have a care what you say, or I may make an example of what will happen to the rest of your people if Arrius is not given up."

As Crixtacus translated, Seugethis considered the merits of doing exactly as he threatened Crixtacus. An object lesson may be more convincing than words. Just as quickly he dismissed the idea not out of compassion but rather because he thought it would achieve nothing. Let the fate of these men, and Arrius for that matter, be on Querinius's head. It was beneath the dignity of a Dacian warrior to play the role of executioner. As they left the village, he reflected on Crixtacus's accusation of him being a Roman lapdog. The remark pricked his conscience. He thought it strange Arrius had never made him feel that way, yet in only a brief time around Tiberias Querinius, he wondered if Crixtacus might be right.

Chapter 21

Tearlach listened carefully and without comment while Bothan related Crixtacus's fate and the Roman demands.

The two men sat on low stools in front of a smoldering fire while around them the construction of the principal Novanti village was already nearing completion. The outer stockade was finished with only the great hall left to be constructed. Despite the bustling activity around them, Tearlach thought there was an air of defeat pervading the encampment and further emphasized by the dour expressions on the faces of men and women alike. It was obvious the displacement of the tribe along with the casualties suffered had taken a toll on the survivors.

So far, Bothan made no direct request to hand over Arrius to secure the release of the hostages, and for his part, Tearlach consciously avoided any hint he would entertain the idea. Still, there was no mistaking the implied notion the exchange of one Roman for fifteen Novanti hostages would be considered a significant step toward a more lasting peace between the two tribes. It was a ticklish situation and demanded care on the part of Tearlach to avoid a direct refusal that would strain an otherwise tenuous peace between the two tribes. Bothan could not ask without making it look as if the Novanti were too weak to resolve the matter without depending on outside assistance. Tearlach had to be careful that nothing he said would be construed as willingness to comply with the Roman demand. If the situation were reversed, the same dilemma would be posed for the Selgovi. As long as Ilya was queen, Arrius was safe with the Selgovi. Even if Arrius was not her husband, he doubted it would change anything. Arrius's defeat of Vadrex at great personal risk to himself was reason enough to protect the Roman. He had gained the Selgovi peace with a tribe that made settling in the north much less risky than it might have been. Tearlach marveled he had lived long enough to hold a Roman in such high regard.

"The Selgovi will provide warriors if you plan to attack the Romans," Tearlach volunteered when Bothan finished speaking.

Bothan grunted and took another long pull from the flagon he clutched in a hand that was noticeably shaking. Tearlach was shocked to see Bothan's diminished physical condition. There was a gray pallor to his face, and the loose folds of flesh on his neck and bare arms sagged. There was no sign of the fire in his eye which made him dangerously unpredictable. The rumor he had been badly wounded was evidently true and the lines of pain etched on his cheeks gave evidence of his discomfort. Reduced to a shadow of his former self, the once loud and robust man now looked as if Cernunnos would soon call him to the next world.

"Good," Bothan wheezed in a phlegm-choked voice. "I need as many warriors as you can give me. Our losses from the Romans were great, and if that was not bad enough, the Epedi have not been friendly. The bastards continue to attack my people and show no signs they're willing to make peace. One day I may take almost as much pleasure in killing Epedi as I do Romans. Unfortunately, my losses are such I am sore pressed to fight either. I have fewer than three thousand warriors still able to fight."

Tearlach tried not to show his surprise at the number Bothan mentioned. In comparison to Novanti casualties, Selgovan losses were far less. He wondered if the Novanti leader was purposely misleading him in a ploy to get more help from the Selgovi. He was about to offer half the number of warriors Bothan announced but reasoned if Bothan was speaking truthfully, their combined strength was inadequate for a successful attack on the Roman camp. Considering Bothan's physical deterioration and downcast manner, Tearlach suspected Bothan was not exaggerating his losses.

"With the small number of warriors our tribes have to fight the Romans, we cannot hope to defeat them," Tearlach said pragmatically. "Perhaps you should consider seeking a truce in return for the hostages," he offered without conviction.

"You mean crawl to the Romans on my belly like a whining dog and beg them to release my warriors on the promise I'll be a peaceful neighbor. I'll fight them until I can no longer hold a sword." Tearlach silently wondered if that day had already come. Suddenly Bothan called out to one of his wives hovering nearby, "Find Neacal and tell him to come here!" Turning back to Tearlach, Bothan said in a voice that sounded firm and resolute, "I'll play the same game as the

216

Romans. If I don't have enough warriors to fight the Romans, I still have enough to catch a few. I'll offer to trade one Roman for one of my warriors, and for any of my warriors they kill, I'll send them two Roman heads."

Under the circumstances, Tearlach considered the plan the only practical alternative to certain failure if Bothan were to attempt to get the hostages back by force. He was openly supportive of the idea and privately dubious of its success. But he was also relieved the Selgovi would not be directly involved.

Neacal listened to Bothan's proposal with mixed feelings. He had planned to leave the tribe before the Roman advance began. Months ago, and before he knew of the planned Roman invasion, he had offered to give the centurion at Blatobulgium information concerning Bothan's intentions in return for a generous reward and safe passage far to the south. On occasion, he had made good on the offer, but of late, he was beginning to reconsider his original plan in the belief he now had more reason to stay than leave. Bothan was good as dead, and Crixtacus, Bothan's expected successor, had been taken by the Romans. Until now, there was little chance for him to become tribal chief. With two of the senior clan chiefs killed in the recent fighting and Crixtacus a Roman captive, he was now closer to becoming Bothan's successor. From all appearances, Bothan's final breath was not far off. His dilemma was as long as Crixtacus lived, there was almost no chance of leading the tribe. It was equally true if he was unable to secure the hostages' release, it would be seen by Bothan and the other clan chiefs as a major failure. His chance then to be Bothan's successor would no longer be certain.

"Why not give the Romans what they want?" Neacal asked.

"Don't be stupid," Bothan said, face clearly showing impatience. "I would do so if I had Arrius, and the Selgovi were willing; but since I do not, and Ilya is not likely to give him to me, I must resort to other means. That is why I summoned you. Take enough warriors to capture as many Romans as you can. Don't kill any more than you have to. Dead Romans are worth nothing to me. We've been given five days before the first hostage is killed."

"What if I'm unable to find and capture any Romans in that time?" Neacal responded with practical concern.

"Then Crixtacus and the others will suffer for your failure. Do not fail me again, Neacal," referring to the clan chief's failure to kill Beldorach two years before when the Novanti and Selgovi had been bitter enemies. It was only because of the Roman invasion the two tribes agreed to an alliance.

Neacal felt the bile rising in his throat. Bothan never seemed to miss an opportunity to remind him of his failure to kill Beldorach. If he been able to bring Beldorach back to Bothan in chains or at least his head, there never would have been the motivation to deal with the Romans. Many times, he had plotted to kill Bothan in retaliation for the ridicule he was subjected to and the humiliation that seemed never to be forgiven or forgotten. His resentment fed the motivation to approach the Romans. In retrospect, it was a foolish and impulsive act. Once the Roman invasion began, it was too late to hold the Romans to the arrangement, and ever since, he lived with the dread his treachery would somehow be discovered. His plots to kill Bothan also never amounted to anything more than idle fantasies. The cold truth was he was afraid of Bothan. Even now, reduced to a shell of the man he once was, there was an aura of invincibility about Bothan that made him back away from the thought. He refused to admit his own fear was the real obstacle.

"The Selgovi will assist you," Tearlach volunteered.

"You see, Neacal, already your chance for succeeding has improved," Bothan sneered. "See to it you manage to get more Romans than Tearlach. I would not look upon you with great favor if I am left dependent on the Selgovi for getting our warriors back."

Tearlach had never liked Neacal, believing there was something furtive about the man behind his outward bluster; yet he almost felt sorry for him. Bothan seemed to go out of his way to goad the clan chief. He wondered why Neacal was willing to put up with such treatment. Without a word, Neacal stood up and walked away, his stiff bearing clearly showing his anger.

"Have a care, Bothan," Tearlach cautioned. "Most men would have drawn their sword for less than what you said to him," thinking Bothan was hardly in shape to resist if Neacal had done so.

"Neacal would never bare his sword to me. It's no accident Neacal has survived where some of my other clan chiefs did not. Neacal is cautious about preserving his life, and while he could defeat me now, his fear prevents him from trying."

"Why then do you entrust him with getting the hostages back?"

"Because I have no one else. I only wish Neacal was taken instead of Crixtacus. Had it been so, I would have left him to his fate."

"It has been on my mind to choose Crixtacus as my successor. If Crixtacus dies, Neacal will probably replace me. That thought alone may keep me alive a little longer, but my wounds tell me it cannot be for long."

As Tearlach walked to his horse, he thought it was possible the survival of Crixtacus and the other hostages might be more dependent on Selgovan efforts than Novantean. While he was ambivalent concerning the hostages in general, he felt the Selgovi had an obligation to Crixtacus. It was Crixtacus who returned the body of Beldorach intact after he was killed by a Novanti archer. Tearlach was surprised at the gesture. Had he killed Bothan, he would have taken his head for a trophy as was the usual practice among the tribes. More important than repaying a debt was keeping Neacal from becoming tribal leader, but just as quickly he considered the possibility Neacal's weak leadership might well serve Selgovi interests. Crixtacus would be a more formidable adversary when inter-tribal warfare resumed as inevitably it would some day. He smiled and thought Beldorach would agree.

Seething, Neacal was oblivious of anything but his own rage as he rode away from the settlement. He decided before Bothan finished speaking he would do anything to prevent the release of Crixtacus. On the contrary, the sooner the Romans took care of his rival the better. It was unfortunate for the other hostages they would have to die as well, but it was a small enough sacrifice. He would have to take care to make Bothan believe he had done his best and not for lack of trying. If he did manage to capture any Romans, he would make certain they would not be exchanged until after he was certain Crixtacus had already been sent to the other world. The one obstacle was Tearlach. The last thing he needed was for the Selgovan dog to somehow capture enough captives for the exchange and lose the opportunity for the Romans to take care of Crixtacus. If Tearlach was more successful, Bothan would never allow him to forget it.

Standing the distance of a thrown spear from the north entrance to the fort, Rufus observed with a critical eye the two legionaries digging the hole. It would have to be deeper than the usual knee-length because of the rain-soaked ground. It would be disastrous if the cross lying nearby toppled over from the weight of the hostage soon to be nailed to it. He thought the turd of a tribune hardly needed much of a reason to order a flogging, and if the crucifixtion did not go well, those responsible would get no mercy.

It had been five days, and Arrius had not been given up in exchange for the hostages. Candidly, he was pleased at the lack of response and was quite willing to see all the hostages crucified and countless more after that as long as Arrius remained out of Querinius's hands. Rufus felt no sympathy or enmity for the hostage about to endure a painful and prolonged death. He had seen enough men, women and even children executed in the manner the hostage was about to experience to be affected any longer. Without looking back at the fort, he knew the rampart was lined with legionaries grateful for the diversion that would briefly relieve the monotony of field duty. He was close enough to hear the undercurrent of low conversations and even recognized some of the louder voices laughing and making bets on how long it would take the victim to die.

Rufus heard the noise from the fort suddenly increase in volume signaling the execution detail was about to leave the fort. He urged the two legionaries to hurry and finish digging the hole to seat the vertical beam. The last bit of loose soil was no sooner removed from the hole when Rufus heard the measured tread of hobnailed boots behind him. He directed the two men to take their positions on either side of the grounded cross. Although he had carefully explained what the two legionaries were to do, he was still concerned they might balk at the last minute and force him to finish the business. It was one thing to stick a sword or dagger blade in a man's gut but nailing someone to a stake was not for the squeamish.

Rufus turned and watched the detail approach under the impassive but watchful eye of Centurion Septimus Cotta, commander of the third century. Rufus spat contemptuously and considered himself fortunate he was assigned to the first century. The unpopular centurion had a reputation for breaking his vine stick on the backs of his legionaries for little reason. What he had done to the deserter only increased Rufus's dislike of the officer. He wasn't surprised to see Tribune Tiberias Querinius trailing along behind the detail. In truth, he would have been surprised if the tribune was not present. Querinius had been a conspicuous spectator at every punishment detail since the campaign began.

Except for a loin cloth, the hostage striding along in the center of the twelve-man detail was naked, his hands bound behind him. He was young and in the prime of manhood. Oddly, his long hair was neatly plaited at the sides, and his body was relatively clean and free of the mud from the small wooden cage where the hostages were confined. From the unconcerned expression on his face, it was apparent the young man calmly accepted his fate. Rufus did not think he would be so calm when the first nail pierced one of his wrists, and by the time the last nail was pounded through both feet, he would be screaming like all the others he had either seen or helped nail to a cross or convenient tree.

When the centurion ordered the detail to halt, four legionaries grabbed the hostage roughly by the arms and legs and carried him to the cross. Before lowering him with his back to the vertical beam, one of the legionaries sliced through the rope binding his wrists. The hostage made no attempt to resist as the legionaries stretched his arms along the cross beam and brought his legs together on the vertical beam with his knees bent slightly to one side with the right ankle positioned over the left. When the first nail was driven through his left wrist, the prisoner groaned audibly, arching his back in pain but otherwise made no other sound. The stillness was broken only by the metallic sounds of the nail being driven into the wood by the heavy hammer. Rufus was wrong. Other than his labored breathing and an occasional groan, the hostage continued to utter no other sound when the last nail was driven through his right arch and into his left foot. With effort, six legionaries lifted the cross and lowered the vertical shaft into the hole. It was then Rufus realized there was no longer any sound coming from the fort ramparts. The grim face of the centurion mirrored those of the legionaries as the detail marched back to the fort.

While his two legionaries tamped the loose dirt into the hole around the shaft to further secure it, Rufus glanced at Tribune

Querinius who stood looking upward at the hostage with an expression reflecting puzzled disappointment. Rufus spat in disgust already regretting his own participation in the detail. As he marched his two legionaries back to the fort, Rufus wondered why the gods permitted a piece of dung like Querinius to become an officer. He resolved to make one of his infrequent offerings to Jupiter and pray that whatever unpleasant fate the gods might have in mind for the tribune, he would be there to see it.

From his concealment on a low hill opposite the fort, Arrius observed the crucifixtion in progress with detached interest. He was too far away to recognize any of the participants including the victim. The possible exception was the individual standing slightly apart and whose helmet plume and glinting breastplate suggested it might be Tiberius Querinius. He assumed the condemned was a legionary judged guilty of a serious offense. He thought it strange the cohort was not formed up in ranks to witness the execution. That the legionary was suffering death by crucifixtion instead of being subjected to the fustuarium was also unusual.

He heard the faint echo of the hammer hitting the nails and was puzzled when he didn't hear any screams. He recalled Cuileán's outraged reaction weeks ago when they found so many of the Votadini tribesmen nailed to trees. He was surprised then by the clan chief's reaction. and explained such a death was purposely designed to be so heinous as to encourage obedience to Rome and Roman law. At the time, he privately wondered why the death was any worse than what native tribes inflicted on their enemies. Now as he watched the vertical beam thrust in the hole, he was no longer so certain.

Deciding he had seen enough, Arrius carefully made his way down the reverse slope and into the draw where Ferox was tethered.

It had been almost two full days since he parted from Decrius, and so far, he had failed to locate Tearlach. He tacked back and forth expecting any moment to come across Tearlach. He wondered that so far there had been no trace of the Selgovan camp. He assumed the Selgovan was still farther west with the Novanti. Based on that supposition, he would keep traveling in that direction until he found Bothan's settlement. As Ilya intended, he hoped Bothan was concentrating on resettling his people rather than engaging the Tungrians and Dacians.

Arrius coaxed Ferox into an easy trot heading west in the presumed direction of the Novanti camp. As he rode, he thought about his new role as an ally of the Selgovi and the possibility of having to fight Flavius and Suegethis. He would sacrifice to the gods that whatever happened, it would not come to that.

Ignoring the occasional attempts to engage him in conversation, Neacal sat staring morosely into the fire and wondered how much longer he was going to be able to convince his clansmen he was making a serious effort to follow Bothan's orders. If the Roman threat to begin killing the hostages after five days was carried out, the first one would die some time today – possibly it had already happened. He hoped Crixtacus was the first victim. In the days of casting about, he had refused to attack the few Roman patrols they saw on one pretext or another by claiming they were either too large or too close to the fort to risk engaging. His clansmen were openly grumbling at their lack of results. Some were beginning to talk of separating into smaller bands to improve their chances of success. The longer he delayed increased the chance Crixtacus would not be among any survivors if they were able to trade for the remaining hostages. But he also worried about Tearlach. It would be disastrous if Tearlach suddenly showed up with Roman prisoners when his efforts had so far produced none. As much as he hated to do it, the time had come to take a more aggressive approach. If the Romans didn't kill Crixtacus, then he would have to find a way to take care of the clan chief himself.

Neacal's thoughts were interrupted when he heard one of the guards call out that a man on horseback was approaching the camp. He stood up and looked in the direction the guard was pointing. He recognized the large black stallion before he identified the rider, and when he did, he knew Cernunnos had given him the answer to his dilemma.

Ferox's hooves made scarcely any noise in the soft earth of the forest floor as Arrius walked the stallion slowly toward the camp. He was cautious at first in case it might be a Dacian patrol encamped, but after seeing the leather garb and blue-daubed face of the guard, he was reassured and urged the horse on at a brisker pace. He thought at first that he had finally caught up with Tearlach until he recognized the heavy-browed, stocky figure of Neacal standing by the fire. The Novantean's startled look was quickly replaced by a tight, humorless smile. Arrius was uneasy when he didn't see Tearlach or any Selgovan warriors among the men. Neacal gave an order, and Arrius had no time to draw his sword before he was quickly surrounded and pulled roughly from the saddle.

"Do not worry, Roman," Neacal said. "I don't intend to harm you although I admit it would give me great pleasure to take your head. The gods have not been kind to you this day, but mine deserve extra thanks for giving me a solution to a problem that until now I had not even considered possible."

"So, the Romans are no longer such a threat the Novanti now make war on the Selgovi?".

"Not at all. For the time being, there is still an alliance between the Novanti and Selgovi. Of course, that may not continue when Ilya learns we've given you to the Romans."

"Why would you give me to the Romans?" Arrius's hands were being tied firmly behind him. "Does Bothan know of this?"

"He will soon enough, but it will be too late to help you. Even if he did, he would not object as long as he thought the Romans might release Crixtacus and the others in return for you." After seeing the puzzled look on Arrius's face, Neacal added, "Some of our warriors are being held hostage by the Romans. They will be released in return for you; otherwise, one hostage every day will be killed until you are brought in." Arrius realized the individual he saw being crucified was likely one of the Novanti hostages. "Bothan wanted Roman captives to trade for our tribesmen, but unfortunately, we haven't been successful. Now we have a better solution, and the chances for the hostages have improved considerably. By giving you to the Romans, I'll get the credit for getting the hostages back."

"What makes you think the Romans will let you and the hostages go once you turn me over to them?" He saw a flicker of uncertainty flash across Neacal's face. That and the tribesman's slight hesitation showed Neacal had not considered such a possibility.

"Well, we shall see if the Romans intend to keep their bargain. If they do not, the Romans will still have you." Neacal paused.

"However, you have a point. I'll send word to Bothan and offer him the honor of taking you to the Romans just in case there is treachery. It appears you will have a little longer to live since Bothan cannot reach us before tomorrow."

Predictably Ilya was not happy the day Decrius returned and informed her of Arrius's plan to find Tearlach. She refused his offer to return and find Arrius in the belief that by now he had surely found Tearlach. Decrius spent the next few days avoiding her to keep from feeling the guilt that continued to gnaw at his conscience.

When the guard in the watchtower reported seeing horsemen approaching from the south, Ilya was among the first to climb the parapet steps and anxiously scan the distant hills. Decrius was not far behind her. Together they maintained a silent but hopeful vigil the riders who had yet to come into view would include Arrius. It wasn't long before they saw a dozen riders cresting the hill a mile distant from the settlement. Even though they were too far away to identify the riders, it was immediately clear Arrius's huge black stallion was not among the horses being ridden.

"I see Tearlach." Ilya nervously grasped the top of the log wall hard enough her knuckles were white.

Decrius had already recognized the diminutive warrior in the lead but made no reply as he continued to stare intently at the oncoming horsemen. The closer the riders came, the more he was filled with forboding that whatever Tearlach said would not be what they wanted to hear.

A short time later, Tearlach soberly confirmed their worst fears when he told them Arrius was Bothan's prisoner and would be exchanged for Novanti warriors being held hostage by the Romans.

Tearlach and Decrius argued heatedly to overcome Ilya's reluctance to go after him. Regardless of her despair over Arrius's fate, she was convinced the tribe couldn't afford to risk a rescue that was sure to cost the tribe more casualties and with so little chance of being successful. It took Cuileán's reminder of what Arrius had done to secure the safety of the Selgovi with the northern Caledonian Tribes that finally persuaded her. Cuileán departed immediately to gather warriors from the outlying settlements. Hours later, flanked by Decrius and Tearlach, Ilya rode grim-faced out of the settlement.

Dressed in leather shirt and leggings with streaks of blue paint on her cheeks, there was little to distinguish her from the several hundred or so mounted men riding behind her. By the time they were half way to Bothan's settlement, their number had increased three-fold.

Chapter 22

The ringing sound of metal on metal coming from beyond the walls of the fort was barely audible over the undercurrent of noise made by the legionaries lining the walls and clustered around the gate. So far, Taidhg had yet to cry out. Crixtacus thought Cernunnos would be pleased to welcome such a brave warrior. He had never been concerned about dying but always assumed it would be on a battlefield with a sword in his hand. He wanted to live long enough to take revenge on the men who would degrade a warrior by taking his life in such a depraved manner. Although he couldn't see what was happening, several legionaries took great pleasure in taunting their captives by graphically describing what was in store for them and how many days it would take for them to die. Torture was rare among the tribes and administered only when an offense or act was so reprehensible a quick death was considered insufficient punishment. But tribal execution was never prolonged or carried out to the extremes routinely favored by the Romans.

Despite his plea to be allowed to replace the younger man, he was not only refused but told as a clan chief he would be the last to die. Taidhg accepted his fate calmly and spent the night quietly preparing himself for the ordeal to come. Earlier that morning, the other captives allowed him some of the contents of the water jar to clean the dirt and grime from his hair and body after which two of the men braided the young man's side locks. When the guards finally came for him, Crixtacus was proud of Taidhg's proud bearing as he was led away. The Novanti would show the Roman dogs how a warrior died.

When Taidhg was marched out of the fort, Crixtacus heard the legionaries laughing and jeering. The clamor gradually begun to subside as the execution progressed until now an unusual stillness descended on the fort. Crixtacus saw the tall bearded Dacian who captured them striding past, a thoughtful expression on his face. The Dacian looked toward the wooden cage, and when he saw Crixtacus watching him, the Dacian changed direction and came toward him.

"Crixtacus, your man dies well. I've never seen anyone so treated endure it and remain silent."

"He still lives?"

"Aye, and likely he will for another day, perhaps longer unless his legs are broken."

Crixtacus was horrified and replied bitterly. "Isn't what you've already done enough? Do you also have to break his bones to make him suffer more?"

Seugethis shook his head and explained graphically. "You don't understand, breaking his legs is an act of mercy and will hasten death when his legs are unable to support him. His body will sag, and he will no longer be able to breathe."

"Would a spear or sword not be more merciful?"

"I suppose, but that's not the way the Romans do things."

"You say you are not Roman, and yet you accept what the Romans do. Is it because you are used to being under the Roman boot?"

"Careful, Crixtacus, That's the second time you've insulted me, and by Zalmoxis, it better be the last."

"What will you do to me worse than what the Romans have already done to Taidhg?"

"There's always the possibility you won't be crucified if Arrius is turned over to Tribune Querinius. Then when you are released, my sword may still your insolent tongue."

"I think you won't have that opportunity, Dacian. Although if I'm wrong, you may find I am not so easily killed when I have a sword or bow in my hand."

Seugethis regarded Crixtacus with amusement and said, "Well, perhaps not, but I would welcome the opportunity to find out." Then with a quizzical expression asked, "Why do you think Arrius will not be handed over?"

"Since Arrius is the husband of Ilya who is now Queen of the Selgovi, it is unlikely she will give him to your tribune for Novanti hostages."

"I thought Ilya's son was the leader of the Selgovi."

"He was killed in battle soon after the Romans invaded our lands."

"Well, it's still possible Arrius will give himself up."

Crixtacus's reply was pragmatic. "Ilya will prevent that. If he did surrender, I do not think the Romans will give us our freedom so that we can continue to kill more of them," and after a slight pause, added, "and Dacians."

Realizing there was more truth than speculation in the response, Seugethis did not reply and instead walked away and headed toward the corral, thinking this was no way to fight a war. There was no pleasure in this sorry affair, and the gods would not look with favor on his role in it. The tribesman had a disquieting effect on him and raised more doubt in private thoughts already made sensitive by Querinius's actions over the past ten days. He had been ready to return to Dacia when Arrius was still in command of Banna when rumors surfaced of a new revolt in his homeland. Perhaps it was past time to go back, but then he wasn't so sure there was anything left to go back to. Crixtacus may have been more accurate than he realized when he called me a Roman lapdog. The realization put him in a dark and unfamiliar mood. The unsettling quiet that remained in the fort that night only intensified his growing belief they were embarked on a punitive campaign that promised little reward and no glory.

Querinius was livid and shaking with rage. The deed was an act of mutiny. The hostage crucified the day before who should have still been alive for at least another full day or more was already dead, and the cause was obvious. During the night, someone had broken his legs causing almost immediate and merciful asphyxiation. Neither the legionaries a few paces away occupied nailing the second hostage to another cross nor the centurion gave any sign they noticed the man was dead. That alone aroused his suspicions. He was convinced they were all secretly laughing at him. Querinius whirled around and scanned the faces of the legionaries hoping to catch one or more of them smirking behind his back, but he saw only impassive faces staring with disinterest as the first nail was being hammered into the wooden crossbeam. Similar to the day before, this hostage was also unnaturally silent, his groans barely audible over the sound of the hammering.

"Centurion Avitus, come here!"

Startled, the centurion in charge of the execution detail hurried over and stopped a pace in front of Querinius. "Tribune?" the officer responded, face expressionless.

"Do you notice anything unusual about this man?" Querinius asked sarcastically while pointing upward.

The centurion glanced up incuriously at the corpse hanging grotesquely from the crossbeam and saw what he expected to see. "The man is dead, Tribune."

"I know he's dead, you idiot. It's why he's dead that's important. His legs have been broken, and after I gave specific orders I wanted him kept alive as long as possible." The centurion looked again and more closely at the dead man. He saw the bruising and unnatural angle of the lower legs, and his eyes widened in sudden comprehension.

"Do you have any explanation for this?"

"No, Tribune. It must have been one of the native tribesmen who did it sometime during the night," he responded with more hope than conviction. He already had an idea of why the native had been killed even if he did not know who did it. Avitus also suspected it was a way to spite Querinius as much as it was an act of mercy.

The explanation was plausible enough, and for a moment Querinius seemed to consider its merits. "I think not. If it had been natives, the guards would have heard something. Natives would have tried to take him away."

The centurion hesitated before responding, reluctant to disagree. He didn't want to say anything to make things worse than they already were. The tribune's volatile temperament was well established and contributed to a growing opinion among some of the officers the tribune was truly mad. The tribune's wide eyes, spittle-flecked lips and steadily mounting wrath over such a trivial incident was only the latest indication.

"But, Tribune, removing the nails is nearly impossible; therefore, they did the only thing they could do and killed him instead."

"You're wrong, Centurion. I believe it was a legionary who did this. A native would not have known that breaking his legs would have killed him so quickly. No, tribesmen would have used a spear or sword." Avitus silently conceded the tribune's logic. "Who was the officer commanding the guard last night?"

Avitus had the uneasy feeling he was about to be made the scapegoat and braced himself for the worst. "I was, Tribune."

"Then I think you know more about this than you're admitting. I hold you personally responsible for finding out who did this, or by

Jupiter, you'll be joining him," pointing in the direction of the latest victim. "When you're done here, detail four men to remain on guard. The guards will be rotated every four hours through the day and night to make certain this man does not die so easily or so soon. Centurion, you have until the mid-day watch to bring me the man or men responsible for this," once again pointing to the dead man.

Standing before Querinius, his helmet cradled under his left arm, Flavius did his best to speak in a casual, persuasive manner. "Tribune, I respectfully request you drop the matter. What's done is done, and there's little to be gained by pursuing it. The guard is in place at the execution site, and I'm quite certain there will be no more such incidents." Flavius held little expectation his request would be granted, but under the present circumstances, he was willing to do whatever he was able to prevent a bad situation from becoming worse. He knew the tribune was right. There was no question a legionary deliberately hastened the hostages's death. It only took a quick look at the corpse to know the death had been caused by an individual with experience in administering the blows that killed him. He had a good idea of the culprit if not precisely a reason, but the last thing he and the cohort needed was for the culprit to be publicly identified. It would not take much more of the tribune's heavy-handed punishment to incite the men beyond where he would no longer be able to maintain control of the cohort.

"Why should I do that, Centurion? To encourage more defiance of my authority? Do not try my patience, or I may feel compelled to order even more severe measures."

"That would be unwise, Tribune," Flavius replied stiffly, face flushed.

Querinius leaped up knocking over the stool in which he sat and leaned forward, his hands braced on the table between them. "Is that a threat, Centurion?"

"Not at all. It's a warning. I cannot speak for the Dacians, but the Tungrians are already restless enough. It would not take much more to incite them."

"Incite them to what? Are you telling me your men might become mutinous? Flavius, have you ever seen a cohort decimated? If there is so much of a hint of truth in what you say, I'll have every tenth legionary put to the sword. My authority here is absolute, and if it becomes necessary to take drastic measures, then that is exactly what I will do."

Too late, Flavius realized now what he said accomplished nothing to lessen the tribune's anger or demand someone be punished. On the contrary, inferring the men were on the verge of mutiny, although true, made the situation even worse. He was tempted to remind the tribune only legion commanders and more senior generals could order decimation but under the circumstances thought better of it. It was obvious Querinius was beyond reason.

"I mean to have those responsible punished. It will serve as an example of what will be in store for anyone who dares to challenge my orders. If those responsible are not identified, I'll have the officers and guards of each watch last night flogged and put back into the ranks."

"Tribune, I urge you to reconsider. The punishment is inappropriate and unjustly deserved. Besides, there's no proof it was done by a legionary. The distance to the execution site is far enough from the fort that it cannot be ruled out it was the local tribesmen who were responsible."

"Flavius, you waste my time. Now get out and bring me the perpetrator, or by the gods, the watch officers and guards last night will be held accountable!"

With the centurions standing in a semi-circle on one side and Seugethis and the Dacian officers on the other, Flavius observed the three optios filing into the tent. Each of the junior officers had been responsible for one of the watches the night before. Flavius was gambling that by going through the motions of an inquiry that produced no results, he would eventually convince Querinius to relent and allow the incident to fade away after reducing the optios in rank and putting the guards in question on half rations for ten days. If Querinius wasn't satisfied with the punishment, he would undoubtedly be relieved of command; he already concluded such an outcome might be preferable to serving under the tribune.

After briefly summarizing Querinius's conditions, he ended by saying, "therefore, I – we – are facing a dilemma. If I carry out the tribune's order, Centurion Avitus and these three officers along with the legionaries assigned to the guard will be severely punished for dereliction. If I refuse the order, then one of you centurions will replace me as commander of the cohort which alone may not be sufficient to end the matter."

"Only General Arvinnius can replace you since it was by his order you were appointed to command," Avitus said.

"That may be true, but I think with General Arvinnius no longer in command and possibly already departed for Rome, it may be a fine point and one easily overlooked by Tribune Querinius."

"Then whoever is appointed to replace you will refuse to carry out the order as well. He will soon run out of officers," Avitus commented further with a mocking laugh.

"I must warn you all, the tribune intends to make an example of someone, and I'm sure I will be that individual. If one of our legionaries is guilty, it is unlikely anyone is going to admit it, and since I have no intention of seeing these three optios," indicating the three junior officers, "and the guards flogged to satisfy the tribune, I don't expect to be in command soon after I inform him of that fact."

After a moment of silence, Seugethis spoke first. "Centurion Flavius, you and the other officers must refuse to execute an order where there is no proof any offense was committed or the guard details were derelict in their duty. I believe only the local tribesmen had a reason to kill the hostage."

There were murmurs of agreement among the assembled officers. "Seugethis, if we do as you suggest, it will be considered mutiny. While the tribune may not be able to do anything about it now, once we go back to the legion, we will all be charged with mutiny for which we will have no defense."

"It's a long way to the Wall and anything can happen including a most unfortunate accident," Centurion Marcellus Cacidus said followed by an undercurrent of approval.

"Enough of this! I did not call you here to listen to mutinous talk." Rufus who until now was silent tried to interrupt. Flavius silenced him by saying sternly, "Not now, Rufus," and continued, "I have a plan that may satisfy the tribune."

Rufus attempted to intervene again, "But, Centurion Flavius—"

Frowning in annoyance, Flavius cut him off impatiently, a note of urgency in his voice, "Optio, hold your tongue until I give you permission to speak."

Ignoring the warning, Rufus pressed on. "Centurion, I did it."

Total silence greeted the confession. Only Flavius, his expression a mix of resignation and exasperation, was not shocked at the admission. He knew as soon as he had seen the broken legs that it been done by an optio's heavy staff. After learning it was Rufus who commanded the middle watch, it was obvious who had done it. The last thing he wanted or expected was a confession that would force him to take punitive measures. Although one problem may have been solved, punishing the popular optio as Querinius expected him to do was bound to cause the very consequences he was trying to prevent.

"Immortal gods, Rufus, for once why couldn't you just keep your mouth shut?" Flavius said quietly. "Did you not understand why I ordered you not to speak?"

"I thought the native deserved to die faster than the tribune wanted, and I wasn't the only one who thought so. We drew lots, and I won," he added with a pleased smile.

"Don't say another word, or I'll be forced to punish these two as well for conspiring with you. You've already said more than I wanted to hear on the matter. It occurred to me to satisfy the tribune by temporarily breaking all three of you to the ranks until the campaign is over and Querinius is gone. I doubt I can convince Querinius reduction in rank is sufficient punishment now that a confession has been made. Querinius intends to have someone flogged. Rufus, pray to the gods the tribune will be satisfied with a dozen lashes."

"You intend only reduction and a dozen lashes!" Querinius said. "I think not, Centurion. It's no wonder you talk of mutinous behavior. It's quite clear to me leniency is the main cause of poor discipline and mutinous behavior. You will make an example of this man. Only then will the men fully understand the consequences of failing to obey orders. You're too soft, Flavius. Perhaps your position demands more of you than you're able to deliver. Your actions for the duration of this campaign will determine whether you will retain your rank and command of the cohort."

Fuming, Flavius said, "Don't threaten me with demotion. Only a legate can reduce my rank. You can recommend to General Felix or General Arvinnius I be demoted, but that's all you can do."

Querinius's face was drained of all color, and his voice was shaking when he responded. "Do not presume to lecture me on what I can and cannot do. As senior commander in the field, I can relieve you and take direct command of the cohort."

"Tribune Querinius, I strongly advise you not do it."

"Why?"

"The morale of the legionaries is low, and should you take direct command, I fear it will become even worse."

"Are you saying I'm the cause of it?"

Flavius knew he had already said far too much. Antagonizing Querinius further might satisfy his anger of the moment, but Querinius would still win. Unfortunately, his own anger overcame reason.

"Tribune, I've served in three legions, and I've seldom seen authority abused to the extent and as needlessly as you've done. If you see fit to take direct command, I'll leave immediately to make a full report of your conduct to General Arvinnius." Privately he was certain Felix and Arvinnius would support Querinius regardless of how egregious the tribune's behavior; however, he wagered Querinius would not call his bluff. A moment later, he was proven correct.

"I'll not permit you to shirk your responsibility even though I have found your capability to command deficient. Contrary to what you say, I believe you're the one who has undermined my authority. I warn you to curb your tongue or else you will find yourself under arrest when this campaign is over. Now, I order you to give the man two hundred lashes. That should discourage any further defiance of my orders."

"That's a death sentence!" Flavius exclaimed, shocked at the severity of the sentence.

"Possibly, but then it has been your laxity that forces me to prescribe the sentence. It's no wonder you were posted to the auxilia instead of a legion," he added with a contemptuous sneer. "It takes more than you've shown me to succeed in a legion command."

"Tribune, I've warned you, a sentence like that will not be accepted by the men, and I take no responsibility for the consequences."

"If you're too afraid or too squeamish to see the punishment is carried out then speak now, and I'll put Avitus in command."

Only twenty years of disciplined service following the eagle restrained Flavius from drawing his sword. Instead, he left without a word and less concerned over the fate of the optio than the reaction the harsh sentence was bound to cause.

Chapter 23

Astride his horse, Flavius watched with forboding as Tiberius Querinius rode forward and came to a halt several paces in front of him. The two officers were positioned near where Rufus was bound hand and foot to a vertical post in the center of the camp. To witness the punishment, the Tungrian Cohort stood in silent ranks on one side while the Dacian cavalry in dismounted ranks were formed up on the opposite side.

"Announce the punishment, Centurion," Querinius said.

Flavius saluted and called out in a voice loud enough to be heard on both sides of the field. "By order of Tribune Tiberias Querinius, the accused prisoner is ordered to receive two hundred lashes for interfering in the execution of a prisoner."

The Tungrian ranks erupted in an angry roar followed by a thunderous drumming sound as the legionaries pounded vigorously on their shields with dagger hilts. An anonymous voice shouted, "Clemency!" and others quickly took up the cry.

"Silence in the ranks!" Flavius ordered in vain. He glanced at Querinius and noticed the tribune's tightly clenched jaw as he anxiously scanned the ranks of legionaries.

"Do something, Flavius!" Querinius said in a low voice.

"What do you advise, Tribune? I warned you the men would not accept a death sentence for so minor an offense." Flavius was privately gratified to see Querinius was noticeably unsettled by the hostile reaction. The arrogant bastard, he thought. But as much as he would have liked to see Querinius humiliated, he was growing concerned the situation the tribune had caused was rapidly getting out of hand. The Tungrian Cohort was on the verge of degenerating into a leaderless mob. Flavius remembered only too well what could happen if there was a complete breakdown as he had seen in the Ninth Legion. Thankfully, at the time he was not an officer; therefore, he was spared the fate of most of those who had been. He thought whatever happened with the Tungrians, Seugethis would still be able to maintain control over the Dacians, but it was obvious from the futile efforts of his own centurions to regain order the situation was beginning to degenerate even more quickly than he'd anticipated. As the clamor increased in tempo, Flavius decided he dared not wait any longer to act for his own safety and that of the other officers.

Flavius guided his mount closer to Querinius's side and shouted over the noise of banging shields and loud cries, "Reduce the sentence to twenty lashes, or we, and certainly not you, will never leave this field alive!"

"I won't do it. If I show weakness now, in the future they won't obey my orders." Querinius said stubbornly drawing himself up resolutely. "Flavius, I hold you personally responsible for this demonstration."

Realizing it was useless and there was no time left to debate the point, Flavius turned away and walked his horse back and forth the length of the formation, hand raised in a demand for silence. Gradually, the din began to subside enough for Flavius to be heard above the remaining shouts.

"Legionaries, listen to me! Tribune Querinius has heard and agreed to your plea for leniency. He has reduced the sentence to twenty lashes. Return to ranks, or I'll charge those who do not with mutiny, an offense punishable by death. Do as I have ordered, or by Jupiter, I vow you will pay the price for your disobedience. Centurions, reform your centuries and prepare to witness punishment." Prompted by blows from centurion vine sticks and vigorous prods from optios wielding their staffs, the legionaries reassembled in ordered if sullen ranks.

Beneath his cuirass, Flavius felt the sweat rolling down his back as he watched the centurions and optios gradually regain control. When order was finally regained and silence prevailed, he heaved a sigh of relief.

Riding back to Querinius, he said in an undertone, "Tribune, I suggest you try to look as if leniency was your idea."

"I'll see you arrested for the mutionous scum you are just as soon as this campaign is over," Querinius said in a low voice.

"Tribune Querinius, as one of the officers reminded me recently, it's a long way to the Antonine Wall."

"What is that supposed to mean? Are you threatening me?"

"Not at all, but there are many out there," gesturing toward the Tungrian ranks now silent, "who would cast lots for a chance to slice your balls off. In case you don't understand what just happened, they do not like you or what is about to happen to this man," pointing to Rufus. "If I were you, I would take great care to sleep lightly until we get back to the Wall. You may have less to fear from the barbarians than you do from them," Flavius added pointing toward the Tungrian ranks.

Shaking with fury, Querinius's face mirrored his hatred when he said, "How dare you talk to me that way. Have you forgotten I am a Tribunus Laticlavus? I will see you pay dearly for what you've said and done here today. I'll have you charged with sedition just as soon as we get back to the legion."

"Tribune, you've managed to increase the risk to every officer by pushing these men to the brink of mutiny with your pointless orders and excessive punishment you mistakenly confuse with discipline. Because of you, I've been forced to reduce and punish one of my best optios for no reason at all, and the legionaries know this. Regrettably, the only purpose for continuing this foolish charade is to preserve some semblance of your authority as a Roman officer. I strongly advise that until we finish this campaign, you exercise your rank and authority as little as possible. Now, Btorix," addressing the legionnairy holding the *flagrum*, "proceed with the punishment, and I expect you to be extremely careful you do not apply the whip too hard."

Btorix had just completed the final stroke when the sentinel at the fort's north entrance called out a warning. A moment later, an orderly approached Querinius and reported, "There are more than a hundred enemy horsemen standing on a hill to the north of the fort. One of them is holding a sheathed sword above his head. I think it may be a signal they want to talk."

"Very well, inform the Dacian commander and tell him to join me and Centurion Flavius at the north gate. Flavius, have the walls manned in case the barbarians have come here to do more than talk."

Flavius gave the order, and the ranks quickly broke as the legionaries hurried to their assigned defensive positions behind the palisade stakes on top of the earthen walls. Seugethis ordered a turma to be positioned and remain dismounted in proximity to each gate. Within minutes, the garrison was fully prepared for any assault.

As the two officers walked their mounts toward the north gate, Querinius regarded Flavius with a self-satisfied smirk. "If the barbarians intended to fight, they would have brought more warriors. I have a feeling Arrius will soon be our guest, and if I'm wrong, then whoever their leader is will be sorry he didn't bring more men. Seugethis wanted a battle, and I think he's about to get the opportunity."

"What if there are more men waiting behind the hills?" Flavius said.

"You're overly cautious after your bold speech to me. Does the sight of a few tribesmen quicken your bowels, Centurion?"

"Not at all, I merely point out we are outnumbered compared to what the tribes can raise against us. Caution would seem prudent. If they do give you Arrius, it would be best to return to the Antonine Wall as soon as possible."

"Nonsense, we'll do no such thing. I mean to have Arrius and as many native heads as we can carry back to Arvinnius. They will speak for years to come of our great success. Who knows, Flavius, because of what we do here today, you may earn a tribune's crest one day – that is if I choose to overlook your recent actions and words. I can be exceedingly generous if there is reason to be. Do you comprehend at all what I'm saying?"

"I understand," Flaaius responded neutrally. "If I behave and you return glorious to Arvinnius, I'll be forgiven."

"You have the general idea. We'll leave what just happened here in the past and look to the future as wise men should," Querinius added with smug satisfaction as Seugethis joined them at the gate.

"Seugethis, I want you to escort the hostages outside the fort so our visitors can see them. Flavius, you will accompany me and see what they want. If they are here to trade Arrius for the remaining hostages, we'll agree to give them the prisoners when Arrius is delivered to me. Once Arrius is in my custody and within the walls, the cavalry will attack the barbarians including the hostages and kill as many as possible. Seugethis, Flavius is worried there may be more barbarians in the hills beyond. I do not share this belief. But in case he's correct,

I'll leave it to your discretion when to break off the engagement and return to the fort."

Smiling broadly at the prospect of battle, the cavalryman saluted and departed to brief his men.

"Now, Flavius, let us meet our destiny and let all of Rome rejoice over what we accomplish here today."

Flavius needed no further evidence the Tribune was not only delusional but dangerously mad.

Neacal had been right concerning Bothan's wounds. As Arrius watched the Novanti gallop toward the two mounted Romans waiting near the crosses, there was little resemblance to the once virile man he recalled many weeks ago. Bothan was not a competent leader in comparison to Beldorach, but he thought he was by far better than Neacal would ever be. For the sake of the Novanti, their gods better look after Bothan.

The Romans were too far away, and the helmet visors and cheek plates covered too much of their faces to identify who they were. One of the Romans wore the plume of a praefectus or tribune and the other the helmet crest of a centurion. He was certain the centurion was Flavius. Even if it was, it would not matter. Flavius would be obliged to follow orders without regard to any personal feelings. He felt a fleeting regret it would be those he last commanded who would be responsible for ending his life. He hoped Flavius would give him a sword and allow him an honorable death by his own hand rather than be taken back to Arvinnius in chains. He smiled at the irony of having survived so many battles and severe wounds only to be slaughtered in a purposeless death.

Neacal interrupted his thoughts by saying, "You smile, Roman, but I think you will find little humor there," motioning toward the fort. "Perhaps they will put you on one of their crosses. I would enjoy watching the ravens feast on your flesh and hear you beg for someone to finish you."

Arrius tugged in vain at the rope binding his hands securely to the saddle. Strangely, he held no malice for those who would soon execute him, but Neacal was another matter.

"Neacal, I doubt your words would be so bold if I had a sword in my hand," Arrius said as he coaxed Ferox toward the Novantean's smaller horse. With his attention diverted to the tableaux below, Neacal was unaware Arrius had moved so close until he suddenly found himself on the ground from a well-aimed kick that would have unseated Arrius if he had not been tied to the saddle. There were smothered guffaws from the other tribesmen as Neacal jumped up, drew his dagger and made the mistake of running toward Arrius. With no more than a light kick to the horse's ribs, Ferox acted predictably. The stallion surged forward and knocked the clan chief senseless to the ground. One of the tribesmen leaned down and grabbed the reins of the black stallion anticipating their captive was about to bolt. Arrius noticed that none of the tribesmen seemed angry and were apparently content to leave Neacal lying on the ground. He thought their lack of concern was a testament to the clan chief's unpopularity.

Arrius heard a distant shout and saw Bothan make a beckoning motion with a sweep of his arm. Flanked by a tribesman on either side with another in front holding the stallion's reins, he was led down the hill at a slow trot.

As they drew closer to the fort, Arrius looked at its construction with a critical eye. The professional in him was pleased at how well the Tungrians continued to follow his exacting standards. Situated on a low hill, the camp was more elaborate than the typical overnight marching camp and looked as if it had been constructed for a lengthy occupation. The defenses consisted of two ditches instead of the usual one.

By the time they were halfway to the fort, Arrius saw the hostages filing out of the gate in a single line. Their hands were bound behind them and a rope around their necks linked them together. Led by Seugethis, the hostages were being escorted by a double file of mounted Dacians. He was close enough to confirm the centurion was, in fact, Flavius. To his dismay, he saw the individual wearing the red-plumed helmet beside him was Tiberius Querinius. No longer did he believe he would get a quick and easy death.

Seugethis came to a halt beside Flavius at the same time Arrius and his Novanti escort stopped beside Bothan. Expressionless, Seugethis acknowledged Arrius with a nod. Arrius glanced at Flavius and noticed the centurion's face wore an expression of resigned regret. By contrast, Querinius's smile was triumphant as he spoke, "Salve, Arrius. I must say you are looking less grand and even more travel-worn than when we last met at Banna. I doubt your physical condition will improve as my guest. In fact, you may count on it."

"Considering your treatment of me in the past, I really didn't expect it would. I don't suppose you would consider giving me a sword to settle matters between us."

"I'm sorely tempted, but I'm afraid I'll have to decline. Your reputation with a gladius gives you an advantage I would be a fool to risk."

Arrius looked at Seugethis and Flavius. "I would have only been surprised if the tribune had accepted the challenge." His voice dripping with sarcasm, he continued. "The hero, or should I say, the coward of Sorek seems to prefer using others and more clandestine methods to try to kill me." Shifting his attention back to Querinius, he said, "It's just as well. I would hate to stain a good sword with the blood of a coward."

Querinius struggled to maintain his composure. "Arrius, I'll personally see you die slowly on a cross for the traitor you are. After you breathe your last, I'll take your head back to General Arvinnius who will no doubt be disappointed, quite possibly even angry, at being denied the opportunity to see how painfully you will die. The rest of your body will be left here for the carrion." Then speaking over his shoulder to Seugethis, Arrius heard Querinius say quietly, "Wait until Flavius and I have taken Arrius inside the fort before you attack."

"Bothan, they mean to attack you!" Arrius warned urgently in Selgovan. "Go now and save yourself. You can do nothing for them," gesturing with his chin in the direction of the bound hostages standing between the Dacian cavalrymen.

With a startled despairing look at the hostages who stared back helplessly, Bothan and the Novanti escort kicked their horses into a gallop and streaked for the distant treeline.

Occupied with regaining control of his horse, Flavius dropped Ferox's reins either accidentally or on purpose, and Arrius saw his chance. He kicked the stallion hard in the belly in an attempt to follow Bothan. Unfortunately, Ferox reared instead of immediately bolting which gave Querinius a chance to snatch the reins and hold on grimly until one of the Dacian cavalrymen came to his assistance.

"Now that I've got you, I've no intention of allowing you to escape," Querinius said. Addressing Seugethis, Querinius ordered, "Get the hostages back inside the fort then go after the others."

As they passed through the gate, Querinius said, "That was clever, Arrius. You spoiled my little surprise; however, I'm confident Seugethis will bring me many more prisoners or at least their heads. You see I intend, along with yours, to take as many barbarian heads back with me as we can carry."

"Are you so certain you'll leave here? You don't realize how vulnerable you are."

"The tribes are finished. They've been routed and no longer have the numbers or the will to fight, and even if they did, which I doubt, they would have attacked by now."

"You're a fool, Querinius. You don't have any idea what you've done. Do you realize who it was speaking for the Novanti? That was Bothan, their High Chieftain. He can neither forgive, nor will he forget your treachery. To preserve his own position and the honor of the Novanti, he has no choice now but to attack. Had you kept your end of the bargain, a bargain I might add you proposed, he would have been content to let you have me and allow you to leave peacefully."

"Your words are nothing but a feeble and vain attempt to get me to release the hostages."

"Why do I care what happens to them? It was Bothan who handed me over to you. I care about the legionaries who will die needlessly because of you and your stupidity. You had the nerve to come here with a combined strength of less than two thousand men. There are eight times as many tribesmen waiting only for Bothan to order an attack." Privately, he thought if the Novanti and Selgovi were capable of mustering half that number, it would be a significant achievement.

"They were once commanded by you. Did you not train them well enough?"

"Aye, but so was the *Deiotariana* and look what happened to it. Have you already forgotten what happened in Sorek, Querinius? How the enemy stormed the walls in overwhelming numbers and annihilated the legion, leaving only a handful of us left to tell of it? How will you conduct yourself this time, or will you hide with the wounded the way you did then?"

"Arrius, I intend to hammer the nails in you myself, and that won't be the beginning of what's in store for you. No, it will not even be close to the end. When they lay you down on the cross timbers, you'll scream with agony from the pain of your scourged back. By the time you breathe your last, you'll wish you had never survived Judaea."

Flavius listened tightlipped to the exchange. "Tribune, he's right. We should release the hostages. You have what you came for. We should leave this place now."

"We'll leave when I order it! Arrius is trying to create panic when there's no reason for it." Then pointing to where Rufus remained tied to the post, he said, "Untie that man and put Arrius in his place." Querinius turned to Arrius and said, "As soon as the Dacians return, you'll receive fifty lashes, and for each day I let you live, you'll get fifty more. Flavius, I want the hostages killed. They've served their purpose, but since they were useful, you may be merciful and put them to the sword. Remember, I want their heads taken with us when we leave."

"Tribune, there's time later to take care of the hostages. It would be better to let them live a little longer just in case."

Querinius frowned and replied after a slight hesitation, "Very well, we'll take them with us. Their execution will provide some amusement for General Arvinnius." The tribune's gaze shifted to Ferox. "You may recall, Arrius, I was prepared some time ago to offer a handsome amount for that stallion of yours. I clearly remember your insolent refusal to sell it. It was another instance when you went out of your way to be disrespectful to me. Now I shall have your horse as a living memento of our time together. Flavius, have the horse groomed and sent to my quarters."

"Be careful with the stallion, Tribune. It takes courage to control the beast, and, Querinius, you have more than proven you don't have it."

"Flavius, give me your vitis." Flavius reluctantly handed the white-faced tribune the vine stick knowing full well what was about to happen. Querinius struck Arrius across the cheek hard enough to leave a bloody and rapidly growing welt. "Consider that a preliminary to what you are about to get." Querinius laughed. "It's a pity you won't live long enough for that to become a scar; it neatly balances the one on the other side of your face."

After Querinius left, Flavius said, "Marcus, I'm sorry for this. I and many others never believed you would be captured or given up. Know this, there is no pleasure in seeing you so ill-treated. I'm afraid there is little I can do to spare what that *mentula* intends for you. Why does he hate you so much?"

"It's a long story and serves no purpose in the telling."

A legionary cut Arrius's bindings and stepped aside to allow him to dismount. Flavius and the legionary escorted him to where Rufus was leaning against the post to keep from falling to his knees. His back was a bloody mess. Arrius knew what it felt like. He still remembered the one time he had been lashed early during his initial training as a new legionary. The offense was minor and hardly merited the punishment, but the senior centurion in charge of training wanted to make an example of him. Then it had been thirty lashes and enough to put him under the care of the *medicus* for two days. He wondered if he could survive the first installment of the two lashings Querinius specified. If he did, and someone provided a blade tonight, he would use it.

Rufus raised his head as he was being cut down by two orderlies under the supervision of a medicus and recognized Arrius coming toward him. His eyes widened in shocked recognition, and he managed to say, "Praefectus, you shouldn't have come here."

"Unfortunately, Rufus, there was little choice in the matter. It seems we've both fallen upon difficult times, but I and the gods think I'll not have much longer to dwell on it." Arrius wasn't certain the legionary heard him for as soon as the rope that bound him was untied, he collapsed unconscious, forcing the orderlies to carry him away.

"Why was Rufus being punished?"

Flavius recounted what Rufus did and the punishment Querinius demanded. "Rufus was fortunate I managed to arrange a demonstration that convinced Querinius his death sentence should not be carried out. In truth, Marcus, it almost resulted in a real mutiny. I thought for a moment I'd lost control of the thing."

"It seems you've had your hands full, and my capture hasn't helped."

"That's true," the centurion admitted with a rueful smile. "I had enough problems without you adding to them. You're still popular, and it's possible the men will refuse to allow the punishment Querinius intends for you. Querinius still underestimates the extent he's hated. He's already threatened the cohort with decimation, and once we return, he could convince Arvinnius to order it. I will do what I can for you, Marcus, but I'll not create a real mutiny even to save you."

"Nor would I expect it."

"Marcus, was it true what you said about Bothan?"

"I spoke the truth. Querinius's intention to kill the hostages is unwise, and if carried out, will not and cannot be forgiven for the reason I said. It isn't just the Novanti you're dealing with either. There's an alliance between the Novanti and Selgovi. If it were just the Novanti you were confronting, your risk would not be so great. Not to overstate my own worth, the Selgovi will not be well disposed to you when they hear of my untimely death and the way it was done."

"One of the hostages said Ilya is now queen of the Selgovi."

"Yes, she became queen after Joric was killed early during the invasion. Whatever happens to me will only give her more reason to hate the Romans and provide additional justification to prolong the alliance between the Selgovi and the Novanti. Querinius has no appreciation for the peril facing you and made much worse if the hostages are not released. I advise you to get the cohort moving back to the safety of the wall before Bothan has a chance to prepare an attack."

"If we're attacked, I would prefer it happen here than on the march."

Arrius thought if he was in command, he would have said the same.

Chapter 24

The all-night ride was punishing for both riders and animals alike. Tearlach allowed only brief stops to rest the horses before pressing on. Ilya began to worry how much longer they could maintain such a pace. There was a quickening of the eastern sky when Tearlach finally called a halt.

"Ilya, we must rest the men and horses, or we'll lose more than we already have," referring to the injuries to both horses and riders sustained during the night. The demanding pace reduced their number by an alarming amount. The only reason they had been able to come this far was the extra mount each rider brought that allowed the horses to be rotated.

"How much farther is it to Bothan's settlement?" she asked.

Tearlach looked for familiar landmarks before replying. "We'll reach it by mid day although not at all if we don't slow down. We can't afford to lose any more men or mounts."

Reluctantly, Ilya was forced to agree. Even though she hesitated at first to commit the tribe, now that they were underway, she resented every delay. "All right, we'll stop here for a few hours."

It wasn't long after the guards were posted and the horses turned loose to graze when most of the men were already fast asleep. Exhausted, Ilya wrapped herself in a cloak and leaned against a tree hoping she, too, would fall asleep as quickly as the others. She closed her eyes, but as soon as she did, her imagination took over and crowded her mind with awful images she did her best to suppress. Betto taught her how brutal the Romans were, and if Marcus was their prisoner, he was in great peril. Initially, she was concerned the warriors would resent extending themselves for a Roman and said as much to Tearlach after his proposal they should try to rescue Marcus. Tearlach reassured her the prospect of a good fight was reason enough even had Marcus not defeated Vadrex.

She heard a twig snap and saw Decrius coming toward her, his hulking figure silhouetted against the dawn sky.

"I'm sorry to have caused this," he said in a low voice without preamble. He sat down next to her and handed her a leather water flask. After satisying her thirst, she gave it back to him with a grateful smile.

"It isn't your fault. If there is any blame, my husband is the one deserving of it. He does what he wishes and sometimes pays little heed to the consequences. I fault him as much as I love him for it. He gave up everything for me and Eugenius, and it may have been better if he hadn't now the Romans have him."

Decrius remained silent. He knew she had good reason to worry and didn't want to add further to her concerns by agreeing. She leaned her head back with her eyes closed, and Decrius thought she was asleep. He started to get up when she spoke.

"Decrius, Marcus never speaks of his time in Judaea. You were with him. What was it like?"

"It was bad. We lost many legionaries, and we would have lost many more if it had not been for Arrius. As the legion's senior centurion, he more than anyone was responsible for saving the eagle standard and was the reason some of us survived; otherwise, I would not be here to say this." He paused then said thoughtfully, "In the end, the Jews lost much more. They lost everything."

"Then we are not so different from the Jews; we lost our homeland as well."

"There is a difference. One day, and I do not think it will be long in coming, we will defeat the Romans. There are not enough Jews left in Judaea to fight the Romans again."

"Do you really believe the Romans can be defeated?"

"Before I left Banna, I heard one of the reasons for building the new wall farther north was that fewer legionaries would be required to defend the frontier and allow Rome to reduce the number of legions in Britannia. Now the war in Judaea is over, there is trouble again in Germania and Dacia. We must be patient and bide our time." He would have said more about the resolve of the Briganti who would eventually rebel again, but he saw she had fallen asleep. It was just as well. He said the things he did more to convince himself than Ilya. In spite of what he told her, he didn't believe he would live to see the Romans leave the island.

It was late in the day when Tearlach confirmed they were but a short distance from the principal Novanti settlement. Shortly after that, the outriders came streaking back to report seeing a band of Novanti horsemen approaching from the south which would eventually intercept their present course. Deciding to wait for them where they were, Tearlach called a halt and allowed the men to dismount and rest the horses. It wasn't long before Ilya saw Bothan emerge from the trees ahead and come toward them leading a large band of horsemen.

Red-faced with exertion, Bothan was uncharacteristically subdued as he reined in his horse and said to Ilya, "I expected to see Tearlach but not you." His eyes refused to meet hers and instead darted nervously back and forth. "What are you doing here?"

"I'm looking for my husband. Do you know where I might find him?"

Bothan gave a hollow laugh and said with a flash of his usual coarse behavior, "Perhaps he has found another woman to bed whose lineage is less royal and is not so demanding as the Queen of the Selgovi." There were a few muted chuckles among the Novanti warriors met by angry muttering from the Selgovi ranks for the insolent response.

Ilya silenced the ominous undercurrent behind her. "Bothan, I've no time to listen to your churlish comments. Our people have enough to worry about from the Romans without looking for reasons to fight each other. Now, have you seen Arrius?"

The leer on his face was replaced with a bland look as he debated a stern denial and riding on. The Selgovan witch made him nervous. It had been the same with her cousin Beldorach whose manner always made him feel inferior. Reluctantly, he decided a version of the truth would be better than a denial, concluding that to say nothing would only make him look weak and afraid when she eventually learned what happened.

"The Romans have him."

Ilya felt suddenly light-headed and found it difficult to breathe. Bothan confirmed her worst fears and what she had been dreading to hear. With effort, she spoke and was thankful her voice was surprisingly steady.

"How did it happen?"

"I sent Neacal to capture Romans to trade for my warriors the Romans seized. He was unsuccessful. Arrius came to Neacal's camp and offered to help get the hostages back. Since it was Arrius they wanted, it seemed Cernunos sent him to us for that very purpose. The plan was to pretend to give up Arrius in return for the hostages. When the Romans brought the hostages out from the fort, Arrius would make his escape during the exchange. Unfortunately, the Romans were prepared, and both the hostages and Arrius were taken prisoner."

"You lie, Bothan," Tearlach said. "I think the only truth in what you say is that Arrius is a prisoner, and if it is so, it's because of Neacal."

"You dare to call me a liar!" Bothan said furiously, drawing his sword and prompting the warriors from both tribes to draw their swords as well.

"Stop, and put away your weapons!" Ilya said. "Tearlach, hold your tongue! The details are not worth fighting over. What matters is that the Romans have the hostages and Arrius, and we must find a way to get them back. Where is Neacal?"

"I don't know," Bothan admitted. "We were pursued by their cavalry, and some of my men did not escape. Neacal was among those."

"How many more warriors than you have here can you gather before tomorrow?"

"Perhaps three thousand and another thousand with more time."

"Well, we don't have more time; therefore, that will have to do."

"What do you mean? If you mean to attack the Romans, we don't have enough men. The Romans have the advantage of being behind walls."

Decrius, who remained silent until now, spoke reluctantly. "He's right, and if we tried, our losses would be great."

Ilya said, "Yes, I know; however, the Romans will not know our strength. We only have to make them think we do, and that may be sufficient to bargain. It may not work, but if we don't do something, Arrius and the others will die while we crawl back to our villages and pretend we tried."

Bothan sheathed his sword and scratched the back of his neck in thought. "Very well," he said in grudging assent. "Let us camp here and discuss how you think we can fool the Romans. I'll send for more warriors, and we'll see how many can be here by morning. If I do not like what you have to say, then we will go back to our villages."

Ilya nodded in relief, satisfied for the time being she preserved a chance to free Marcus and the other hostages. The immediate problem remaining was she had absolutely no idea how they would do it.

The tribal camps were established separately at opposite ends of a valley. Ilya agreed to come to Bothan's camp later that evening after the details of her plan were worked out. Sharing a small fire with Tearlach and Decrius apart from the other men, Ilya anxiously broke the gloomy silence. "Decrius, you know the Romans better than anyone. What will it take to convince first Bothan and then the Romans we have a plan and enough warriors to demand terms?"

"I don't know," was the disappointing response. "The Tungrian Cohort has almost eight hundred men and the Dacians another five hundred, perhaps less. For a successful attack, we would need to field at least four thousand men. Even then success would not be guranteed. I do not wish to give offense, but neither the Selgovi nor the Novanti are as skilled or disciplined as the Tungrians and Dacians. If we did attack and were able to defeat them, I doubt we would find the hostages alive."

"I've no intention of proposing a real attack. As I told Bothan, we only need to make it look as if we will. The question is how. Tearlach, what does the country around the fort look like? Is it situated on flat ground, surrounded by bare fields, forest – describe it to me."

"Rolling hills, some tree-covered while most have low vegetation growing on them. The fort is situated on a low hill."

"How close can archers get without being seen?"

"Not close enough, I'm afraid," Tearlach responded, shaking his head.

Decrius, absent-mindedly poking the fire with a stick, said, "It won't matter. In fact, the more visible they are the better."

"What do you mean?" Tearlach said with a perplexed frown.

Ilya's eyes were shining, and Tearlach was nodding in admiration after Decrius finished describing the plan they would present to Bothan.

"It's a good plan," Bothan said grudgingly after Decrius finished speaking. "I'll send more men back to the villages to bring as many horses as we can gather." Then directing his attention exclusively to Ilya, he said peevishly, "I do not like turning Novanti horses over to this man," pointing to Tearlach. "I do not trust him. He's a thief and has taken many of our horses in the past. The Romans have reduced my herds enough without having to lose more horses to him."

Exasperated, Ilya shot Tearlach a meaningful look before directing her attention back to Bothan. "I'll guarantee every horse turned over to the Selgovi will be returned when this is over. Since you have more men, it only makes sense the Selgovi use the horses to deceive the Romans into believing they are facing a force many times their number. It is also well-known the Novanti have the finest archers among all the tribes," she added smoothly and with only slight exaggeration. "They will be more effective in pressing the Romans at close range while my warriors fool the Romans into believing we have more horsemen than we actually do. If they remain far enough away, they will not be able to see most of the horses have no riders."

Bothan considered the response in silence before nodding in assent. "We'll do as you say, but I'll be in command, not you, Ilya," he said resolutely with a mulish expression indicating he expected her to disagree.

Ilya glanced at Tearlach and rolled her eyes. "Of course, you will be the senior commander," Ilya assured serenely. "You're far more experienced in these matters than I am. You've only to explain to your men what they must do and when. My Selgovi will do their part when you give the signal."

"I'll allow you to talk to the Roman commander," Bothan said craftily making the offer sound as if he was according her an honor. He had no intention of being duped and nearly captured again.

Before Ilya had a chance to reply, Decrius said, "It would be better if I do it. They know me well, and I believe for that reason I can persuade them to hand over Arrius and the hostages in return for allowing them to leave unharmed."

Bothan looked at Ilya. "Very well, let it be so," not caring who dealt with the Romans as long as it wasn't him.

Back at the Selgovan camp, the initial satisfaction of having convinced Bothan to accept the plan was beginning to give way to a sober assessment of their chances for success. Shifting her gaze first to Decrius then Tearlach, Ilya asked anxiously, "What do you really believe our chances are for succeeding?"

The two men exchanged looks, each hesitating to say the words Ilya did not want to hear, and they did not wish to utter.

Finally, Tearlach said, "If we try hard enough, the *Morrigu* will use her magic and trick the enemy into believing what they see is more real than it is."

Decrius had intended to keep his private thoughts to himself and say nothing of his own misgivings until Ilya asked him directly, "What do you think, Decrius?"

"Tearlach is right. The *Morrigu* is our only chance. We must convince them quickly they are vastly outnumbered. When the Roman commander eventually realizes there will be no attack, only volleys of arrows, he will know it is a bluff and attack with his cavalry. The archers are exposed and will be at greatest risk."

"Do you think Bothan realizes the danger to the archers?" Ilya perceived the weakness of the plan for the first time.

"No, or else he wouldn't have agreed to the plan. Pray he doesn't think of it, or he won't go through with it."

Already she was beginning to have some regret for pushing Bothan into accepting the scheme. "Why didn't you speak of this before now?" she asked.

"Because I couldn't think of a better plan." He did not volunteer his private belief Arrius, if still alive, would not be for long once the deception began. He thought the only thing which would be accomplished in the end was a quicker death for Arrius than he would get if they did nothing.

Chapter 25

Arrius saw horsemen coming toward the fort with the flamboyant Seugethis in the lead. Behind him, the crunching of hob-nailed boots as the cohort for the second time that day was formed into ranks to witness the punishment.

"Remove his tunic," Querinius ordered the legionary holding the lead-tipped *flagrum.*

Arrius stared straight ahead and tried to prepare himself mentally for the ordeal by concentrating on the mundane activities taking place in his field of vision. He noted the attention of the sentries guarding the gate and the ramparts were directed more to what was taking place inside the fort than out. He looked through the north gate and saw the two crosses. Even more ominous was the detail exiting the gate and carrying a large wooden cross presumably intended for him.

Arrius heard Flavius's urgent warning, "Tribune, don't do this! I cannot allow you to risk consequences similar to what happened this morning."

"What do you mean you won't allow it? Have a care, centurion, or you may find yourself in his place if you dare to challenge my authority!" Querinius replied in a low voice shaking with anger.

"Tribune, do as Centurion Flavius said!" thundered a voice Arrius recognized as belonging to Seugethis. "End it now with a sword. He deserves a better and quicker death than this."

"Dacian, don't presume to address me in such manner and don't interfere in a matter that does not concern you. I am carrying out the punishment General Arvinnius would doubtless prescribe if he were here."

"Well, I am interfering. I don't like what you're doing, and from the looks of the Tungrians behind you, I think they do not care much for it either." Arrius twisted around to look over his shoulder and saw scowling legionaries watching the proceedings with hostile looks.

"I'm warning you, Seugethis, leave now, or I'll have you placed under arrest."

"I don't think so, Tribune," Seugethis responded in a steely voice.

"What do you mean?" Querinius replied in a voice less certain.

"Simply that you do not have the capability to arrest me, and I strongly advise you not to try."

"Seugethis, there is no need to dispute our differences like this in front of the men," Querinius replied in a more conciliatory tone of voice. "It would be better to discuss this further in more private circumstances."

"What is there to discuss, Tribune? I'll not see this man treated this way. Send him to his gods befitting a warrior."

"I'll consider your request; however, it's not my pleasure that Arrius will die now." Querinius replied in an attempt to rescue a modicum of his rapidly deteriorating authority. "He will have the rest of the day and night to think about his death tomorrow."

"And it will be by the sword?" Seugethis reminded.

"Yes, it will be by the sword," Querinius said between clenched teeth.

"Good, I would not like to hear later that you changed your mind."

"You will be here to witness it."

"No, Tribune, I will not."

"What do you mean by that?" Querinius asked clearly perplexed.

"It means I'm leaving early tomorrow at first light. Arrius has been captured, and there is no enemy to fight; therefore, I see no reason to stay any longer. I consider this campaign at an end."

"You can't leave," Querinius replied, the tone of his voice a cross between outrage and concern. "If you leave without my permission, you'll explain to General Arvinnius why you left."

"I'll remind General Arvinnius what you've obviously forgotten or never knew. The Dacian ala has been posted to Germania. I am merely obeying the orders of Imperial Rome – a few days sooner, but then I and my cavalrymen are most anxious to be closer to our homeland. I'm not sorry to leave; there's no pleasure or honor in any of this," he added, lips curled in disdain. Arrius saw the shocked look on Querinius's face. It was obvious from the tribune's expression he had been unaware of the Dacian's orders.

Seugethis started to move away only to rein the horse in after a few paces. He reached behind him and retrieved a human head tied by the hair to the back of his saddle. "I nearly forgot, Tribune. Here's at least one head you can take back with you in celebration of your triumphant success." Seugethis tossed the head in the general direction of Querinius where it fell close to Arrius. In spite of the blood and dirt encrusted on the grisly trophy, he recognized the face. Neacal was no longer a candidate to replace Bothan.

"Flavius, the prisoner will remain here until the Dacians leave tomorrow. I want a guard to remain here in case one of your legionaries tries anything. Give him some water. I want to be sure he's alive and well for what awaits him tomorrow.

"Do you still intend to crucify him?" Flavius asked.

'Just as soon as that Dacian son-of-bitch is far enough away he can't hear Arrius screaming when I put the first nail in him."

The night was long and sleepless. His cheek was painfully swollen from the blow Querinius gave him with the vitis, but it might have been worse. Flavius draped a sagum over his shoulders and ordered him released from the ring at the top of the post that forced him to remain standing. His wrists were retied with an arm on each side of the post. While still uncomfortable, the arrangement allowed him to kneel or to sit with his legs outstretched. However sympathetic the guards may have been privately, they were diligent in following their orders to make sure the prisoner would be there and alive the next morning. He thought the fear of Querinius eclipsed any residual loyalty they may have for him. He finally gave up any hope Flavius would somehow find a way to supply him with a gladius or pugio.

The sun had yet to crest the eastern hills when Arrius heard someone call his name. He opened his eyes and saw Seugethis sitting astride his horse while behind him the Dacian turmae made final preparations to depart the fort. The jingling of harnesses, the muffled stamping of hooves in the hard dirt and the occasional curse provoked by a stubborn mount were all familiar sounds.

"Arrius, I've done what I could for you," Seugethis said with sincere regret. 'I would have wished your gods had seen fit to take you on a battlefield than like this even if it had been my *spatha* that sent you to them."

When Arrius spoke, his voice was slightly hoarse. "Are you so certain you would have succeeded?"

"Who but Zalmoxis knows what the outcome might have been? You would have been a worthy opponent, but I think in the end my sword would have prevailed," he said confidently without hesitation or a trace of false modesty.

"I would prefer your sword than what Querinius intends for me."

"So, the bastard plans to ignore my warning." He paused and his face assumed a thoughtful expression. "Perhaps I should remain here a little longer to make certain he does not."

"It will do no good. He will either crucify me here or take me back to Arvinnius who will see to it. I think whether I die today or a few days from now doesn't matter. I knew this could happen to me before I left Banna and came north. My only regret is I didn't put a blade in Querinius before I left."

"I would do it for you, but Rome does not approve of Dacians killing its tribunes. May his gods piss on him in this life and in the next. Well, I must go. I'll pray to Zalmoxis in your behalf although he has no regard for Romans. Perhaps he will make an exception for you and allow you to dwell among the Dacian immortals," he said expansively. "Then you and I will ride swift horses and talk of things pleasing to warriors."

"What if he doesn't listen to you?"

Seugethis lifted an eyebrow and replied philosophically, "I confess there have been times when he has not, but I will try. This I promise, Marcus Arrius."

Arrius watched Seugethis ride off toward the south gate with the Dacian turmae cantering after him. A part of him envied the cavalryman's uncomplicated existence. Lost in his own thoughts, he didn't hear Flavius approach from behind him until he heard him speak.

"Marcus, Querinius has decided to take you back and turn you over to General Arvinnius. For what it's worth, you have at least another three days to live."

"Do I have the gods to thank or Seugethis for my reprieve?"

"Both, I think. The tribune is concerned he will not have enough time to do a thorough job of crucifying you now that the Dacians have gone. He correctly believes we are *too vulnerable* to remain here. He has a point if what you say concerning Bothan is true. With Seugethis gone, Querinius has just lost more than half of his force. In my opinion, our brave tribune is suddenly less enthused about executing you than he is in seeking the safety of the Wall. I believe with some justification there is another reason for keeping you alive a little longer. He's concluded he can no longer trust the Tungrians to carry out the execution and fears mutiny if he tries. For once, I agree with him. As soon as we load the wagons, we will leave."

It was approaching mid-morning and preparations for departure were proceeding with orderly precision. The oxen and mules were already hitched to the wagons and waited placidly as goatskin tents, grain bags and other boxes of tools and equipment were loaded. Last to be struck were the *tribuli*, the three stakes sharpened at both ends and tied together to form triangular caltrops lining the parapets.

He heard a commotion near the horse corral. Excited voices shouted in alarm. He heard the shrill neighing of an angry horse and knew immediately it was Ferox. There were too many wagons lined up and blocking his view for him to see what was happening. By then all activities had ceased with attention directed toward that end of the fort. A moment later, Ferox galloped past him and through the east gate. Arrius smiled in satisfaction, knowing Querinius would never have the stallion. As preparations for departure gradually resumed throughout the fort, he glimpsed a disheveled Querinius. The tribune was limping and grimacing in pain while massaging his left shoulder as he walked toward a wagon. It required no explanation for him to know Ferox had reacted predictably to a rider unfamiliar and unprepared to cope with the stallion's irritable nature. He recalled being catapulted into the air when he first tried to ride the horse.

"Rider approaching!" one of the gate sentinels shouted.

In response to the alert, Arrius watched Cotta interrupt his inspection of a loaded wagon to hurry toward the north gate. He never liked or particularly trusted Cotta. The centurion had been the only officer who remained steadfastly loyal to Betto. The centurion jumped up on the low rampart and looked in the direction the sentinel was pointing. A few curious legionaries wandered over to the northern rampart to see for themselves. Cotta turned and said something to a legionary standing below the rampart. The legionary immediately left and returned several minutes later accompanied by Flavius leading his horse. After exchanging a few words with the centurion, Flavius mounted and rode alone out of the fort. Flavius no sooner departed than the sentinels on the other three sides of the fort were reporting signs of movement. Gradually, more and more legionaries spontaneously stopped whatever they were doing and began moving to the walls only to be restrained by angry centurions and optios ordering them to resume their assigned tasks.

A short time later, Flavius reentered the fort at a faster pace than when he left. He dismounted and after a brief conversation with Cotta, one of the *cornicinies* positioned at the gate lifted his horn and blew the signal to arm and prepare to defend the walls. There was an orderly scramble as legionaries grabbed helmets, shields and pila and moved quickly to occupy their assigned defensive positions. The tribuli were unpacked and quickly reassembled and placed on the earthen walls.

Much later, Arrius was still puzzling over what was happening when Rufus, taking advantage of the excitement, limped toward him and said, "It was Decrius who met with Flavius. He says that if you and the hostages are not released unharmed by mid-day, we will all be killed. If there's a battle, I'll come back and cut you loose. At least then you may have a chance to kill that prick of a tribune unless I do it first. No matter what happens, as long as I live, you'll not die on a cross.

"Rufus, you always seem to be at hand when I need you. My debt to you continues to increase."

Rufus grinned, saying over his shoulder as he walked away, "Arrius, maybe if you paid more attention to the gods, you wouldn't need so much help."

Arrius marveled how Fortuna curiously bound their destinies together. He reflected on the significance of Decrius delivering the message to Flavius and wondered if by chance Ilya had learned of his capture and joined Bothan. He hoped if it were true, she wouldn't be foolish enough to take an active part in the assault but knew she undoubtedly would.

Chapter 26

Rivulets of sweat streaked the blue paint on the warrior's excited face as he reined his lathered horse in front of Ilya and Bothan.

"The Roman horsemen have left the fort and are traveling south with their wagons."

"What about their foot soldiers? Are they leaving as well?"

"I cannot tell, but they do not appear to be."

Bothan turned to Ilya. "Then the plan has changed; we no longer need to make them believe our strength is greater since we now outnumber the Romans. Instead, we'll attack the fort as soon as we can get into position; your warriors will join the attack," Bothan said decisively.

"But if we attack without first finding out if they will give us the hostages, they will have no reason to keep them alive and every reason to slay them," Ilya responded.

"Ilya's right," Tearlach said. "We must talk first. If they accept the offer and give us the prisoners, we can attack them after they leave the fort."

Bothan remained silent considering the argument before reluctantly agreeing. He wanted to avoid giving in too soon to keep from giving the impression he was incapable of thinking clearly, a conclusion Ilya and Tearlach reached long ago.

"Very well, I agree. Now we must move quickly and get into position. Ilya, take your warriors and place them on the north side of the fort. I will position my warriors on the other three sides. The carnyx will signal when it's time to attack."

Decrius was inwardly less confident than his outward appearance suggested as he rode toward the fort and came within arrow range of the walls. He hoped a single horseman would be looked upon more as a curiosity than a threat. Bareheaded, he also counted on being recognized, and if not welcomed with open arms, he would at least be given an opportunity to deliver the message before attracting a volley of arrows.

It was apparent from the absence of tribuli on the earthen walls the cohort was prepared to march. The braying protests of mules were familiar sounds and brought back vivid memories. Once they could have been nostalgic recollections but all he felt now was bitterness and regret for what he had once been.

He was close enough to the crosses to see the two men hanging from them, one of which was already dead. Another cross with a hole dug beside it was on the ground close by in preparation for the next victim; he had a good idea who that might be. Decrius was relieved to see Flavius riding toward him.

"So, the report a centurion from the auxilia has declared war on the Roman Army was true," Flavius said after stopping a few paces from Decrius. "I feared you would be too late to find your wife and son when I last saw you. When an optio in the Sixth legion reported a Brigantian wearing the helmet of a centurion killed his men and allowed him to live to tell of it, I suspected it was you."

"If I had known a day earlier of the attack, I might have saved them."

"I'm sorry you did not. If I had known of it sooner than I did, I would have told you in time to save your family."

"You knew I would be too late when I left you."

"I did not. Querinius's messenger arrived just before you left and informed the Briganti would be attacked soon – he didn't say when."

"Then it was Querinius and not Arvinnius who was responsible?"

"He was acting commander of the legion at the time. Whether he actually led the attack, I cannot say."

"Cannot or will not?"

"What does it matter, Decrius?" Flavius replied with a trace of irritation. "What's done is done and cannot be changed. It was unfortunate your wife and son were caught up in it. There is nothing more to be said. Why are you here?"

"Bothan and Ilya are willing to trade your lives for the hostages and Arrius. Do they still live?"

"They do, except for the one crucified yesterday, and he would still be alive if Rufus hadn't broken his legs last night."

"Rufus did it?"

"Aye, he confessed. The Novanti was brave, and the men thought he deserved a better death. Tribune Querinius ordered Rufus flogged."

"Querinius is here?"

"Unfortuately for all concerned, he's in command."

"You must convince Querinius to agree to the terms by mid-day, or there will be a battle in which you and the cohort cannot possibly survive."

"As much as I personally do not wish to see any harm come to Arrius or the rest of the hostages, I do not believe Querinius will agree to the terms. But I'll tell him even if I cannot recommend he agree to them. I also doubt Bothan intends to attack, or else he would have done so by now."

"That may have been true before the Dacians left. Now you have no chance of leaving here alive except the one Bothan offers. Even as we talk, the Novanti and Selgovi are surrounding the fort with numbers far greater than you have."

Flavious looked beyond Decrius at the far hills and saw a large dust cloud rapidly expanding both North and South. He turned around and looked past the fort and observed the same thing. He faced Decrius and said, "Bothan will do what he thinks he must, and I will do the same. Know this, if there is to be a battle, I'll take no pleasure in it, but nor will I hold back my sword."

"Nor will I. You have only a few hours left to save the cohort. Even if you do decide to surrender Arrius and the hostages, I will personally see that Querinius never reaches the new wall alive. For now, there is nothing more to be said."

Flavius watched the former centurion ride away and hoped Decrius was bluffing about the number of tribesmen ready to assault the fort, but the dust clouds suggested otherwise. He cursed Seugethis for leaving; however, there was no anger behind it. He couldn't really blame the Dacian for going and might even have done the same had their positions been reversed. By the time Flavius rode back into the fort, his thoughts were focused only on preparing for battle.

Although pale, Querinius remained surprisingly calm as he listened to Flavius summarize the meeting with Decrius.

"I think they're bluffing. Do you agree?"

"I do not. I think they mean to attack even if we give up Arrius and the others."

"Then there is little point in meeting their demands."

"We have no choice but to fight."

"Can we defeat them?"

"If their numbers are what Arrius and Decrius have said they are, we have little hope."

"But in your opinion, there is a possibility we can prevail?" Querinius queried anxiously.

"There is always a chance. Despite your poor opinion of the Tungrians, they know how to fight. Arrius trained them well."

"But you do not think the chances are very good."

"No."

"Very well, we have a few hours to prepare for an attack. You may go and see to our defenses. If our survival is as doubtful as you seem to think it is, we may as well kill Arrius and the hostages now."

"On the contrary, we need to ensure they survive in case their terms become more acceptable later."

"What do you mean?"

"Duty demands we aquit ourselves well; however, it may be necessary to use them to bargain later when we believe we've done enough to protect the honor of Rome."

"Ah, yes, I see what you mean. Given our circumstances, it's good to be flexible. Put Arrius with the other hostages."

Flavius noted with contempt the eagerness in the tribune's voice. There would be no additional attempt by the barbarians to negotiate, but then there was no reason Arrius should be the first casualty.

Arrius saw Cotta walking toward him accompanied by two legionaires When the centurion drew his dagger, he wondered if his time had finally come. Amazingly, Cotta leaned down and sawed through the ropes that bound him to the post. Motioning for him to stand up, Cotta said, "Tribune Querinius is concerned you may be harmed in the event we're attacked." The centurion gave a mocking laugh. "He wants to be certain he isn't cheated of the spectacle of seeing you crucified, and for that matter, neither do I."

Arrius tried to stand and found his legs were painfully cramped. Evidently, the centurion thought he was moving too slow and grabbed Arrius's arm, pulling him roughly to his feet before shoving him in the direction of the low-roofed wooden cage where the hostages were confined. His legs still stiff, Arrius stumbled and fell to his knees. Cotta began prodding him with his dagger hard enough to prick the skin. When they reached the cage, Arrius whirled around and before Cotta and the legionaries could react, he snatched the dagger from Cotta's hand and grasped the left cheek plate of the centurion's helmet while bringing the dagger up underneath Cotta's mailed apron. The centurion's eyes bulged, and he gasped in shock as he felt the point of the blade pressing against his genitals.

Arrius looked meaningfully at the two legionaries, one of whom stood frozen while the other remained relaxed and unconcerned clearly enjoying the spectacle. "I suggest no one make any sudden moves or the centurion's balls are mine," he said loud enough for a number of other legionaries nearby who stopped what they were doing to watch the unfolding drama. "Cotta, that includes not pissing on my hand."

"Don't cut me, Arrius," Cotta whispered between gritted teeth. "If you do, you'll never get out of here alive."

"You're right, Cotta, and for that reason I'm not going to try. I'm a dead man no matter what I choose to do; consequently, I don't have anything to lose which is more than I can say for you. I don't like you, Cotta, and I never did. One of my true regrets is that I didn't run you and Betto out of the cohort soon after I took command. I'll try to resist the pleasure it would give me to push this blade up as high as it will go."

"What do you want?"

"First, I want you to apologize for treating me so poorly."

"I won't do it."

Arrius pressed the blade more firmly, forcing the centurion to stand higher until his boot heels cleared the ground. "What did you say?"

"I apologize," Cotta said in a low voice through clenched teeth.

He moved the blade upward even harder. "Louder, I couldn't hear what you said, and no one else did either. Try again, and this time I want the divinties in the celestial clouds above to hear it."

"I'm sorry for what I did!" Cotta said louder, voice strained, face flushed in humiliation. Arrius heard some of the onlookers snickering.

"Very good, Cotta, now send someone to find Tribune Querinius and bring him here."

"You heard him!" Cotta said harshly, addressing the nearest legionary watching the tableux with mouth agape. By now, virtually the entire garrison was aware of what was happening near the hostage cage and paused in whatever they were doing to watch what would happen. A few started to drift closer to get a better look.

Following the legionary's departure, Arrius glanced in the direction of the other guard who still appeared to be enjoying the spectacle and said, "While we wait for the tribune to get here, I want you to draw your gladius and hand it to me hilt first." After the legionary surrendered the sword, he brought the tip of the blade up under the centurion's chin.

It wasn't long before Arrius saw Flavius approaching at a fast walk accompanied by Avitus and the legionary Cotta had sent for the tribune. Avitus was sternly ordering idle legionaries back to their duties as he passed by them and vigorously applying his vitis to the backs and shoulders of those not moving fast enough to suit him.

Flavius came to a stop a few paces away and said quietly, "It's no use, Arrius, he isn't coming. You may as well let Cotta go."

Disappointed but not surprised, Arrius shoved Cotta toward Flavius. When Cotta started to draw his sword, Flavius lashed out firmly, "Let it be, Cotta, and see to your century. I'll handle this." After the centurion left, Flavius said, "You really didn't expect Querinius would come."

"I don't suppose I did."

"It would be better if you gave me the dagger and sword," Flavius said, an anxious note in his voice, fearing Arrius was about to turn the sword on himself. "Alive you may still be able to help them," gesturing toward the cage.

"Why? It would seem a sword is a better choice than what Querinius intends for me."

"It may not come to that, Marcus. Our situation here is precarious if the tribes attack. I give you my word, if I lose the battle, you and the hostages will not suffer for it."

"Then let us go now, and I'll talk Bothan and Ilya into allowing you and the cohort to leave unharmed. The only condition is that you leave Querinius behind."

"As much as I would like to, I cannot agree to do that, and if you were in my position, you wouldn't either."

"Probably not," Arrius responded in resignation tossing the pugio and gladius at Flavius's feet. He heard the legionary behind him unfastening the shackle locking the cage door. Without further comment, he turned and ducked through the low entrance into the gloomy interior and heard the rattle of the lock after the door closed behind him.

After the bright sun outside, the interior of the cage was dark and fetid from the number of men confined in such a small enclosure. The stout wooden poles used to construct the walls and roof were spaced a hand's length apart. The floor was similarly constructed to discourage any attempt for the prisoners to dig their way out. The odor from a large earthen jar in the corner to the left of the door proclaimed what it was intended for. On the opposite side of the door, there was a smaller water jar with a clay cup resting on top of the wooden lid. There was room for only a few to lie down at any given time, and the roof was so low only the shortest among them was able to stand upright. When his eyes became more accustomed to the gloom, Arrius spotted Crixtacus sitting close to the door with his back to the wall staring at him.

The clan chief spoke first. "Did you come to the fort thinking to set us free?"

"I did not come willingly. It was Neacal's idea, and Bothan agreed to it."

"The Romans will never release us, and Bothan was a fool to think they would." The comment was made objectively and without any sign of bitterness. "We're all dead men," he added in the same resigned tone.

"It may be, but there may yet be a chance you're wrong."

"How can that be?"

"It seems Bothan with the possible assistance of the Selgovi is prepared to attack the fort if we aren't released. Even now the fort's defenses are being prepared."

"Then I think we will die sooner than later when the attack begins."

"Perhaps not. In fact, there may be a better reason to keep us alive in case the battle is decided in Bothan's favor."

"If Bothan wins, he'll kill every Roman who survives," Crixtacus responded pragmatically.

Arrius considered the remark and silently thought the clan chief was right. The realization was a grim prospect that emphasized he was caught between two worlds with conflicting loyalties to both and helpless to prevent what was going to happen.

"The cavalry left the fort several hours ago to return to the new wall; consequently, Bothan may now have the advantage in numbers for a successful attack, but it will not be an easy victory. The Romans won't risk leaving the fort without cavalry protection. The only chance they have is to remain here until Bothan leaves or the Romans learn of the attack and send reinforcements."

Further conversation was interrupted by the eerie, unsettling notes of a carnyx. Arrius peered through one of the narrow slits and observed Querinius conferring with Flavius near the north entrance. He thought Flavius and the Tungrian Cohort would be better off if Querinius found a safe place to crawl into leaving the centurion to fight the battle without interference. There was a cry of warning, and the sky was suddenly filled with arrows that prompted any legionary with a shield to kneel under it and others without scurrying to find a wagon to dive under. Several arrows impacted harmlessly in the dirt near the cage with a few more thudding into the log roof above.

The smaller and rounded shields carried by the auxilia infantry offered considerably less protection from missiles than the larger rectangular shields standard in the legions. Even though the legionaries' shields offered sufficient protection from high-arching arrows, they were vulnerable to those launched at close range in a flat trajectory. Occasional gaps began to appear along the walls as wounded legionaries, ignoring the angry curses of the optios and centurions, left the walls to seek the comparative safety of the wagons. He recalled the deadly accuracy shown by Crixtacus and Neacal during the archery competition with the Venicones and saw how ill-matched the Tungrians were. Roman spears were no match against arrows. Without the benefit of cavalry to keep the archers from coming close enough to reduce their effectiveness, the defenders were at a distinct disadvantage. He thought the battle would be brief if Flavius didn't consolidate his force into a smaller perimeter. Arrius saw an ox hitched to a wagon struck in the flank by an arrow. With a bellow of pain, the panic-stricken animal set off in a lumbering gait forcing its teammate to do the same. With the wagon bouncing and weaving precariously from side to side, the oxen charged up the nearest berm trampling a legionary and knocking aside several tribuli before plunging into the outer defensive ditch. Arrows continued to wreak havoc on the other draft animals. In their frantic haste to escape, those animals not struck down broke free of their handlers and began stampeding throughout the fort, strewing baggage and posing as much danger to the Tungrian defenders as the missiles raining down from above. Some animals disappeared through the gates while others charged up the berms only to fall helplessly into the outer ditches. There were now numerous gaps along the walls further eroding an already threatened defense.

The chaotic scene was reminiscent of the battle in the Sorek Valley, but at least in Judaea, the legion had more time to prepare for the Jewish attack. Flavius had been caught at the worst possible time. The Dacian cavalry's early departure left the fort extremely vulnerable and too large to be defended by a single infantry cohort. If the Novanti were persistent, there was little to indicate the Tungrians were going to be able to hold out unless Flavius consolidated the defense to a smaller section of the fort. As if reading his thoughts, he heard a trumpet blast and legionaries defending the south end of the fort left their positions and rushed past him to form a triple line stretching from the east to the west entrances. Silently, ranks stood waiting with no overt signs of panic. Centurion Avitus barked a command, and the legionaries in the first and second ranks hefted their pila while those in the third rank drew their swords.

Moments later, the first wave of mounted tribesmen swept over the south wall and charged toward the ranks of legionaries. The leading Novanti horsemen, faces and bare torsos liberally daubed with blue paint, took the brunt of the pila that thinned their ranks with devastating results. Before the horsemen could recover, another volley of spears blunted the charge creating more confusion as the survivors turned back only to collide with those following behind. Successive blasts from a carnyx signaled assaults commencing at the north end of the fort. He saw several Novanti armed with lances breach the top of the wall; however, their success was short-lived, and they were quickly cut down.

The Novanti who gained access to the fort from the south regrouped and prepared to charge again. With a shock, he recognized Tearlach and Cuileán among those in the vanguard confirming that Bothan was being assisted by the Selgovi. He prayed to every god he could think of he wouldn't see Ilya. In dismay, he glimpsed her slender form toward the back urging her horse over the south wall.

The second assault was more successful than the initial one, and the Tungrian line would have given way if not for Avitus who managed to rally them in time. Now dismounted, the Novanti continued to press the Tungrians on all sides. Even though the Novanti were suffering heavy casualties from the disciplined Tungrian defense, it was only a matter of time before the tribesmen prevailed.

Above the din of battle, Arrius heard a sound growing steadily louder that alternated between a shriek and a prolonged howl. It was the distinctive and unmistakable sound of the Dacian *draconarius* standard. For whatever reason, the Dacian cavalry had returned, and their arrival raised enthusiastic cheers from the Tungrian defenders. The cavalry was about to add another dimension to the battle with an outcome now very different than was certain only moments before.

Cries of alarm followed by the sound of a carnyx indicated the Novanti had seen the approaching Dacian cavalry sweeping down on them. Abandoning the fight, the tribesmen turned and fled back the way they came. With relief, he saw Ilya, still mounted, disappear over the earthen wall. From the sounds of the battle beyond the walls, the fighting was intense. The assault on the north and west sides of the fort continued unabated. When the north wall seemed on the verge of being overrun, Flavius led a counterattack in time to blunt the native assault and regain control of the ramparts. It was impossible to tell which side was dominating the other as the din of battle continued for some time without any sign of lessening.

Arrius watched the desperate fighting inside the fort and heard the all too familiar clamor of battle beyond the walls with growing sadness. Until now, he had never harbored any personal thoughts much less doubt about spending a lifetime of fighting during which the enemy was defined by Rome. Eventually, personal feelings gave way to professional detachment. As a legionary, it was easy to be loyal to the eagle; obedience to it did not require and even discouraged any thought concerning the legitimacy of the orders he followed or gave. Now the conflict raging between the men he once comanded and the tribesmen only served to emphasize his conflicted loyalty for both sides of the battle.

His first indication the battle was over, at least for now, was the gradual silence that descended on the fort broken only by the occasional pitiful cries of a wounded animal or the groans of the injured legionaries lying near the wooden cage. Arrius took in the devastation and realized if not for the timely arrival of Seugethis, the cohort would have been destroyed to a man. He estimated less than half the legionaries remained alive, and many who did bore wounds serious enough to make them ineffective. The fighting had been terrible and relentless with neither side ready to accept defeat. Here and there, legionaries and Novantii warriors were locked together in death. The few surviving draft animals stood in small groups as if trying to seek comfort from each other's presence. He saw an ox with several arrows protruding from its heaving body standing a short distance away lowing pitifully; suddenly, the animal's front legs buckled, and it pitched forward.

He heard the drum of hooves and saw the Dacian cavalry, or what he presumed was left of it, coming slowly through the north and east entrances; Seugethis led the column entering the north entrance. That Seugethis was not in pursuit of the withdrawing tribesmen and the comparative few cavalrymen straggling into the fort suggested the Dacians had suffered casualties too great to pursue the fleeing tribesmen. Seugethis dismounted and gave the reins of his mount to another cavalryman before slowly walking toward Flavius standing on the east wall. The usually exuberant Dacian seemed uncharacteristically subdued. Arrius wished he was close enough to hear what the three men were saying. After engaging in a brief conversation, the three men parted. It soon became obvious from subsequent activities that the legionaries and cavalrymen were preparing for another assault.

Seugethis turned and looked back at the battlefield littered with the dead and dying, and said to Flavius, "They fought well. I think if their numbers had been greater, Zalmoxis wouldn't have been able to save us."

"Why did you come back?" Flavius asked.

"My rear guard saw native horsemen heading in the direction of the fort. I thought it was possible you might be in trouble, and I've never been one to overlook the possibility of a battle," he said with a trace of a smile.

"We would have fared better if you never left."

"True, but then if I'd stayed, I was afraid I might have to kill your tribune. Now it seems I will have to remain."

A few minutes later, Querinius joined the two men still standing near the east entrance. "Do you think they'll come back?" Querinius asked. Apart from the tight grip on the hilt of his gladius, the tribune was composed. Before either Flavius or Seugethis answered, Querinius followed with another reasonable question already on the minds of both men. "If they do, can we withstand another attack?"

Flavius spoke first. "If I were Bothan, I would press the attack. He knows we've suffered badly. Arrius was right that Bothan cannot afford to lose. They'll attack again, possibly today, perhaps tomorrow. Their losses are heavy, but then so are ours."

"I agree with Flavius," Seugethis said, "but the day grows long and the tribes seldom fight at night. I think if there is another assault, it will be tomorrow."

"What if we give up the hostages in return for allowing us to leave?" Querinius asked hopefully.

"Arrius as well?" Flavius asked.

"Never!" The tribune replied emphatically. "I'm willing to consider handing over the hostages if it comes to that, but Arrius will die no matter what happens here. I will see to it myself if we are overrun."

"Arrius still lives?".

"He does. The tribune decided it might be better to take him and the hostages back to General Arvinnius. I think the opportunity for that is long past. We can only hope by some chance the legion will learn of our situation and send relief. Seugethis, do you think you can get a message back to General Arvinnius?"

"It's possible, and I'll try; however, it would be two or three days at least before we can expect reinforcements. If they keep on fighting, I doubt we can last that long. It's more likely the natives will be able to increase their numbers before we can."

"It seems we have little choice for the present except to prepare for the next assault," Querinius commented, eyes shifting nervously back and forth between the other two officers before adding, "I recall in

Judaea how Ar…" he quickly corrected what he was about to say and said "*I* consolidated what was left of the *Deiotariana* Legion in the northen half of the fort. We'll use the baggage wagons for a barricade between the east and west entrances."

"I've already given the order to do so, Tribune," Flavius replied evenly. "It's a tactic Arrius taught the cohort. Decrius once told me if the primus pilus of the *Deiotariana* had not suggested doing such a thing, there would have been no survivors. I believe it was Arrius who was the *first spear* at the time."

Querinius flushed and without comment stalked off, presumably to inspect the realigned defense now feverishly underway. Flavius and Seugethis watched the departing tribune, each lost in his own thoughts. Flavius broke the silence saying in disgust, "When I face the gods, which now may be sooner than I wish, I will ask why they ever let that bastard be born and become a Roman officer."

Seugethis nodded. "I may yet kill the son of a bitch if the natives don't, but for now we need every sword, even his."

"Both sides have suffered greatly," Crixtacus said to Arrius as the two men surveyed the activities in the fort. Throughout the afternoon and into the evening, the two men watched the Tungrians preparing for the next attack. Damaged walls along the northern half of the fort were repaired, and tribuli from the southern side were implanted in front of the overturned wagons now forming a wall connecting the east and west sides of the fort. The new makeshift breastwork was located only a few paces from the rear of the wooden cage. The legionary that had been posted just outside the entrance was no longer present; Arrius suspected the cohort's reduced strength was responsible for removing the guard.

"I think both sides will keep on fighting, but if Bothan chooses not to, the Selgovi will," Arrius said.

"How do you know the Selgovi are here?"

"I saw Ilya and Tearlach. I suspect somehow Tearlach learned I was a prisoner and told Ilya."

"Then Ilya knows Bothan betrayed you."

"True, but it's unlikely she'll call Bothan to account until the battle is finished. Unfortunately, Bothan's actions will not improve relations between the Selgovi and the Novanti."

"Bothan did what he had to do," Crixtacus replied stiffly, sounding defensive. "I would have done the same."

Arrius wasn't surprised at the comment and took no offense. Under the circumstances, there was no point in arguing the matter, and he attempted a conciliatory response.

"I don't fault Bothan, and if we leave here alive, I'll try to convince Ilya not to either."

"Why?"

"Because the Selgovi and Novanti have a better chance of survival if they stay together. The Romans will always prevail if the tribes don't fight as one."

"That may be so; however, the alliance will not last. It never does," Crixtacus added with a fatalistic shrug.

Arrius thought it was better to drop the subject of tribal unity that if achieved would make them less vulnerable to Rome and each other. He recalled his talks with Beldorach. The High Chieftain was an exception to the other Britannian leaders he had met including Crixtacus. Beldorach was a visionary and had he lived, he would have posed a formidable obstacle to Roman expansion. He wondered if one day it would be his son's destiny to achieve Beldorach's vision.

Chapter 27

In the flickering light of the fire, Ilya anxiously searched the faces of Bothan and the Novanti clan chiefs for any sign of defeat and intent to withdraw. Bothan was lying on his side with his eyes closed as another warrior bandaged a deep gash extending from the tribal leader's right shoulder to his elbow that was still bleeding and dangerously so. Bad as the arm wound was, it was minor in comparison to the right side of his chest where the metal shaft of a Roman spear protruded and imbedded too deep to remove. The wound was mortal, and Bothan accepted the reality with stoic calm. Tearlach as well suffered a grievious wound to the left side of his face; if he managed to survive, he would never have the use of the eye again. Ilya surveyed the council made up equally of Novantian and Selgovan chiefs and saw that she and Decrius were the only ones present without wounds. Decrius had not participated in the battle except to remain close to her. His refusal was not held against him when he voiced his reason. Because of Tearlach's insistence, along with the other Selgovan clan chiefs, she had reluctantly left the battle after realizing all she could contribute was moral support by being close by and visible.

Their losses were much greater than anticipated, and she wondered if she should be the one to suggest terminating the battle, given Bothan's condition. Even if he managed to stay alive through the night, he would not mount a horse again except in the next world. She reluctantly accepted what Tearlach and Decrius insisted that if the Novanti did leave, the Selgovi alone would not be capable of taking the fort. Perhaps, the only recourse was to wait until the Romans left the fort and then attack them in the open.

Ilya was relieved to hear Bothan announce, "We'll be better prepared tomorrow. If not for their cavalry, we would have destroyed them. I think their commander will not sleep well tonight after what happened to his fort today." A moment later, Bothan added philosophically, "I may sleep better – perhaps much longer."

"Did anyone see where the hostages are being held?" Ilya asked.

"They would be held in a small cage fashioned of logs or poles with a log floor to prevent digging out," Decrius said.

"I saw such a thing near the center of the fort close by the east wall," Tearlach volunteered.

"Then concentrate on the east wall," Bothan said. "Their losses will make it more difficult for them to defend the fort."

"They won't try to defend the entire fort," Decrius said.

"What do you mean?" Bothan managed to ask before a racking cough caused him to lie back with his eyes closed. Ilya saw that his chin was flecked with blood.

"The commander will consolidate his defense on the northern half of the fort."

"How can you be sure of this?" Bothan asked his voice barely above a whisper.

"Because that is the way they've been trained. The wooden stakes the Romans call tribuli have been removed from the southern half of the fort."

His eyes still closed, Bothan pursed his lips in thought as he considered the new information. "Well, it changes nothing and may even make the task that much easier. Ilya, your horsemen will attack the east wall while mine will assault the other three. Keep enough men back to deal with their cavalry when it leaves the fort."

Frowning, Decrius looked at Ilya and said in a voice too low for Bothan to hear, "We should attack on foot. Horses will not be able to get across the outer ditches and through the additional tribuli now on top of the walls."

Ilya immediately addressed Bothan. "The Selgovi will attack the east wall on foot. I fear the horses may be less effective in breaching the obstacles the Romans have constructed."

"Do as you see fit," Bothan said dismissively. After a moment of silence, he opened his eyes and sat up and regarded the council comprised of senior clan chiefs of both tribes. "I'll not be with you tomorrow; therefore, it's my wish since Crixtacus is a prisoner that Tearlach lead the attack in my place." He directed his attention to the Novanti clan chiefs who sat scowling at the surprising announcement. Aware of the tension his decision created, he forestalled the inevitable objections and potential rift by saying, "Tearlach is the most experienced among you. It is for that reason I've decided." Bothan looked at each clan chief and repeated the question, "Do you swear by Cernunnos and the memory of your fathers that you will obey my order?" To Ilya's relief, each Novanti clan chief acknowledged with a curt nod. He sank back and spoke what would prove to be his final words, "If Crixtacus survives, I name him High Chieftain of the Novanti."

Arrius estimated it was well into the middle watch when he heard the rattle of the iron shackle locking the cage door. He thought at first it was his imagination or caused by the wind blowing in fitful gusts. The usual noises of the fort coupled with the stamping and snorting of the restless Dacian mounts tethered on the other side of the makeshift wall made it difficult to tell. A moment later, he felt a wave of cool air wash over him, and he realized the door had been opened. He heard a low voice asking for him and knew it was Rufus. The hostages began stirring restlessly.

Arrius made his way to the entrance and crawled out. Rufus, face a pale blur, was standing by the open door. The legionary was carrying a balteus, helmet and pilum.

"Arrius, come with me, and I'll lead you out of the fort," Rufus whispered. "Put these on," he added while handing him the helmet and belt of a common legionary.

"Not without the others," Arrius said restraining the legionary's attempt to close the door.

"The arrangements are only for you."

"Then I won't leave."

Rufus hesitated and then relented, "All right, wait here until I return. I'll have to make new arrangements." The legionary left, and Arrius was tempted to take a chance and leave with the hostages now to reduce the risk Rufus was taking. He knelt down and whispered for Crixtacus. When Crixtacus managed to gain the entrance, Arrius leaned close to the clan chief's ear and told him what was happening.

"There's a legionary loyal to me who will show me a way past the guards. He intended only me. I told him I would not leave without the hostages. He's gone to see if whoever is helping him will include you and the others as well."

Crixtacus cupped his hand close to Arrius's ear and whispered, "Go with him when he returns. We'll wait a short time and make our own way out. Even if we fail, I'll give thanks to you and your man for giving us the chance."

Arrius conceded it was a reasonable compromise considering the larger risk of getting thirteen captives past the fort's defenses instead of a single individual. He was still debating whether to accept the proposal when Rufus suddenly reappeared. "He won't agree. He claims the risk is too great."

"Then we'll try another way. Crixtacus, have your men get ready to come out when I return, and for the love of your gods, tell them not to make a sound." He quickly told Crixtacus and then Rufus what he intended to do. He concluded by saying to each of them separately, "If my plan doesn't work, make your own way out the best way you can." Arrius turned to Rufus and whispered, "Let's find Querinius."

Ever a light sleeper, Tiberias Querinius thought the night would never end. He dreaded the coming dawn and the prospect of more fighting. He thought the waiting was far worse than the actual fighting. He was pleased with how he had acquitted himself so far and how effectively he had managed to overcome the terror that paralyzed him in Judaea.

The sides of the tent flapping noisily in the gusting wind added to the difficulty of trying to sleep. The occasional soft patter of raindrops instead of being soothing was just another irritating sound. The flickering oil lamp on the table nearby cast restless and distracting shadows on the tent walls. He considered blowing out the flame but thought the darkness would only stimulate his imagination even more. His greatest worry he would be unable to maintain his composure tomorrow was surprisingly greater than the possibility he wouldn't survive. He felt like screaming and brought a fist to his mouth to stifle the urge. Nothing was going the way as it should. His authority was badly eroded, the capability to withstand the next major attack was questionable and his aching head made it impossible to think clearly. Instead of helping, the quantity of wine he consumed succeeded only in making the pounding in his head worse. A wave of self-pity swept over him. Why did Fortuna always seem to abandon him when he needed her more than ever?

Querinius sat up and reached for the wine jar sitting on top of the table next to the lamp. It was empty. He called irritably for the orderly sleeping on the other side of the screen that partitioned the tent into two rooms. When there was no response, he stood up somewhat unsteadily. Before he had taken a step, the screen parted. Querinius froze in shock when he saw a grim-faced Arrius standing before him holding a gladius.

The camp was more restless than usual for such a late hour. Arrius heard a muffled scream at the far end of the camp and knew the medicus was busy tending the wounded. He heard legionaries talking quietly inside their tents as they passed by. The bloody battle the afternoon before and the prospect of another one in a few hours was enough to leave even the most battle-seasoned legionary unable to sleep. He was grateful for the cold blustery wind and occasional spatter of rain, incentive enough for the wakeful legionaries to remain in their tents instead of gathering outside. As it was, there was little activity except for legionaries returning from or leaving for guard duty or seeking relief in a latrine trench. The few they encountered hurried past them without curiosity, eager to return to the drier and comparative warmth of their blankets.

The tribune's tent stood in the center of the compound adjacent to the *principia* and apart from the parallel lines of leather tents extending on either side housing the eight-man *contubernia*. He knew with certainty from the standard way a Roman fort was always configured, Flavius's tent would be on the other side of the headquarters tent. In the event of a night attack, a standard layout ensured confusion would be minimized when every legionary would be able to find his way through the fort even in the darkest night.

Arrius waited for Rufus to approach the guard standing at the entrance and silhouetted by a torch sputtering fitfully behind him. He had tried to convince Rufus to return to his tent before his role in the escape attempt was discovered. The legionary was predictably adamant in his refusal as he was with his insistence he intended to leave the fort with Arrius. Reluctantly, he finally agreed knowing there was no time or point in debating the matter further.

The guard came to attention when he recognized the optio. After a brief exchange, Rufus beckoned Arrius forward to replace the sentinel. The legionary quickly disappeared in the darkness without questioning why he was being relieved sooner than expected.

Arrius pulled the tent flap aside and stepped inside the vestibule. He waited quietly until his eyes grew accustomed to the dark interior illuminated only by the faint glow of an oil lamp shining through the thin inner screen. He drew the gladius slowly when he spotted the orderly asleep on a pallet next to the tribune's field desk. Arrius heard the creak of the cot in the next room followed by the tribune's querulous voice calling for the orderly. The orderly awakened and started to get up only to stop, his eyes opened wide when he took in the tall figure standing over him and the sword blade hovering inches from his face. Arrius put a finger to his lips gesturing for silence. When Rufus entered the tent behind him, Arrius pointed to the orderly and then pulled the screen aside.

"Since you refused to accept my invitation earlier, I decided to come to you." The white-faced tribune stood frozen with an expression of shocked disbelief that slowly turned to resignation.

"Go ahead and kill me and get it over with, but if you expect me to beg you not to, I won't give you the satisfaction," Querinius said in a thick voice that quavered slightly.

"As much as I would like to run this sword through your belly, your time hasn't come yet. I need you alive, and if you cooperate, the gods may persuade me to let you live."

"What is it you want?"

"It's quite simple. I'm leaving here with the hostages, and you're going to help."

"Why should I help you?" Querinius protested. "If I help you, you're going to kill me anyway."

"That is a certainly a possibility, and I confess a tempting one at that in return for all you've done or tried to do to me. You're contemptible, Querinius. You should have died in Judaea. I could spend the rest of my life, as I've been doing since then, wondering why the gods allowed you to survive when better men than you did not. I would gladly kill you now except that would do nothing to help the hostages. I need you, Querinius, and you may thank the gods you are worth more to me alive than dead. Do what I tell you, and you may yet live long enough to leave Britannia."

Querinius hesitated, a gleam of hope in his eyes. "If I do as you say, you won't kill me?"

"Let me put it another way. I can promise you won't live to see the sunrise if you don't."

"All right, tell me what you want me to do."

"Orderly, come in here," Arrius said without replying to the question. When the wide-eyed orderly appeared, he surprised him and the tribune by saying, "Find Centurion Flavius and tell him to come here alone. You may tell him Arrius and Tribune Querinius request his presence as soon as possible."

Following the orderly's hasty departure, the astonished tribune shook his head and said, "Soon, the entire camp will be awake and ready to kill you before you take three steps outside this tent."

"Perhaps, but I think not. Flavius understands better than you if he were to do that, you will die now. Unlike you, Flavius is an experienced legionary who can appreciate a situation in which his commander's life, regardless of how worthless it may be, will be forfeit should he call out the garrison and force an unfortunate conclusion for both of us. Flavius also has another quality you've never had. He will do as I ask because he's a loyal, honorable man and pledged to do his duty in behalf of you and his command regardless of how distasteful. Even though I've explained it, I doubt you're capable of understanding what I just said."

A few mintes later, Arrius heard Flavius in the outer vestibule say to Rufus, "I might have guessed who was responsible for this. Rufus, I'm afraid I'm finally out of patience with you." Arrius smiled, recalling the many times in the past when he dealt with the legionary's habitual and intractable behavior.

Flavius entered the room fully dressed in cuirass and helmet, lines of fatigue etched on his face. The crusted blood on his arms from several gashes gave evidence of his personal involvement in the battle. After a quick glance at Querinius, Flavius ignored him completely and addressed Arrius.

"Well, Marcus, I see you weren't able to sleep either," Flavius said with a sardonic smile. "Perhaps it might have been better for all of us if you had simply left while you had the chance." Before he could answer, Flavius's eyes widened in sudden comprehension. "Of course, it's about the hostages."

Arrius nodded. "I need you to improve our chances of getting me and the hostages out of here without causing a lot of unnecessary deaths including mine or the brave Tribunus Laticlavus here whom I am pleased to say has agreed to cooperate." Flavius arched an eyebrow and listened as Arrius continued. "You and Querinius will leave here with me and Rufus to go and get the hostages now waiting for me. I will, of course, have a dagger ready to end the tribune's life if he should be foolish enough to alert the garrison. If the alarm is given, the hostages have been told to fight their way out. If they are not able to, they will still have a better chance than before. From the hostage cage, we'll go to the east entrance where you will instruct the guards to let us pass."

"What happens to the tribune when you leave the fort?"

"He goes with me. If all goes well, I'll consider releasing him. If things do not go well, he will die. When I see Bothan and Ilya, I'll do my best to persuade them to allow what's left of the cohort to leave unharmed with the dead and wounded. Naturally, I cannot guarantee they will agree, but I promise to try. With the hostages free, the tribal leaders might be willing to withdraw in the belief their honor has been satisfied."

"It seems I've little choice but to agree, and I confess it will be difficult to hold out much longer. However, we must be careful not wake up the garrison for if the legionaries wake up and realize the tribune's life is in jeopardy, they're more likely to let you kill him than try to save him."

While Rufus tied Querinius's hands behind him and wrapped a cloth around the tribune's mouth, Flavius looked curiously at Arrius and asked, "What will you do if you are successful in getting away?"

"I'll find Ilya and my son and try to stay away from Roman patrols and forts."

"Do you have any regrets you didn't go back to Rome?"

"No. I had no reason to go. What became and remains important to me lies to the north. It may well be the same for you when some day this life is no longer important." Arrius could tell from Flavius's doubtful expression the centurion had no idea what he was talking about.

With Flavius in the lead, the four men made their way down the center of the camp toward the wooden cage. Arrius maintained a tight hold on Querinius's tunic as they walked. The point of the dagger blade in the tribune's back was a persuasive reminder to cooperate. Before they reached their destination, the clouds above began to thin and reveal a crescent moon bright enough to further increase the risk of discovery. A few paces from the wooden cage, Arrius signaled Flavius to stop and urged Querinius into the lead. He found Crixtacus crouched by the entrance.

"Crixtacus, get them out now." Arrius whispered. The hostages quickly and silently exited the cage. When the last man cleared the entrance, Crixtacus formed the Novanti into a column, two abreast, as he instructed. He hoped the darkness would conceal the fact the guard detail wore no helmets and were unarmed. If they were noticed, he counted on Flavius's presence to dispel any suspicion. If the alarm was given, he depended on Flavius's ability to control the situation long enough to get safely over the outer ditches. With Flavius again in the lead and Arrius close behind keeping a tight hold on Querinius, the silent column moved along the row of upturned wagons toward the east entrance. With the cavalry horses tethered on the other side of the makeshift wall and the Dacian cavalrymen occupying the south side of the fort, there was no threat of running into a sentry.

Without incident, they neared the last wagon and approached the narrow space allowing foot passage to the east entrance left open to allow the cavalry to pass through when and if the attack was resumed. Arrius saw the dark shape of a sentry walking his post on the rampart ahead of them; the shape disappeared when a cloud obscured the moon and cast the fort once more into darkness.

Flavius no sooner made his way past the wagon when a voice challenged him.

"Flavius, I see you don't trust your centurion in charge of the watch to ensure the fort is secure." To his dismay, Arrius did not need to see the speaker to recognize who it was. Of all men to be on watch duty, it had to be Cotta.

To his relief, Flavius reacted calmly as if nothing was amiss. "Had I not been checking the guard, then you and the other centurions would have wondered why. I think tonight there is additional reason for concern, don't you agree?"

"Aye, although so far there hasn't been a sound, only their fires tell the bastards are still out there. We showed them," the centurion blustered, "and we'll give them more of the same if they try again."

Then as if was an afterthought, Cotta added, "I wouldn't be surprised if they've gone and left the fires burning just to keep us awake."

"I'm no longer surprised by anything including the possibility you may be right. But if there's another attack, we need to be prepared. Now go and find Seugethis and then the other centurions and tell them as soon as the third watch has been posted, I want all officers to report to the principia." Arrius breathed a sigh of relief. Finding Seugethis would oblige the centurion to go to the south end of the fort.

"You can send an orderly for that," was the surly response.

"But I'm sending you instead. Now go find him. The third watch will soon be posted."

Arrius heard Cotta moving away in the direction of the Dacian camp. A moment later, Flavius appeared. "Marcus, the way is clear, but you don't have much time before the sentry returns."

"Thank you, Flavius." The centurion made no reply as he watched the men file past him and quickly disappear.

"Bothan is dead."

Tearlach's cryptic announcement was not unexpected. When Ilya left the Novanti camp the night before, it was evident the tribal chief would not live much longer. Her reason for sending Tearlach to visit Bothan's camp as the eastern sky began to brighten was less to confirm what she expected and more to assess Novanti resolve to continue fighting. Bothan was not a particularly skillful leader in battle, but when he was alive, he did claim the loyalty and obedience of his warriors. Now that he was dead, would they obey his edict to keep on fighting?

"What do you think they will do?" she asked.

Tearlach shrugged. "They are discussing it now. Some want to return to their villages. They believe the Romans cannot be defeated and fear the hostages have already been killed. There are just as many who want to stay and fight, but even those who do say they will not follow a Selgovan into battle."

"A Selgovan?" Ilya asked.

"It was Bothan's wish I lead the next attack. The Novanti clan chiefs are not ready that it be so."

"When will they decide?"

Shaking his head, Tearlach said, "I don't know, but I believe they will leave. If they remain, it's because Bothan named Crixtacus to be High Chieftain, and that may oblige them to keep on fighting."

Ilya folded her arms and fought back the tears threatening her composure. She was thankful it was still dark enough Tearlach and the others couldn't see the desperation on her face.

"Even if the Novanti decide to leave, we can still fight the Romans," Cuileán said behind her.

"We cannot fight them without the Novanti as long as the Romans remain in the fort," Ilya responded firmly. "If the Novanti leave, we'll wait to see what the Romans do. It's possible when they leave the fort, there may be an opportunity to free Arrius and the other hostages – if they still live."

"What if they do not?" Cuileán asked.

"Then we will leave as well. Our losses have been too great to fight only for revenge." The murmur of approval was an indication she made the decision they were waiting to hear even if it wasn't the decision she wanted to make.

As they reached the first defensive ditch, Querinius began to struggle in an attempt to break Arrius's firm grasp. The noise and the tribune's muffled cries were loud enough to arouse the sentry who called out to the other sentries along the wall. In moments, the growing noise behind him signified the fort was on full alert. He heard the whispering thud of spears striking the ground nearby. He knew the chance of a pilum finding a target in the darkness was remote. Unfortunately, the clouds were thinning rapidly, and the moonlight, faint as it was, would improve legionary marksmanship. Also cause for concern was the time it was going to take to cross the two V-shaped ditches.

Resisting the urge to cut the tribune's throat and catch up with the others who wasted no time in passing him by, Arrius instead reversed his hold on the dagger and brought the heavy hilt down on the back of Querinius's head, and the tribune slumped unconscious to the ground. Arrius picked the tribune up and threw him into the waist-deep ditch and jumped in after him with Rufus close behind.

"Finish him!" Rufus whispered. "We have to keep going!" His words were given greater urgency when another spear impacted close above where they were just standing.

"He goes with me!" Arrius lifted Querinius up and shoved him over the edge of the ditch. "Go on without me, Rufus," Arrius urged as he prepared to climb up beside the tribune.

"My chances of surviving a native spear or sword will be much better if I'm with you."

Arrius thought the legionary's concern was justified. Neither Crixtacus nor any of the other hostages would recognize Rufus if they saw him. A Roman who did not speak any of the local dialects would be killed without hesitation if found outside the fort.

"Fine, but get rid of the helmet." He heard the hollow thump of the helmet as it landed at the bottom of the ditch.

Arrius slid over the edge first and then reached down for Rufus's hand to assist the shorter man over the top. Arrius swung Querinius over his shoulder and headed for the next ditch a few paces away and dropped the unconscious tribune into it. By now, the approaching dawn and disappearing cloud cover was rapidly increasing visibility and improving both the accuracy and number of missiles coming their way. Arrius peered back at the fort and knew they were still within range of the pila arching toward them. He gave silent thanks that the archers had not joined the effort. A little farther and they would be out of spear range, but arrows would present a much greater problem. Arrius looked toward the nearest hill whose outline was just starting to become visible. With no sound or sight of Crixtacus and the other hostages, he assumed they were probably more than halfway to safety.

Arrius paused long enough to catch his breath before depositing Querinius on the opposite edge of the ditch. He helped Rufus scramble to the top then climbed up after him. He was in the act of heaving the tribune to his shoulder when he heard a gasp followed by a curse. Out of the corner of his eye, he saw Rufus stumble and fall to one knee. At first, Arrius thought he may have tripped over one of the many bodies or horse carcasses littering the field. When the legionary stood up and began a shambling run, he knew something was wrong. Rufus remained in the lead, but he was also moving too slowly. The tribune seemed to grow heavier and heavier with each step he took, and the rapidly brightening sky was giving the archers a visible target.

His lungs began to burn, and his breathing was becoming more labored with each step. He felt Querinius's body suddenly jerk about the time he heard the familiar swish of an arrow passing close by. A part of him knew it was foolish to keep on carrying the tribune only to find out later he was already dead. It took only another arrow whizzing past and narrowly missing him for him to decide he had been foolish long enough. Just as he was about to drop Querinius, Crixtacus appeared at his side.

"Give him to me!" said the clan chief.

Arrius was too winded to argue the point and paused only long enough to drape the tribune's body over the smaller man's shoulder. At the same time, he saw Rufus lying face down with an arrow imbedded in his back. As carefully as he could, he gathered Rufus up in his arms and staggered on.

When the fusillade of arrows ceased, Arrius thought he was finally out of range. His relief was short-lived. He heard shouts and the drum of hoofbeats behind him. Realizing the futility of reaching the nearest hills and safety, he stopped and lowered Rufus gently to the ground. He stood up and drew the gladius then waited for the oncoming horsemen. It was light enough to recognize Seugethis and Cotta in the lead followed by a dozen or more Dacian cavalrymen.

Arrius was quickly surrounded. Seugethis wore an expression of thoughtful concern in contrast to Cotta's gloating smile.

"Put down your sword, Arrius," the centurion ordered triumphantly, "unless you intend to put the blade in your own belly."

"Get off your horse and take it from me, Cotta."

"I don't think so. Even if I were fortunate to defeat you, I would rather forego the pleasure and see you die a more entertaining and slower death."

Seugethis looked at Cotta and said, "Centurion, if you want Arrius, I advise you do as he said and get off your horse."

"What do you mean? He's our prisoner. We'll take him back to the fort along with that scum," pointing to Rufus.

"No, they're your prisoners. Do with them as you will; however, think carefully on the matter before you take them back alone. If I were to wager on the outcome, it would not be on you, Centurion." Seugethis shifted his attention to Arrius and with a faint smile said, "Marcus Arrius, I think Zalmoxis is looking after you this day." Then almost pensively, he added, "However, it would be best not to depend on him too much in the future." Arrius acknowledged the cavalryman with a slight nod and watched as the Dacian troop galloped off toward the fort.

Attempting to put a brave front on his sudden reversal, Cotta said, "Pick him up and start walking back toward the fort."

"Cotta, leave now while you can."

The centurion never had a chance to reply. Behind him Arrius heard the faint twang of a bow string a moment before an arrow slammed into Cotta's left eye. Without making a sound, Cotta fell backward off the horse. The incident happened so suddenly and quietly, the centurion's mount remained calmly where it was. Arrius slowly approached the horse and took hold of the reins. After guiding the horse to where Rufus lay, he lifted the unconscious legionary and placed him face down over the saddle. He walked slowly beside the horse with one hand on Rufus to keep him from sliding off. He didn't have to go far before he saw Ilya running toward him.

Chapter 28

"Will he live?" Arrius asked Ilya after she removed the arrow and started to bandage Rufus's wound.

"The point was lodged between two ribs and fortunately did not penetrate as deep as I feared. He has a chance if the wound or the lacerations on his back don't fester."

Arrius breathed a sigh of relief and gave silent thanks to the gods for the optimistic prediction. "It seems I continue to be indebted to Rufus." With Ilya and Decrius listening attentively, he related how the legionary made their escape possible.

When he finished, Decrius asked, "Why did you bring Querinius with you when it would have been safer to kill him once you left the fort?"

"I thought to use him to bargain with Bothan in the belief he would spare the fort from further attack. With Bothan dead, I will make the same offer to Crixtacus."

"The Novanti losses were heavy, and they may not resume the attack. Our losses were also considerable," Ilya added. "Tearlach is in their camp now to see what the Novanti intend to do. With Crixtacus as Bothan's likely successor, the Novanti will choose based on what he will say."

"What about the Selgovi? Do you and Tearlach intend to keep fighting?" Arrius asked, keeping his voice and expression neutral.

"I pledged to help the Novanti free you and the hostages. With Bothan dead and you and the hostages free, I will tell Crixtacus I see no reason to keep on fighting." The answer was what he hoped for.

"Arrius, come with me to the Novanti camp. I want to try to persuade Crixtacus to break off the assault before Tearlach succeeds in convincing him otherwise. I believe both sides have suffered enough."

"What if Flavius decides to keep on fighting?" Decrius asked.

Arrius shook his head. "He won't. Flavius as much as said he would be content to get what's left of the cohort back to the new wall. Even Seugethis may have his fill of fighting for the time being."

"I hope you succeed, but I wouldn't say that if it was a Roman cohort." The hard look in Decrius's eyes confirmed the Brigantian's burning hatred of Romans had not abated.

Arrius and Decrius approached Querinius standing with his back to a tree, ankles lashed together with his wrists tied securely to a low-hanging limb above him. The tribune's face showed the pain of the broken arrow shaft protruding from his right thigh. Scowling to mask his fear, Querinius said, "Arrius, you broke your word. I did what you asked, now let me go."

"I never gave my word. I said only that I would not kill you, and I won't. I cannot say the same for this man," indicating Decrius standing next to him. "Given the chance, Decrius would gladly slit your throat or a lot worse. It was his wife and son who died when the Sixth Legion, under your command, attacked the Briganti. You may recall Decrius. He was one of the few survivors of the *Deiotariana* who served Rome well in Judaea and certainly far better than you. Until recently, he was a loyal centurion assigned to the Tungrian cohort at Banna."

"Then he's as much a traitor as you are, Arrius. I'm sorry he wasn't with his wife and son when we killed them."

The blood drained from Decrius's face as he reached for his sword.

"Hold, Decrius!" Arrius said placing a restraining hand on the Brigantian's wrist. "We'll let the Novanti decide his fate."

At first, Arrius wasn't certain Decrius was going to heed him. If the former centurion did not, it was doubtful he'd be able to prevent him from killing Querinius. Gradually, Decrius regained control, and he thrust the half-drawn gladius back into the scabbard.

With a mocking laugh, Querinius goaded Decrius, "Was your wife comely? Well, it probably didn't matter if she was or not. I wonder how many legionaries used her before they killed her, or after—"

The tribune never finished what he was about to say. Decrius stepped toward Querinius, and this time Arrius didn't try to stop him. The Brigantian grasped the arrow shaft in the tribune's thigh and began slowly twisting it. Screaming in agony, Querinius tried to kick Decrius away but was unable to loosen the Brigantian's firm grip, and his movements only added to the excruciating pain. Querinius fainted long before Decrius, with a final tug, pulled the shaft free.

"What have the Novanti decided," Ilya asked Crixtacus.

"I still have many warriors who want to keep on fighting, but I have almost as many who wish to return to their villages. What of the Selgovi?"

Ilya frowned. "I will not leave if the Novanti decide to keep on fighting, but I think it's time to stop fighting – both of our tribes have lost too many warriors."

Crixtacus looked at Arrius. "I would like to hear your thoughts."

"I know the commanders and those men well. They will never surrender, and if the fighting continues, many more men on both sides will die. It is my wish to see the legionaries who have survived so far be permitted to leave unharmed. They were once loyal to me, and it is difficult to watch them destroyed. There will be no winners if the battle continues, only more dead legionaries and warriors. Except for two, the hostages are free, and the Roman commander is now your prisoner to do with as you wish; this alone may be the only victory the Novanti can achieve."

Crixtacus glanced at Querinius sitting trussed and ashen-faced on the ground and. turned to Ilya. "I will tell those who wish to continue fighting the battle is over. We will fight the Romans another day. Arrius, I give you my thanks for helping us. You will always be a welcome guest in our villages." Then with a sidelong and meaningful look at Tearlach, he said, "The invitation may one day include other Selgovi as well." Tearlach frowned but tactfully refrained from commenting.

Unable to understand any of the exchange, Querinius looked beseechingly at Arrius. "Arrius, tell them to let me go, and I swear by all the gods I'll ensure Rome will let you live in peace for the rest of your life."

"You're a liar as well as a coward. The only reason you decided to take me back instead of crucifying me here was because you worried Seugethis would stop you. You schemed first with Aculinieus in Judaea and Betto here in Britannia to have me killed. What I never understood was why. Well, I no longer care what answer you might give. I don't even care what Crixtacus will do with you. Whatever he intends, it will not be pleasant and possibly bad enough to almost pity you. Querinius, make your peace with the gods, but I think you will fare as poorly in their domain as you have in this one."

Decrius went over to Crixtacus and said something too soft for Arrius to hear. Crixtacus nodded his assent.

"Arrius!" Querinius screamed when Arrius and Ilya with the rest of the Selgovi walked to their horses, "I beg you, give me your sword, and let me take my life in the Roman way."

Arrius never looked back, and he didn't need to ask Decrius why he remained behind with Crixtacus.

The fort and battlefield were unnaturally quiet. As if by tacit agreement the battle was over. There was no move by either the fort's defenders or the tribesmen to interrupt the mutual and solemn task of seeing to the wounded and retrieving the dead. Although well within arrow range from the fort, the two crucified hostages were taken down without incident under the watchful gaze of the Tungrian sentries. If the sentries wondered why the tribesmen took the cross once intended for Arrius with them, they did not voice it. Standing on the rampart, Flavius watched without surprise. He knew why. He thought if he were in their place, he would probably have done the same. The centurion left the wall and began giving orders to abandon the fort.

The Selgovi were silent as they rode north with the only sounds of their passage marked by the thudding of the horses' hooves, the creak of saddle leather and the occasional hollow thump when a wooden shield bumped a low hanging branch.

Arrius heard the tribune's screams gradually becoming fainter and fainter behind them until they faded away altogether. He took no joy in Querinius's death, nor did he believe Decrius was content the tribune's brutal execution was enough to atone for the loss of Iseult and Rialus. There would be a part of Decrius that would never allow him to forgive or forget. He thought by contrast the recent battle, a battle in which he was no more than an unwilling observer, marked a change in him that had nothing to do with Querinius. When he left Banna, he was no longer a Roman, but just living with Ilya did not mean he was a Selgovan either. He wondered whether it was his defeat of Vadrex that secured his place with the Selgovi, but he realized that was not it entirely. The Selgovi had accepted him before

292

he really accepted them. It wasn't Ilya alone responsible for coming to his rescue. The tribesmen had come because they wanted to.

Arrius gave Ferox a gentle pat and said to Ilya riding beside him, "For the first time since I left the Wall, I feel like I'm going home." He thought both Philos and Beldorach would have been pleased.

Epilogue
160 C.E.

Arrius sat dozing with a blanket wrapped around him to ward off the late winter cold. He roused briefly when either Eugenius or Rufus exclaimed triumphantly after one or the other managed a particularly successful parry or thrust with their blunted swords. They still looked to him for the finer points of swordfighting even though he privately thought both were now better than he was or possibly ever was. Not surprisingly after recovering from the arrow wound in his back which nearly claimed his life, Rufus refused to consider going back to the Antonine Wall claiming Turbo had come to him in a dream and ordered him to continue looking after Arrius. He had been secretly pleased. He would have missed Rufus more than he cared to admit.

In the intervening years since leaving Banna, he persisted in his refusal to participate in any engagements with the Romans. However, this was not true on the countless occasions when he had drawn his sword during frequent tribal conflicts that seemed to erupt over often trivial reasons. He became frustrated and impatient when the cause of conflict appeared to be manufactured simply because fighting was so deeply ingrained in the native culture.

He thought he had seen too much of war. For much of his life, he accepted war as a natural condition of both the empire and his life. It wasn't until Judaea that he began to comprehend what Philos until then failed to make him understand. There were more important things to be concerned with than his legionaries and the next battle. He wondered if the death of Sarah, the Jewish woman who jumped to her death, had become a catalyst for change. He hoped when Eugenius became High Chieftain, it would not take as long for him to understand there were other and better ways to settle matters than with spear and sword. Ruefully, he supposed it was something Eugenius would have to learn for himself.

He missed Decrius. First, it was Tearlach who failed to come back from one of the attacks on the wall fifteen years before. It wasn't long after Tearlach's death when Decrius did not return. As he feared,

294

Decrius refused to let the past go and never missed a chance to kill Romans. Even his Selgovan wife was not enough to still the Brigantian's hate. He hoped the gods had given Decrius peace.

He thought it was a curse for a soldier to grow old. He wondered why the gods allowed him to live longer than he ever wished. It had been weeks since he was able to climb on the back of a horse without assistance or the aid of a mounting block. Ever since the fluttering in his chest began, he seemed to have little strength to spare. He was quite willing now to sit quietly in the sun dreaming or thinking of the past. Now and then as he drifted off, he fancied he heard the legion trumpets, the rhythmic crunch of hob-nailed caligae on a mettaled road and the marching chants. It was sadder but easier to spend the remaining time left to him sifting through fading memories. He smiled and thought memories were like leaves floating on a swift-moving stream, they turn and twist in the current, pausing briefly when detained by some obstacle before swirling away to disappear downstream.

He realized he was no longer certain if what he recalled was real or simply imagined or some combination of both. He considered the possibility truth is not so much about fact at all but what people choose to believe, and most of all what he chose to believe. But no matter, even if he had been inclined to speak of the past, there were few left to care what he had to say, and that, he reflected, was perhaps the saddest thing of all. He was no different from others who fought and lived to tell of it only to wonder in the end why he survived when others as much or more deserving did not. There were many times in a hard-fought battle when he thought the time to kneel before the gods had come. He thought it would be wise not to expect too much from them; after all, they were known to be capricious, and it is not always possible to make sense of what they do. Whatever the gods decided, he thought, he would not mind if they would allow him to be with Ilya. It was her face he wanted to see last in this world and forever in the next. He sacrificed equestrian rank and wealth when he decided to leave Banna and Rome behind over twenty years ago. He traded it all for the woman he still loved and the son who would soon become the leader of the Selgovae Tribe. He looked across the valley below, smiled and thought, *No, I didn't sacrifice anything at all.*

They were all that was left of the noisy throng that braved the snow and harsh winter wind to view the strange object so foreign to Selgovan customs. The Selgovi had been tolerant and respectful of Arrius's simple instructions but privately horrified his body was to be burned. It was a measure of their respect for him and their devotion to Ilya that overcame their reluctance to have it done.

"Mother, I understand the first four lines – they are what he was as a Roman officer, but what do the last two lines mean?" Eugenius asked with a puzzled frown as he looked at the stone slab upon which was inscribed:

Marcus Junius Arrius
Primus Pilatus Legio XXII, Deiotariana
Praefectus, II Cohortes Tungrian Equitatae,
I Ala Dacorum, Legio VII Victrix

Sapientia per Immanitas bellum
In parte acuta quasi gladius altera manu

The slab was in a sheltered grove of trees where Marcus asked that it be located along with his ashes. The falling snow was already starting to cover the profusion of offerings the villagers had left around it.

"I don't know. I never learned to read or write Latin. Do you know, Rufus?" Ilya asked. He was studying the inscription as if by staring at it long enough he'd be able to decipher the text.

Rufus shook his head. "I don't know either. He gave me the writing on a tablet and asked me to find a stone carver. When I asked what it meant, he wouldn't tell me. He said it didn't matter, and that it was intended only for the gods in case when he came before them they no longer recognized who he was and what he had once been."

"Father never spoke to me of his time in the Roman Army," Eugenius said. "Why didn't he?"

"I believe he would say his time here in Caledonia with the Selgovi was more important for us to remember."

"I miss him," Rufus said, squinting to conceal his eyes welling up.

Ilya merely nodded. Respecting her need to be alone, Eugenius and Rufus quietly left the grove and made their way back to the settlement. Deep in thought, Ilya remained long after the two men left. Although sad, she wasn't grief-stricken. She knew Marcus had been ready to leave. Aimlessly, she brushed the blowing snow that was beginning to obscure the inscription. He asked her to tell Eugenius what the last part of the inscription said only after he experienced the desolation of war, claiming Eugenius would then be more able to understand its meaning. She mouthed the words, *Sapientia per Immanitas bellum* – wisdom through the brutality of war. *In parte acuta quasi gladius altera manu* – a sword at the side is as sharp as one in the hand. She recalled on the occasions when Eugenius was young and enthralled with weapons and tales of battle, Marcus would find opportunities to remind him it was better to keep a sword sheathed until there was no longer any other alternative but to draw it.

Ilya turned and slowly made her solitary way back to the village. Long before she reached the settlement, the blowing snow obliterated the writing on the stone slab. As she walked, she reflected on the information the messenger had brought a short time ago. The Romans were abandoning the wall and moving south. The news was received joyfully by the tribe, and the warriors were already preparing their weapons for a new spring offensive. She thought it wouldn't be too many years before she told Eugenius what the inscription said. She only hoped to live a little longer until Eugenius was old and experienced enough to truly understand its meaning as Marcus intended.

Historical Notes

Very little is really known of the tribes inhabiting Britain at this time. Unfortunately, the Celtic tribes left no written language for modern day historians to draw upon. From the time of the Roman occupation, Latin was the only written language, and that tended to be restricted to those in the upper strata of the indigenous peoples or those who were engaged in trade with the Romans. Historians interested in early Britannia have had to rely on oral history, archaeological evidence and manuscripts written by monks long after Roman occupation of the British Isles effectively ended in the fifth century. Most of what we know from contemporary sources of the period was provided by a few notable Romans such as Julius Caesar and Tacitus writing about his father-in-law, Agricola. Therefore, the reaction of the northern Caledonian Tribes (encompassing modern day Scotland) to the wall, which notably included the Selgovae, Novantae and Votadini Tribes, is not really known. In one sense, Hadrian separated the latter tribes from the Brigantes Tribe which represented the largest federation of tribes south of the wall. The wall may have had the positive effect of reducing the constant predations between the Brigantes and the northern tribes. It is probably safe to assume that it was the Brigantes who became somewhat more Romanized than the northern tribes simply because of their greater exposure to the Romans. That is not to say the Brigantes were complacent about Roman occupation. By the sheer size of their lands and numbers, the Brigantes continued to be the principal threat to *pax Romana* in central/northern Britannia.

The physical descriptions of the local population regarding appearance and dress were consistent with the few contemporary writers that chose to record their observations. Julius Caesar commented on the widespread use of blue dye to color faces and arms both in Gaul and in Britannia as well as the elaborate hairstyles of the Celtic warriors they fought. Others described the large stature of the Brythonic Tribes and the use of animal skins to make their clothing. Tattoos were common and apparently reflected Celtic designs still popular today. I found it curious there were reports the Brythonic tribes used a type of soap and had a habit of bathing that may have equaled or surpassed the hygienic practices of the Romans.

The hierarchy of the Brythonic Tribes is mainly open to conjecture. I found references to "high chieftains," "kings/queens," and "clans" during my research. For simplicity, I ended up modeling the tribal organization and leadership along the lines of the later Scottish clans. There is much to suggest the Celtic tribes may have been matriarchal with women accorded a degree of autonomy and expression far greater than popular myth accepts today.

How the tribes selected their leaders is not at all clear, but I believe hereditary rights had much to do with passing on claims to tribal leadership. What happened to the tribes? Many of those in the south became Romanized during the 400 odd years of Roman occupation only to be assimilated in later centuries by other invading cultures from the continent, Ireland and Scandinavia. I do not think it is a stretch of the imagination to believe the fractious nature and penchant for intertribal warfare characteristic of the early Caledonian Tribes were at some level responsible for the clan rivalries that characterized so much of Scotland's later history.

Eboracum (York) was the headquarters of the Ninth Legion and later the Sixth Legion, *Victrix* during the period of the novel. The capitol settlement of the Briganti was only a short distance from Eboracum – a likely reason for the *Victrix* Legion to be located there. The Brigantes Tribe was one of the largest tribes dominating the central and northern regions. It would have made sense for the Romans to keep a close eye on this particular tribe along with the means to quell any unrest. General Arvinnius's concerns about the possibility for a Briganti revolt were justified. The tribe did rebel on at least two occasions.

Unfortunately, the only remaining physical evidence of the legionary fort is beneath York Minster Cathedral. Some of the foundations of the fort were discovered during 20th century excavations done to shore up the cathedral. There is an excellent museum beneath the main cathedral floor that includes a model of what the fort may have looked like.

The Sixth legion was responsible for the security of the northern frontier. The description of the mission of the Sixth and the role of the Roman auxilia described is historically accurate.

Hadrian's Wall, or the "Wall" as the Romans referred to it, was a "tripwire" manned by foreign troops from provinces across the breadth of the Roman Empire. It was the practice of the Roman Army to position non-Roman auxiliaries on the frontier. The legions were placed in rear positions to act as the main defense should hostilities break out. Hadrian's Wall was intended to be less a defensive position and more a means for population control, tax collection and most importantly, to define the border between Rome and the barbarians.

The legions cited in the novel were actual and assigned to the locations specified. The overall command of Hadrian's Wall was believed to be at Uxellodonum (Stanwix) in the extreme western section of the wall. The main unit stationed there was a cavalry unit of over a thousand strong. In the event of a general mobilization along the wall, the cavalry would have been used to screen the western flank of the legion or legions moving to the northern region. The latter concept was a key feature of Arvinnius's battle plan for invading the north. The Novantae and Selgovae Tribes were regarded as the predominant and most belligerent of the northern tribes with the Votadini the most closely aligned with Rome.

With the death of Hadrian in 138 C.E., his adopted son Antoninus Pius assumed the imperial throne. Unlike Hadrian, who spent most of his life traveling the length and breadth of the empire, Antoninus Pius had seldom left Rome or Italia. By all reports, he was a popular choice, and the empire continued to enjoy relative stability during his reign. It seems somewhat surprising the new emperor would have ordered the movement of the Britannian frontier nearly 100 miles north by 140 C.E., thus virtually abandoning Hadrian's Wall. The reason may have been the practical necessity of reducing the expanse of the northern frontier from the 78-mile length of Hadrian's Wall to the smaller 37-mile length of the Antonine Wall located between the Firth of Forth and the north shore of the Clyde.

The Roman reasons for moving the Britannian frontier north into Caledonia as suggested by the characters in the novel are accepted by most historians. Antonninus Pius needed *dignitas* which a successful war would give him. There was also a practical reason. A smaller border would require a smaller force to safeguard it, necessitating fewer troops and making the prospect of vexillations from Britannia more available to shore up other parts of an empire under the continued threat of rebellion.

General Arvinnius's battle plan for the invasion of Caledonia is hypothetical, but I think it is based on reasonable conjecture for how it may have occurred. Epigraphic evidence from legionary monuments indicates at least parts, if not all, of the three legions stationed in Britannia were engaged in the invasion of Caledonia and subsequent construction of the Antonine Wall. In traditional Roman doctrine, the auxilia would have represented the vanguard with the legions representing the heavier and more decisive battle formations following close behind.

The Antonine wall was abandoned 20 years later around the year 160 C.E., and Hadrian's Wall was reoccupied.

Glossary of Terms and Place Names

Terms

Ala (alae [ah lye] -pl): Wing; refers to Roman cavalry units of strength varying from 500-1000 men. During the time of Julius Caesar and the republic, the Roman Army depended on foreign cavalry, placing its emphasis more on heavy and light infantry to win battles. Caesar's battle experience in Gaul taught him the importance of cavalry, and gradually the Romans began to place more importance in cavalry capabilities for reconnaissance patrols, skirmishing, and flanking maneuvers. By the second and third centuries, the Roman army completely embraced the use of cavalry and had become proficient in its use. The cavalry *alae* were the highest paid in comparison to the infantry units attesting to their increased value.

The auxilia cavalryman wore boots with spurs, a lighter cuirass and carried a longer sword. Their shields were considerably smaller and round instead of the rectangular, curved scutum of the foot soldier. In addition to the sword that all cavalry wore, some were armed with small javelins or darts carried in a quiver attached to the saddle. Other cavalrymen carried longer spears that were not thrown but were used to jab downward.

The saddle during the period had four pommels which helped to maintain a firm seat since there were no stirrups. Stirrups weren't used until sometime in the fourth or fifth century. Accordingly, it would have been very difficult if not impossible for a rider to remain securely in the saddle if the spear was used as a lance as was the case by cavalry and mounted men in later centuries.

Aquila (a qwee la): The legion standard represented by an eagle gilded in silver clutching gold thunderbolts

Aquilfer (a qweel fer): Legion's senior standard bearer ranking just below a centurion

Auxilia (owks eel e ah): Auxiliary refers to the non-Roman forces that frequently manned the frontiers. In Britannia, legionaries from Tungria (northern Belgium) and Hispania (Spain) and many other Roman provinces garrisoned the forts along Hadrian's Wall. It was common practice during the empire to relocate indigenous troops to locations along the Roman frontiers in other than their own tribal lands. The latter provided further assurance against internal rebellion. The legions frequently remained behind the line of auxiliary forces as reinforcing elements to the frontier lines. This practice also left legionary forces available for vexillations to other parts of the empire where border incursion or local rebellions threatened or must be contained. There were three main elements of the *auxilia*: cavalry *ala* organized into *turmae* (troops), the infantry *cohortes,* and the mixed cavalry and infantry called the *cohortes equitae.* Auxilia forces were either designated as *quingenaria* (500 strong) or *milaria* (1000 strong). Surprisingly, it was the cavalry *ala* that was considered the senior command over the infantry *cohortes* which in turn took precedence over the mixed cavalry and infantry unit when they were of similar size.

Balteus (bal tay oose): The Roman military belt that more than any other item distinguished the legionary. Divestiture of the belt was considered a severe punishment and a disgrace.

Brigantia: The principal goddess of the Brigantes. She embodied the spirit of the earth and air.

Caligae: The hobnailed boot-sandal all Roman officers and legionaries wore. They varied in thickness if not in basic design according to the weather and terrain. Somewhat open around the upper foot they were laced to mid-calf or higher, depending on the weather. In winter and cold regions, legionaries wore socks and wrapped their legs in felt or wool cloth for additional warmth. The Emperor Caligula derived his name from the time he was a small boy and spent much of his time in uniform around legionary barracks. Because of that, he was given the nickname *Little Boots.*

Carnyx: A type of tapered trumpet used in battle by the celtic tribes in ancient Britannia. It was as long as six feet and held vertically when played to allow the sound to carry farther, and presumably above the battlefield. Only pieces from the top (animal or dragon heads) of the instruments have been found. Depictions on Roman coins and decorative objects give some idea of the size and shape. Modern reconstructions have been included in celtic music ensembles. The sound, mournfully rich and not unpleasant, ranges from a deep bass to a high-pitched blast. The notes would have traveled a great distance and made them both effective for signaling as well as inspiring warriors to give it their best. Sample audios can be heard by Googling 'Carnyx' on the internet.

Castigato: Corporal punishment as when a centurion would strike a legionary with his vine (vitis) stick.

Centurion: The rank of centurion was both prestigious and highly coveted. The role of centurion in the Roman Army has no direct counterpart in the U.S. Army today. It is fair to say, the centurion performed the duties with the commensurate responsibility of a modern day commissioned officer, warrant officer or senior non-commissioned officer depending upon the centurion's seniority and specific position in the Roman military hierarchy. For example, the most senior centurion in a legion of typically 5000 strong could be legitimately compared to a battalion commander and normally in the grade of lieutenant colonel, while the most junior centurion was assigned duties more in line with a first sergeant or sergeant major. The centurion above all represented the senior, combat-tested leadership of the legion, which represented the primary fighting unit of the Roman Army. Unlike the tribunes and even the legion commanders who normally served only brief periods in the army, the centurions were the professional backbone upon which legion and field commanders absolutely depended upon to maintain discipline and win battles.

Entry into the centurionate was achieved in diverse ways. He could receive a direct appointment if the candidate enjoyed sufficient political clout or served in various positions below centurion considered to be possible steppingstones but not necessarily within the legion. Being the son of a centurion was a decided advantage. Coming up through the ranks, where after about 12 years a legionary would become eligible, was undoubtedly the more traditional and preferred means of access as it allowed the selection process to focus on proven ability. Literacy was essential and may have been the greatest determinant for preventing a ranker from being appointed to the centurionate. Eligibility might be accelerated by extraordinary conduct in battle. Military governors of a Roman province had the authority to make appointments to the centurionate. The senior centurion was the *primus pilus,* First Spear, a reference to the pilum or javelin that with the gladius, or short sword, was the premier weapon of the Republican and Imperial Roman Army. As the senior centurion of the legion, he led the first and largest of ten cohorts in the imperial legion. Each cohort was assigned 480 men in six centuries except for the first cohort, which was nearly double the size of the others. The duties and responsibilities of the *primus pilus* were considerably greater than that of the other centurions. By tradition, the position was held for only one year after which transfer as *primus pilus* to another legion was possible. Just as likely, it was a significant steppingstone to promotion to procurator in the civil service or as a *praefectus castrorum* (see below).

Century: A unit of 80 men commanded by a centurion; 60 centuries to a legion. The century was divided into ten *contubernia* with eight men assigned to each *contubernium.* Each *contubernium* shared a mule to carry their baggage, a tent in the field, a room or rooms in garrison and were allocated rations as a small unified mess

Cernunnos: (Ker noo nos) The Celtic god of nature, fertility, reincarnation, wealth and warriors. The deity is also known as Cernowain, Cernenus and Herne the hunter.

Cohort (Cohors): A unit of 480 men; ten cohorts to a legion. The exception was the first cohort nearly double in strength and led by the senior centurion, the *primus pilus.*

Consilium: Military council.

Contubernium (contubernia) (con tu bern ium): See 'century' above.

Cornicin (ies): Horn blower(s).

Cornicularius (corn e cue lah rius): Senior administrator of a
military headquarters.

Cunnus: Obscene reference to female genitalia. Undoubtedly
derived from the word cuneous or "wedge-shaped,' a descriptor
the Romans also applied to a cavalry formation.

Dignitas: The literal meaning meant dignity; however, the term
conveyed much more than the modern literal definition. It
represented the sum total of a man's stature gained from military
and service to the state. Romans placed more importance and
emphasis on maintaining dignitas than we do in modern times. In
particular, Roman nobility and officers would seek death before
the loss of dignitas, a loss of stature that could only be redeemed
by suicide.

Decurio(nes): An officer commanding a *turma* or cavalry troop.

Denarius (denarii): The largest Roman coinage denomination. It
is estimated the legionary foot soldier was paid about 180 denarii
a year with the combined infantry and cavalry legionaries earning
more. The cavalryman was the highest paid legionary. The
centurions were at the top of the army pay-scale and depending
on seniority, earned as much as five times the amount of an
ordinary legionary. It can be assumed centurions were also paid
according to their seniority and years of service. There are two
difficulties in assessing what the actual pay and the relative value
of the denarii in terms of modern day buying power. Legionary
pay was withheld to pay for rations, equipment and fodder;
therefore, it is impossible to say with any certitude precisely what
the legionary had left for discretionary spending, but it is safe to
assume it wasn't very much. Withholdings were even made for
burial.In the event the legionary died, he would be assured of
appropriate ceremonials and offerings in his behalf. Low or no
pay was a common complaint and the underlying reason for
various mutinies, punctuating the importance then, as it does
now, the effect soldier pay has on morale. It is believed common

practice was to pay the legionaries three times per year. The *auxilia* was paid according to a more reduced scale in comparison to the regular army.

Dolubra(e) (doe loo breye): Combined pick and axe the legionary used to dig trenches and fell trees for constructing fortifications, obtacles and roads.

Donativum: A beneficence or bonus.

Draco: The dragon standard signifying a cavalry unit and carried by the *draconarius*. A tubular cloth sleeve, fashioned serpent-like, was attached to a metal dragon, wolf or snake head. A noise device in the jaws was activated by the wind that also filled the body of the sleeve. The wind-filled body and the accompanying noise must have been impressive to see and hear when carried on parade or in battle. Apart from the psychological impression the standard was intended to convey, it may have had a practical use for indicating the wind direction to the mounted archers. The use and design of the *draconarius* was not original to the Roman cavalry but was copied from the Dacians (see Dacia above). By the third century, the standard was in widespread use by the Roman cavalry.

Ferox: Axe. The Dacian axe resembled a scythe-shaped blade on the end of wooden handle and was considered by the Romans as a formidable infantry weapon that forced them to wear additional armor on the left leg and sword arm.

Fasces: A bundle of tied birch rods around an axe that symbolized the *imperium* (authority) of a high official including the emperor and provincial governors. The fasces were carried by *lictors* walking in front of the official when he attended a public event. The fasces continue to be used in modern day and are represented on U.S. coinage and as part of the formal seal of the U.S. Congress.

Ferrata: Legion name meaning iron

Flagrum: Also, *flagellum*. A whip consisting of three leather thongs and sometimes tipped with lead. Lighter whips without the lead were used for less severe punishment while the heavier version was reserved for major punishments and to scourge a victim prior to crucifixion.

Fustuarium: A harsh sentence reserved for particularly serious offenses such as sleeping on guard or cowardice. The condemned man was set upon with cudgels, usually the wooden portion of the pilum with the metal shaft removed, by members of the individual's own unit, probably his century. The punishment was occasionally administered to an entire unit including a legion when the charge was cowardice. In such cases, lots were drawn and every tenth man was condemned. The term 'decimated' refers to this practice. In most cases, the individual or individuals died from the brutal beating. If an individual somehow managed to survive which was probably rare, he was summarily dismissed from the army in disgrace.

Gladius (glah dee oose): The short sword carried by officers and legionaries.

Gravitas: A derivation of 'gravis,' yet the word connoted much more than a 'grave' or dignified demeanor. To possess gravitas was to have not just the appearance of substance but the reality of it as well. Much like the oriental concept of 'face,' the individual who had gravitas commanded respect and authority far beyond the prestige accorded only by title or position.

Legatus (le gah toose): Legate, a provincial governor

Legio: Legion; approximately 4,800 men

Lilia: Holes dug in the ground with sharpened stakes at the bottom constructed as a part of the defensive obstacles protecting a Roman fort. They were called 'lilia' presumably as an imaginative reference to lilies which the upthrust stakes vaguely resembled.

Medicus (medi coose): Medical doctor.

Mentula: Vulgar reference to the penis

Morrigu: The Celtic supreme war goddess, queen of phantoms and demons, shape-shifter, user of magic; also known as the great white goddess who occasionally appears as a crone; also known as Morrigan and Morgan. The goddess was observed in Britain, Wales and Ireland.

Optio(nes): A rank below centurion. The *optiones* carried knobbed staffs and were generally positioned in the rear to prod legionaries who appeared to be ready to break ranks. Most likely they were equivalent to senior sergeants.

Pilum(a) (pee loom; pee la): Spear (plural). Although one generally thinks of the short sword, or gladius, as the weapon that most characterized the Roman legionary, it was the heavy javelin which defined the Roman Army. Slightly over six feet in length, it had a long pyramidal shaped point that took up almost a third of the total length of the weapon. The opposite end was encased in a short metal sleeve. The Roman Army depended on volleys of pila to deliver a punishing barrage before the front ranks charged. The metal shafts of each pilum were not tempered and bent easily on contact. The latter was an intended consequence and resulted in weighing down the shields of the opposing ranks allowing more lethal opportunity to wield the gladius at short range.

Praefectus: A position associated with equestrian rank and one step above a centurion.

Principia (prin sip e ah): The headquarters building or tent in a Roman fort.

Primipilatus (pree me pee lah toose): Former senior centurion.

Primus pilus (pree moos pee loose): It literally means "first spear" and was the form of address and title of the senior centurion commanding the first cohort in a Roman Legion. Prestigious and coveted, the position was the apex of the centurion's career. The position was usually held for only one campaign season before it was surrendered. There was no limit on the number of times an individual might hold the position, but it was probably unusual for a centurion to be so privileged multiple times. Once a centurion attained the position, he was automatically accepted into the equestrian class, a distinct step up in the social hierarchy of the Roman Republic and Empire. The vast majority of centurions never achieved the rank. See Primipilatus.

Pugio (pu gee oh): The dagger each legionary wore on the *balteus* on the opposite side from the *gladius*. Centurions wore the dagger on the right side while the legionary wore his on the left.

Sacramentum (sahc rah men toom): The oath each legionary took to the emperor after recruitment and later during the empire to the legion commander to assure personal loyalty

Sagum (sah goom): Military cloak made of rough spun wool worn by the common legionary

Salve: Hail. Used as a greeting.

Scutum (Scuta) (skoo toom; skoo tah)): Shield; (plural)

Sesterce (ses ter chee) (pl- sestertii): A coin worth approximately a quarter of a denarius (see above) and two and a half 'asses,' the smallest of the three denominations.

Testudo: A tight defensive formation named for the tortoise in which the inside ranks placed their shields over their heads while the outside ranks kept their shield facing outward. The formation provided protection from arrows and other missiles from above and the sides.

Torque (tor kwee): Military decoration worn around the neck.

Tribuli: (thistles) Thick stakes 5-6 feet long and sharpened at both ends used as part of the defense of a Roman fort or marching camp. Three stakes were lashed together at the center to form a large caltrop which were then embedded in the upcast obtained from the forward defensive ditch below the low rampart walls. The stakes would have been a deterrent to any foot or mounted attack but would have provided no protection from arrows. When the camp was moved, the stakes were pulled up, untied, and loaded on mules or carried by the legionaries for use in building the next camp.

Tribunus Laticlavus (tree bun oos lah tee clah voose): Senior tribune in the legion and a senator designate. He wore a cloak with a wide purple strip differentiating himself from the narrow stripe of worn by the junior tribunes. He was second in command of the legion in the event the legion commander was incapacitated. The other more junior tribunes assigned to a legion served mainly in administrative capacities and to give them experience in serving in a legion against the day when they might also be given command of one.

Triclinium: The dining room in a Roman villa or the *praetorium* (fort commander's quarters).

Turma(ae): Cavalry troop consisting of 32 men and led by a decurio.

Valeria: Valorous.

Vexillation (vex eel lat shun): A term used to describe a detachment to or from a legion. Typically, the Roman legions lost or received vexillations from other legions according to tactical or strategic requirements. The vexillation concept was more likely to have been exercised at the cohort level to maintain unit cohesion.

Via Principalis: One of the two main streets that crossed in the center of a Roman fortress at a right angle with the *via praetoria*. Near the intersection of these two roads is where the headquarters or principia would be located.

Victrix: Legion name meaning 'Victorius'

Vicus (vee coose): Settlement, village

Vitis (vee tis): The distinctive twisted 'vine' stick a centurion carried symbolizing his rank. It was also frequently used as an instrument for administering corporal punishment.

Woad: A plant from the mustard family from which a blue colored dye was made and which the Celts tribes used to paint their bodies.

Place Names

Aesica (Eye see ka): Greatchesters, England. It was one of the sixteen major forts on Hadrian's Wall located approximately ten miles east of Birdoswald (Banna).

Banna (Bah na): Birdoswald, England. In Latin *Banna* means tongue or spur and refers to the geography of its location at a sharp bend of the River Irthing.

Belgica (Bel gee ka): Generally modern-day Belgium and part of northern Germany.

Blatobulgium (Blato bul gee um): Birrens, Scotland, located east of Dumfries. This fort was the farthest forward post in the tribal lands of the Novantae.

Britannia (Bree tah nee ah): England, Wales and Scotland.

Castra Exploratorium (Kahs trah eks plora tori oom). Netherby, England, located near the border between Scotland and England and approximately ten miles north of Carlisle

Dacia (Datiae or Datia (Da-chee-ia): Extended over what is now is now the Carpathian-Danube region consisting roughly of Romania, parts of Hungary, Bulgaria, Yugoslavia and Moldavia.

Deva (Dew ah): Chester, England.

Eboracum (Eh bor a coom): York, England. The ruins of the headquarters of the former Ninth followed by the Sixth Legion lie under York Minister Cathedral and were discovered in the last century when the cathedral foundations were being repaired. They can be seen today via a self-guided tour of the crypt.

Fanum Cocidii (Fanumcocium) (Fah num Co cee dee): Bewcastle, England, located 7-8 miles northwest of Birdoswold (Banna). The Latin name "Shrine of Cocidius" probably derives from the local Britannic god Cocidius who was variously associated with the forest and hunters but was also depicted in statues and stone etchings as a warrior. Fanum Cocidii was the only known Roman fortress named after a deity. It is possible Fanum Cocidii was a fortress used by local British tribes before the Romans arrived, and the Romans either adopted the existing name or coined it out of respect for the deity. The worship of Cocidius was fairly widespread in Britannia and bore similarities to the Roman god Sylvanus which may account for the Roman willingness to continue honoring and worshiping the deity.

Rutupiae (Rootoo pee-aye): Richborough, England, ten miles or so north of Dover and about five miles south of Ramsgate.

Uxellodunum (Ucks el lo do noom): Stanwix, England, a suburb of Carlisle in northwest England. It is thought this was also the probable location for the command headquarters for the entire wall defense. For command and control, this far western location may have been favored over a more central site simply based on the greater threat posed by the Novantae and Selgovae Tribes populating the west and central sections respectively. Positioning the largest cavalry unit on the wall at this particular location would have offered a rapid response in the event the far northern outposts were attacked. It also makes strategic sense for the Romans to locate a large body of cavalry here as a cavalry *ala* (wing) was traditionally used to screen the flanks of an attacking legion. Should the Romans launch an attack north of the wall, the cavalry wing would have been used to screen the western flank.

Voreda: Old Penrith, approximately 12 miles south of Carlisle.

Bibliography

Blair, PH. *Roman Britain and Early England 55 B.C. – A.D. 871*, W.W. Norton & Company, New York, London, 1966.

Bowman, A.K. *Life and Letters On the Roman Frontier*, first published by the British Museum Press, London, 1994; subsequently by Routledge in the U.S. and Canada, 1998.

Breeze, DJ., *The Antonine Wall,* first published by John Donald, an imprint of Birlinn LTD, Edinburgh, 2006

Burke, J. *Roman England*, W.W. Norton & Company, New York, London, 1983.

Caesar, Julius, *The Gallic War*, translated by H. J. Edwards, Loeb Classical Library, Harvard University Press, Cambridge Massachusetts, 2004.

Churchill, W. *The Island Race, Volume I*, Cassell and Company, Ltd, London, UK, 1964

Cowan, R. *Roman Legionary 58 B.C. – A.D.* illustrated by A. McBride, Osprey Publishing, Botley, Oxford, UK, 2003.

Ehrlich, E. *Amo, Amas, Amat and More,* with an introduction by William F. Buckley, Jr., Harper and Row, Publishers, N.Y. 1985.

Goldsworthy, A.K *The Roman Army At War, 100 BC- AD 200*, Oxford University Press, 1996..

Luttwak, E. N. *The Grand Strategy of the Roman Empire From the First Century A.D to the Third*, The Johns Hopkins University Press, Baltimore and London, 1979.

Renatus, Flavius Vegetius *Roman Military*, translated by John Clarke 1767, Pavillion Press, Inc, Philadelphia, 2004.

Speller, E. *Following Hadrian,* Oxford University Press, Oxford, U.K. 2004

Tacitus, *The Agricola,* translated with an introduction by H. Mattingly (1948) and revised by S. A. Handford (1970), Penguin Books, London England, 1970.

Webster. G. *The Roman Imperial Army, of the First and Second Centuries A.D.,* University of Oklahoma Press, Norman Oklahoma, 1998.

Wilmott, T. *Birdoswald Roman Fort,* English Heritage, London 2005.

CPSIA information can be obtained
at www.ICGtesting.com
Printed in the USA
LVHW091709080322
712899LV00015B/184

9 781945 181610